The Lost Paladin

Written by Matthew Marcellus

Artwork by Christopher Lloyd Wright

Oneonta, New York 2021

Table of Contents

Character List

Talar Stoneking- Prince of Stonedom, brother to Cynfor

Cynfor Stoneking- Prince of Stonedom, brother to Talar

Cadoc Stoneking- King of Stonedom, father to Talar and Cynfor

Tomlin Stoneking- Cadoc's father, Talar's grandfather, deceased

Alwin of Stonedom- Talar's bodyguard, brother to Hartwin

Hartwin of Stonedom- Talar's bodyguard, brother to Alwin

Tiberius- Captain of the Emperor's Guard

Lord Commander Volga-Commander of the High Keep in Capa

The Emperor- Supreme leader of Capa

General Initium- The Emperor's father

Calbrius-Headmaster of the Academy

Dobervist the Dwarf- Former Champion of the Arena

Aemon- Ancient Elf

Malnar-Teacher at the Academy

Mona of Mercium- Daughter of the King and Queen of Mercium

Dalir Hannoson- Son of Hanno

Hanno Hannoson- Koristan's ambassador to Capa

Clavis- Commander of the Third Legion

Gunther- Clavis' Riken bodyguard, father to Ansgar

Ralphin- Son of Brigantium's leader, student at the Academy

Ansgar- Ralphin's bodyguard, student at the Academy

Marcus-woodcutter from Capa

Tarquin-woodcutter from Capa

Evander-leader of the woodcutters

Sorel-woodcutter from Fort Carillon

Cyprian- Capan Hunter

Tadius- Capan Hunter

Ragonius- Capan Hunter, former Arena champion

Axius- Capan Hunter

Madoc- Owner of the Oakbridge Tavern

Sigrid-A Queen of the Rikens

Brimhilt- A Knight

The Sargent- Capan soldier at Fort Carillon

Justus- Capan soldier at Fort Carillon

Randlo- Capan soldier at Fort Carilllon

Chapter I- A Queen's Fury

The young Queen stared across the field at her people, who were emerging from the forest. She turned her head left, then right, and smiled as the wave of humanity reached its peak. They had all braved the plummeting late winter temperatures and miles of unforgiving terrain to assemble here. Abandoning their homes and those too weak to travel, her people had forgotten past transgressions amongst themselves to unite. Only together could they survive this horrible enemy.

The Queen looked up at the cloudless, grey sky. The wind kicked up, blowing cold air down her back. Despite having barely slept over the past few days, a renewed sense of energy swept through her as the proximity of thousands of her people overwhelmed her. The Queen climbed a wooden cart next to her. Before her eyes, the tips of wooden spears, pitchforks, and clubs bobbed up and down. The younger fighting people moved towards the front, and she could sense their anger. She looked over the crowd and saw the fierce eyes of a particularly fearsome warrior. He smiled at her through his thick beard, nodded, and raised his ax high. The grass around the ox cart was being turned into a soupy, muddy mess by the mass of people.

Above the noise of the army, a lone voice cried out. "My Queen! My Queen! What do you say?" she shouted.

A silence fell upon the gathering mass of tribesmen. They waited for their leader to answer the question. "Will we fight them, my Queen? Will we fight?" the elderly woman asked.

The Queen's eyes scanned across the breadth of her tribesmen, then across the field, where the enemy waited. They looked so weak compared to the warriors surrounding her. She tried to count them anyways. She gave up counting after feeling the impatience of the mass of fighters around her. She was not her father, not a general, but any fool could see that the small Legion in front of her was no match for the combined strength of her tribe.

"We will not fight them," the Queen yelled to the astonishment of all present. "We will slaughter them," she quickly followed. "They killed my father for no reason! They put us in chains, they rape our women, they steal our food. They will die!".

The crowd around her roared in approval, and for the Queen, any sense of uncertainty about leading her people to war vanished. They could not be defeated, not today, not with this many fighting. The enemy had been foolish to leave their fort, and now they would die.

"Show them no mercy, for they show us none," the Queen screamed, and her people roared even louder.

She could feel their voices reverberating through the wagon's floor. She jumped down to the ground and walked through the mass of people until she was out in front. The Queen grabbed a short sword from the nearest warrior and raised it high. "We will kill them all!" she screamed furiously.

The tribesmen were in a frenzy, some screaming uncontrollably. Their hatred of the red-caped enemy had boiled over past the point of reason. Several female warriors joined their Queen in the front rank and began screaming wildly. The female warriors were even more enraged than their male counterparts. They had lost their husbands, sons, and daughters to the enemy. Their logic had been replaced with rage.

"Follow me. We will kill them all," the Queen yelled out. She began walking towards her enemy, across the barren field. The tribespeople followed, some of the women warriors running ahead of the mass.

"Move forward," the Queen shouted, and she could feel her people behind her. They would succeed. They would win. Her people would have their revenge. They would be free of their enemy.

"Slow down and wait for me!". It was Galar, her father's oldest friend and a well-respected warrior despite his age. Reaching out, Galar grabbed his Queen's shoulder and stopped her. The tribespeople passed on screaming.

"What?" the tribe Queen shouted. Her eyes were ablaze with rage; she held the sword in both of her hands. She looked ready to use it.

"You are our Queen. You are not our best warrior," Galar said.

"It does not matter; we will crush them," the young Queen replied.

"You are our Queen. If you die, a part of us dies," Galar screamed, for he needed to be heard, and the tribespeople were still streaming past the two. "I promised your father I would look out for you, and I will," he asserted.

"Get off me. They will die!" she screeched, turning towards the enemy. With no other options, Galar grabbed her shoulder with his other hand, spun her around, and slapped her as hard as he could. A few young, bare-chested warriors paused to intervene. After seeing Galar's black bear vest under his brown cloak, they quickly ran forward. Only the bravest could wear the fur of the great black bear, only the most respected warriors.

"You bastard Galar, let me fight!" the Queen screamed in defiance. With no other choice, Galar slapped her again, this time rendering her unconscious. He slung her over his shoulder and carried her through the remnants of the tribesmen. He carried her through the mud to the wagon. Elderly tribespeople and those too young to fight, pushed more wagons together. They began to set up to watch the elimination of their enemy. Galar heaved his Queen onto the wagon and told one of the elders to watch her. He gently brushed her hair out of her eyes. Slapping her had been hard, for he had known her since birth, but she must live no matter the cost. She was nobility to Galar and to his people, a being who had descended from the Gods themselves. Having fulfilled his oath to her dead father, Galar pulled his long knife from its sheath and his hatchet from his belt. He was a respected warrior and hunter. He hated the enemy as much as the others. Trotting quickly from the wagon, he looked back at his friend's daughter and thanked the Gods that he had a Queen as bold as she was.

"With me, we will kill them all," Galar bellowed at the lagging tribesmen. Galar ran towards the slaughter, which had just begun.

Chapter II- The Third

Clavis smiled as he saw the horde of barbarians begin their ascent towards him. It was an ascent. Clavis had walked the barbarians' current route the day before and had been pleasantly surprised at the hill's uncanny ascent. He had been encouraged by how muddy it had become after his entourage had followed his path. There was a line of springs along the top of the route. The spring's water leaked towards where the barbarians now rushed. The hill was not nearly steep enough to impede an enemy's attack, but Clavis hoped that it would spread his enemy thin, stopping a brutal crushing charge. Clavis' wishes were coming true. The fastest and most eager barbarians were already out in front, jeering and cheering in their sleek bear coats. The older and less enthused were falling behind, weighed down by their weapons and the thick mud that their eager comrades had created. They were all still screaming in anger, howling like mad Men. One of the Legionnaires standing near Clavis began shaking, causing his long rectangular shield to clatter against his spear. Clavis smiled. He remembered his first battle, the gut-wrenching fear, the uncertainty, the vomit-inducing anxiousness before the battle. Now he longed for it. Only in battle could Clavis gain the fortunes necessary to become rich enough to retire in style. Become rich enough to gain office, become a Senator. A Senator of the Empire. One day soon, Clavis thought. A man could not fight forever, but today Clavis would fight. He would win. He must.

A Captain of the Legion snapped at the shaking, green recruit, and he suddenly stopped. He did have reason to fear, Clavis thought. The barbarians outnumbered his Legion roughly three to one. Ten thousand barbarians, Clavis reckoned. The Legion's line snapped to attention when Clavis began walking past the front line. His eyes were locked on the approaching barbarian mass.

Despite the shaking recruit, Clavis thought his Legion was as tough as any. This was not going to be their first scrap. They had fought the Koristans during the construction of Badatoz Castle, fought back the marauding Barons of Borisco, and helped conquer the Kingdom of Mercium. They had helped crush the back-stabbing Knights of Mempacton. Of course, Clavis was not alive when Mempacton fell, but his Legion had been there. The Third Legion had been in existence since the creation of the Empire nearly three hundred years ago. Clavis had joined as a poor youth. He had been hungry, sick, and frail, but the Third Legion had taken him in. The Third had fed him, taught him how to fight, how to survive, how to be a Man. Clavis had excelled in his time as a Legionnaire. To the point to where he now commanded the Third Legion, the same Legion that had fathered him. Clavis loved the Third Legion. The Third loved him.

Most Legion commanders seemed elderly to the Legionnaires they commanded, but not Clavis. He fought on the first line when he could, amongst them, amongst the danger. He was lucky. The Third had not lost a battle under Clavis despite bad odds and heavy casualties. They believed in their general.

Clavis continued strolling in front of the Legion's most advanced line, the shield line. The barbarians continued their path towards him. The barbarians were close now, close enough to see their facial features. Clavis could see the screaming Women amongst the barbarian Men and could barely stifle a laugh. Reaching the center of the Legion, Clavis cleared his throat, adjusted the red cape that hung over his shining armor, and pulled his sword, raising it high. Looking at his Legionnaires, Clavis bristled with pride. There was no fear in the veterans' eyes, no worry on their weathered and scarred faces. In his deep and commanding voice, which he was known for, Clavis addressed his troops. "Men of the Third Legion, are you scared of a bunch of screaming Women?" he bellowed.

"NO," the Third thundered in response.

"Are you going to kill these rebel barbarian scum?" Clavis roared.

"YES, General!" the Third replied.

"Good! Listen up. Archers aim at their flanks. Shield line will advance upon contact and keep moving no matter what." Shifting his attention to the secondary line, Clavis kept up his battle speech. "Once the shield line advances, throw your javelins, then your spears, then draw your swords. Finish off anybody the shield line leaves. Understood Legionnaires?

"YES, General," they replied in unison.

Clavis had gone over his battle plan with his officers the night before, and they had relayed the battle plan to the Legionnaires. He felt confident they understood. They were veteran soldiers, and they understood how the Legion fought. Some of his junior officers had questioned the need to fight in the open against greater numbers, but his senior officers had faith in him. They knew the battle-hardened Legion could fight a rag-tag group of wandering barbarians.

"Show no mercy, Men of the Third. No Mercy!" Clavis shouted.

"NO MERCY," the Third replied. The barbarians were making their final approach on the Legion, and Clavis quickly stepped behind the shield line. He took his spear from his personal bodyguard, who began buckling his metal helmet's chin strap. Clavis took his place on the spear line and saw through the shield line that the barbarians were not massed together anymore. They were strung out in lines with stragglers connecting them. The front-line barbarians were still screaming, their long hair wild and unkempt. Their faces were distorted in anger. Clavis could clearly see their bearskin vests and the yellow teeth of his enemy. If he could kill their best warriors, Clavis figured the day was his. The deciding moment was here.

"Hold shield line, HOLD!" Clavis bellowed, and the officers up and down the shield line echoed his words. The barbarians were even closer, and Clavis could now smell the collective stench of the unwashed pagans. "HOLD!" he shouted again, as finally, the first barbarian line closed the gap and smashed into the Third Legion. The sound was deafening. Human flesh and bone collided with the cold wood of the Legion's large shields. One barbarian managed to hurdle the shield line, but he was impaled by the Legionnaire on Clavis' left. Another huge, ax-wielding, bearskin-clad barbarian smashed his way through, but Clavis' bodyguard downed him by throwing his javelin. Clavis looked up and down the shield line, and for the most part, it was holding. Adrenaline rushed to Clavis' head as the thrill of battle erupted within him. "Throw javelins," he shouted, and the Legion responded. About one thousand Legionnaires were on the shield line. The archers kept firing their missiles into the barbarian horde. The javelins and arrows rained down on the barbarians. Many of the barbarians did not have shields, leaving them defenseless against the aerial onslaught. The effect was immense. Those wounded howled out in pain as arrows and javelins protruded from their chests, stomachs, and shoulders. The dead littered the ground. Those lucky with shields found them worthless, with the javelins stuck in them.

"Throw spears!" Clavis barked above the chaos of the battle. The second round of aerial missiles was even more devastating than the first, with more barbarians crying out in pain. Thousands of them now were wounded, dead, or were dying. The javelins and spears were having a brutal impact on the advancing barbarian horde. The Legion's archers kept pouring volley upon volley on the enemy's flanks, forcing them to the shield line. The bearskin line was almost completely wiped out, with only those locked against the shield line surviving. The brown soupy mud was turning red under the barbarians. Clavis checked his line again and knew it was time. "Forward, Legion, forward!" Clavis shouted, and the Legion responded. The spear line, now without spears, drew their swords. They pressed forward, giving weight and extra force to the shield line.

The bearskin barbarians were in a precarious spot. With their brethren wounded behind them, retreating meant trampling them and leaving them to the enemy. A minute ago, they outnumbered the cursed red capes, but now they were outnumbered. More importantly, the rest of the horde had stalled under the arrows and spears. They were alone. The Legion moved forward, stabbing, and hacking over the back of the shield line. The barbarians either ran, were run over by the sheer weight of the Legion or were stabbed to death. The Legion marched on. Those barbarians wounded by the projectiles were stepped over by the shield line and finished off. The Legion reequipped itself with its spent spears.

The second main body of barbarians tried to rush the Legion but was entangled by their own wounded and the thick mud. They were stopped outright by another volley of spears and arrows. Clavis did not bother giving any more orders. His Legionnaires and officers knew what to do. He focused his attention on the immediate battle in front of him. It was time to bloody his sword. With a nod to his bodyguard, Clavis withdrew his sword from its scabbard and pressed forward towards the shield line.

In front of Clavis, the shield line Legionnaires pressed forward. Their shields were locked together. Their knees were bent, and all the strength they could muster was pressed into their shields. To Clavis' left, a Legionnaire fell from a club blow to the head. A ragged, bearded barbarian with beady eyes and a pointed chin swung at Clavis when he stepped over the fallen Legionnaire. Clavis blocked the club with his sword, to the barbarian's shock. Another Legionnaire decapitated him with a swing from his sword. His beady eyes stared up at Clavis. The blood from his body drenched Clavis' boots and bare legs. Clavis pressed on, leaning over the nearest shield line Legionnaire. He thrust his sword into a screaming woman's mouth. She grabbed her mouth, trying to stop the blood, and was knocked down by the shield line Legionnaire. After the Legionnaire stepped over her, Clavis brought his sword down, killing her.

The barbarians were in a panic now. Some were desperately carrying the wounded back to the woods. Some tried to press forward to fight the hated enemy. Those upfront could not hold the shield line back and were forced back. It was chaos; the Legion left behind it nothing but corpses, bloodstains, and entrails. In front of the Legion, the barbarians screamed. When their Queen had yelled at them to fight, they had screamed back in anger. Now the barbarian horde screamed in terror.

The slaughter continued. The Legion was now facing the elderly and the youngest of the barbarians, those at the rear who had not run the fastest.

Many were bare-chested, as the youth apparently saw it a sign of bravery to fight this way. Clavis shook his head in disbelief as they ran up like this to the shield line, only to be easily cut down. A lucky barbarian threw his spear at the line, hitting a Legionnaire in the throat, killing him. The young recruit who had been shaking went berserk, breaking formation and impaling the barbarian. "Form Line!" Clavis ordered. The shield line continued forming around the young recruit. The young recruit was soaked in his opponent's blood. Clavis clapped his back and urged him forward. Clavis looked ahead and could see a ring of wagons parked next to each other. Wounded barbarians were frantically trying to climb over the wagons as those too wounded to move cried out for help. Those last brave few who were still fighting either ran or died at the shield line.

As the Legion approached the wagons, Clavis could see a beautiful barbarian warrior standing on top of the wagons, shouting at her comrades to stay and fight. Clavis could not help but admire her bravery. "That one is mine!" he yelled, pointing at the Queen. She seemed to notice Clavis before she jumped down from the wagon and began approaching the Legion. "Gonna kill us all?" Clavis yelled. The warrior woman was stopped by an elderly warrior with a hatchet and knife. They seemed to argue. Before the Legion could attack them, the elder threw her backward and rushed the shield line. Clavis's bodyguard threw his javelin. The javelin hit the old man square in the head with such force that it caved most of his skull in on top of itself. The Legion and Clavis howled in pleasure, and Clavis clapped his bodyguard on the back. The barbarian woman howled in rage and grief. She dove over the wagons, grabbing a wounded man by his ankles before retreating to the woods.

Clavis called for the Legion to halt and surveyed the carnage. Behind him, thousands of barbarians lay dead or were withering in pain. Those who survived would become the Legion's slaves, to be sold at auction with the proceeds split amongst the men. Clavis looked forward into the woods. He could not see any sizable force and could only hear the screams of the wounded. The day was his. The Third Legion of the Capan Empire was victorious. He was victorious. The men around him were screaming in joy, laughing as they finished off the gravely wounded barbarians. Clavis summoned a runner over to him.

"Send word to Capa, tell them the Third Legion is victorious."

"Yes, General," the young blood-soaked recruit replied.

Clavis climbed aboard one of the wagons and gazed upon the field of battle. Vultures and crows were already descending upon the dead, but Clavis was not dead, he was victorious. Which meant that tonight he would get drunk, rape a barbarian, and eat as much as he could. In the morning, the Legion would retire to the more sophisticated realms of the Empire. It was good to be Capan.

Chapter III- A Prince's Duty

Talar adjusted his cloak and spat out a mouthful of road dust as he sauntered along the Great Road. Talar did not know why anybody thought the Road was Great. He had been looking down upon its grey cobbles for two weeks now, and he was sick of looking at it.

To the right of him, the regular people filed past, dressed in their woolen tunics, short pants, and sandals. The climate near Capa was consistently warm for most of the year. Only the occasional storm passed overhead. The common people, as Talar liked to think of them as, were the farmers, smiths, masons, millers, and the laborers who were helping build the Empire. Talar envied their simple lifestyles, for no commoner faced the problems that he did. Talar rode past on his horse, looking down on the often dirty but carefree faces. Life was good for most Capan citizens. Food was plentiful and affordable. The Legions provided security and maintained order, and most importantly … taxes were low. But not all those who traveled past Talar wore wool and made a living with their hands. Rich merchant trains with horse-drawn wagons, armored guards, and servants passed by. The silk-clothed merchants made their fortunes transporting the goods that Capa provided. The occasional Legionnaire, on leave or furlough, marched past, with citizens clearing the way for them.

This went on for miles. Hundreds, if not thousands of people, walked past Talar as he rode on. The two guards his brother had ordered to accompany him rode next to him. Talar still scoffed at the idea of his brother requiring him to ride with guards. With the trip almost over, Talar looked forward to his freedom once again. For the guards, Alwin and Hartwin, brothers no less, were watchful of Talar beyond what he thought was sane.

The mid-day sun beat down upon Talar, who was not accustomed to such high temperatures. The young man drank from his clay water jug and wiped his brow of sweat. Stonedom was much higher in elevation and seldom saw temperatures this high. Talar took another drink from the clay jug and wished for a breeze to relieve his discomfort. Hartwin looked over at Talar and tried to gauge his mood. The young Prince had kept to himself since they had left Stonedom. Nonetheless, Hartwin was proud of his young Prince's composure.

Another half-hour passed until the odor changed for the worse. Hartwin and Alwin looked at each other and pressed on. Talar lingered briefly, trying to swat the offensive odor away from his nose. It did not work. Talar caught up with the brothers, and the three from Stonedom crested the last hill in their long journey. They gazed with awe at the vast city before them, for Capa was the heart of the Capan Empire.

The three from Stonedom wheeled their horses off the Great Road, and the locals passed smiling. They had seen awe-stricken tourists before. Capa expanded across the horizon, a massive city situated against the Shimmering Sea. Capa seemed to stretch forever in the distance. Talar shook his head in disbelief as the enormity of the city began to sink in. Talar could see massive columned buildings spread out amongst the hills that reared above the sea below. Talar had never seen such huge buildings. He wondered how they were constructed.

Talar's gaze turned southward across the vast pillared city down to the bay where giant concrete piers stuck out into the greenish, blue water of the Shimmering Sea. Thousands of people milled upon the docks. Talar could see ships with square ends and double sails moored up and down the concrete piers.

"How can they withstand the sea?" Talar asked Alwin, but the Stonedom warrior merely shrugged. Still in disbelief, Talar's inspection of the massive port was interrupted by Hartwin's grasp upon his shoulder. Talar followed where Hartwin's finger pointed, and his jaw dropped. "It cannot be! How did they build it?" Talar asked. His question was drowned out by all the commoners walking past them.

Talar dropped the reigns to his horse down to his lap. He simply could not believe it. Before his eyes, above the vast city, a massive castle stood. The castle was formidable, to say the least. Eight massive turrets symmetrically surrounded a grey stone spire that seemed to touch the clouds. The turrets all had ballista and catapults strategically placed amongst the walkways, but what made the castle truly impregnable was its steep location. The castle seemed only accessible through a single gate. From Talar's position, that massive gate seemed the only link between the castle and the rest of the city. To the rest of the world, really, Talar thought.

"We'll only be up there a few nights at the most, Your Highness," Alwin solemnly said to Talar.

"Yea, Alwin, I know," Talar replied. "To be honest, I already miss Stonedom; I already miss the lake, the mountains, the woods. I miss Cynfor as well," Talar said after taking a deep breath.

Turning his horse away from the city, he turned backward-looking back over the vast fields of wheat he and the two brothers had ridden through for so long. "I hope he is well, along with my father. He looked so weak when I last saw him last. I should have acted sooner Alwin, it is my fault that we are here," Talar said gloomily.

Alwin shook his head after hearing his Prince's words. "You fought bravely to save your father, Talar. You fought well, with honor. A Goblin is no easy foe. You killed two."

"My father might die because of what I did not do, Alwin," Talar said, his voice trembling slightly.

Hartwin and Alwin looked at each other with alarm in their eyes. "You fought bravely, Talar. There was nothing you could have done. These things are out of our control. You have heard the Druid's teachings. Do not forget them," Hartwin said. Talar's hands began to shake as the memory of the hunting trip in the Stone mountains began to replay itself in his head. Hartwin and Alwin again looked at each other with alarm again. "My Prince, what happened to your father should have never happened. No matter what you think, you did save his life," Hartwin said.

"I watched like a little boy as those beasts skewered him, Hartwin," Talar replied.

A deep silence fell upon the three Stonedom men. Hartwin and Alwin had tried to keep Talar in good spirits on the long journey with ale and stories of foreign lands. Talar had gotten to pass through those foreign lands, and with them, he had found some sort of relief. Talar looked up at the imposing castle. He knew of the danger of entering that castle, but he knew that he must go there. Fear gripped Talar as he realized how small Stonedom was compared to Capa. Now the fate of his people rested upon his shoulders. Cynfor, his older brother, would have made the trip, but his father's grievous wounds prevented him from leaving the King. "Cynfor would have kept Father from being harmed," Talar whispered.

"You don't know that Talar, you don't know that", Alwin said. The younger brother grabbed Talar's shoulder, and with Hartwin still grabbing his hand, Talar suddenly felt trapped. Talar threw his arms up, brushing off the brother's attempts to console him. He urged his horse forward, then looked back at the brothers.

"Let us enter this grand city. I am ready to make my pledge to the Empire and return home to see my father. The young Prince of Stonedom sighed, for he and his people had been totally free once. The brothers nodded, and they could see that their Prince was thinking of the past. They thought Talar was thinking of his father, their King. "I suppose it will be quite the spectacle," Talar stated.

"They will make you pledge fealty to Capa and to her Legions. You will be on your knee in front of the Emperor and the High Court. You must do anything he commands, and you must seem willing and obedient. For you know...the consequences of...disobedience," Hartwin said sadly.

Talar turned his head slowly so he could look squarely into both brothers' eyes. "I know the consequences, Hartwin. The end of Stonedom. The end of our people. The end of everything that we are." He thought about his grandfather Tomlin, the first king of Stonedom to pledge fealty to Capa. "Is this how Tomlin felt when he was forced to come down here?" the young Prince asked. Both brothers pondered their Prince's question.

"When Mempacton fell, we were alone, Talar. Trolls to the north, Goblins to the east, Capa to the south. We had to side with them, Talar. Or face Mempacton's fate," Alwin said softly.

"They caused Mempacton to fall, Alwin. They wage war against everyone they can," Talar exclaimed. Anger flashed thru Talar's eyes as he continued speaking. "They kill Dwarves and Elves, Alwin. Elves, Alwin. The Gods' gifts to Men, and they kill them. Why would anyone kill an Elf?" Talar's voice was rising. Commoners passing by were starting to notice. Hartwin moved his horse over and again clasped Talar's hand.

"Your task is not easy, my Prince. The fate of our people rests upon you kneeling and saying the words of the pledge. You are right Talar, Capa is waging war on our neighbors. If we fought with the Dwarves against them, our people would be slaughtered. To the last child... slaughtered. Our names, our history, our deeds forever wiped out. Like Mempacton," Alwin stated.

Talar shook his head. "I will say the pledge for my people," he stated. "I know Cynfor would if Father was not wounded." For Cynfor had always looked out for his people. Talar loved his older brother. He still remembered the look of shock on Cynfor's face when he had entered the glen where Talar stood defending their father from the Goblins. Talar had already slain one of the Goblins and was battling the other when Cynfor attacked it from behind. Talar had then lunged with his broadsword, impaling the grey, wiry, foreign Goblin. Goblins were not native to the mountains south of Stonedom. Because of this, no one had bothered to stay with the King, and Talar's father had been stabbed through the back by one of the Goblins. The King still lay weak in his bed. He had not opened his eyes and was breathing shallowly when Talar had left.

"He may be dead. Do you realize that Hartwin? Talar said. He looked at his sword pommel when he said the words.

"King Cadoc is a fighter. Only a strong man would have made it out of the glen with such a wound alive, Talar. The healers are doing the best they can, this I am sure of," Hartwin replied with confidence. Despite his youth, his young Prince was also a strong Man, but Hartwin still worried for him. An ailing father coupled with the fate of his people was a heavy burden to bear.

"If only the Elves still roamed freely, Hartwin. My Father and your King would be standing in good health….and Cynfor would be here, not me," Talar complained.

"But you are here, Talar. The time has come. Put aside past transgressions, gather yourself, go up to that castle, kneel, and say that pledge. Then we will go home. We should be heading back north in the morning," Hartwin said optimistically.

Spinning his horse back around to look again at the might of Capa, Talar straightened his back, gripped his sword for reassurance, and nodded to both brothers. "Let us go see this city and get this done then."

Talar urged his horse further down the hill, with the two brothers flanking him. Commoners made way, for they could see the fierce look upon all three of the Men from Stonedom. Talar felt small when the main gate of Capa's outer wall became larger as they approached. He was about to kneel in front of the Emperor of Capa, arguably the most powerful Man in the world. His people's fate depended on what he did and how he did it. A chill went up Talar's spine as he rode towards Capa.

Chapter IV-The Empire's Capital

The massive metal gate was open now. Open to all commoners, merchants, farmers, and traders. As such, there was a hold-up at the gate as the gate's guards looked over those trying to enter the great city. When the three from Stonedom approached the guard station, a Legionnaire barked at them to halt. The brothers and Talar stopped their horses and peered down at the red-caped Legionnaire. "Are you from Stonedom by any chance?" the Legionnaire inquired. When Talar nodded, the Legionnaire grinned. "I knew it, I knew it. It is those big horses you are riding on. Only northerners have horses that big. Sir, Sir, Sir, over here, Sir, it is the Lords of Stonedom," the Legionnaire shouted.

Talar looked up from the loud Legionnaire and out into the street, past the gatehouse. A squadron of Capan soldiers was quickly advancing toward them. Talar had never seen Capan soldiers like these. They did not wear the red capes and metal armor of normal Legionnaires, but rather yellow animal skin cloaks with black spots, along with metal breastplates. The crowd cleared away as the squadron abruptly halted directly in front of the three from Stonedom.

A middle-aged soldier with black hair stepped out from the side file of the squadron and approached the Stonedom Men. "Lord Cynfor, my lord?" the soldier inquired.

"Who are you?", Talar demanded. Despite being in Capa and having to swear an oath to the Emperor, he would not be bullied around by a common soldier.

Sensing the hostility in Talar's voice, the strangely dressed soldier dropped to a knee and bent his head. "I'm looking for Lord Cynfor, my Lord. My name is Tiberius; I am Captain of the Emperor's Guard."

Hartwin looked at Talar, and Talar realized his mistake instantly. Adjusting his broad sword, Talar easily slid off his horse, approached the still kneeling Captain, and cleared his throat. "No need to kneel, Captain Tiberius. My apologies. My name is Talar Stoneking, brother to Cynfor Stoneking."

Tiberius immediately stood up, looking right into Talars' green eyes. Both the older soldier and the young Prince were the same height. "No need to apologize, my Lord Stoneking. We did not know exactly when you were arriving. Young nobles usually travel in larger parties. Usually with more guards as well," Tiberius noted dryly.

"I can defend myself just fine, Captain," Talar replied. Talar hoped he would not have to defend himself against the Capan Captain. His face was marred with scars.

"I'm sure you can, my Lord," Tiberius sarcastically said. The comment drew laughter from the red-caped Legionnaires, but the Emperor's Guard remained silent.

A few awkward seconds later, Captain Tiberius finally cleared his throat. "Let us go up to the High Keep, and welcome to Capa, my Lord. The First City of the Empire."

Talar simply nodded at Captain Tiberius and gestured for him to lead the way. Alwin, who had rolled his eyes at the Captain's last comment, drew a harsh glare from his elder brother, Hartwin. Capans liked to think of themselves as the first Men of the world, and they taught their young this. The three from the north knew better.

As the Stonedom Men rode past the Emperor's Guard, Talar examined their razor-sharp spears, short swords, and leather armor linked with metal chains. Their steel helmets were finely crafted, extending down the sides of their faces, and protecting their noses as well. They did not wear long pants as the Stonedom men did, but rather short pants made of sturdy white linen. The men looked to be in good physical condition, and as the three Northmen lumbered by on their horses, the entire troop snapped to attention and reversed their course in unison. Talar was impressed and let Captain Tiberius know it.

"Yes, my Lord Talar, highly trained battle-hardened veterans, each Man of the Emperor's Guard is willing to die for Capa, for his fellow Guards, and for the Emperor. Each Man has a sworn oath to this. The Guard receive the best pay, the best equipment, and upon retirement, should they reach it, the finest land available to veterans," Tiberius noted.

Talar nodded again at Tiberius, not saying any more, for he seemed out of place looking down upon the grizzled veteran from his high horse.

Continuing through the vast city, Talar soon began to quit thinking about his current dilemmas. The sights and sounds of the foreign city began to overwhelm him. The Emperor's Guard had formed a perimeter around the three from Stonedom, with the Sargent of the Guard barking at civilians to clear the way. Around the perimeter, an array of sailors, merchants, dockhands, masons, and shop keepers shouted, hustled, and bustled their way through the narrow streets. Above the streets, simple homes with terraces and balconies jutted out over Talar. All the windows had iron bars to deter thieves. To Talar's left, a baker toiled away at his oven, while to his right, a blacksmith fanned the bellows to his forge. Both Men seemed to live above their respective shops. As the group progressed through the city, Talar saw a pair of drunks stagger out of a rough-looking tavern. Talar saw merchant shops with fine spices and cloths from Koristan and fishmongers selling strange blue crabs that were larger than any crab that he had ever seen. The strange sights and sounds of Capa washed over Talar. His head spun from side to side, trying to catch every detail of the foreign city. The mass of people around him seemed to teem with energy, and that energy perked Talar up, putting a big smile on the young Prince's face after so many miserable miles on the Great Road.

The Guard and the three from Stonedom continued through the strange city without speaking, passing hundreds and hundreds of different people from all walks of life. A Senator of the Empire passed the group, and Captain Tiberius saluted the elderly statesman. A rich merchant riding upon a silver gilded wagon drawn by two massive oxen went by. Three horsemen with long lances with ribbons hanging down trotted around the wagon, acting as guards. The horsemen had odd-looking short brown leather jackets with black trousers and high leather boots. Talar wondered who they were and where they were from. Tiberius, who was walking alongside Talar, read the questioning look on his face. "Merchant guards from Borisco, mercenary cavalry, my Lord," Tiberius said. Talar looked at the three from Borisco again, this time catching a look at their short-curved swords and their short horse bows.

"The Barons of Borisco's famous horse troop," Talar exclaimed. Talar had heard of the stories of how the Barons of Borisco had led charge after charge into hordes of Trolls during the fall of Mempacton. They had not saved the great city, but they had saved thousands of people, some of whom had settled in Stonedom.

"Famous for what? Drinking and whoring, my Lord?" Tiberius replied with a sly grin. While Capa tolerated Borisco, there was little love between the giant Empire and their neighbors to the northwest

"They are famous in the north, in Stonedom, for fighting Trolls, Captain Tiberius," Talar replied evenly.

"Trolls............. I hear they are stupid and fight with sticks and stones, my Lord. Only slightly more dangerous than the even dumber Goblins. The races that came out of the caves should have stayed there, in my opinion. Including Dwarves." Upon saying the last word, Tiberius smiled, then continued marching forward. Sensing the mood of the other Guardsmen, Talar felt that this idea was prevalent amongst them.

"Captain Tiberius, have you ever personally fought against a Goblin or a Troll?" Talar inquired.

"I have fought in the East, in the South, and in the West," Tiberius answered.

"But never against a Troll or Goblin, Captain?".

Slowly and with reluctance, Tiberius answered, "No, my Lord, I've never fought a Troll or a Goblin."

Instead of mocking the grizzled veteran, Talar remained silent. He knew he was a foreign noble in a foreign land, surrounded by thousands of strangers. He did not want to make any unnecessary enemies. Alwin could not help himself, loudly snorting while shaking his head.

Tiberius, who had been waiting for two days in the hot sun at the gate for the three from Stonedom to arrive, sarcastically asked the young Prince if he had ever killed a Troll.

"No, Captain, I've never fought a Troll, but I killed the two Goblins who wounded my father."

"Two of them?" Tiberius inquired. Talar nodded along with Hartwin and Alwin.

"Slew them both, he did. Saved our King, our Prince Talar did," Hartwin remarked with pride.

Captain Tiberius looked Talar in the eyes and shook his head. He did not know this young Lord from Stonedom well, but he liked him. Tiberius looked him over better. The young Prince from Stonedom was an even six feet tall, with green eyes and a fair complexion. The Men from Stonedom wore their hair short, and Talar was no exception. Tiberius hoped the young noble fared well in front of the Emperor, for he had heard rumors that the Emperor was mad with Stonedom for not helping with the war against the Dwarves.

Tiberius looked at Talar again and hoped his own son, who was a similar age, would be successful as Talar in his first fight.

"Have you talked from anybody from the Senate or from the Emperor's Council, my Lord?" Tiberius asked of Toman.

"No, Captain, you're the first Capan I've talked to since I read the summons from the Emperor." The summons had come by official messenger, who had run three horses to death bringing the piece of parchment to Stonedom.

"Out of the way, drunk!" Tiberius roared. He pushed aside a staggering sailor, who began puking in the gutter. Small children ran over and took his money as he helplessly floundered in the gutter. One of the Guardsmen gave him a good kick in the groin to teach him a lesson.

Looking down from the flailing drunk up to the street, Talar noticed that they had entered the harbor area of the massive city. The strong smell of saltwater hit Talar's noise. Gulls flew above Talar, landing on the masts of the giant ships anchored in the harbor. The concrete harbor rose out of the sea, with giant piers too numerous to count. The party continued passing the harbor front. Merchants and sailors passed by. Some toiled preparing the giant ships for sea. Others were celebrating the ship's return to the harbor. Talar began to get lost in the buzz of the city, with his head whipping around and looking all over at the strange sights. Tiberius smiled, remembering the first time he had entered Capa.

After making their way through the harbor, the party began ascending into a residential neighborhood. This one was more prosperous than those by the cities entrance. Talar noticed that the sewer smells and gutter trash began to disappear along with the shabbier common folk. The buildings and houses to his left and right had low walls and arched gates. Red tile roofs and open courtyards with overlooking balconies sprung up into Talar's view. They passed house after house as the party continued to climb up towards the Keep. Suddenly Alwin spoke up and asked Tiberius about the location of the fabled Arena.

"The Arena is on the other side of the city. The area you just rode through is what we Capans call the Old City. It was built before the Troll Wars. The Arena borders the River Capulus and the New City, the area on the other side of the High Keep."

Talar nodded in understanding. The centralized location of the Arena made it easily assessable for all those in Capa who wished to attend. Alwin spoke again, asking: "Is Malfoy still champion, Captain? News of the Arena is sparse in Stonedom."

"Yea, that big bastard from Riken is still the Champion. I am starting to think he cannot be beaten. Too quick with those swords, he is. Unless they bring in a proper Cyclops, I think he will not be beaten anytime soon," Tiberius answered.

"A Cyclops?" Alwin asked.

"Yea, it has been years since the hunting teams caught one, but the last one took down three champions at once then tore the arms off a full-size Ogre," Tiberius noted. "It wasn't even armed with anything," he added.

"How do you catch a Cyclops? And aren't all the Ogres dead?" Alwin had plenty of questions.

"The hunting teams have their ways, and no, the Ogres aren't all dead. There are a few of them hiding out in the rocks west of Borisco. Since the Arena opened, there has been an open bounty on all Ogres of all sizes," Tiberius dryly noted as if all knew this basic information.

Hartwin glared again at Alwin, this time for embarrassing them all with his giddiness about the Arena. Fighting to the death for money was banned in the remaining northern kingdoms but was revered in the Empire. While all the fights and battles were popular, none were as popular as the fights between the Empire's champions and the non-human races.

"The hunting teams did get a new batch in though, that's the word on the street anyway," Tiberius smiled at the men from Stonedom. "New batch of Dwarves for Malfoy and the rest of the boys down in the Arena."

Talar clenched the reigns on his horse as he heard Tiberius' words. He looked over at the brothers and could see anger in both of their eyes. Dwarves were forced to fight in the Arena. It was disgusting to think that any Dwarf was forced to fight to the death, let alone in front of thousands of drunk cheering Capans. The thought made all three from Stonedom sick to their stomachs. The Dwarves of the Great Hall had traded with, worked with, and fought with the Men of Stonedom for over a thousand years. Until the Trolls Wars. Until Mempacton had fallen. Until Tomlin, King of Stonedom had kneeled. Now his grandson would kneel again. Talar's grip on his reigns tightened more to the point where his horse reared up. Talar was an excellent rider, but he still almost toppled off his mount, only saving himself by desperately grabbing his saddle.

With a look of confusion on his face, Tiberius looked back at Talar from his marching, reached out, and grabbed the reigns to Talar's horse. "What the..." Tiberius began, but Hartwin cut him off by saying that a dog had run under his horse.

"Well, he's settled down now, my Lord. Damn dogs, anyway. Do nothing but spread disease. Let us keep heading up. The High Keep is near. And watch your head around the next corner. The aqueduct drops down. You might hit it on that high horse of yours, my Lord," Tiberius said.

"Capa has aqueducts Captain Tiberius?" Talar asked politely, interested in the Empires' engineering feats.

"Yea, they start miles outside of the city, bring fresh water in from Lake Hurzon. The tides bring salt water into the River Capulus. We started building them after the Troll Wars when Capa expanded. The Emperor's grandfather ordered the construction of the first aqueducts as a matter of fact," Tiberius again noted as if explaining directions to an out of towner.

Talar was about to ask another question about aqueducts but remained silent. The group rounded the next corner and saw the concrete aqueduct spanning the width of the street. Riding closer, Talar heard water moving as the aqueduct funneled water across the street to the next block of houses. "Where does it go?" Alwin wondered out loud.

Tiberius was starting to grow tired of the foreigner's questions and abruptly stated to Talar, "Downhill to a series of public fountains and smaller aqueducts. Any more questions, my Lord?".

Talar shook his head and continued riding forward, looking back now and then to gaze at the aqueduct. It was another foreign wonder to the young noble. Rounding another corner and then another, the group and their guards remained silent, passing through the wealthy area of Capa. Finally, after riding another corner, Talar gazed up and lost his breath. For before his eyes, he could finally see the massive castle that he had spotted outside the gates of the city.

Shaking his head again, Talar urged his horse forward. He strained his head as high as it could go, so he could see the tops of the eight turrets and the central spire. The castle's stones were light grey in color, arrow slits and ballistae crowded the tops of the walls, and red-caped Legionnaires lazily milled about. Despite seeing the castle, Talar had not a clue how to enter it, for an almost sheer granite cliff rose behind the row of houses directly to

Talar's right. The group kept riding, and Talar kept shaking his head in disbelief at the size of the fortress.

"Impressive, isn't it, Young Lord?" Tiberius inquired of Talar.

"Yes, Captain, impressive, to say the least," Talar replied. The group continued riding underneath the massive castle until they finally approached another wall and gate. This wall was not as high as the outer wall, but Talar still had to strain his head to look up at the Legionnaire's manning their posts. Tiberius went over to the officer in charge of the gate's guard detail, and the two quickly exchanged words. Returning to the group, Tiberius dismissed his Men, and they began to leave the gate area.

Approaching Talar, Tiberius gently grabbed the reigns to Talar's horse and gestured for him to dismount. After dismounting, Tiberius turned to Talar. "Lord Talar Stoneking, you may advance into the High Keep. Your Men can stay in the barracks with my Guard. There is a spare room. Gather what belongings you desire to keep with you. Horses are not allowed past the gate."

Talar nodded in understanding, then turned to Hartwin and Alwin, who were still mounted on their horses. He looked in the eyes of Alwin, then turned and looked at Hartwin for a few seconds. Talar could not find the words to say, the words to reassure his friends and mentors that he would not fail them. That he would not fail his people.

The words never came to his lips, so Hartwin broke the silence instead. "Remember what I told you, Talar Stoneking, remember what our people need." Talar nodded. He could not bring himself to say farewell to his companions.

Tiberius spoke up again, "The Emperor and the High Court would have heard of you entering the city by now, young Lord. If you want time to clean off the road dust before you meet the Emperor, you must cross the drawbridge now and enter the High Keep. I will escort you."

Talar nodded, looked again at the brothers, grabbed his sack of clothes and belongings, and began to approach the steel gate. A giant Legionnaire smiled at Talar and opened the gate for him and Tiberius. Talar could not help the feeling that he was in trouble, that something bad was happening to him. He felt like he did when he had heard his father scream out when the Goblin had attacked him. Everything was slowing down. He felt as if he could not breathe. Talar thought about his father, Cynfor, and the rest of his friends in Stonedom. They were all depending on him. He represented them all, all the citizens of Stonedom. Thousands of people depended on him. He thought about his father again. How weak and pale he looked the last time he saw him. He thought about all the things that he wanted to say to his father, wondering if he would ever get the chance too. Talar's body began to unconsciously shake a little. The wide drawbridge that connected the Emperor to his Empire and the rest of the world stood before him. Tiberius, a veteran of numerous battles, could sense Talar's restlessness., He saw Talar slightly shaking and reassuringly put his hand on his shoulder. Talar looked over at Tiberius with a wild look in his green eyes. Tiberius had seen that look before, a mix of fear and excitement. "The Emperor waits on us. Shall we proceed Talar Stoneking?"

Once again, Talar could not say anything, so once again, he simply nodded. The young Prince of Stonedom set his foot upon the drawbridge, not knowing what lay beyond.

Chapter V- The Emperors of Capa

The Emperor of Capa smacked his lips as he munched on a fresh piece of bread. Grabbing the bread knife to his right, the Emperor cut another piece and dipped it in vinegar. A young servant placed a piece of parchment beside the Emperor. The words on the parchment were laws that the Senate had overwhelmingly approved. The laws guaranteed that the veterans of the Dwarf war would be granted tracts of land to farm and settle once the Dwarves were gone. The Emperor continued eating, reading over the law. Breadcrumbs spilled from the corner of his mouth, landing on the parchment below. The Emperor finished reading the laws and signed his name upon the parchment. If the law were popular and served the Empire's purpose, he would sign it. For the Emperor had learned from his father that the people were the true power to this Empire. The Legions fought and won wars and new lands, but the people were the true power. The Emperor knew it. He also knew the secret to rule this Empire. Keep the people content and occupied, and in the absence of their curiosity, you could do anything.

The Emperor looked up from his simple meal into the eyes of the Men who were seated at the long rectangular table around him. He cut another small piece of bread, dipped it into the vinegar, and ate it whole. It was a simple meal for a simple Emperor. The Emperor did not treat himself to the tasty sweets and pies that were popular in Koristan. Nor did he feast on the wild boar and deer roasts that were common in the northern territories. The Emperor preferred the diet of his people. Fish and bread. Water and wine. The Emperor pushed the bread out in front of him, and without saying a word, the servant reached down, picked up the bread and vinegar, then left the room. The Emperor kept the bread knife in his hand as he again looked around the table at the Men around him. For around the Emperor sat the Men who governed the Empire.

Generals with red capes, leather armor, and steel breastplates made up most of the table's occupants. All the Generals had a small, silver skull ring on their right hand. White-robed Senators, most with graying hair, were also present. The Empire's three Admirals made up of the rest of the occupants of the table, and for that matter, the room. For this plain room was below the Emperor's personal chambers in the highest part of the center Spire. Only a few of the men at the table had ever been this high up in the center Spire. Most of them had met the Emperor, maybe not in person, but on the battlefield or in the Senate. Today was different, for meetings like this were rare.

"Has anyone heard from Clavis?". The words seemed to pop out of thin air, and to an outsider, one might have thought that the Emperor was talking to himself.

Lord Commander Volga, who oversaw the High Keep, and who sat immediately to the Emperor's right, spoke. "Yes, Emperor, a messenger pigeon just came in this morning."

Smiling, the Emperor raised his eyebrows and, in a low voice, asked Volga why he had not been informed of this when the pigeon arrived.

"You were in the Senate, my Emperor," Volga replied evenly. His gray hair and weathered face betrayed nothing. "The bird arrived just as you were walking in, my Emperor."

"I understand, Lord Volga, thank you for clearing that up," the Emperor replied kindly, his voice trailing off slightly at the end. He always ate after going to the Senate, and this was the first time Volga had seen the Emperor all day.

"What did Clavis have to say, Lord Volga?". This time his words did not trail off, for the Emperor could already read his trusted advisor's eyes. The Emperor smiled again, this time broadly.

"Clavis was VICTORIOUS," Volga said loudly. The room erupted in cheers, hoots, and howls. The Senators shook the Generals' hands, the Admirals cheered, and the Capans banged their hands on the wooden table. Only one Man in the room did not smile. The Man on the Emperor's left, General Initium, remained silent. General Initium oversaw the upcoming Dwarf invasion, and everybody knew that Clavis would want his job now that he was done with the northern barbarians.

"How many Legionnaires did we lose, Lord Volga? Is that tribe of barbarians done?" the Emperor asked. His words silenced the men in the room immediately.

"Clavis reports minimum losses. He routed the barbarian tribe, killed at least three thousand, wounded twice that much, and took a few hundred as slaves," Volga replied in his deep, monotone voice.

Everybody in the room again started pounding their fists on the table, all except the Emperor and Initium. The Emperor looked over at Initium, and he began to slightly bang his clenched fist against the table. The Emperor smiled, then raised his hand, silencing the assembled men.

"Finally, some good news, some good news!" the Emperor beamed. "Excellent, excellent! Clavis can join the main Legion group for the invasion. The Third Legion deserves a rest here in Capa before they head out and join the main group, though. Volga, see to it," the Emperor commanded.

Volga nodded and began writing the Emperor's orders down. The Emperor began pacing around the room, behind the seated men, with the bread knife in hand. He kept pacing until he remained standing behind Initium. The mood in the room switched quickly from celebration to uneasiness. The Emperor began to speak slowly, patting his left hand with the blade of the knife. "What do you have to say about Clavis' victory, Initium? Pretty impressive, isn't it?" the Emperor asked.

"Yes, my Emperor," Initium replied in his thick Capan accent. "Very impressive."

"Very impressive indeed! Clavis took on ten thousand barbarians with a single Legion Initium! He killed thousands of them, scattered the rest, damn Man is a hero of the Empire!". The Men around the room shouted and pounded on the table again, for they could sense the shift in the Emperor's mood. For a minute, everyone had thought that Initium might find that bread knife in an uncomfortable spot. This would have been a shock to all there. For the Emperor had always liked Initium, promoting him early in his career, despite his youth and background of growing up in the slums of Capa.

"What about you, Initium? How many thousands of Dwarves has your Legion killed?" the Emperor asked the question quietly. His eyes scanned the room briefly. He then shifted his gaze to Initium and looked into his brown eyes.

"The Fifth Legion is the only Legion under my command that is in Dwarf country, my Emperor," Initium replied.

The Emperor looked around the room with amazement in his eyes, leaned over the table, slapped his own head in jest. "I know this Initium! How many have they killed? How many Initium?". The amused look on the Emperor's face faded to cold anger. "How many Initium?" the Emperor asked again. Some in the room wondered if Initium's rise was about to end.

Commander Initium had been looking down at his hands while the Emperor questioned him but now raised his head slowly. There was no fear in his eyes, only determination. "My Legions have not killed any Dwarves recently, but…. we will slay them all my Emperor, ALL OF THEM!". With that statement, Initium slammed his fist down on the table.

The Emperor walked back over to his seat at the table, sat down, began cutting the bread up, and dipped it in the vinegar. "We will crush the Dwarves. We must. Our ancestors demand it. Our people need it. All the Dwarves. Those in that mineshaft of theirs and those north of Badatoz, they will all perish. All of them," the Emperor stated.

The men around the table all nodded solemnly. They all had heard these anti-Dwarf speeches before. They had grown up hearing them. The Emperor kept eating, shifting his attention away from the Dwarf scum and to the affairs of the Empire. A pox had broken out in the slums beyond the tanneries. Medicine was in short supply. Legionnaires would be banned from the area. Tax collectors in eastern Mericam had been attacked recently. More Legionnaires would be sent. The entrance fee to the Arena was being raised to help fund the additional Legions that were being formed and trained. New ships for the Empire's navy were being built but slowly due to a lack of timber. With that, the Emperor looked back at Initium.

"Can your Fifth Legion provide any protection to the Capans that go up the Cold River?" the Emperor asked. Anger flashed in his dark eyes.

"We can't provide good protection past the last outpost, Fort Carillon. The timber cutters have cut all the timber around the fort. They head upriver where we cannot travel in force," Initium replied. The Emperor nodded, but his eyes still burned with anger. The land up the Cold River was rugged, but the timber was immense. The kind needed for warships. The Empire needed ships, for Koristan's navy badly outnumbered them.

"Well, for the price they are getting for timber, they can risk a few pesky Dwarves, right Generals?" the Emperor stated. The Generals all nodded in agreement, for timber cutters who could manage to bring timber down the river could make a small fortune. "Little tree bastards, with their little arrows anyway. Shouldn't stop a big ax swinger!" the Emperor laughed at his own joke. He then recapped the priorities of the Senate. A trade representative from Monger was expected soon. "We got enough fish, right boys?" the Emperor jested, the Generals and Senators chuckled. The Emperor kept eating his bread, soaking it in the vinegar. The harvests from the Fertile Crest were expected to be good this year. A member of the Resistance had been captured. He had killed himself before making it back to Capa.

"Damn lucky bastard," Volga muttered under his breath. The Master of the High Keep was known to spend considerable time in the torture chambers.

"What was that Volga?" The Emperor had heard Volga curse already but liked to keep him on his toes.

"The Prince of Stonedom, Talar, has arrived at the High Keep. Just walked in a few moments ago, my Emperor," Volga replied, ignoring the emperor's jest.

The Emperor seemed surprised that Volga had not told him this yet. Before the Emperor could speak, Volga did. "I thought you would want to hear of Clavis' victory, my Emperor." The Emperor nodded again and asked Volga if he was sure if it was Talar and not Cynfor who had entered the High Keep. "No, Talar Stoneking entered the Keep. That is the name he gave to Captain Tiberius," Volga replied.

The Emperor asked how many Men were in the Stonedom Princes' escort. "Just two, my Emperor," Volga replied.

"Just two, Volga?" the Emperor inquired. Volga nodded again. The Emperor found it strange that only two Men would attend to the Prince of Stonedom. He was slightly irritated that the elder Stoneking had not sent his eldest son Cynfor to pledge loyalty. He had heard that he had been wounded in combat. Maybe the old King needed him for protection. Either way, it gave the Emperor a reason to raise the taxes on Stonedom.

"Just as well, the Emperor muttered. "We'll hold Court in an hour to take stock of this Prince of Stonedom and to make him swear his allegiance to this Empire and me. Generals, Admirals, Senators until then…" the Emperor said with a sweeping hand gesture.

With that, the Generals, Admirals, and Senators began to get up from their chairs and file out of the room. All of them except General Initium. Some of the older generals shook their heads in contempt of Initium. Some sneered but not too obviously for fear of the Emperor's watchful gaze. At long last, the door shut, and only Initium and the Emperor were left at the wooden table.

Initium visibly eased, reached over, grabbed the bread knife and food from below the Emperor, and began to eat.

Standing up and pacing around the table again, the Emperor made sure no one was outside the door. "Sorry about that, Father." Initium simply nodded and continued eating. The Emperor walked back to his chair. Taking a seat, the Emperor asked Initium how he was feeling.

"Just fine, Son, and do not apologize. We must maintain this ruse for obvious reasons," Initium said. The Emperor smiled and kept eating. The Emperor watched his father eat. He ate vigorously. For his youthful frame required a lot of food. He also required Elf blood. For despite looking younger than forty, General Initium was over a hundred years old. The Emperor just sat and stared at his youthful-looking father in amazement. He still could not believe that just so little Elf blood could maintain a Man's life for so long. The public did not know this, of course, only Initium, the Emperor, and the few chosen Men who hunted the Elf blood down for them.

"How is Cyprian doing anyway, Son?" Initium asked, thinking of those same Men who hunted the Elves for them.

"He's out there on the hunt for us, Father. As soon as I hear word from him, I will let you know as always," the Emperor replied.

"Good, if I am to remain visible for the duration of the campaign, I will need at least a pint of fresh blood," Initium said. He had instructed Cyprian to take an Elf alive. Dead Elves only produced a few pints of blood. They would need more eventually.

"A pint Father! We barely have that much left. We do not know when Cyprian will get more. Or how much. As I have said before, and now after his victory... we should allow Clavis to take command of the main Legion group. A hundred thousand Legionnaires are a lot to command Father."

"I've done it before, or have you forgotten," Initium replied sharply, looking into his son's eyes. "I led one hundred thousand Legionnaires against the Great Troll army AND the Dwarf army, and we won. Damn near killed all the Dwarves. Secured the Fertile Crest for us. Secured an Empire for you, Son," Initium said determinedly.

"I know what you have done, Father. The history books sing your praise. The King who turned Capa into an Empire," replied the Emperor. He had lowered his voice to not anger his elderly father.

Upon hearing his son's praises, Initium nodded his head. "My actions changed history once, Son and they will change it again. Remember, Son, I helped write those history books. We lost forty thousand Legionnaires and nearly the same amount was wounded during the Great Battle, a good number to the Dwarves. I hope we do not lose that many again. That amount of carnage is awful, Son. Inevitable in war, though," Initium stated with no regret.

"Yes, Father, but you killed almost all the Dwarves seventy years ago. They do not reproduce like us. That is known. We will crush them, even if they hole up in that mineshaft. The Legions will not be stopped. You will lead them to victory," the Emperor said confidently.

Looking up at his son with love in his eyes, the youthful-looking father nodded, patted his son on the back, and began to proceed to exit the room. The Emperor asked one last question of his father. "Will you be at the young Stoneking's allegiance ceremony Father?".

"Yes," replied the Emperor's father. "His grandfather bent down on his knees in front of me, and now I will watch his grandson do the same with you. Make sure there is fear in this Talar's eyes. Make sure there is obedience. I will see you, Son; may the Gods be with us both." With that, the elderly General Initium, who looked younger than forty, and whose son was Emperor, left the room.

Chapter VI- A Prince's Pledge

Talar glanced nervously to his left and right. Before him, a set of golden doors encrusted with shining red gems stood shut. To his left was Captain Tiberius, who was vigorously shaking off the road dust from his trousers. To Talar's right was an older Capan in a perfectly clean white robe and sandals. Captain Tiberius had introduced Talar to the white-haired Man and had said that he was the Keeper of the High Court. After shaking Talar's hand, the Keeper had simply nodded his head and motioned for the two of them to remain in front of the massive golden doors. Talar looked at the gems, the only bright spot the young Prince had seen since setting foot in the massive Keep.

Talar began to feel uneasy and began sweating profusely. He wiped his clammy hands on his trousers. The ruling class of Capa was behind these doors, along with the Emperor. Talar did not really know what to expect or, for that matter, what to do. There was no specific loyalty oath that he knew of. The Keeper of the Court sensed Talar's nervousness. "Keep your head bowed the entire time, young Prince. Wait for the good Captain to be relieved of his duty. Then do as the Emperor instructs and always address him as Your Emperor, understood Prince?".

"Yes, Yes," Talar sputtered.

"Do not mutter and mumble, like you just did," the Keeper stated and then rolled his eyes. The Keeper heard a gong from inside the High Court and began to unlatch the gem-encrusted door.

"Remember what I said, young Prince," the Keeper whispered while pushing open the great golden doors to the marble courtyard below. Talar gasped in astonishment as hundreds of Capans turned around at once and stared at him. Most of the people were dressed as the Keeper was, in clean white robes and sandals. Legionnaire officers and generals stood out amongst the crowd, as most in the courtyard wore the white robes. Unlike the Keeper, most in the courtyard were adorned in gaudy necklaces, bracelets, and rings. They were flashier and larger than any rings or necklaces that Talar had ever seen. Some of them even had jewel-encrusted dagger sheaths.

Tiberius nudged Talar's shoulder, and the two walked down the short staircase to the Courtyard below. Talar could not see the Emperor yet. The robed Capans were peering around the great marble columns of the High Court, trying to catch a glimpse of the foreign Prince. Tiberius and Talar kept walking, the crowd of Capans giving away, until finally, Talar stood before a great golden throne. The throne stood in the middle of the Court and was immense. Jewels, gems, and rubies all decorated the great throne. Two silver swords jutted from the top of the throne, pointing toward the Court's ceiling. Talar was wondering where the Emperor was when he heard the gong again.

The gong's noise reverberated through the Court, and the crowd of Capans kneeled. Talar did as well, but a second later than the others. Keeping his head down but looking out of the corner of his eyes, Talar could see a small contingent of bodyguards escorting a middle-aged, balding man. The soldiers were dressed as Tiberius was, with the strange yellow animal skin with the black dots and the metal breastplates. As the bald man approached the throne, the soldiers spread out around the throne, a ring of swords and shields surrounding him.

"Rise, good citizens of Capa," the bald man said in a surprisingly deep and baritone voice. The balding man, who Talar assumed was the Emperor, was not a large man by any standards. The crowd of Capans around Talar and Tiberius began to rise. Talar noticed that Tiberius' head was still bowed, so he copied Tiberius' actions.

"My Emperor, King of all Kings, Lord of all Lords, and Protector of Mighty Capa, I present Captain Tiberius of the Emperor's Guard, and Talar, son of Cadoc, Prince of Stonedom," the Keeper of the Court said. He had followed Tiberius and Talar, unbeknownst to Talar. His loud words spoken close to Talar's ear had startled the youth. With the crowd of Capans all staring at him, the young Prince began to feel uneasy again. Talar felt sick to his stomach, but remembering Hartwin's words and his training, he gripped the handle of his sword and steeled his resolve. Talar took a deep breath, and while looking down, exhaled slowly.

Silence filled the High Court. It hung in the air until Talar could hear Tiberius' breathing. Someone in the crowd coughed. Finally, after what seemed like an eternity, the Emperor began to speak. "Raise your head and look at me, boy," the Emperor's deep voice pierced through the Courtyard. Talar raised his head and looked into the eyes of the Emperor, the most powerful Man on this continent. Talar was probably only ten feet from the Emperor, and with him sitting on top of his golden throne, Talar could get a good look. The Emperor's blue eyes stared icily back at Talar. Talar could see the intelligence in those blue eyes, the brutality.

"Where is your brother, young Prince?" the words seemed to hang in the silent Courtyard. Talar tried to speak but could not. He could sense the crowd's uneasiness, their hidden hostility, their impatience with the youth. Clearing his throat Talar finally regained enough of his composure to speak.

"He is in Stonedom, attending to my Father, my Emperor," Talar had remembered to address the Emperor correctly. Tiberius nodded just slightly, encouraging Talar to keep speaking. "My father was wounded by a Goblin and is in bad shape, my Emperor."

The balding Emperor with the icy blue eyes just stared at Talar. Talar could still feel the uneasiness in the crowd, and to him, it did not feel like curiosity anymore. It felt like apprehension. Speaking slowly and looking directly into Talar's hazel eyes, the Emperor said: "I sent for your brother, Cynfor. Yet only you are here. Why did your family disobey me?". The words washed over Talar, and fear started to rise from the bottom of his spine to his neck until a chill gripped his entire body. Talar had heard of the horrors that befell Capa's enemies. Those horrors were the main reason Talar's grandfather Tomlin, and his father, Cadoc, had pledged to Capa and not to their ancestral allies, the Dwarves and Elves.

"He is attending to my father. I am sorry, my Emperor. My father was gravely wounded and might not live for much longer. He requested Cynfor to stay. I am sorry again, my Emperor. I did not mean to offend with my presence."

"So, your father was wounded by a Goblin. And he might die. Your brother Cynfor is staying with him. Against my command." Pausing for a minute, the Emperor could feel the hostility towards Talar throughout the assembled Capans. He was going to build off it. "Your Stonedom tribe is quite rebellious, young Prince. Are you proud of that?" the Emperor asked, his eyebrow arching as he did.

"I don't know what you mean, my Emperor. I am sorry if I or any of my family offended you. I am sorry, my Emperor," Talar stated, at a loss for further words. Talar knew of the Court's bloody history. People had been killed in the High Courtyard before. Talar looked over at Tiberius as the Captain slowly began shuffling away from him. This scared Talar even more. The fear built up more when Talar saw one of the Emperor's yellow-clad Guards with his sword slightly out of the sheath. The Guard's fingers tapped the sword, eager to use it on the foreign Prince.

The Emperor could see the young Prince trembling in fear and continued to speak in his loud, deep voice. "Stonedom sends no soldiers to our Legions. Your father refuses it. While Capans die to protect the Empire, you Stonedom people live in no fear. Our enemies, the Dwarves, do not attack you, even though you live so close to them."

Talar was shaking quite visibly now, the fear gripping him, for he was sure that the Emperor was going to order one of his Guards to execute him. Talar looked over at Tiberius again and, to his horror, saw that Tiberius had his hand on his short sword. There was nothing but emptiness in Captain Tiberius' eyes. The crowd around Talar began to curse Stonedom and "Cadoc the coward." Talar was sure he heard one Capan wish for his father's death.

"You better kneel before you fall down, you disobedient northern Coward!" the Emperor roared at Talar, and Talar instantly got down on both knees. The yellow-clad Guards now towered directly over Talar. Talar looked up and could only see the Emperor's face as he leaned over the heads of his Guards. The crowd of Capans now openly cursed Talar, calling him and his family cowards and traitors. "Dwarf lovers," they shouted and sneered. The crowd surged towards Talar, and he kept shaking in fear, certain now that his death was imminent.

"Enough, enough!" the Emperor spoke loudly in a commanding voice, and the crowd stepped back at once. The Emperor made a show of scratching his chin and seeming to think over his options, even though he had hashed this plan earlier with his father. "I have made my decision about Talar, the cowardly Prince of Stonedom," the Emperor stated. The gathered crowd awaited eagerly, some wondering if the prince would be killed here, sent to the Arena to die, or tortured in the dungeons below. Few thought he would survive; the Emperor did not raise his voice often.

"The Young Prince of Stonedom needs to find his courage. He shall be trained here at the High Keep's Academy. That way, he will learn proper Capan culture and how to properly rule and defend his people," the Emperor said.

The Emperor looked down at Talar after speaking, and Talar could see the disgust and disdain in his blue eyes.

Talar's eyes bulged in surprise. He could not believe what he had heard. Despite enjoying the exotic sights of the Capa, Talar longed for Stonedom already. Training at the Academy meant living in Capa. Away from his family, from his wounded father. Talar was almost about to foolishly protest when he realized where he was and who he was speaking to.   "Yes, my Emperor," was all Talar could manage to say.

The Emperor continued, "Stonedom will also finally join the war effort." Talar could hear the words but could not comprehend them yet. "I expect your brother Cynfor to lead a raiding party south to the Cold River," the Emperor said. Talar still could only barely hear the words, the shock of the entire Courtyard experience paralyzing him while he knelt. "I want half of all Stonedom soldiers to report for training duty here in Capa. It is about time Stonedom entered the ranks of the Legions," the Emperor stated in a matter-of-fact tone. Talar could not imagine Stonedom soldiers stripping their metal armor for the red capes of the Legions. He also could not believe that the vast Empire needed half of Stonedom's soldiers. Fearing for his life and the lives of his citizens, Talar merely said: "Yes, my Emperor."

"Those two soldiers who escorted you will join the Legion immediately after their training here in Capa, of course." Talar risked the Emperor's wrath and looked up at him wearily. Seeing the young Prince's dejected look, the Emperor smiled, and his icy blue eyes narrowed as they met Talar's eyes. There was no remorse in the blue eyes and a chill went up Talar's spine. Talar quickly looked back down at the white marble floor of the Courtyard. "Do you understand, Prince of Stonedom?" the Emperor asked. He had mockingly said the word Prince, and the Court erupted in laughter.

"Yes, my Emperor, I understand," Talar replied, saying the words softly.

"Good. It would be a shame for that city of yours to be destroyed over the actions of its young Prince," the Emperor said loudly. The chill that had run up Talar's spine now returned at the mention of Stonedom's destruction. "Now pledge to me, Talar, Prince of Stonedom, that you, your family, and your countrymen will serve me. Will serve the Emperor and Capa until death takes you. Your life and honor are bound to this pledge, so do not say the words unless you mean them, young Prince!" the Emperor coldly stated.

Talar nodded, not wanting to upset the Emperor or the mob of Capans around him. The moment that he had been dreading had now finally come, and he knew what was required. Still kneeling, Talar raised his right hand and began to speak.

"I, Talar Stoneking, Prince of Stonedom, pledge upon my life to serve the Emperor, and Capa, faithfully until death," Talar said loudly. The Emperor was satisfied with the pledge and the dejected look and overall fear that permeated from the young Prince of Stonedom. The boy had learned his place. The Emperor was about to conclude this session of the High Court when the gong rang out again, and the Keeper of the Court announced the envoy from Monger had arrived. Looking surprised at the unexpected guest, the Emperor merely shrugged his shoulders and motioned for the Keeper to usher in the Monger delegation.

Following Captain Tiberius' lead, Talar managed to follow the Captain to the side of the Courtyard without falling. He was still overwhelmed with all that had happened but, for now, he watched silently as the Monger delegation emerged from the Capan crowd to stand before the Emperor.

After the Keeper made the proper introductions, the Emperor motioned for the Monger delegation to rise. The delegation was dressed in the dull gray woolen shirts and matching trousers that were common in the far north. None of the Monger envoys had metal jewelry, but all had bear claw necklaces. The bears' hides served as their coats and cloaks. Their wind-swept faces and pale skin stood in contrast to the tanned and soft Capans. The people of Monger made their living by fishing the Ice Sea and hunting the barren landscape surrounding it. They had no King, no government, and only met up once a year in the spring to trade with the outsiders. While Volga had mentioned the trade envoy earlier, the Emperor did not think they would be arriving today, for the trip was long. Glancing at Volga, the Emperor raised an eyebrow in question. Volga remained expressionless. Not wanting the awkward silence to continue, the Emperor spoke in his deep voice, welcoming the Monger envoy. The Mongers remained silent until finally, an elderly man, draped in a black bear cloak, stepped forward and began to speak.

"Thank you for receiving us, my Emperor," the elderly Man said in a slow and soft voice. His Capan was accented with the harsh native tongue of the north. "We do not wish to take up your time, Oh Great Emperor," the elderly man said while falling to his knees, and the rest of the delegation followed suit.

Blinking his eyes in confusion and looking at Volga for answers, the Emperor again motioned for the Monger delegation to rise. Slightly annoyed with the Mongers' peasantry, the Emperor asked the elderly spokesman why he was here.

"To ask the Emperor to send his red capes north, to defend us." The words of the elder Monger were barely audible, but they drew a loud exclamation from the crowd of Capans. The Mongers were well known for their durability. Three Legions had to be sent to establish order in the far north seventy years ago, immediately after the Great Battle. Monger, like many other northern states, resisted Capan rule and revolted. All the Legions suffered great losses in the ensuing war with Monger, but the simple fishermen and trappers were no match for the Capan war machine. The treaty which settled the war saw the best Monger men sent to the Legions and trade prices set by Capan merchants. The treaty also guaranteed Mongers' safety, even though no Legionnaires were currently posted there in the far north.

"Who do the people of Monger need protection from, Old Man?" the Emperor had to raise his deep voice to be heard over the rumbling of the crowd, for the only thing that could threaten the resolute people of Monger were Trolls. At least that what the Emperor and his fellow Capans thought.

After not speaking for a moment, the Emperor asked the elderly Monger envoy if it was Trolls attacking his people. The old Man took a step forward, and his soft voice silenced the courtyard. "A great band of barbarians raided our villages. They burned our homes, killed our young men, and captured our women. Will you send your red capes north, my Emperor?" the old fisherman asked. The Emperor nodded then instructed Volga to dispatch a Legion to secure Monger. The Emperor assumed the barbarians were the remnants of the Riken tribe that Clavis had destroyed.

The Emperor thanked the old Man for his service to Capa and instructed Volga to give them all fifty gold pieces for their troubles. The entire Monger delegation fell to their knees and thanked the Emperor. He rolled his eyes as they groveled. The Emperor was ready for a glass of wine and some privacy and was about to adjourn the High court when General Initium's voice suddenly rang out from the crowd.

"Old Man, have you seen or heard of that villain and piece of rubbish, Dobervist?", Initium's words silenced the High Court again. Most Capans would not have dared mention the name Dobervist around the Emperor. For the outlaw Dwarf was hated throughout the Empire for escaping the Arena and embarrassing the Emperor himself. Ten years had passed since Dobervist's escape, and the price for his bounty was the highest in the history of Capa. The bounty had never been paid, and Dobervist still remained on the run.

"No, my Lord, I have not seen the Dwarf Dobervist, nor have I heard of anybody seeing him," the old Man had been taken back at the question. No one in his village had ever seen a Dwarf, for they lived on the other side of the continent.

The Emperor's father seemed satisfied with the answer, and not wanting to hold the people up any longer, the Emperor motioned for the Keeper to end the High Court Session. He also motioned for Lord Volga to come over to him. After whispering to Volga, the Emperor pointed at Talar. Talar knew his future was being decided for him by the two Capans. Lord Volga approached Talar and told him gruffly to follow him. As the Capans left the High Court, Talar followed Volga to a rear exit. His whole world had been spun upside down. There would be no going home. At least not anytime soon. He could not believe it. He was stuck in Capa as a prisoner. He felt selfish at once. Hartwin and Alwin had been sentenced to the Legions. They would be forced to fight the Dwarves. Forced away from their families. He thought about the other Stonedom soldiers that were being drafted into the Legions. He thought about Cynfor and wondered what his brother would do with the orders to attack the Dwarves near the Cold River. He thought about his Father, weak and frail after the Goblin attack, and the look he had given Talar after being stabbed. As Cadoc had laid on his bed after the attack, he could barely talk, but he had looked at Talar a certain way. Talar's father had never looked at him before like that. Talar would never forget the look. There had been pride and confidence in Cadoc's eyes. Talar thought of his actions that fateful day. There had been no fear when he had fought with the Goblins because it had been so quick. Today was different. The fear had built up in Talar to the point where it overcame him. Knowing that fear like that could kill him one day, Talar vowed to not let it happen again. His hand went to the hilt of his sword, and he gripped it like his life depended on it. Besides the clothes on his back, his sword was all that he possessed. Talar looked out at the Courtyard as the white-robed Capans left. Those that caught his eye sneered at him in disgust. For the first time since the Emperor had spoken, Talar realized he was alone, and another chill went up his spine.

Chapter VII- A Lonely Dwarf

Dobervist looked up at the tree through the light darkness of the pre-morning dawn. It was a scrubby pine, but it was rugged enough to hold his weight. Slinging his bow over his shoulder, the Dwarf began to climb the bushy pine tree. His strong hands gripped the sticky branches, and he easily hauled himself up, despite his stocky frame. The bow tangled a few times on some smaller branches, but Dobervist was able to make it to a limb that faced the game trail below him. Settling in, with his back to the tree, Dobervist unslung the bow from his shoulder. He then fetched an arrow from the quiver at his side and prepared himself for the upcoming hunt. The pre-dawn darkness was slowly fading as the sun began to crest the ridge ahead of the dwarf. The sun's brilliant orange-yellow light lit up the sky, and Dobervist began to scan to his left and right, looking for any signs of movement. The Dwarf saw nothing.

The sun slowly rose, and soon the darkness was finally gone, and Dobervist could see further out. The game trail below him led to an old field stone wall ahead of him. The wall was a remnant of Mempacton, the lost kingdom, and was used by Mempacton farmers to delineate property. Seventy years of disuse and weathering had not helped the wall, and it was fallen over in numerous spots. Still looking for movement, Dobervist heard the snapping of a twig and the rustling of leaves behind him. The leaves had just begun to turn color, but Dobervist's sharp eyes caught the culprit behind the noise. The grey squirrel pounced along thru the woods, occasionally stopping to peer around. To Dobervist, the squirrel was making quite a racket, but there was nothing he could do. The noise would not affect his hunt. The squirrel continued his journey until it stopped and dived into one of the holes that the fallen stone wall provided.

A few hours passed like this, with Dobervist constantly looking around, only to stare at the red and grey squirrels that passed below. The Dwarf had picked the spot due to the game trail and the marks the stags had left on the trees around his perch. No stags seemed to be in the area. His legs cramping and his hands cold, Dobervist was about to climb down and call in Stripe when he heard the dogs' barks ring out from the forest beyond the wall. Dobervist quickly knocked an arrow, for the dog only barked when he was on a stag. Or a boar. Dobervist hoped it was a stag and hoped the nimble beast would pass close enough to give him a shot. Stripe continued to bark, his short, loud barks becoming louder as he closed in towards Dobervist. The dog's barking was becoming louder, but now Dobervist could hear the breaking of dead tree branches and the snap of pine saplings as something large charged through the brush ahead of him. His view was impeded by the old fieldstone wall, but Dobervist knew Stripe could smell him and knew both animals would be in view shortly. Taking a deep breath, Dobervist began pulling back on the arrow slightly, preparing himself for the shot, which he knew would come quickly.

The crashing through the brush was loud now, right behind the stone wall, and Dobervist now heard the grunting and snarling of a boar. He immediately began to worry about Stripe, for the small dog could easily be gored to death by the tusked boar. He had been cut open by one before but still was fearless. His thoughts about Stripe passed as both the boar and dog finally came into view, both animals hurdling thru the gap where the grey squirrel had hidden hours before. The boar was old and tough and swung his tusks sharply around at Stripe. Stripe continued to bark and hound the boar, biting the boars' tail which forced it towards Dobervist. The boar was forty yards away from the Dwarf, usually an easy shot, but Dobervist view was blocked by brush and saplings. He held the arrow back slightly still, waiting for the boar to come closer. Stripe continued to bite and nip at the big boar until finally, the boar kicked him in the ribs sending the small dog flying back into the stone wall. The boar took off down the game trail, right at Dobervist and the Dwarf knew it would be a tough shot. His only shot was down at the boar's top instead of hitting him broadside. As the boar approached, only ten yards away now, Dobervist pulled back on the arrow. The Dwarf's hand came up to his cheek for just a fraction of a second before the wooden arrow flew away from Dobervist, hitting the boar with a thud.

Dobervist's head bobbed from side to side as he strove to look where the boar had been hit, but the boar screamed in pain and kept running. The wounded boar, tough and old, ran through the brush until he was out of sight. Dobervist remained in the tree, and Stripe finally came over, unharmed from the hunt. The Dwarf was certain he had heard the boar crash, and he hoped it was a final crash into the forest floor. Taking a deep breath and exhaling, Dobervist looked down at Stripe and smiled. The small brown dog with the white stripe down his backside smiled back at the Dwarf. The two were friends.

Climbing down from the scrubby pine took the Dwarf a few minutes as he did not want a broken foot from a fall. The Dwarf and dog were miles and miles away from the nearest trace of civilization, except for the forgotten stone walls. After reaching the ground, the Dwarf went over to Stripe, who was already lapping up the blood from the boar's wounds. The Dwarf could not see any pig fat mixed with the blood, which was a good sign. Stripe peered anxiously up at the Dwarf, ready to begin tracking the wounded boar. Dobervist knew better. It was better to let the boar lay down and die. Boar tusks were viscous, and he did not want to be wounded, and he certainly did not want any harm to come to Stripe. Bending over to pet the dog, Dobervist looked up at the sky and figured he had plenty of time before dark. Before the wolves and Trolls came out. Stripe jumped up, interrupting his thoughts, and began licking the Dwarf's face. Laughing, the Dwarf continued petting the dog, biding his time, and hoping the boar was dead.

After what seemed like an hour to the Dwarf, he and the dog began tracking. The Dwarf had hit the boar in the small stand of scrub pines, but the blood trail led away into the hardwood forest to the east. Dobervist let the dog do his job and instead began taking mental notes of where they were going, for he was not too familiar with the forest around him. Dwarves, boars, stags, and squirrels were not the only creatures in the woods. The packs of wolves were viscous, huge bears were common, and wandering bands of Goblins occasionally passed through. Not to mention the most dangerous creatures; the Trolls...and Men. Dobervist had been in these remote woods for nearly ten years now. Hunting, fishing, and trapping consumed his time. He had learned how to survive through the harsh winters. He lived alone in this wild forest for a reason. While he hunted the boars and stags, pheasants, and turkeys, he knew all along that he was being hunted. The Emperor of Capa wanted him dead, and bands of Capan hunters had been dispatched to kill him. Only a few ended up finding him, and those who did were never seen again.

The blood trail ran into a stand of old-growth beech trees. Stripe was beginning to track a little too fast for Dobervist's liking, so he whistled to stop the dog. Stripe immediately stopped, looking back at the Dwarf, patiently waiting. Dobervist bent down next to the small dog and looked at the blood trail. It was thick and consistent. Dobervist looked around but saw nothing but the ancient beech trees, their massive smooth grey trunks supporting a canopy of green leaves whose tips were just turning orange. Looking ahead, Dobervist could tell that the blood trail was shifting downhill, which he took as a sign that the boar was beginning to tire. Pushing aside the branches of a maple sapling, the Dwarf continued slowly, the dog matching his pace. The blood trail was beginning to get bigger, with the dark spray from the boar's wounds easily becoming visible against the orange leaves on the ground. Dobervist knocked another arrow and proceeded with caution. The Dwarf and dog kept this slow pace up for another hundred yards, with the Dwarf occasionally stopping to check the trail and to scan the woods. A massive hawk soared ahead, catching Dobervist's eye for a moment, but he quickly focused his attention back on the blood trail. The Dwarf and dog slowly kept tracking until finally, after half a mile, the Dwarf spotted a massive pool of boar blood and his arrow. The Dwarf smiled; he knew the boar was his now.

The arrow was bent where the boar had managed to reach around and pull it out with his teeth. The shaft was worthless, but the dwarf was going to be damned if he left the metal arrow tip behind. Forging arrow tips over an open fire out in the woods was not easy by any standards. The pool of blood was a good sign, and not wanting to wait any longer, they kept tracking.

They did not have to go far. The pair walked down the slight hill, and Dobervist spotted an ancient beech that had fallen. The green moss covering the blowdown hid its gray bark, and its massive root system stuck up some twenty feet in the air. The Dwarf whistled twice now, and Stripe stopped, not moving a muscle. The blood trail looped around the raised roots of the fallen behemoth, and the Dwarf had a feeling the boar was lying on the other side. Creeping forward slowly, the Dwarf tried not to rustle the leaves under his feet but was unsuccessful. If the boar were there and living, it would have moved. Relaxing a bit, the veteran hunter knocked an arrow and made his way around the roots of the fallen beech. He stopped, peered around the edge of the roots, and smiled again. The boar lay dead not ten feet away, lying on his stomach in a pool of blood. The Dwarf raised his fist in celebration, and Stripe bounded ahead, rounding the corner, finally gazing at the boar again. The hunting dog began biting the dead boar's hide vigorously. Dobervist walked over and began looking over the boar. It was massive, much larger than he had originally thought with long weathered tusks. The boar's thick black hair was matted with blood from the wound. The shot had been good, close to the heart, but the boar still had run close to a mile. The Dwarf began to plan how to get the boar back to his camp.

After calming down Stripe and making sure nothing was tracking him, the Dwarf got down to the business of dressing the boar. He put aside his bow and quiver, unsheathed his knife, and quickly field-dressed the boar. Stripe began tearing into the gut pile, and Dobervist whistled, then threw a piece of liver away from the guts. The dog chased it and began eating it. Dobervist finished his task and began wiping his hands clean on leaves. He had cut the edible boar meat into two pieces. He now fished out two pieces of thick vines that he kept in the small knapsack that he carried around his waist. After tying the two vine pieces to the two hunks of meat, Dobervist hung the smaller one from one of the raised roots that jutted out in the air. The Dwarf slung the bigger hunk over his right shoulder, the bow over his left, secured his quiver and knapsack and started the trek back up the hill to his camp. Stripe followed the Dwarf, the dog easily keeping up with him. He paced himself for two trips up and down the hill. The Dwarf could have taken both chunks at once, but he figured he had plenty of time before dark and did not want to accidentally fall.

The Dwarf steadily made his way back up the hill, through the ancient beeches, past the scrubby pine he had hunted in, past the stone wall, until finally, he made it to his camp. The Dwarf had found his "camp" two years ago, just as winter was setting in. Dobervist and Stripe had been forced from the ruins of an abandoned Mempacton farm by a pack of Goblins seeking shelter in it. With little food, Stripe and Dobervist had set off into a blinding winter storm. The Dwarf had spotted the massive pine tree from a distance away and was planning to simply shelter underneath it. Then he had found an opening in it and realized it was hollow. It was also quite spacious, for the massive hollow pine was nearly eight feet in diameter. The dwarf and dog had now been living in the hollow pine for two years now and since had made it quite cozy, at least by his standards.

Approaching the tree branch gate that he had fashioned as a door, Dobervist opened the gate and entered his home. After hanging up the large chunk of boar meat, he took a sip of water from a wooden bowl he kept on a column of rocks that he had stacked. The stacked rocks served well as a table, and they retained the heat from the small fire pit that Dobervist maintained. Stripe liked to lay against the stone table, and he did so now. After munching on some black berries that he had picked the day before, Dobervist tossed Stripe a berry, watching as the dog devoured it. He then grabbed his bow and quiver, then motioned to Stripe. They left their pine tree home to fetch the smaller chunk of boar meat. The trip down to the raised roots was uneventful. After grabbing the meat and heading back up the hill, the Dwarf stumbled upon a magnificent stag just twenty rods from his pine tree perch. The bow was still on the Dwarf's shoulder, and he knew the stag would spot any quick movement. Stripe looked at the stag, only thirty rods away, and then looked back up at Dobervist. Dobervist remained still. After gazing at the duo for a few minutes, the stag turned and began slowly walking away, his massive antlers scraping against the overhanging saplings.

"I'll get you tomorrow," Dobervist said, his first words spoken in three or four days. The days all seemed to blur to Dobervist now. He judged time more by the change of the seasons. He was close to home now, and with only a few hours before dark, Dobervist hung up the other chunk of boar meat and quickly began cutting the hunks into smaller strips. It then took Dobervist a few minutes to collect some tinder, but he quickly started a small fire in his stone fire pit and began hanging the strips above, the smoke from the oak tinder preserving and flavoring the meat. Satisfied that the meat was properly smoking, Dobervist went outside to survey the woods around his home. In the ten years living in the wilds of Mempacton, the Dwarf had learned to constantly look out for danger. A few of the bounty hunters had managed to sneak up on him, but none in recent years. After a while, the familiar sounds of the forest returned. The birds were chirping above, squirrels were jumping through the leaves, and an owl was hooting out in the distance. Looking up at the sky Dobervist realized he had been out of his home longer than he thought and quickly went in as dusk approached.

The hunt had taken Dobervist and Stripe all day, and the dog wearily looked up as he entered the hollow pine. Taking a seat next to Stripe and rubbing the dog's belly, Dobervist threw another piece of tinder into the fire with his other hand. The owl hooted again outside; this time closer. The night was settling in now, and Dobervist cleaned his bloody knife off on a piece of stag hide he kept as a rag. Staring into the fire, he thought about the events that had led him to this solitary life. The Legion's attack on his family's small hunting camp had been swift and without warning. At only five years old, Dobervist could not comprehend what was happening, but he remembered his father being run down by mounted Legionnaires. His mother had screamed upon seeing his father's death, a scream that still was fresh in his mind, even after sixty years. Dobervist did not know what had happened to his mother. He had been captured by a Legionnaire as he wept over his father's corpse. For the next forty years, Dobervist had lived as a slave. He had thought that he was a Man, and so did those around him. He had been owned and traded by rich Capans, who had worked him in the mines. The marks of their whips still scarred his skin.

Dobervist, along with other slaves, had tried to escape those mines south of Capa. Their attempt had failed, and all the slaves had been sent to the newly erected Arena. All the other slaves perished in that Arena, all of them except Dobervist. The crowd roared when he had killed an Ogre. The crowd, like his former slave owners, had thought Dobervist a short, stocky Man. For five years, Dobervist fought as the champion of Capa, becoming the pride of the Empire. During those five years, Dobervist fought almost every manner of creature that had ever lived on both continents. Including Dwarves. Finally, his identity was uncovered by his enemies, and he was sentenced to certain death in the Arena. Against the odds, against the will of the Emperor, and in front of all Capa, Dobervist had escaped the Arena and the city of Capa itself. He then headed north, making his way through the Fertile Crest, where he had found Stripe.

The dog had been abandoned by a farmer for being the runt of the litter. Alone and numb from the life of slavery and killing that he had endured, Dobervist had found an unexpected friend in Stripe. Nursing Stripe back to health, Dobervist had kept moving north until he finally had reached the wilds of Mempacton, where he lived now, ten years later.

Stoking the fire, Dobervist leaned against the boulder, which was beginning to warm up. Stripe rolled over, looked up at Dobervist, then back to his stomach, expecting a belly rub. Dobervist inclined him. The dog was the only company Dobervist had, and he loved the small animal fiercely. While scratching Stripe's ears with one hand, Dobervist pulled off his boots with the other and prepared for bed. He pulled a stag hide blanket over him, and Stripe jumped up to his side, laying his head on Dobervist's chest and staring into the Dwarf's eyes.

"Good boy, Stripe. Good boy. Go to sleep, boy, sleep now," Dobervist muttered to the dog, and the dog took his advice and closed his eyes. At ten years old, Stripe was getting older, and Dobervist dreaded the day he would be without him. Staring up at the inside of the hollow pine, Dobervist thought about what his life would be if not for Capa. His father and mother would probably still be with him. He probably would have found a wife. Maybe he would have a child by now. Maybe a home where all those he loved lived. It would never happen. Dobervist was hated by the Capans as much as he was by his fellow Dwarves. He had unknowingly killed three Dwarves in the Arena, their faces masked to make them look like Goblins. He still remembered the look in the young Dwarf's blue eyes as his mask had fallen off. The fear. The pain. Dobervist had not picked up a sword since then.

The pain and fear on the young Dwarf's face still haunted Dobervist's thoughts, and as he lay in the hollow tree, miles and miles from his homeland, a single tear escaped from his eye.

"I'm sorry young boy. I am so sorry. I'm so sorry," Dobervist whispered the words as he wiped away the tear. For hours, the Dwarf lay there, not being able to sleep. The Dwarf boy's face haunted him. Finally, after long hours, the Dwarf drifted off to sleep. Stripe, who had stayed up with his master, curled up to the Dwarf as the embers of the fire slowly faded.

Chapter VIII- A Chance Encounter

Dobervist's eyes snapped awake when the last ember in the fire popped. He took the stag hide blanket off him and looked over at Stripe. The older dog was still sleeping, tired from the previous day's hunt. Not wanting the small dog to be cold, the Dwarf placed the stag blanket around him and got ready for the morning's hunt.

He checked the smoked pork meat and then sampled a piece for breakfast. The Dwarf checked his weapons next. His bow was in good shape. He had five arrows left, all with metal broadheads. His knife was still sharp, despite the previous day's butchering. After placing the bone-handled metal blade in his leg sheath, Dobervist slung the bow and headed for the door. Stripe looked up with one eye, turning over in the blanket. "Stay boy, stay," Dobervist whispered. The Dwarf opened his makeshift door and stepped out into the wilderness.

The moonlight shined down on top of Dobervist's head as the Dwarf headed to his scrubby pine tree post. He hoped the big stag he had spotted the night before would be in the area. After reaching the pine, he climbed up, repeating the events of the previous morning. After settling in, he looked around, his Dwarven eyes trying to pierce through the darkness. It was still twenty minutes before light, and Dobervist had a feeling something was out in the woods.

The Dwarf's instincts were right. Just as Dobervist turned his head to the right, a sudden burst of sound erupted, piercing the morning's stillness. Something large was crashing through the woods, past the old stone wall. Stags did not make this much noise, and Dobervist did not think it was a boar either. The Dwarf was momentarily caught off guard. If it was not a game animal, then whatever was making the noise might want to kill him. If he tried to exit the scrubby pine, the noise would surely give away his position. He decided to remain where he was, and preparing for anything, he knocked an arrow to his bow string. The crashing sound kept coming closer and closer, only twenty yards away, until it suddenly stopped. The Dwarf remained motionless; the arrow ready to be drawn back when the odor hit his nostrils. The foul stench, which reminded Dobervist of rotten meat, overwhelmed him. The Dwarf had smelt this vile stench before but only once.   A chill immediately went up his back, for the stench of a Troll was usually associated with the smell of death.

The Dwarf began to panic. He did not have any long weapons or armor to properly fight a Troll, and as far as he knew, there were at least two of them out there. Dobervist had only seen a Troll once before, at dusk while hunting. The beast had passed right under the tree Dobervist had been perched in. The image of the massive horned beast was instilled in his mind. Dobervist began to worry about Stripe, for the dog would be trapped inside the tree, and the smoked pork meat might attract the Trolls. A massive shadow emerged from the opening in the stone wall, and Dobervist's thoughts about the dog went to the back of his mind. The shadow took another step, and now Dobervist could clearly see the beast behind the noise.

The Troll was massive, at least half a rod tall. The Troll's head was as large as a brown bear with two massive horns protruding from the top of the head. It had eyes like a Man and a large snout with sharp teeth. The huge Troll looked around, raising his head to the wind. The Troll raised his snout, searching for the scent of its prey. The Dwarf had fought massive Ogres in the Arena, but he had been properly armed for the battle. With only a bow, a few arrows, and his small hunting knife, he doubted he could kill one of the legendary beasts. The Troll kept moving, now fully in the moonlight, and Dobervist could see that the Troll had a large wooden spear in his hand. The large hands of the Troll were tipped with claws and covered in thick, brown hair. The Troll's feet mirrored his hands, and Dobervist heard the Troll's claws scrape across a stone on the ground. The rest of the Troll was covered in patches of black and brown hair. Dobervist figured the beast weighed around thirty stone, maybe more.

Hoping that the Troll would keep moving, Dobervist slowly settled back in the scrubby pine, careful not to make any noise. The Dwarf slunk back into the shadows of the pine, letting the tree branches and needles obscure him from sight. The Dwarf was not in luck, though, and instead of continuing along the stone wall, the Troll turned, heading towards the Dwarf. The crashing sound to the Dwarf's right resumed, meaning that another Troll was coming over. With no move to make, Dobervist remained still as the other Troll joined the one Dobervist had seen before. The Trolls were similar, except the new one was slightly shorter and with a different array of fur. The new Troll also was carrying a large round stone, instead of a spear, as well as a horn. After signaling to each other silently, the Trolls split up, taking up ambush positions. Dobervist knew the Trolls were hunting something, but he did not know what. He was thankful it was not him.

Time seemed to stop to the Dwarf. The stench of the Trolls wafted over Dobervist, and he struggled not to cough, fearful of alerting the hulking beasts. The two Trolls had taken up ambush spots, with one hiding behind the stone wall and the stone-laden Troll concealing himself behind a large oak tree. Dobervist again wondered what the pair of Trolls were hunting, for they had scared away all the game with their loud approach to the clearing. He did not have to wait long to find out, for a loud Troll horn bellowed out in the distance behind the Dwarf. It was still too dark for the Dwarf to see, but he could hear more crashing through the ancient beech forest behind him. The Dwarf could also hear more Trolls yelling at each other in their guttural tongue. The Dwarf's heart began to race, for he was now surrounded by a pack of Trolls on the hunt.

Dobervist figured that the two Trolls in front of him were posted to stop what the pack behind him was pushing forward. The crashing sounds were getting louder and louder now, and looking down from the tree to his left, the Dwarf saw a slender figure dart silently out into the opening ahead of him. The Dwarf's eyes opened in disbelief as the slender and lean figure bounded effortlessly between the trees, running faster than any Man that the Dwarf had encountered before. To the Dwarf's horror, the slender figure was sprinting right towards the two massive Trolls!

The Troll behind the oak tree moved first. The Troll jumped out from behind the tree, breaking the dead branches underneath and alerting the slender figure. The Troll then displayed his awesome strength by hurtling the small boulder with one hand directly at the slender figure. Meanwhile, the other Troll behind the wall began to make his move. The stone from the first Troll flew at the unknown figure, but at the last moment, the slender being was able to duck under the flying boulder. The stone struck a smaller tree and burst through it, sending the top of the tree down. The crashing sound behind the Dwarf was getting closer, and the slender figure was not wasting any more time. After regaining his footing from the attack, the figure started forward, right at the other Troll. The Troll behind the stonewall had witnessed his brethren's failure but now gripped the end of his spear with both massive hands. Swinging the spear back as if it were a scythe, the huge Troll then swung the spear forward and released it. The Troll's actions sent the massive wooden spear end over end sideways at the slender figure's legs. The spear flew, then bounced off the ground once, then struck the slender figure in the legs causing them to fly up in the air. Both Trolls rushed forward, grabbing the stricken figure by the arms, and restraining whomever it was roughly.

The sun was now beginning to crest the ridge, the first rays just barely making through the forest canopy to the floor below. Dobervist could see better now and now could make out the blonde hair of the captive before him. He also spotted movement below him, and to his horror, another Troll walked out into the opening along with five or six Goblins. Remaining silent and still, the Dwarf could not help but to wonder who this awful hunting party had captured. For no civilized beings had reason to be in the wilds of Mempacton.

The smaller grey Goblins howled in glee at the sight of the captive. Their hunt had been successful, and now their bat ears twitched in anticipation of the violence to come. Two of the Goblins prodded the blonde prisoner with their short spears, the wooden tips causing him to squirm. The newly arrived Troll strutted over to his brethren, slapping them on the back. This Troll was shorter but much stockier and carried a massive double-sided ax. Holding the captive, the Troll now picked him up by his hands, raising the prisoner in the air and shouting in his native guttural tongue. The sun's rays had by now crested the ridge, and in the morning light, the Dwarf could now see that the slender captive was an Elf!

Catching his breath, the Dwarf began to think over his options. The Elf continued to be prodded by the Goblins, his slender frame absorbing the pain. The Elf looked small compared to the Trolls, but Dobervist could see the Elf was much taller than the short Goblins. The Dwarf already knew that he was going to help the Elf. A dark-haired female Elf with unforgettable green eyes had saved Dobervist from illness as a child. His mother had cried in joy as the fever broke and as Dobervist's breath returned to normal. Since the Dwarves had emerged from underground two millennia ago, they had protected the peaceful Elves. It was a mortal sin amongst Dwarves to not give Elves aid. Dobervist would be damned if he did not help this Elf.

With only five arrows and his small hunting knife, he knew he could not kill all the Goblins and Trolls below him. The Dwarf knew that he had the element of surprise on his side, and he knew that he could outrun both the Goblins and Trolls. The ax-wielding Troll now signaled to the other Trolls and walked over to the stand of saplings only ten yards from Dobervist. The Troll looked up, and fearing that he had been spotted, Dobervist froze, not moving a muscle. The Troll was oblivious to the Dwarf's presence, though, and began bending over a good-sized sapling over. The Troll exerted all his strength, bending the pine sapling over until the top of the tree was on the ground. Seeing what his brethren were doing, the other Troll began to follow suit, bending another sapling over. Dobervist now figured out what the Trolls were up to, for he had heard about these horrors from an old Legionnaire during his captivity in Capa. The Trolls intended to bind the Elf's legs and arms to the tops of the bent trees, then let go of the trees, causing the Elf to be torn to pieces. Apparently, this was an old Troll tradition.

The Goblins then came over, with two of them climbing a sapling until the top bent over enough for the overs to pull it over. Dobervist realized that only one Troll was holding the Elf captive now, the other Trolls and Goblin preoccupied with the bent pine saplings. Knowing that time was not on his side, Dobervist pulled back on the arrow slightly, thinking over the upcoming shot. The Dwarf knew that if he missed and the Troll did not unleash his grip on the Elf, then both were probably dead. For only in the confusion of the Elf's escape could Dobervist make his own. Feeling a slight breeze on his left cheek, the Dwarf stepped forward within the scrubby pine tree. Dobervist pulled the arrow back, his right hand brushing his cheek as the string was pulled back. Quickly adjusting for the wind to his left, Dobervist let the arrow go, and the ash bow sent the arrow speeding towards the horned Troll. Dobervist had aimed for the Troll's throat, hoping to put the arrow through the huge beasts' windpipe. His shot was slightly off and hit to the right of where he had aimed, the arrow getting entangled in the fatty jowls of the Troll. The shot achieved what the Dwarf intended, and after howling out in pain, the Troll immediately released his grip on the Elf. Dropping to his feet and looking up, the Elf spotted Dobervist in the scrubby pine and nodded in appreciation.

Not wanting to waste the surprise, Dobervist rapidly pulled another arrow from the quiver at his side and knocked the arrow. The Goblins and two unharmed Trolls below him still had the pine saplings bent over, shocked at hearing the guttural screams of the wounded Troll. The wounded Troll had collapsed to his knees, soaked in blood that was flowing from his jowls. One massive hand grasped the entrance wound while the other desperately grasped the arrow. Both were covered in dark Troll blood. The ax-wielding Troll moved towards his wounded brethren now, sending the pine sapling hurtling back to its original form. The other Troll followed suit. Not having any other shots, Dobervist pulled back on the arrow, the string touching his cheek for a split second before the arrow was speeding through the air towards the side of the closest Goblin. The smaller grey creature howled in pain as the arrow penetrated deep into his side, breaking through the Goblin's ribs, and puncturing one of the creature's lungs. The Goblin collapsed to the ground, the arrow protruding from his side, as he kicked his legs in pain and howled.

The bent pine saplings had now sprung back to their original form, but they were still bobbing back and forth, shielding Dobervist temporarily from sight. Dobervist stepped forward and, not thinking about it, leaped straight out of the tree. Dobervist hit the ground with a thud, but he had saved the bow from any damage. Looking up, he could see that the Elf was already moving out of the clearing and figured he should do that as well. After rising to his feet, Dobervist took off in the direction of the Elf, sprinting only three rods from the grey Goblins who now surrounded the wounded Goblin. The wounded Goblin had begun spewing up blood, and Dobervist knew the Goblin would die. One of the Goblins noticed the Dwarf sprinting and howling in rage, stepped back, and hurled his wooden spear. Dobervist stepped behind a tree as the missile passed by, then resumed running. Out of the corner of his eye, Dobervist saw the ax-wielding Troll begin to pursue the Elf, as the other Troll tended to the wounded one. Dobervist ducked through honeysuckle underneath tree branches and jumped over down trees as he sped forward. The Dwarf had lived in these woods for years and easily outpaced the five Goblins pursuing him. Taking a moment to survey his surroundings, the Dwarf looked to his right and saw the Elf sprinting through the woods to his right about one hundred yards away. The ax-wielding Troll still gave chase, breaking through the brush and undergrowth like a charging bear. Worst yet, both the Elf and Troll were heading straight to the Dwarf's home and to Stripe.

With the Goblins behind him and the Troll charging at the Elf, Dobervist did not know what to do. He figured that the Troll would find his tree home and the locked-up Stripe if he did not do something quick. The Elf was heading right at the large hollow pine, and not wasting another moment, Dobervist knocked another arrow and began running at the Elf and trailing Troll. Jumping up on a fallen beech, the Dwarf ran across the top of the fallen tree until he reached the end. The elevated perch provided him a good shot at the trailing Troll, who was now only five rods away but still running. By the time the Dwarf brought the arrow back to shoot, the Troll was now six rods away, but the Dwarf let loose nonetheless, sending the arrow at the Troll's back. Dobervist jumped off the fallen beech, landing on the ground then heading to the large hollow pine which he called home. The ax-wielding Troll yelled out in pain, and Dobervist knew he had hit him, but now he only had two arrows left.

Dobervist kept running, pushing through the thick undergrowth and skinny saplings until he reached the clearing around the hollowed pine. Running forward with one of his two remaining arrows knocked, the Dwarf reached the makeshift door to the hollow pine tree and opened it. Stripe jumped up and down, nervously whining, for the small dog had heard the Troll cry out. The Dwarf quickly grabbed the stag hide blanket, threw it on the boulder, and dumped the bowl of berries in it. Taking out his knife, he cut a large chunk of the half-smoked boar meat down and threw it in with the berries. Dobervist then sheathed his knife and tied up the ends of the stag hide, making a crude sack. Slinging the sack over one shoulder, Dobervist grabbed the bow and arrow with one hand. The Dwarf motioned for Stripe to follow him, and after opening the makeshift door, the Dwarf gazed at his hollow tree home. It then hit the Dwarf that this was probably the last time he would see his home, for the Trolls would not forget about his ambush. After trying to take a mental note of his small home, the Dwarf shut the door and turned around, ready to continue his escape. He had not been quick enough.

The leading Goblin of the five chasing him finally caught up, and the Dwarf dropped the sack of food, freeing up his left hand. Dobervist dropped to his knee and knocked the arrow. The Goblin charged into the clearing; the short wooden spear leveled at the Dwarf. Only 2 rods away and with no obstructions, Dobervist drew back and released, dropping the Goblin. The shot had stopped the small grey creature in his tracks. The rest of the Goblins emerged from the forest but were hesitant to proceed. Out of nowhere, the ax-wielding Troll burst through the thick undergrowth, sending saplings, twigs, and branches up into the air as he landed in the clearing. Dobervist's arrow remained buried in the brute's back, and for a second, the Dwarf and Troll locked eyes.

"Run Dwarf, run!" a voice called out behind Dobervist, and not bothering to see who it was, the Dwarf picked up the sack and turned around. The blonde Elf stood before him, waving his arm frantically, motioning to the Dwarf to hurry up.

A simple "Yep" was all Dobervist could manage to say before he started sprinting out of the clearing, away from the tree he had called home for two years. Stripe was already ahead, waiting with the Elf. The trio now all sprinted forward, the nimble Elf taking the lead, Stripe in the middle, and

Dobervist trailing behind. The wounded Troll and four Goblins gave chase, the Goblins following behind the massive Troll who continued to crash through the undergrowth, despite his wound.

The trio kept this up for another ten rods but they were not making much ground on their pursuers. "Where are you taking us," Dobervist shouted at the Elf, who simply shrugged as he kept moving.

"I haven't been around here in three hundred years, Dwarf!" the Elf replied, his voice surprisingly calm. "Go right, right, Elf. Right!" the Dwarf shouted at the Elf, who followed his directions. The trio had now been running for a fifty rods and was below the spot where the boar had died the day before. Dobervist knew if they kept heading downhill, there was a stream below, for he had caught brook trout in it many times before. He also knew that eventually, the stream dropped over a rock ledge, and suddenly an escape plan came into the Dwarf's mind.

The trio kept running downhill, now through an open hemlock forest that pitched even more. Dobervist glanced behind and could see the massive Troll only 5 rods behind him, the Goblins trailing behind the Troll. "To the stream!" Dobervist shouted as the Elf looked back. Stripe was out of sight; giant green ferns grew on the forest floor, obstructing the dog from the Dwarf's view. Dobervist knew the dog was down there somewhere.

The Elf and Dwarf now reached the end of the forest, jumping off the bank and landing on giant slabs of moss-covered stone. The Dwarf looked around in fear as Stripe was nowhere to be seen, but then the dog jumped down from above, emerging from the ferns and landing in the Dwarf's arms. Dobervist had dropped the sack of food to grab Stripe, and the Elf reached over, picking up the sack. "Which way, Dwarf?" the tall blonde Elf asked.

"Downstream," Dobervist spoke the word hurriedly, for all three of them could hear the ruckus the Troll was making above them. The trio proceeded downstream, jumping from moss-covered boulder to moss-covered boulder, slipping occasionally. The three avoided the deeper pools of the stream but still got their feet and ankles wet as they ran downstream.

"They're still behind us!" the Elf shouted after glancing backward. The Troll and Goblins were catching up now, their clawed feet better suited to the wet mossy rocks. The Dwarf motioned to keep going, so the Elf obliged. The trio kept making their way downstream until they reached a bend in the stream that was surrounded by huge boulders on all sides. The trio jumped down, and Dobervist could hear the falling of water up ahead. Rounding the bend, the Dwarf spotted the pair of hand-stacked stone walls that emerged from the banks to his left and right. The walls jutted out from the bank, with the stream flowing between them: an old mill site, another relic of Mempacton. The Troll roared from behind. He was only four rods away and was not slowing. "Keep going!" Dobervist shouted.

The trio passed through the old stone walls, their feet splashing through the stream. In front of them, the stream dropped off a rock ledge and landed into a shallow pool, some three rods below. To the trio's left, the stone was also a sheer drop but to the right, across the stream, there was a ledge that led below. That ledge was not directly connected to the top of the ledge they were currently standing on. At least one rod separated where the water fell off, to where the ledge began. Looking around, the Elf spotted the ledge and nodded at the Dwarf in understanding. Make the jump and escape. Looking down over the falls, a ball of terror formed in the Dwarf's stomach. If they did not make the jump, they would surely die.

The Troll roared again, now only two rods behind. The Elf, still grasping the sack, calmly walked back near the Dwarf. "Can you make it with the dog, Dwarf?" the Elf asked.

"Yea, I think so. Go ahead. I'll catch up," the Dwarf replied. Dobervist's deep voice was in sharp contrast to the Elf's voice. It was also the most talking Dobervist had done in months, and the Dwarf began coughing. Shaking his head, the Elf reached down, petted Stripe, and then sprinted towards the edge of the falls. The Elf's agility was apparent, for even with the sack of food and slippery rocks to run on, he easily sailed from the higher falls' ledge down to the ledge below. The Elf landed deftly, rolling on his shoulder as he landed and coming up on his feet before banging into the sheer cliff. The Dwarf shook his head in amazement. He looked down at Stripe. The dog looked back and barked. Dobervist secured the bow as best he could and picked Stripe up. Looking to his right, he could see the Goblins climbing over the abandoned grist mill's walls as the angry Troll strode down the creek through the opening of the old mill's walls.

The Elf beckoned to the Dwarf from the ledge below, but the Dwarf knew he did not possess the agility the Elf did. Dobervist was much shorter than the Elf and probably weighed twice as much. And that was without Stripe. With no other option and with the Troll now sprinting directly at him, Dobervist took off. The Dwarf stared at his feet below and at the ledge before him, trying to time his steps with his takeoff point. The stream's water hit his feet, chilling them through his buckskin boots. Stripe whimpered, and Dobervist could feel his warmth. Still staring below, Dobervist now approached the last step before the fall's ledge ended. Gathering all his strength, the Dwarf sprung out as far as he could but immediately realized escaping via the waterfalls was a bad idea. Dobervist fell, but the end of the ledge and the Elf's outreached hand seemed so far away. Not thinking that he was going to make it, the Dwarf rashly threw the small dog at the Elf, catching the Elf off guard. Stripe landed in the Elf's arms sending the slender Elf reeling backward. Looking down, Dobervist was shocked to see the end of the ledge was in sight. He stretched out his arms, and his hands hit the end of the ledge. Only the top third of the Dwarf had made it onto the ledge, and his hands frantically searched for a finger hold. Not finding any, the Dwarf began to slide off the ledge, and Dobervist was certain he was going to die. At least Stripe made it, he thought. Then suddenly, the Elf's hand grasped his, and using all his strength, the Elf pulled the Dwarf up, saving his life.

Both the Elf and the Dwarf heaved in exhaustion from the league long run and the frantic jump. Stripe panted and licked at the wet rock that made up the ledge. They all had made it. The Elf was staring back from where they had jumped. Dobervist turned and saw the huge Troll in the daylight finally. The beast was furious. Its' dark brown fur was even darker from the blood that had dripped from the arrow, which still protruded from its back. The Troll's horns, like a small cow's horns, were covered in leaves and twigs. The beast stirred back and forth, its clawed feet clicking on the rock ledge above. The Goblins cowered back, afraid of the Troll's wrath. Dobervist realized that the Troll was thinking of making the jump below. To where they now sat.

"He won't do it, no way. No way," Dobervist said nervously.

"I think he might, Dwarf. He looks mad. Wants to kill us all, you know. Especially me. With that being said, I think we should be going," the Elf said in a wily manner, handing Dobervist his sack of food and starting down the ledge.

"If I barely made it, no way that big bastard makes it. No way. Not with that arrow sticking out of him. No way, Elf," Dobervist said confidently. The Dwarf looked at the taller Elf and nodded at him with confidence. He had fought enough foes to know when to run and when to stand his ground.

"So, what do we do, Dwarf?" the Elf asked, a smile starting to cross his face.

"Step back and keep Stripe back," Dobervist answered, a smile crossing his face, for he liked this Elf, who was not nearly as solemn as the Elf Dobervist had met before.

The Troll raged above, swiping at the Goblins who tried to remove the arrow from his back with his giant ax. The Goblins failed, so instead, they reared back, and threw their spears at the trio. All four of the spears hit the sheer rock above the trio and, besides making a racket, caused no harm. The Dwarf now picked up one of the spears and looked it over, getting a feel for its' weight and balance. The Troll now looked back and forth, trying to figure the distance of the jump. Enraged at the trio for ambushing them after their long hunt, the Troll trotted back to where the Elf and Dwarf had started their sprint over the ledge. The Troll howled one last time, threw his ax to the ground, and raced towards the ledge, intent on murdering the trio below.

"I can't believe it," the Dwarf said loudly.

"Told you so, Dwarf, let's get going, shall we," the Elf replied hurriedly.

The Troll, meanwhile, was already past the stream and now took his last step, his clawed legs thrusting him out with force. The Dwarf, meanwhile, picked up the spear and walked towards the end of the ledge. The Troll flew down, farther, and farther until he finally crashed into the end of the ledge, like the Dwarf's approach. The Troll's eyes were barely visible as his clawed hands wildly grasped at the smooth rock, the claws screeching along the end of the ledge. Without saying a word, the Dwarf walked over and stabbed the Troll in hand with the spear, twisting the spear as he plunged it in.

"That is just awful, Dwarf. Just awful," the Elf said, for Elves hated violence, even against their enemies. The Troll, meanwhile, with only one clawed hand to support his massive body, was slowly slipping off the ledge as the Dwarf held the spear and the Troll's right hand off the ledge. The Troll approached the end of the ledge, and throwing the spear away from him, Dobervist stomped on the Troll's other hand, sending the Troll off the ledge. The Troll howled in anger, then in terror, as he fell below. The Goblins screeched and shrieked wildly. The Troll's hairy body hit the rocks below, his body and blood bouncing off the rocks and landing in the stream below. The Goblins, full of fear now, ran off, disappearing behind the abandoned mill's walls.

Despite his disdain for violence, the Elf smiled at the Dwarf. "Well done, Dwarf, we should be going now," the Elf said. Dobervist looked over the Elf, and his jaw dropped when he saw his eyes. Bright flashes crossed through the Elf's pupils. Dobervist looked closer, and he saw a starry night sky within the Elf's pupils.

Bending over to pet Stripe, the Dwarf kept examining the Elf. He was dressed in forest green wool trousers and had a rough brown woolen cloak with a similar undershirt. Besides his boots, he had nothing else. "Who are you, and what are you doing out here, Elf?" the Dwarf asked.

"I could ask the same of you, Dwarf, but for now, just know those are not the only dangerous things tracking me. I will explain as we move, but we need to keep going. Is that alright with you, young Dwarf?" the Elf asked.

The phrase young Dwarf sounded odd to Dobervist, but he nodded at the Elf, stood up, and checked his bow. It had somehow survived the jump, but he had only one arrow left. The Dwarf picked up one of the Goblin's spears, and nodding at the Elf, they headed down the ledge to the small pool below. The ledge leading below was above the hemlocks and the shallow pool. The ledge took them along the side of the cliff below, gradually meeting the forest floor. The giant hemlocks soared up above, and the giant green ferns returned as well. The green fronds stood out against the orange needles below them. The gentle murmur of the stream seemed to calm everything. Stripe ran ahead, lapping at the stream's running water. The Dwarf looked at the Elf and asked him where he was headed to.

"Oakbridge, Dwarf, but I haven't been in these woods in ages," the Elf replied, wondering if the Dwarf would continue to guide him. His Elven instincts told him that he would need the Dwarf's help again. Dobervist's mind was already set, though. He was getting tired of lonely nights in the deep woods by himself and desperately needed company. The Elf seemed alright, and it was his Dwarven duty to protect him anyway.

"I know the way. Follow me, friend," Dobervist said while extending his hand. The Elf shook it, and the trio took off downriver, the stream silencing their footsteps.

Chapter IX- The Academy

Talar stared at the walls of his room. It had been a few hours since Volga had escorted him out of the High Court, leaving him behind the Emperor's throne to a walkway that led higher up into the Keep. Volga had not said a word until the two of them had met a pair of High Keep Guards. The High Keep Guards were all highly decorated veterans of various Legions. Most were big, hulking Men with stocky shoulders and thick necks. The High Keep Guards carried the short sword of the Legion and were dressed like the Emperor's guard, sans the fancy yellow animal cape. Volga and Talar approached the two Guards in the narrow hallway.

"These two will take you to your room. Food and drink will be brought later. An instructor from the Academy will fetch you in the morning." Volga then turned abruptly and left the way they had entered. Talar was left alone with the two weathered Guards. Without saying a word, one motioned to Talar with his hand, and Talar followed obediently. The other Guard fell in behind Talar, and Talar began to feel helplessly trapped between the two brute Guards.

After climbing a few spiral staircases, the lead Guard suddenly halted in front of two large wooden doors with large bronze handles. The Guards led Talar through a bleak, windowless hallway. Sturdy oak doors were uniformly spaced out on both sides of the hallway. The lead Guard then stopped and unlocked one of the doors. The Guard gestured for Talar to enter, and he obeyed and walked into the room. The Guard shut the door wordlessly, the bang of the heavy door echoing through the quiet hallway.

Talar looked around at his room. It was windowless, with a simple cot, wooden desk, and chair. That was it. A grey blanket was folded on the cot, and he went over, picked it up, and placed it on the chair. Talar, Hartwin, and Alwin had all ridden almost non-stop from Stonedom, and the long journey was catching up to the youth. Talar did not know what to do, did not want to think about anything, so he simply stared down at the grey stone of the High Keep. After some time, he got up and sat at the desk, thinking about what had happened.

Talar eventually nodded off and woke up a few hours later, his head slumped over the desk. Someone had entered the room and left a plate of fruit and cooked chicken, which Talar began devouring. There was a lit candle on the desk. There was also a small pitcher of red wine with the food. Talar poured himself a glass and tasted it. The bitter liquid was foreign to Talar, who always had drunk ale with his meals. He gulped down the wine, decided he enjoyed it and poured himself another. The day's events began to wash over Talar, and he instantly felt ashamed. For a while, he sat here dining and drinking wine. Poor Hartwin and Alwin were already in the Legion's barracks. Besides that, he had brought shame to himself, to his family, and to all Stonedom. Talar drank from the glass greedily and remembered himself shaking like a coward in front of the Emperor. He remembered kneeling, shaking, the fear paralyzing him. Talar knew he had to do it for his own safety and for the safety of Stonedom. He still hated himself for being so afraid, though.

"Never Again," Talar said over his wine glass, speaking to no one. At that moment, the youth vowed to never show fear in front of his enemies again and vowed he would be fearless in front of the Emperor and his Guards again. Finishing his glass of wine, the youth poured another and another, finishing the pitcher. His body buzzed from the strange alcohol, and Talar fell onto the bed. "Never again, never again," he whispered drunkenly until he fell asleep again.

Talar awoke to the noise of someone pounding on his door. The sound immediately jolted the youth from his deep slumber, and as Talar woke from his sleep, he found that his head was ringing. The young man's first experience with wine had left him with quite a headache. His head pounding, Talar groggily walked to the door, still dressed in the clothes he wore the day before. Talar opened the door, not knowing what to expect.

A middle-aged man with short dark hair and a finely trimmed mustache stood before Talar. He was dressed in the white robes popular among the elites of Capa. The man frowned instantly at the sight of Talar. "Where are your robes?" he demanded.

"What robes are you talking about?", Talar answered, looking around the small room and noticing his sword and boots were missing. "Hey, where's my sword? Where are my boots?", Talar demanded of the robed man, sending a look of shock across his face.

"I am the Headmaster of the Academy, and I will not be addressed in such an insulting manner," the look of shock had faded quickly. Anger had replaced it. "I ask you again, where are your robes?" the headmaster asked. His words were quick and sharp. Talar shook his head and told him that he had not seen any robes and again demanded to know where his sword and boots were.

"Master, pupil, you will address me as Master, or your questions will not be answered," the headmaster harshly said. Motioning to a servant down the hall, the headmaster told the servant to fetch a set of robes. Talar's head was still ringing from the wine, and his stomach felt sick from the fact that now he was required to call this worm of a Capan master. For upon closer inspection, the headmaster was quite frail-looking, but he still sported a bloated belly from too much feasting.

"Where is my sword, my boots?" Talar said, raising his voice, remembering his vow from the night before. The headmaster simply sneered at Talar, then grabbed a set of robes from a servant and roughly tossed them into Talar's hands. "You stink of filth, Northerner, change quickly, your already late for class," the headmaster snarled, shutting the door in Talar's face.

Talar stood before the slammed door in outrage. His sword was not anything special, a normal sword from his father's armory in Stonedom. Cynfor carried the family's ancestral sword, the broadsword forged centuries ago by the Dwarves. The sword still reminded Talar of home, though, and he wanted it back. Anger seethed through his body. His head still pounded from the wine. He was dirty and filthy from the journey here. He wanted the sword back but knew he could not get everything he wanted while a prisoner here in the High Keep. Better to pick battles he could win. Keep Stonedom safe. Taking a deep breath, Talar began to change, disrobing from his dark trousers and green tunic to the white wool robes the headmaster had thrown at him. The white robes were not itchy, surprisingly, but Talar still felt awkward with only the robes on. The headmaster banged on the door again. Talar turned and opened the door.

"Much better," the headmaster exclaimed, clapping his petite hands together. "Now, take these sandals, and follow me," the headmaster dropped a pair of leather sandals on the floor. Talar awkwardly put them on and gingerly followed the headmaster, his feet unaccustomed to not being in boots.

"You can address me as Headmaster Calbrius, pupil, understood," the headmaster proclaimed. He expected an answer from Talar, but Talar was going to be damned if he was going to call him Master. Talar maintained his silence, and Calbrius snorted in disgust. "You will learn your place, pupil. There are consequences for your actions. I speak directly to the Emperor. You do not want to see him again, do you boy?", Calbrius asked loudly.

Talar did not say anything, instead of shifting his gaze from Calbrius' dark eyes to the floor. Calbrius, happy to see the look of defeat on the youth's face, smirked in delight. The pair continued, rounding a few corners until Calbrius stopped in front of two large wooden doors with the large brass handles.

"This is the entrance to the Academy. You will learn the route in time. You are only permitted to walk from your room to here. That is all. Remember what we talked about earlier, pupil," Calbrius then opened the door and beckoned Talar inside.

A room with a marble floor,like the High Court lay before Talar. Four large columns stood in the middle of the spacious room, forming a large square. Within the columns, roughly thirty robed students were bent over their desks. Upon Talar's arrival, they twisted back, looking at the Northerner. Calbrius waved at another teacher, who waved back at the headmaster and motioned for Talar to enter. The teacher stood between the farthest stone columns, but what lay beyond the teacher is what caught Talar's eyes. A large window, half a rod in width, and spanning the length of the room dominated the background. The window offered a stunning view over the New City, which seemed to stretch to the horizon.

Talar, heeding to the beckoning teacher, walked closer to the marble columns until he was in front of his fellow students. The teacher introduced himself as Instructor Malnar and pointed to an empty desk in the first row. Talar walked over to the empty desk, noticing that some of his fellow pupils wore gaudy gold necklaces and rings. Their linen robes were better woven as well. After taking a seat, Malnar nodded at Talar and was about to speak when from behind Talar, a weasel-like voice spoke up.

"Shaking like a leaf, he was, northern coward!" a short Capan with dark hair said, his golden necklace bobbing as he spoke. Talar turned and glared at the Capan. "Look how mean he is, dirty barbarian." This remark drew a round of laughter from most of the students. Knowing there was nothing much he could do, Talar remembered the face of the boy who had spoken and remained quiet.

Instructor Malnar continued with his lesson, a history of Capa before the Troll War. Malnar possessed a monotone, bland voice, and after a few minutes, Talar began to stare out of the window at New City below. Talar wondered if Hartwin and Alwin were down there, enduring the training rigors of the Legion. Alwin was young enough to handle it, but Talar worried about the aging Hartwin. He also worried about his ailing father, wondering how his recovery was doing. Talar wished he had spent more time with his father now that he was so far from him. Cadoc had always been preoccupied with governing Stonedom and patrolling Stonedom's borders. Even so, Cadoc had always treated Talar well, always made time to go hunting and fishing with him. Talar closed his eyes and prayed to the Old Gods that his Father and Cynfor were well. Time went by, and Malnar seemed content to ramble on about Capan history when a gong suddenly rang out. The gong startled Talar out of his daydreams, causing him to jump in his seat.

"I told you he was jumpy!" the same weaselly voice from the short, pudgy Capan behind him rang out again. The same students who laughed before joined in again, but Talar noticed a few who did not. Looking to his left, Talar caught the eyes of a beautiful red-haired student who seemed older than the rest. Her green eyes caught Talar's, and his heart began to race.

Malnar collected his books and told the students he would see them tomorrow. Not knowing what was going on, Talar looked around. He spotted servants bringing in various dishes of food. Talar realized it was time for lunch. The students around him began to stand up and mingle around. Talar caught the red-haired girl looking at him and decided to introduce himself. Being the second son of a king meant that Cynfor had received most of Stonedom's young ladies' attention. Still, Talar had brought more than one young woman to the King's hayloft before. Talar smiled at the green-eyed girl and was about to introduce himself when the short, weasel voiced Capan grabbed him by the shoulder. Turning around, Talar found himself looking down upon the short, pudgy Capan along with four of his friends.

"Barbarian scum, shaking like a leaf in front of the entire High Court," the pudgy Capan shrieked, repeating his previous insult. "Trembling like a scared little girl, wasn't he, Ralphin," a taller freckle-faced boy to the right of the pudgy Capan said. Talar figured that the short, pudgy, dark-haired Capan with the weasel eyes and black eyes was Ralphin. "Yea, Tobias, he is just a northern coward. Just like their famous Paladin. Just like their famous Knights. They all ran from battle shaking just like he was. Without us, his people would have been Troll food!", Ralphin replied. All five of the boys laughed now, and Talar grew angrily. It was one thing in to insult him, another to insult his people's history. Clenching his fist, Talar hauled back and was about to punch Ralphin when a strong hand grasped his arm. Looking back, Talar looked into the brown eyes of a stocky student with short light hair. The stocky student released Talar's fist once Talar had turned around. "Right where he's supposed to be," Ralphin cackled, and the rest of his cronies joined in. The stocky youth pushed Talar aside and stood beside Ralphin, making his allegiance to the spoiled Capan known.

Knowing that he was outnumbered, Talar instead walked over to a large table that was ladled with food and water. Talar grabbed a plate, loaded it up with strange-looking berries and crab meat. After tasting the crab meat and finding it delicious, Talar walked over to the window, keen to gaze down upon the New City. Talar picked at the crab meat and gazed down below, seeing the tiny figures of the common Men and Women below. The New City looked hastily constructed to Talar, with aqueducts, shops, temples, forges, and taverns all built together in the same area. It also seemed to lack the nicer tile-roofed buildings Talar had seen on his way up to the keep. Looking to his left, Talar almost spurted out one of the berries he had just popped in his mouth. The Arena, which had not been visible from Talar's desk, now loomed to his left, its giant walls casting a shadow down on the shops below. Talar's mouth dropped for the size of the Arena was just dawning on him. The Arena looked about ten rods high, its massive walls constructed of concrete and built with arches for support. Talar marveled at the engineering masterpiece and was quite content to stare at it and eat crab meat when Ralphin's voice called out again.

"His people can't build like us Capans. That's why he's staring," Ralphin explained to Tobias, drawing a laugh from his cronies and some of the other classmates. "I guess his Druids, with all their knowledge, do not know about arches!" Ralphin said sarcastically. Talar turned and realized that he was the only one standing, that the rest of the class had returned to their respective desks to eat. Not letting Ralphin's words go to his head, Talar merely turned around, resuming his lunch and marveling at the Arena.

After some time, the servants returned, removing the leftover food. The males of the class then began to shuffle towards the side of the courtyard, where another double wooden door was. The females split off to the other side, and not wanting to cause a disturbance, Talar followed the rest of the young Men. The stocky student who had grabbed Talar's hand began to stretch his arms out as if preparing for some physical activity.

"Weapons training, my friend," the student to Talar's right said. The student was a little shorter than Talar and had dark eyes. His skin was also darker than the rest of the students, contrasting with the white linen robe he wore. Talar realized that the student who had spoken was Koristan and wondered why a Koristan would be in Capa's High Academy. Talar nodded in understanding, and the Koristan continued speaking. He told Talar that nearly half of their days would be dedicated to weapon training.

"Apparently, this is higher learning in Capa," the Koristan added, assuming Talar would know that higher education amongst Koristan nobles was much stringent. Talar nodded again and, after introducing himself, learned that the Koristan's name was Dalir. The two young men shook hands, walking with the rest of the male students into another large, open room, this one absent of columns.

In the middle of the room, three grizzled-looking Men in Legionaries' colors and armor waited for the boys. The rest of the students began to pick up shields and short wooden swords, which were assorted on benches along the perimeter of the courtyard. Talar, not knowing what to do, instead waited patiently, his hands clasped behind his back. Talar had plenty of experience with sword training but not with the weapons the Capans used. The short swords the other boys had picked up were half the size he was used to. The shields, too, were much larger than the standard Stonedom shield, and Talar struggled with its size when one of the Legionaries handed him one. Reaching down to pick up one of the wooden swords, Talar struggled to maintain his balance. The shield was heavier than any that he had used before.

The eldest of the Legionaries, a stocky man with a horrendous slash across his bald scalp, split the boys up, assigning Dalir to be Talar's training partner. Talar was relieved at first but panicked when Dalir initially attacked him. Dalir's wooden sword pelted Talar's shield rapidly, and Talar had all he could not topple over from the attack. After laughing at Talar's awkwardness, Dalir informed Talar that he had been just as clumsy with the shield when he had started.

"I doubt it," Talar replied, and both laughed. The two trained with the rest of the male students for the rest of the afternoon. The three Legionaries gave advice and showed them different techniques. They could break for water whenever they wanted to, and Talar remarked to Dalir how relaxed the weapons training seemed to him.

"We arere nobles, you know, not gladiators. We are not going to fight in the Arena against Ogres and champions," Dalir noted dryly, drawing a laugh out of Talar.

"I guess you're right, Dalir, but back home in Stonedom, Cynfor and I would train for hours without a break. It just seems strange to me," Talar said, wiping his forehead with a towel that the servants had brought in.

"There are plenty of strange things in this city, you'll see," Dalir replied.

The gong sounded, and the eldest Legionnaire clapped, signaling to the boys that the training session was over. Talar looked around and began following the rest of the boys back into the main courtyard. There were no teachers present, and as they emerged from the training room, the young Women emerged from their side. All the students began to walk to the double wooden doors that Talar had first entered with Headmaster Calbrius, and Talar realized that the school day was over. Wondering what he would do with the remainder of the day, he exited the entrance with his fellow students, trying to remember the way back to his door. With little to do in his room, Talar thought of exploring the High Keep. His explorations were cut short due to a stern glance from Headmaster Calbrius, who stood watch over the filled corridor outside the classroom.

Talar filtered among his fellow noble classmates, his white robes feeling as foreign to him as the people around him. After making his way down the corridor, Talar was not quite sure where his room was, but one of the High Keep Guards pointed it out for him. Talar entered and once again was surprised to see fresh ale, cheese, and sliced bread on a tray waiting for him.

"They do feed me well," he muttered under his breath as he sat in the chair. Talar looked over his small plain room and began eating the cheese. His hangover had disappeared, but the anger over his missing sword and boots still gnawed at his pride. Talar poured himself a glass of fruity wine and began to think over his situation. He looked around the room as if the grey stone walls would provide inspiration. It was clear to him that the Emperor wanted him alive, but Talar could not figure out why. If the Capans wanted to take over Stonedom, their massive Legions easily could. They then could appoint their own ruler, somebody loyal to the Emperor. "So why keep me alive?", Talar wondered out loud.

Talar sat in the chair, drinking the fruity wine, and he thought about the question he had asked out loud. No answer came to him. To Talar, killing him seemed much easier than the forced schooling the Capans envisioned. Talar continued to think about the issue until a sudden knock on his door interrupted his thoughts. Talar rose, walked over, and opened the door. A bemused Dalir stood in the doorway, a broad smile on his face.

"This used to be a closet. Did they tell you this, Northerner?", Dalir asked sarcastically. Talar smiled and welcomed Dalir into his "closet," drawing a laugh from the young noble Koristan. Talar shut the door and bid Dalir sit in his only chair, which Dalir did.

"I would pour you a drink, but they only gave me one cup Dalir," Talar said.

"Yes, they do treat you quite badly Northerner, Volga probably tortured somebody in here once." Dalir's remark caused Talar's eyebrows to shoot up, drawing another laugh from Dalir. After catching his breath, Dalir asked him what he thought of his first day of schooling.

"The arms training is easy enough, and the history classes are boring enough, I suppose. The green-eyed girl who sat in the back caught my eye, though," Talar said. Dalir smiled.

"Yes, Mona is quite a beauty. Too bad she is from Mercium. Ralphin or one of his cronies will probably end up marrying her." Dalir's comment caused Talar's jaw to drop. He could not imagine any girl wanting to marry the crude Ralphin, let alone the green-eyed beauty. Dalir saw Talar's reaction and just then realized how naïve the northern Prince was. Shaking his head in disbelief, Dalir looked at Talar as if he was a child. "You don't understand Talar?" Dalir asked.

"I guess not, Dalir. Everything here is foreign to me," Talar replied. Still shaking his head, Dalir went on to explain how Ralphin's father was the Prefect of Brigantium, which had sent the most Legions to help conquer Mercium some twenty years ago. The noble family of Mercium, having lost their sovereignty, were now forced into marriage with Ralphin's family. Talar shook his head in disgust, swallowed his wine, and just stared at Dalir. Dalir could feel the hostility in Talar's eyes. "The Capans are not my people Northerner, I am only a guest here," he stated defensively.

"A guest?" Talar asked. "Why are you in a Capan school if you're only visiting Dalir?".

Dalir nodded. The Koristan had to explain this often. "My father is Ambassador of the High Court of Koristan and has been dispatched to our northern neighbors here in Capa. My father and the Emperor thought it fit for me to study Capan life and history. Probably because I will be the next Ambassador if I don't screw up," Dalir said. Talar nodded in understanding. Talar knew enough of politics to know that Koristan and Capa had traditionally been enemies, but an uneasy peace now existed between the two nations.

Dalir, who was sick of Talar's plain surroundings, asked him if he would like to go back to his chambers, where they could both drink. Talar immediately agreed but wondered aloud if Headmaster Calbrius would approve. "Calbrius will not pester me, do not worry about him. C'mon," Dalir motioned to the door to exit, and Talar followed suit. Both young men glanced up and down the empty hallways. No one was out of their rooms. Talar followed Dalir down the hallway and, after making a few turns, approached Dalir's room. Dalir opened the heavy wooden door, but from there, the similarities between their rooms ended.

Dalir's room was at least four times as large as Talar's. Bright tapestries with symmetrical shapes and patterns adorned the walls, plush red couches ran against the walls, and in the center was a table whose base was made of the tusks of some foreign beast. Talar saw all of this but, his eyes were fixed on the view between the stone arches that were in the back of Dalir's room. Dalir's room had a small balcony that overlooked the New City. Dalir smiled at the shocked Northerner and waved his hand towards the balcony. The two youths went under the arched entrance and stood on the balcony. Talar looked out across the New City. From this high up, he could see endless rows of four-storied stone buildings, packed together like spruce trees on the top of a mountain. Smoke lingered above the New City, and suddenly, a foul odor hit Talar's nose. Looking over at Dalir accusingly, the Koristan threw up his hands while laughing.

"It is Capa's stench! Let me light some candles so you can finally view the other half of Capa without holding your nose", Dalir exclaimed before going back into his room.

Dalir returned after a few moments with a few lit candles. Setting the candles around the pair, the foul odor subsided, and Talar resumed his study of the New City. Below Talar, the New City residents went about their daily hustle and bustle. Talar noticed that, unlike the Old City, the streets were not lined with cobbles. A permeant haze of dust stayed suspended above the New City. Talar could see cattle and goats being herded through the nearest street below, presumably to the local butcher. While the New City was just as busy as the Old City, Talar could not help to notice that the residents seemed shabbier in appearance, with fewer Men wearing shirts instead of going bare-chested. Talar kept inspecting this section of Capa. A strong concentration of smoke in one area seemed to be a bunch of forges and armories. A row of taverns lined both sides of a dirt-filled street. Throngs of Capans fought and wrestled on the bare ground outside. Unconcerned local citizens just walked by, trying not to step on the fighters. A square directly below him looked like an open market, with vendors selling a variety of products. A Woman's scream drew Talar's attention. He and Dalir watched as far below, a young scantily dressed Woman was being harassed by a small group of Men. The Men were trying to pin her up against a wagon filled with hay. Talar began to fear that he was about to witness a rape. Luckily, her screams drew the attention of a pair of Legionaries on duty, who quickly dispersed the group. Talar shook his head in disbelief. While Old City had been foreign, it had seemed civil. New City was wild.

"Yes, I know it seems barely civilized. Sometimes I just come out here and drink wine, enjoy the spectacle," Dalir said before waving his arm above New City.

"The spectacle?", Talar replied. "That Woman was going to be raped."

Dalir assured him that the Legionaries did not allow Women to be raped out in the open during the daytime. "But at night, the streets are dangerous down there. The drunks and thieves take over. The Legionnaires only go out in force and only when they must." Talar shook his head in disbelief. In Stonedom, there was safety day and night, despite Goblins and Trolls. In Capa, chaos reigned as the sun fell.

"Enough of this, Talar, let us go back in and drink. I've got more than one cup anyways.", Dalir said with a smile. Talar nodded and followed Dalir back inside, sitting at the tusk table, as Dalir readied the glasses of wine. Dalir handed Talar his drink and took up a seat opposite of him. "The New City is quite awful; I avoid it at all costs. I advise you to do the same." Talar shook his head in agreement and asked Dalir why the Emperor would let half of his city fall into such an unruly state. "I'll tell you about my opinion on the matter, but you must promise to keep this talk to ourselves," Dalir stated. Talar nodded, and Dalir kept speaking. "The Capans have been at war almost constantly for the past seventy years. This massive slum below us supplies a good amount of the Legionaries in their Legions. It also does not have many jobs, which forces its young to go outside of Capa. Start over in new places. Colonize new lands. It is all part of the Emperor's plan. Do you follow me, Talar?"

Talar nodded in understanding as Dalir sipped his wine. It all made sense to him. Loyal Capan citizens being forced into new territories. "Hopefully, the Capans do not want to colonize Stonedom," Talar said, but Dalir laughed at the notion.

"Colonize Stonedom? Fight off Trolls and Goblins for rocky farms. I don't think so," Dalir said. Dalir leaned forward with a smile on his lips and a question in his eyes. "At the High Court, you spoke that your father was wounded by a Goblin. We do not have Goblins or Trolls or any creatures like them in Koristan. What happened to the Goblin that attacked your father? What are they like?", Dalir asked slowly, remembering that Talar's father was wounded.

Talar's eyes fell as Dalir spoke of his father and the Goblin who attacked him. Images of the grey goblin and its horrendous attack on his father flashed through his mind. He still could hear his father's scream after the Goblin had attacked him. Talar remained silent, and Dalir was about to change the subject when Talar finally began to talk. "We were hunting on a steep ridge, on the mountain just south of Stonedom. We have all hunted there before many times. Goblins are not common south of the city, but with the Dwarves focused on Capa, their patrols missed the Goblins that come out of the mountains east of Stonedom. A boar was running below us, and the main hunting party took off after it. My father's bodyguard: his old friend Gareth went off a little way in search of the boar. I had actually tripped over a fallen branch and was recovering from the fall when I saw it," Talar said, remembering the faithful day.

"You saw the Goblin then?" Dalir asked. He was fascinated by the strange creatures of the Northern continent.

"Yes, Dalir, I saw the Goblin. It was perched on a large boulder behind my father, who was on his steed. I can remember seeing his grey skin. Well, I yelled immediately, but it was too late. The Goblin jumped off the boulder and attacked my father. I then rushed up and fought the Goblin, killing it. Another Goblin, who had killed Gareth, attacked me as I was about to tend to my father. Cynfor had heard my scream and attacked the second Goblin, and I finally managed to stab that creature in the back, killing that Goblin as well," Talar said, finishing his story. Dalir poured him another glass of wine.

"I'm sorry that this happened to you, Talar. I will pray for your father, the King of Stonedom tonight," Dalir said solemnly. Dalir then raised his glass in respect. After taking a moment to study his new acquittance and to think over Talar's story, Dalir began to speak of Koristan. He told Talar of its' numerous territories, peoples, and different geography. Dalir's curiosity had taken the fun out of the evening, and he knew it. So, he talked about Koristan, his homeland, which he sometimes missed. Talar listened attentively, interested by Dalir's strange homeland, which he had only seen on maps in his father's library. Dalir continued speaking about Koristan, and one cup of wine turned to two, then three. Talar's thoughts drifted to his homeland and to his ailing father. He wished above all to be done with Capa, return home, and tend to his father. That would not be happening anytime soon, though, and the thought of being trapped in Capa infuriated Talar. Talar just could not figure out what the Capans wanted with his family and Stonedom. Stonedom lay on the other side of Stone Lake, which was nearly twenty-five leagues long. It was the closest civilization to the Dwarf's stronghold. There was a stone road that led directly to Thendara, the Dwarf's high castle. Stonedom's citizens expected to send supplies to the Legions during the upcoming campaign. Cadoc had built a warehouse to store Stonedom's tribute to the Legions. This still was not enough for the Capans. Just what else could they want? These questions flooded Talar's mind until an idea flashed through his head. Dalir had made him promise to keep a secret, now he would demand the same.

"...the Shallow River, aptly named, of course, makes its way through the Great Dune Desert all the way to the Shining Sea. If one were to stand at that point, you would only be forty leagues from the great Capan fortress of Badatoz," Dalir rambled on about northern Koristan until Talar cut him off abruptly. "Dalir, you made me promise to keep a secret tonight. Will you do the same for me?", Talar asked softly.

The question caught Dalir off guard, but he nodded after drinking from his wine glass. "Dalir, you have been here in the High Castle for much longer than me. You seem to understand this city and the Capans better than me. Why do you think the Emperor is keeping me here? Why not just kill the rest of my family and me and be done with it?", Talar asked. Dalir's eyebrows arched when Talar had asked the frank question, and he took a few moments before answering.

"Despite what you might think, the Capans are not barbarians," Dalir stated. Now Talar's eyebrows were arched in disapproval, and he was about to voice his objections, but Dalir now cut him off. "Let me continue, Talar; the Capans are not barbarians. They are not going to slaughter one of the lost Northern Kingdom' Princes for no good reason. They value hereditary, royalty, and most of all, loyalty. The Emperor is giving you a chance to prove your loyalty to himself and the Empire. If you and your father do as they command, I see no reason for the Capans to annihilate you and your people. Stonedom is important now but after the siege of the Dwarves? Why annihilate a frontier trading outpost that stands as a warning between you and the unknown?", Dalir stated factually.

Talar thought over Dalir's comments and, after a while, started nodding in agreement. Dalir was right. Past the Stone Mountains and Thendara, the land was unsettled and unknown. Few dared to climb over and past the snow-capped peaks of the Stone Mountains. This still did not explain why Talar was required to stay in Capa or why the Capans had attacked the Dwarves and Elves in the first place. Talar voiced his first question to Dalir, who patiently smiled and then poured himself another glass of wine.

"Capan Generals, Senators, and other nobles are going to be living in Stonedom soon, Talar. The siege will begin next spring. The city labors daily to ensure the Legions are equipped for the campaign. Some Legions are already being staged in Brigantium.", Dalir stated. Upon hearing this, Talar's mouth dropped, and he almost spilled his wine. Only having just arrived in the massive city, this was all news to him. He had not expected the siege to begin anytime soon.

Dalir seeing the confusion and bewilderment on Talar's face, could not believe that he had not known this. "How do you not know this Talar, has news not reached Stonedom yet," Dalir asked. Talar told Dalir that the merchants visiting Stonedom had not talked of it, and no one on his travels to Capa had mentioned it either. Dalir shook his head in disbelief at the total lack of communication. The pieces to all the puzzles that had plagued the Prince of Stonedom were now falling in place. War was coming to Stonedom. To his home. The siege of Thendara would be a battle for the ages. Now Talar shook his head in disbelief. Everything in his world was coming unhinged. He did not know what to do or what to say, so he drained his wine glass and looked at Dalir with fury in his eyes. "I will not let my people suffer; I will not let them be massacred. I will not, Dalir, I will not," Talar said.

"Then fulfill your pledge to the Emperor and to Capa, and like I said before, you and your people will survive Talar. As far as I know, the Capans have no other motives to conquer Stonedom except to use it as their main base against the Dwarves," Dalir said. Talar nodded in understanding, but his stomach felt squeamish at the thought of the Elves and Dwarves being wiped out by the Capans. For the Legions would outnumber the Dwarves by the thousands. Talar thought of the few Dwarves he had met as a child. They all had been the same height as he was, for he had only been eight or nine when he had met them. He still remembered the intelligence in the Dwarves' eyes and the strength of their hands as they shook. Still feeling squeamish, Talar thanked Dalir for his hospitality and half staggered, half walked to the door. Dalir smiled at Talar's drunkenness and helped him to the door. Dalir had one last question for Talar before he left, though.

"What did that imbecile Ralphin mean earlier? I did not understand his words. What is a Paladin? What is a Druid?" Dalir asked. Talar was surprised by Dalir's questions but answered quickly.

"The Druids are my people's link to the Elves. They are the only ones allowed into Thendara. The only ones allowed to see the Elves," Talar said. Dalir remained silent, hoping Talar would keep talking about the fabled Elves. Most Koristans thought Elves were myths, something the Capans had invented. Dalir could tell from Talar's tone that he believed in them, though. "The Druids also oversee the Summer Solace and the Winter Solace rituals. They conduct weddings and funeral rituals. They also crown the new Kings of Stonedom when the old Kings are burned. They help the poor and sick. It is a great honor to be a Druid," Talar said. He was about to bid Dalir goodnight when the curious Koristan asked him another question.

"Is a Paladin another word for a Druid?" Dalir asked, hoping he was not upsetting Talar.

Talar thought for a moment before answering Dalir's question. "The Paladin was not a Druid, Dalir. The Paladin was a Knight of Mempacton. He was their immortal leader. So, no Dalir, the Paladin is not a Druid," Talar said.

"Immortal? This Paladin was immortal?", Dalir asked, intrigued by the thought of immortality. Talar nodded after leaning against the wood door.

"The Paladin is immortal Dalir. Just like the Elves. He has not been seen, though. The Druids say that he is lost," Talar said, almost slurring his words as the wine started to affect him. He had not thought of the Druids or their teachings for some time. The Druids had educated him along with Cynfor, and now Talar thought of the white-haired Druid who had taught him. The Druid had told him that the Paladin had become lost after the fall of Mempacton. Neither Cynfor nor Talar had inquired further about the Paladin's whereabouts, but now he wished he had. The Paladin was supposed to be the protector of the Elves, and he would be needed in the upcoming spring. Talar brushed the thoughts of the lost legend out of his head and opened the door.

"Do you believe in this immortal Paladin? In immortal Elves?", Dalir asked as Talar walked through the doorway.

Talar looked down at the grey cobbles below him, then nodded. He had never seen an Elf or the Paladin, but he believed the Druid that had instructed him. "Yes, Dalir, I believe in them. I believe in the Old Gods, not the new ones the Capans created. It is late Dalir, and your wine is strong. We will talk tomorrow. Until then..." Talar said with a wave. He staggered down the dimly lit hallway, and Dalir watched him leave before shutting the door.

After Talar had left, Dalir poured himself another glass of wine and made himself a plate of fruits and fish meat for dinner. He left his comfortable couches and exotic table and exited his room under the arches to the balcony outside. Dalir relit the candles to stop the constant stench and stared out across New City. Somewhere a child was wailing and sobbing uncontrollably. The lights from the street filled with taverns seemed to be the only bright spot below him, for the sun had fallen while he and Talar had drank and conversed. Dalir thought of his new classmate and of his strange beliefs. He had begun to like the northerner after he had tried to take a swing at Ralphin. Ralphin had teased Dalir exhaustedly, and being the only Koristan student, Dalir had to put with him and his bullies. Dalir would have never thought of punching Ralphin despite his callous name-calling. Violence had been completely foreign to him. His father, the Ambassador, condemned violence, and despite having three older siblings, raucous behavior was not commonplace in his home. Dalir had been aghast at his first day at the Academy, the hours of weapons training had at first seemed scary to him. After a few days of training, and after besting Ralphin, Dalir had begun to like the training. He also liked that Ralphin's taunts had, for the most part, ceased.

Weapons training and actual combat were two different things, though, and Dalir was aware of the differences. Besides the grizzled Legionnaires who trained them, Dalir had never talked to another person his age who been in combat. Dalir had been shocked at Talar's description of his battle with the two Goblins. His own classmate had slain two Goblins! Dalir raised his glass to Talar's braveness, and he wondered what Goblins really looked like. He drained the wine glass and thought of the immortal Elves. He thought that they must be a myth. He extinguished the candles and stared out over New City, enjoying the effects of the alcohol. Dalir enjoyed the sense of the unknown about this strange city. He enjoyed seeing its' different people, its' foreign foods, and customs. Capa was known to all in Koristan, though.

Dalir wished to experience the far reaches of Capa, to be the first Koristan to map and explore the lands where his people had never traveled before.

The stench of New City brought Dalir out of his drunken daydream. There would be no exploring soon. He was bound to be Ambassador, a duty he knew was honorable. Maybe once he was Ambassador, he could arrange a tour of the Capan Empire. As he made his way to his couch, Dalir thought of touring Capa as Ambassador and thought of Talar's bravery. Would he be that brave in front of a Goblin? These different thoughts flowed through Dalir's mind. Laying down on the couch, Dalir looked at the candles burning around the room. If he got up to extinguish them, he would sleep better, but then the stench of New City would make its way in. Dalir stayed put and eventually drifted off to the sounds of the lively New City below him.

Chapter X- A New Life

Fresh, clean, crisp air filled the young Man's lungs. The air was so clean that a bright smile erupted on his face. The air was much cleaner than New City's foulness. The youth shook his head, for only a few weeks ago, he had been utterly homesick for New City. Now, he did not want to go back. Staring down at the clear waters of the Cold River, the youth looked at his reflection. His light brown hair and beard had grown out, and for the first time in his life, the Capan youth had a suntan. New City's foul air, constant commotion, and sewage-filled streets did not entice its' youth to spend their time outdoors.

Refocusing on the task at hand, the Capan studied the clear water below him. He stood up to his knees in the cold water that gave the river its' name. His hands gripped a spear. The slender wooden spear had been carved by one of his new friends, Claudius. Claudius had grown up in Brigantium's slum. From Claudius' description, it was a place he would not want to visit. The spear remained motionless, and so did the Capan. The cold water was causing his legs to go numb, and he was about to give up. Then his prey entered the water below him. Taking his time, the youth tracked the trout until it was just below him, then he swiftly launched his attack. The spear flashed through the water, impaling the trout. The youth twisted the spear and pulled up, heaving up a mighty trout at least three feet in length. The sudden movement sent some warmth through his legs, and the youth now headed to the shore.

"Well done, Marcus. Well done! Now catch another!" yelled Claudius. Claudius, like Marcus and the others, was dressed in brown linen pants and white vests. At the sound of Claudius' yelling, the other Capans in the group stopped their tasks and came to the edge of the river. Marcus continued out of the water and threw the spear and the mighty trout down in front of his companions. His feet and legs were warming up now that he was out of the brisk water. Evander, the companion's leader, came down and started cleaning the fish. His large hands and thick fingers made quick work of cleaning the trout. Grasping the two long filets, Evander motioned for Soren, the eldest of the companions and the shortest. Soren's short and powerful arms reached out to Evander, grabbed the filets, and then made his way to the companion's campsite. Evander now motioned to Marcus, apparently for his spear.

"Go up with Soren and start a fire. Tell Tarquin to stop working on the raft, and help you two with dinner," Evander's deep voice made his words seem like a command, but that was just how he talked. Marcus nodded and took off towards the fire, which Soren was attempting to start. Despite Evander's gruffness, Marcus liked his leader. At twenty years old, Marcus was in a world completely unknown to him, and having an experienced woodsman like Evander around was crucial. The vast pine forests that expanded out from the Cold River were the definition of wilderness. The massive pines along the river had never seen humans until recently. Now the sounds of axes being worked into the huge pines filled the woods. Around Marcus were at least ten other similar-sized groups. All were cutting the timber. The price was worth the risk of being injured by the falling giants and the risk of the Dwarves.

Capa had never provided much to Marcus. His father died at sea and his mother at birth. He had grown up working in a tavern, witnessing the ways of the world from a young age. One day a large, stocky fellow walked right up to the bar Marcus was tending, set his ax on the counter, and ordered drinks for all. Marcus had never seen anyone with so much gold in his pouch, and he could not resist asking the bearded brute where he had procured it.

"Up the river, boy, up the river. If your tough enough, you could join me next time!" Evander had replied. Marcus had taken Evander up on his offer, and now seven weeks later, he strode barefooted through the ancient forest. Brown pine needles stuck to his feet, but after making his way back to the campsite, he wiped them off before putting on his dark leather boots. Soren had already successfully started the fire and was beginning to cook. Marcus guessed that they were done working for the day, for the sun would be setting soon.

"Are we done for the day Soren," Marcus asked? The elder woodcutter replied that they were and instructed Marcus to hurry on to Tarquin. "Don't want him by himself around dark," Soren had barked. His gravelly voice, like Evander's, was deceptive; that was his normal tone. Marcus kept walking past the campsite and began climbing the ridge where they all had been cutting. As he entered the clearing, he jumped up on the massive tree stump which he had helped create. The stump was at least five feet in diameter and jutted up from the ground giving the youth a good perch. Marcus needed the perch, for when the giant pine had fallen, it had created quite a bit of brush. The giant's entire top end lay off to Marcus's left, unwanted by the woodcutters. It was not big enough for a warship mast. The companions had cut that giant and one other over the past four weeks. Falling the giants was hard enough work, and Marcus' hands bled when he plied the crosscut for the first time. Days of paddling up the Cold River had strengthened his muscles, but nothing compared his hands for that first week of wood cutting. Evander, Soren, and Claudius had not taken it easy on the two younger Capans either. Both Tarquin and Marcus were expected to do more ax work due to their young age and inexperience. As the days wore on, the youths had figured out that dropping the giant pines was much easier than moving them to the edge of the ridge, where the trees were too windswept for masts. After bucking the logs into three rod long sections, the woodcutters had set off on cutting numerous smaller logs to use as rollers. Days of stripping eight-foot logs ensued. By then, the youths had proven their worth, and the older woodcutters relaxed, not having to worry about a useless tag along. But nothing prepared them for the ordeal of moving the monster logs. Three weeks of constant work had exhausted the group, but finally, after using every trick Evander and Soren knew, they had moved the two giant logs to the edge of the cliff.

Marcus scanned the thick brush in front of him until he finally located Tarquin, who was working on the raft that would steer the two giants pine logs down the river. The old loggers had learned that the logs could easily get hung up on other trees on the riverbanks. A simple raft with a rudder could help guide the two logs down the river. Tarquin's long blonde hair swung from side to side as he fastened two small logs with a thick length of rope. Tarquin had grown up with Marcus, and the youth's blue eyes flashed up towards Marcus as he called out to him.

"We're done for the day Tarquin, have a drink!" Marcus shouted to his lifelong friend. Tarquin shook his head in disagreement and motioned for Marcus to help him. "Help me finish fastening this, Marcus," Tarquin replied. Marcus hesitated, for it was getting dark, but then saw that the task could be completed quickly. Marcus walked over to the raft, which was about finished, and helped his friend secure the rope around two logs. "Let's do the other side," Tarquin said methodically as he began to walk to the other side of the raft. Now it was Marcus's turn to shake his head before he reminded Tarquin about Evander's rule about being out after dark. Tarquin nodded in understanding and began packing up the tools. Marcus helped him after slavering some bear fat across his arms and neck. The bear fat kept the bugs at bay.

"I don't know why Evander and Sorel worry about those little Dwarf bastards anyway," Tarquin stated. "Haven't they ever been to the Arena? I once saw Malfoy split one of the em' right in two. Right down the middle, never will forget it!" Tarquin added. Marcus nodded in agreement. He had been at Tarquin's side, gloriously drunk as Malfoy had split the Dwarf from head to toe into two halves. It was not the only Dwarf the two had seen slaughtered in the Arena.

"I don't know either Tarquin, as big and rugged as Evander is. I don't know why he frets over the Dwarves. But being that he is big and rugged, and he is in charge, let's hurry up and get back before the sun sets," Marcus said.

Tarquin nodded as he jumped up to the massive fresh-cut stump that Marcus had just been standing on. "I'll lead the way, old pal. I want the first crack at any Dwarves we meet on the way back to camp!" Tarquin cheerfully stated as he swung his ax playfully in the air. Tarquin led the way, and Marcus followed his friend out of the logging clearing, down the ridge, and back to the campsite where Sorel had a large fire burning. The two youths could see other fires starting around them as the other logging camps settled in for the evening as well.

"How's the raft going, Tarquin?" Evander asked in his deep voice as he flipped the trout over in the skillet below him. Evander, Sorel, and Claudius all waited anxiously for Tarquin's answer because when the raft was done, and the logs were in the river, then they could all depart this wilderness.

"It'll be done first thing in the morning, Evander. I could probably finish it tonight if we started a fire near it," Tarquin replied. Tarquin's previous employment as a shipbuilder had been the main reason Evander had let him come along.

Evander scoffed at Tarquin's suggestion. "You know my rules, Tarquin. You youngins aren't scared of anything, but there are all sorts of things in these woods that will kill you!" Evander replied, his voice rumbling over the cracking pine branches in the fire. "I know you three don't care much about Dwarves, but there is more out there than just them. I killed a giant black bear with a crossbow last time I was here. Ain't that right, Sorel?" Evander said, taking the trout-laden skillet off the fire. Evander had included Claudius in his rant, for the red-haired Mercium was only five years older than Marcus and Tarquin. "Now, come over and eat dinner, boys. Have a drink too," Evander beckoned to the three youth, his gentle eyes lit up due to the glow of the fire.

The three youths took their share of the trout, and all the Men were quiet as they feasted on the fish meal. Evander had caught another trout bare-handed, and the two-trout provided plenty for the five hungry woodcutters. The party's supplies were running low. They usually ate salted pork and smoked beef. The expedition was coming to an end soon, though, for with the raft nearly done and the logs ready to be dropped in the river, all five would be headed down river soon. Marcus and Tarquin did not know when they would be leaving. It was Evander's decision to make. It all depended on the water level, according to Sorel. If the river were too high, the logs could be lost. If it were too low, they would be stuck in the river until it rained.

The five of them finished their meals, and Evander produced a bottle of wine and began passing it around the campfire. The three youths all took long sips of the fruity wine. When Sorel grasped the bottle, he did not immediately slug it down as was customary. When first meeting Sorel, Marcus had wondered why the eldest man in the party of five was not in charge. Then after being with the elder for a few weeks, Marcus had figured out why. Sorel drank more than the four of the others combined. He was often so hungover that swarms of flies and gnats would hound him no matter how much bear fat he put on. The elder timber cutter was worth the trouble for his knowledge of the wilderness, of the river, and on how to move the giant logs was priceless. It was Sorel's idea to use ropes and pullies to move the logs the last one hundred yards to the side bank.

Sorel looked over all three of the youths. After giving them all a stern look, he took a long pull from the wine flask. After drinking from the flask, the elderly timberman issued a warning to the three youths. "You boys weren't even born when I saw my first Dwarf. It was not in the Arena either. It was at Fort Carillon. The first Fort Carillon. Before it was burned," Sorel said, his deep voice trailing off.

"Before it was burned?" Marcus and Tarquin asked in unison, disbelief across their faces. A few loggers from the other camps had come over, probably to trade with Evander, but now they listened to Sorel.

"Yea, before it burned," Sorel replied, finally drinking from the bottle. "Back thirty, thirty-five years now, but yea, ole Fort Carillon burned, the Dwarves took it." The other loggers now shook their heads in disbelief. Marcus looked over at Tarquin and rolled his eyes, much to Tarquin's delight. The loggers were muttering in disbelief amongst themselves, not believing the wine swelling woodcutter. Evander finished his meal and threw another log on the fire. He beckoned to Sorel for the bottle, which his elderly friend handed over after taking another swig for himself.

Claudius spoke up, questioning Sorel's claims over Fort Carillon. "I've never heard of that in my life. Never. The Dwarves sacking a fort manned by Legionaries? Your drunk Sorel, but that's alright with me!". Claudius spoke the last words joyfully, and the rest of the loggers laughed at his simple joke.

"He may be drunk, but he is right. Carillon fell to the Dwarves." Evander's deep voice silenced the other men in an instant. The crackling fire was all Marcus could hear now, but his eyes were fixated on Evander's face, which seemed to shine above the fire. "The Dwarves attacked at night. They busted right through the front gate. Started killin' before the Legionnaires could be rallied. They killed just about everyone: children, women, the old ones too. They took the livestock, burned Carillon down. It happened quick, just twenty minutes or so. Sorel nodded his head and took the bottle from Claudius, who was just staring at Evander in shock. The rest of the woodcutters stayed silent. None dared to challenge the giant woodcutter. The campfire's flames flickered, and Sorel reached over and adjusted a few logs to keep the flames up. Marcus did not know what to think. He had not believed Sorel for one second, but Evander was known as a Man of his word. Marcus looked around at the other axmen and then looked over at Tarquin. His friend from Capa was thinking the same thing as he was. If Fort Carillon had fallen to the Dwarves, why did no one know?

Marcus assumed one of the old loggers would speak up and question Evander, but none did. The crackling of the fire was that all that could be heard. The silence was driving Marcus crazy. He wanted to hear more of Carillon. Not heeding Tarquin's warning glance, Marcus spoke up. "I don't question you, Evander." His words brought the eyes of all the woodcutters to him. He began to sweat from the attention and the heat from the fire. "But how do you know what you said is true? How do you know Fort Carillon fell?" Marcus asked. Evander looked at Sorel and gave the elder axmen a quick smile. Sorel smiled back in return and took another long swig from the wine bottle. Evander then slowly looked around the fire, into the eyes of each woodsman, until his unflinching gaze settled upon Marcus.

"I was there, young Marcus. Sorel was too. As a matter of fact, ole Sorel here rescued me from those damn Dwarves. Ain't that right, Sorel?" Evander said. Sorel took another pull from the wine bottle and simply nodded in agreement. Marcus's jaw dropped in disbelief. Evander laughed at seeing Marcus's expression. Chuckling to himself, Evander continued speaking. "I was just a child, just five or six. My parents had sent me there to be in service to the Commander's family. I don't know what Sorel was doing there?" Evander asked.

"I was drinking," Sorel replied, bringing out a laugh from the others and breaking the tense mood. Looking back at Marcus, Evander continued telling the others that Sorel had saved him by catching him as he jumped off the fort's walls. "How did you catch him?" asked one of the loggers behind Marcus. The question brought more laughs, and Sorel said that Evander was not as big back then. "He was only a kid, heavier than a hog, though!" Sorel said. The last joke brought more laughs, and sensing that the mood was broken, Tarquin spoke up, asking Evander why no one back in Capa knew about this. The question brought a pause to the laughs, but they started back up after Evander said: "Go ask the Emperor!".

The woodsmen continued laughing, and the other loggers finally got down to their trading business with Evander. The other loggers knew that Evander and his crew would be leaving soon and traded hard for the groups remaining goods, especially the salt. Evander countered, telling the logger he was trading with salt he might need if it did not rain soon, and they were stuck here.

The other logger, whose name was Valens, spoke just as rough as Evander and was just as wide but not as tall. Valens looked like a keg of ale to Marcus while Evander was two kegs. Valens told Evander that he thought it was going to rain soon. He had seen dark clouds gathering to the south. Evander threw more wood in the fire, and as he and Valens continued bartering, Marcus's thoughts drifted back to Fort Carillon and the Dwarves. How did the Dwarves capture a Legion's fort? How did they kill all the Legionnaires inside? Dwarves cannot even pick up Man weapons, for they lack the strength. And why didn't no one in Capa know about this? Marcus looked over the fire at Evander as he traded with Valens. He wondered if Evander was pranking him and his youthful companions. Tarquin slapped his arm to get his attention, then handed him the wine bottle. Taking a long swig, Marcus passed the bottle to Claudius, who took a swig and then played at being a Dwarf by bending his knees. Claudius jokingly jabbed at Tarquin, acting the part of a ferocious Dwarf. The gesture was not seen by Sorel or Evander. The young Men from the Capan Empire could not help but laugh at the idea of dangerous Dwarves.

Later in the night, Evander traded most of the remaining salt for wine (at Sorel's behest), and the group of woodsmen finished their last bottle and prepared for bed. Evander informed them that they only had a few hours of labor to get the logs and raft in the river. He also said they would need more water in the river to float the logs down. Tarquin and Marcus smiled at each other in the dying light of the fire. They both thought of how they would spend their cut of the log's sale in Capa. Marcus was thinking of Women while Tarquin dreamt of his own ship. The woodsmen prepared their simple beds of hemlock boughs and wool blankets. Marcus began to think of Capa and its' gorgeous Women. Just as Marcus was about to drift off into sleep, Tarquin broke the silence of the quiet night. "That Valens said it was going to rain soon."

"I hope so, Tarquin. I hope it rains soon. We will get back to Capa. Back to Capa." With those final words, Marcus fell asleep, thinking of rain, Women, and his home.

Chapter XI- Ready for the River

When the first drops of rain hit Marcus's face, he thought that he was dreaming. He did not bother to stir from his makeshift bed, for this dream of rain hitting his face was too good to leave. The rain picked up, and when Tarquin exclaimed, "Good Gods," Marcus knew he was not dreaming and opened his eyes, only to see the darkness of night still.

Marcus wiped the sleep from his eyes. He looked up at the sky, then over to the horizon. The sun had not made it up over the distant mountains, but Marcus figured it would be light in a few hours. The rain continued down, and the reality of the situation was dawning on Marcus and on Tarquin too. With this sudden rainstorm, the river would certainly rise high enough to float the two giant logs down to Fort Carillon and eventually to Badatoz. The rain picked up now, and the young Men from Capa covered themselves with their wool blankets, pulled on their leather boots, and walked through the pine forest towards the others in their group.

Evander and Sorel had already lit torches that were burning bright despite the rain. Claudius was hunched under the large canoe they had paddled upstream. The canoe would carry them home, minus Evander, who would steer the raft. At thirty feet in length, the wooden canoe was heavy but now provided excellent shelter from the storm. After spotting Marcus and Tarquin approaching, Sorel and Evander retreated to the canoe where the boys joined them, thoroughly soaked by the rain at this point. Evander shouted over the rain, the torchlight illuminating his face. "This storm will get us home. Let us get breakfast going. We should be ready to work once it is light out!". Evander seemed to bark the words out, but by now, Marcus, Tarquin, and Claudius could sense when he was in a good mood. The whole crew of axmen ate their breakfast of bread, beans, and leftover trout in silence. It was too wet to get a fire going. The youth hoped it would quit pouring rain by sunlight but remained optimistic over the thought of getting home with their prizes.

As the sun peaked over the horizon, the rain slowed down to a drizzle, and the loggers were forced to wait a little longer until their eyes could see through the undergrowth of the pine forest. Usually, the birds were chirping their morning melodies, but the rain deterred them today. Finally, Evander gave the word, and the three youth and two seasoned woodsmen sprung to work. Evander had deemed getting the canoe and their remaining supplies to the river bank a good first task. The five woodsmen strategically got under the canoe, with Evander in the front, his giant shoulders supporting the massive canoe while the others threw their hands up to support it. The five cautiously went through the still semi-dark woods. The sun was rising, though, and soon the group could see much easier. As the group passed around a base of a massive pine, they could hear the Cold River in the near distance. After another twenty rods, the loggers set their wooden canoe down in a small clearing near the riverbank and gazed out at the Cold River. The rising sun shining through dark clouds seemed to light up the wide river. Trout jumped up at their breakfast, some hitting their mark, some missing. Tarquin spotted a blue heron and pointed it out to Marcus. The youths laughed at the sight of the strange-looking bird scooping fish out of the river with its long-curved beak. Evander motioned that it was time to get back to work, and with a sigh, the youth followed him back to their campsite. Arriving at the camp, Evander told Tarquin and Marcus to accompany Sorel up towards the raft. Claudius and Evander would finish bringing their supplies to the canoe while the others finished the raft. Grabbing his ax, Marcus followed Tarquin and Sorel up the ridge through an open pine forest, which in this section was clear of undergrowth.

Sorel, Tarquin, and Evander finished working on the raft and started dragging it towards the edge of the cliff. The youth had thought they would carry it down, but apparently, Sorel intended to just drop it over the cliff. "We'll hook the rudder up once we're down there, no need to kill ourselves, that raft is rugged as an Ogre boy!" Sorel had said. Marcus nodded in agreement, and the three picked up their axes and began to work on felling the few remaining trees which blocked their prize logs from the cliffs bank. The ax felt good in Marcus's hands now, and he smiled for only a few weeks ago he had hated it. Marcus and Tarquin teamed up on large hemlock, which needed to be cut. The rhythm of their axes hitting the hemlock made Evander smile as he and Claudius approached. Quickly surveying the situation, Evander assigned Cladius a tree to cut then began helping Sorel cut the pine he was working on. By now, the rest of the logging crews were well into their morning work routine, and the sound of trees dropping and ax blades sinking into the pines was everywhere. The five worked frantically despite the drizzle. They could almost smell Badatoz and the shipbuilders who paid well for the perfect logs. After a few hours, the drizzle stopped, and from the perch, atop of the cliff, they could see the river below them rising. Only one large scraggly pine now blocked their prize logs from the cliff banks. Evander gripped his ax and began attacking the pine with a ferocity that the youth had not seen before. Sorel motioned to the others to quit staring at Evander and help him out. Sorel turned back down the ridge towards their campsites. Looking over his shoulder as he walked down the ridge, he saw Evander step aside as the scraggy pine collapsed over the cliff. Their last obstacle was gone. They were ready for the river.

The boys followed Sorel through the camp and down to the clearing by the river, where their canoe waited. After putting the canoe in the river and getting Sorel situated in the back, the three youths grabbed the line from the front of the vessel and began pulling the canoe upstream from the bank. Evander had chosen this spot to cut not only for the prime timber but also for its accessibility, for the river's current was nearly nonexistent under the cliffs. The three youths still had to work, though, for the canoe and Sorel were not light. They kept pulling and finally passed the spot where the logs up above rested. The scraggy pine which Evander had cut floated in the water and smacked against the canoe harmlessly. After they tied the canoe off to a large tree and after pulling Sorel in, the four woodcutters walked down the riverbank under the cliffs, marveling at the beauty of the wilderness around them. Reaching the clearing where they had previously stashed the canoe, the group turned and headed back towards the camp. Evander was waiting for them and was grinning like a child.

"Were bout' ready, boys! I talked to Valens and some of the others, and they agreed to help us with the last push to the river!" Evander stated. His giddiness was apparent.

"What did you trade for that," Soren asked Evander, who replied that he gave half of the wine to Valens. Sorel just shook his head in disgust but did not complain. Fort Carillon had wine, and he expected to be there soon. The five woodsmen walked up the ridge, where to their surprise, almost all the other axmen were waiting for them. Valens stood in the middle; his thick arms crossed over his white vest. The rest of the axmen stood around him, drinking wine and smiling. Apparently, pushing the massive fifty feet logs over the cliffs together was a tradition amongst the woodsmen. It also was good entertainment, for the long days and short nights could be quite boring sometimes. "What's the plan, Evander?" Valens asked in his rough voice, the other woodsmen looking to Evander for directions.

"Sorel, go take Tarquin and get down to the canoe. We will tip the raft over to you, and you and the boy will hook up the rudder and get it out of the way." Tarquin was chosen because he was the smallest of the youth, but he was also the best paddler. Sorel smiled, then nodded to his old friend and started back down the ridge, Tarquin following behind him with the rudder over his back. "Claudius, Marcus, get the rocks from under the logs out and be careful," Evander said.

They obliged their leader and carefully removed the rocks holding the logs back without getting their fingers or hands pinched. Meanwhile, about half of the woodsmen picked up the raft and easily hurled it off the cliff to the river below. Tarquin and Sorel had not reached the canoe yet, but the raft was not going anywhere in the still water below. It was time to push the massive logs now, and the fifty or so woodsmen grabbed their long pine poles, which they usually used to push trees over during the cutting process. Forming a long line behind the first log, the woodsmen began prying and pushing, grunting, and cursing until they finally got the massive log moving. Spinning slowly, the massive log started to gain speed and began rumbling down the ridge towards the cliff. A few saplings stood in the massive log's way, but the force of the log easily plowed over these. The log bounced over a large boulder and then was gone over the cliff. The log seemed to float in the air, gracefully falling before hitting the water with a loud smack that bounced off the cliff walls and filled the wilderness with sound. The woodsmen cheered out loud and peered over the cliff bank some three hundred feet below where Tarquin and Sorel were floating toward the log in the raft and canoe. "We got to give Sorel some time to get it out of the way and get it hooked to the raft," Evander said with a grin on his face. The other loggers were clapping his back and handing him wine, which he drank. Marcus took a swig for himself and stared out below, where Tarquin was steering the canoe himself. Sorel was in the raft hooking up the log with strong ropes. Tarquin stayed back, not wanting to capsize the canoe. In a matter of minutes, Sorel had the giant log fastened to his raft. Evander peered over the cliff next to Marcus and saw that Sorel was ready for the other log below.

Pointing to the other log then to the cliff, the woodsmen cheered as they got the signal from Evander to put the other log in the river. Marcus joined them this time, and a rugged ax man handed him a pine pole to push the log with. Joining the line of other woodsmen, Marcus gritted his teeth and began to push and pry at the log until finally, the huge piece of timber began to move. Slowly rotating, the log began to pick up speed until it was rolling easily down the ridge toward the cliff. The log hit the same boulder as the last one and then fell over the cliff bank. A few seconds later, the now-familiar smack of the log hitting the river rang out again, and the woodsmen cheered.

Valens strode over to Evander and was about to shake his hand when he suddenly grabbed his neck and bent over at once. Marcus wondered if he had been stung by a bee when he heard another woodsman cry out. It was the rugged ax man who had handed him the pine pole. The large man grasped an arrow that protruded from the middle of his stomach. The rugged man fell to his knees, and Marcus saw the disbelief in his blue eyes before he fell to the ground. Marcus and Claudius just stood there in shock, but Evander did not. The massive axmen bellowed out: "Dwarves, Dwarves, Dwarves!" then knocked both Marcus and Claudius to the ground. Marcus was now looking up at the blue sky, which still had dark clouds here and there. He looked over and saw that Claudius was beginning to stand up. "No, boy! No!" Evander shouted but to no avail. Claudius stood, only to have an arrow strike him square in the chest. The force of the arrow threw Claudius back, and his legs flopped for a few seconds before stopping. Marcus knew Claudius was dead after seeing his lifeless eyes below his red hair. His stomach began to sink as he saw his friends' bloodstain his white vest and then the rocks below him. An arrow whizzed past Marcus's head and brought him back to the reality of the situation. Marcus screamed Evander's name, and the big woodsmen grabbed him by his white vest and began pulling him up. "We gotta get out here, boy! Now!" Evander screamed. Behind him, a Dwarf jumped out a pine tree onto the back of woodsmen. The woodsmen threw the Dwarf off and were about to stomp on him when a hatchet struck Evander in the shoulder, drawing blood. The sounds of the forest had been replaced with the screams of the woodsmen and the war cries of the Dwarves.

Evander and Marcus bounded away from the clearing of the cliff and down the ridge. Ahead of them, the woodsmen camp was in chaos as Dwarves attacked from every direction. A short Dwarf suddenly popped out from behind a tree and lunged at Evander. The giant axmen caught the spear with one hand then swiped at the Dwarf with his other hand. The Dwarf easily ducked the giant axmen, drew a knife, and now lunged at Marcus! Marcus stepped back and tripped on a tree branch, falling to the ground. The Dwarf jumped on top of Marcus, and Marcus frantically fought the Dwarf off, keeping from being stabbed by grasping the Dwarves' wrist, which held the knife. The Dwarf was strong, though, and finally got in a position to stab the young Man. The knife reached for the soft skin of Marcus's stomach when Evander violently struck the Dwarf in the head with a large rock, killing the bearded Dwarf instantly.

The Dwarf died on top of Marcus, and Marcus had to brush the Dwarf's long black hair out of his eyes, so he could see. Looking down at the camp, Marcus could see Valens frantically swinging his ax with his back to his overturned canoe. Valens' neck wound had soaked his white vest, but the stocky woodsmen fought on. Valen pinned a Dwarf under his foot and was about to sink his ax when a stocky Dwarf jumped off his overturned canoe and tackled him to the ground. The Dwarf he was about to kill rolled over, pulled his knife, and slit Valens' throat.

Evander pulled Marcus to his feet. "C'mon boy," he yelled, and the two kept running down into the camp, which was a battleground. The screams and howls were all around them now, and Marcus's head snapped back and forth as he tried to avoid arrows, hatchets, and Dwarves. The two did not make it far, though. After only going four rods from where Evander crushed the Dwarves skull, a Dwarf popped out from a large pine and sank his ax into Evander's left knee, bringing the giant axmen down with one swing. Evander screamed in pain as the Dwarf tried to wrench the ax free. Without hesitation, Marcus charged forward, pushing the Dwarf back into a stand of thick brush. The ax was still buried in Evander's leg, and blood poured from the wound. Evander writhed on the ground in pain. Around him, the battle cries of the Men turned to screams of horror as they realized their fate. Marcus stood above Evander and the fallen Dwarf, not knowing what to do. As Evander leaned forward to try to stop his wound from bleeding, a short Dwarf came behind the gentle woodsmen and stabbed him in the neck from behind. Evander grasped his neck with both hands in vain. The giant woodsmen looked Marcus squarely in the eyes and muttered the words "Run Boy!" before he spat up blood and collapsed to the ground.

The short Dwarf sprung up and lunged at Marcus, but the young Man from Capa had been in enough bar brawls to know how to fight. Marcus kicked the Dwarf in the chest then stepped back, surveying the carnage around him. In front of him, the path to the clearing by the river was blocked by Dwarves and woodsmen struggling to fight them back. An arrow struck the tree next to him, and Marcus looked up to see a Dwarf knocking an arrow from a tree limb some five rods in the air! Marcus retreated up the ridge, past the Dwarf Evander had killed, not knowing what to do. Ahead of him, there was nothing but chaos and death. Marcus continued up the ridge in a panic. He did not want to die today. His heart was racing in his chest, and he thought it was going to burst right out. He kept racing up the ridge to the clearing near the cliff. Claudius still lay on the rocks, along with a few other dead woodsmen. He looked around fearfully for the Dwarves, but none were around. Marcus considered his options, and none of them were good. He could not make it to the riverbank the normal way without being killed by Dwarves. He could not just run into the woods; how would he survive with Dwarves everywhere? Marcus began to pace back and forth, not knowing what to do but filled with fear. Marcus heard a tree branch break and snapped his head around at the sound. A group of Dwarves had seen him retreat up the ridge and had followed him up. The four Dwarves were armed with axes and spears, and they fanned out as they approached the unarmed Capan.

"Please no, please, please, spare me!" Marcus begged. The Dwarves showed no pity or remorse. Marcus had never seen a Dwarf up close, and now for the first time, he was amazed at how human-like their faces appeared to be. The Dwarves kept advancing, forcing Marcus back. Marcus continued to plead, but the Dwarves kept advancing anyway, their buckskin pants already covered in blood. Marcus noticed Claudius from the corner of his eye and knew he was getting close to the cliff's edge. An idea suddenly hit Marcus's panic-stricken brain. As a boy, he had once jumped off the docks in Capa to escape a bully. He remembered the feeling of falling through the air. The biggest Dwarf among the four suddenly raised his spear as if to throw it at Marcus. Knowing that it was now or never, Marcus suddenly turned, and without thinking, he ran and jumped right off the cliff. The Dwarves looked at each other in disbelief, then cautiously approached the cliff. The young Man was gone. They could not tell from this distance if he emerged from the river. The four Dwarves collectively looked up from the river, then at each other, and began laughing. They slapped each other on the back, and the largest Dwarf pointed back to the camp, where the carnage continued.

Chapter XII- The Hunters

Cyprian looked over the Troll corpse from atop the waterfall. The stench of the dead Troll had alerted him and his three companions. Stepping back from the waterfall's sheer edge, he gazed out at the valley which lay before him. His prey was down there, but where? Cyprian glanced over at Tadius, his cousin and companion. Tadius was lounging against one of the old stone walls of the old Mempacton mill. Ragonious lounged against the other wall, studying the Troll's discarded ax, as Axius stood guard upstream away. Cyprian and Tadius had been hunting these wildlands for almost seventy years and had learned the importance of constant vigilance long ago.

"You think he teamed up with another? That pine tree back there seemed to be somebodies' home. Maybe there are two of them now?", Tadius's soft-spoken voice carried into Cyprian's ears as he looked over the valley. Looking down again at the Troll, the companion's leader spotted an arrow protruding from the Troll's shoulder. He now nodded his head, for the day's events were starting to make sense to him.

"He's not with another Elf. That Troll has an arrow sticking out of him," Cyprian said to no one in particular. Elves were incapable of violence, so the arrow signified to Cyprian that the Elf had come out here looking for a protector. That made sense to Cyprian, for if he were his prey, he would want protection as well. Now Cyprian wondered who this protector was, and suddenly it dawned on him who it might be. He began to become excited at the thought. It made sense, for who else would be living in a pine tree in the wilds of Mempacton?

"He might be with Dobervist," Cyprian said the words to no one but turned now to see the expressions of his companions. Tadius was nodding in agreement, a slow smile emerging from beneath his sharp eyes and close-cut brown hair. Ragonious was smiling broadly, for the former Arena champion had wanted a shot at killing Dobervist for years now. Cyprian had brought him on to his team some fifty years ago after watching Ragonious become champion in the Arena. Axius seemed unfazed by Cyprian's revelation. Cyprian had harbored high hopes for Axius, but the big Mercium Man just was not smart enough for Cyprian. He was handy in a fight but got drunk every chance he got. The former Legionnaire had been the best soldier in his Legion, but Cyprian needed hunters, not brutes.

"What do you think, Cousin? They obviously went down that valley, but to where? Towards Carillon or back north towards Oakbridge?". Tadius asked the question, but Cyprian was already thinking about it. Not knowing what to say to his cousin and his other companions, Cyprian tucked his pants back into his knee-high leather boots. Tadius and Ragonious looked at each other and smiled. They had been together long enough to know each other's habits. Cyprian was not sure which direction the Elf and his still unknown companion had gone. He was about to tell Tadius this when suddenly a Troll hunting horn sounded from the deep woods to the north of them. A few seconds another horn answered from the west.

All three Men nodded at each other now, for, with the Trolls to the north and to the west, the Elf would have to go downstream. Picking up their light packs and bedrolls, the companions prepared to move out, and Ragonious signaled to Axius that it was time to move. Cyprian grabbed his bow, as did Tadius and Ragonious. Tadius quickly took out his small leather pack, which contained various poisons, and produced a vial of the Troll killing serum. The poison could kill a Troll in a matter of minutes but could only be found in the far southern jungles of Koristan. Tadius nonetheless brushed a healthy coat over all his companion's arrow tips, except for Axius, who used a crossbow. His bolt was covered as well. Trolls were too dangerous not to use the poison. Tadius put away his poison pack and began adjusting the dark green wool vest which hung over his brown woodsman's shirt. All four were dressed similarly. Cyprian had learned that Capan robes and cloaks served no purpose in the wild.

"Go upstream a little bit Axius, we will be right behind you," Cyprian said in his naturally low voice. Decades of hunting in the wilderness turned your voice down a few decimals. Axius nodded and took off upstream, making his way through the stone walls of the old mill. "It's about high noon," Cyprian stated, then nodded to his cousin. Tadius produced three very small shot glasses from another pack. Carefully unwrapping the glasses from their soft leather pouch, Tadius quickly passed a glass to Ragonious. Cyprian now took the vial that was wrapped around his neck out and carefully poured each one of them a drink. The glass vial was covered in two layers of leather for protection. The Men drank the watered-down Elf blood as soon as it was poured.

Feeling immediately better, Tadius carefully put away the small shot glasses and shouldered his bow. The three companions all smiled at each other, for everyone would be dead of old age without the vial around Cyprian's neck. Now they youthfully bounded upstream where they found awaiting Axius perched on one of the large moss-covered boulders that littered the stream bank.

"There is a trail up," Axius said, pointing to a game trail that would lead the companions past the waterfall and to the southeast where the stream flowed. Axius did not speak the common tongue well, and his thick Mercium accent made him a target for Ragonious' jokes. Ragonious had a feeling Cyprian would be getting rid of Axius soon, and he usually ended up doing the deed himself. Ragonious could not wait. The dumb ex-Legionnaire from Mercium had almost got him killed in a bar brawl he had started a few weeks past.

"Trail up," Ragonious said mockingly, and both Tadius and Cyprian smiled to themselves. Axius did not seem to hear Ragonious and just kept going up the trail. Cyprian began to climb up the steep stream bank and kept smiling. They were still on the hunt. He had thought they had lost their prey at the waterfall, but the Trolls were helping him out now. Hopefully, they would pick up a foot trail at the base of the waterfall. Tadius came up and laid his hand on his cousin's shoulder. The two were closer than brothers after all their years together.

"We are still on the hunt, young cousin," Tadius said softly even though Cyprian was far from young. He was over a hundred years old.

Cyprian smiled at the small joke and took up his usual position behind Ragonius. He was in a great mood, and he could sense his cousin was as well. They had gotten Elves with less to go on before, and they knew they were close to this one. If only they could get Dobervist as well! The Emperor would surely give them a few months off if they got Dobervist. Cyprian smiled at the thought of being in Capa for months instead of weeks like he was used to. The companions traversed down the steep rocky side of the waterfall quickly and almost howled when they found a double footrail at the base of the waterfall. The hunt was on.

Chapter XIII- The Arena

Talar stared out into the vastness of New City, which stretched out before him through the window of the High Keep's classroom. Malnar's dull voice rang through the background of his thoughts as he gazed down on the bustling city below. A few days had passed since he had visited Dalir's room. The days had been filled with more Capan schooling and Capan weapon training and more Capan snobbery. Most of the class treated him as a barbaric peasant. No one acknowledged him except Dalir, and of course, Ralphin and Tobias, who went out of their way to harass him. The Prince from Stonedom was frustrated and relentless. Being cooped up in the High Keep was bad enough but enduring the taunts and jests from Ralphin, and his cronies were becoming unbearable.

Malnar noticed Talar staring out the window at New City beyond, stopped his lecture about the fall of Mempacton, and called on the young Man from Stonedom. "Talar, how did the Dwarves betray the Mempacton army during the Great Battle?" Malnar asked. The entire class turned a little to look at Talar, and he heard the shuffling of their white robes.

Talar shifted his gaze from New City and just stared at Malnar as if he were the Goblin who had stabbed his father. Dalir saw the look on his new friend's face and saw the rage in Talar's hazel eyes. Talar had heard these lies before as he traveled south from Stonedom through Capan lands. He just could not believe these lies were being peddled from the High Keep itself!

"By not attacking the Capan Legions!", Talar sarcastically replied. He immediately heard the gasps of his classmates and looked back to see their shocked faces. Malnar was shocked, too, not expecting the answer nor the hostile tone. Malnar had dealt with far worse students than Talar and decided to be patient with him.

"Now I know your still a new student here, Talar, and maybe you have not been told all of the truth about the history of Mempacton," Malnar stated.

Talar was fired up and cut Malnar off. "The truth? The truth? The truth is Capa betrayed Mempacton and attacked them and the Dwarves from behind! Mempacton had the Troll army beat, then Capa attacked them!". The class was looking at Talar like he was crazy, and he could hear their whispers about him. The classroom was filled with whispers now, for no one had challenged Malnar for quite some time.

"The Dwarves allied with the Trolls the night before the Great Battle," Malnar stated, but he was cut off again by Talar.

"The Dwarves have been fighting the Trolls since the beginning of their existence. Why would they ally with them then and betray Mempacton? Why?", Talar asked defiantly.

Malnar had been caught off guard by Talar's first statement, but he was ready for his second barrage of questions. One did not rise to a teacher in the High Keep by not being keen-witted. "The Dwarves attacked the Mempactons because they are greedy and jealous little creatures," Malnar said while spreading his hands apart. The Empire's propaganda was embedded deeply within Malnar, and he honestly believed that the Dwarves had joined their eternal enemies. "The Dwarves were jealous of the greatness of Capa and Mempacton. Jealous of Men," Malnar stated, and the students at the long table around Talar all nodded in approval. "The Dwarves knew our ally, Mempacton, would be vulnerable while fighting the Troll army. Then they attacked the Mempactons from behind, and with the Trolls, crushed them completely. Only the strength of our first Emperor, Titus, and the strength of our mighty Legions kept the Dwarves and Trolls from conquering Capa itself! Talar turned around in amazement at the sight of his classmates nodding in solemn approval and could not believe they accepted these lies as the truth.

Malnar could still see the disbelief in Talar's eyes and knew how to convince him. "Alright, Talar, it is clear to me that you still do not accept my words as the truth. So, tell me, where did you learn about the Great Battle? Who taught you about it?", Malnar's usually monotone voice had captured the attention of the entire class. Talar had calmed down and now realized he was challenging Malnar's authority, and he did not want to risk any repercussions to his friends or people.

"The Druids taught me the history of the Great Battle," Talar stated evenly. He glanced over at Dalir, who shook his head at his brazenness. Malnar thought for a few seconds, his dark hair and long beak-like nose staring at the wooden desk in front of him. The middle-aged teacher looked up at Talar and began to speak in a sarcastic tone.

"Yes, the famous Druids, and who taught them, your famous Paladin?" Malnar asked. The teacher's sarcastic manner caused most of the class to erupt in laughter. Malnar looked over the class, pleased at their response. Malnar looked down at Talar, who was turning red with embarrassment. "Yes, the Druids and the Paladin, they are ancient Mempacton myths students. Their Paladin was supposed to protect Mempacton forever, according to their myths. Yet, Mempacton is now in ruins and its people gone," Malanar said.

"Enough talk of his stupid northern legends," blurted Ralphin. "The Games are today, and we're wasting time talking about his Mempacton myths," Ralphin sneered. His cohorts and cronies laughed and jeered at Talar. It was the sixth day of the week, and classes were being cut short, giving the students time to see the Games, which started in the afternoon. Malnar continued his false narrative of the Great Battle until Calbrius entered quietly through the set of wooden doors behind the class. The headmaster's head was scanning back and forth across the class as if to ensure compliance. Talar noticed the headmaster and focused on Malnar to avoid Calbrius' gaze.

Calbrius rang the gong, and the class turned in their wooden seats to face him. "You all have permission to watch the Games in the Arena today. Listen to the Keep's Guard, or you will face my discipline. And Ralphin? If you get so drunk you need to be carried out, I will have you scrubbing the floors of the Keep for a week! Is that understood?", Calbrius asked loudly. The class nodded solemnly, the wooden doors behind Calbrius swung open, and the class started to filter out of the classroom. Malnar informed them that they would be leaving in an hour and to meet back at the classroom. Talar walked out of the classroom and spotted Dalir, who was leaning against the stone walls of the hallway. Talar started to make his way over to Dalir but was cut off by Tobias and Ralphin. The duo looked at him and sneered, but he did not let their sour looks spoil his mood. He would finally be free to leave the High Keep, even if it meant going to the Arena.

"Lunch in my room before we leave?", Dalir asked, and Talar nodded. The two kept walking towards their rooms while Talar asked Dalir about the Arena and the Games. Boxing, wrestling, and horse racing were all common forms of entertainment in Stonedom, but gladiator combat was not. Talar could not comprehend why the fights to the death were called "Games." He did not know why people would want to watch them either. "It is more than the blood and gore, even though some do come just to see the brutality," explained Dalir. "Once you see a quality match between two experienced gladiators, you will know why the Games are so popular," Dalir stated. Gladiator matches were just as popular in his native Koristan as they were in Capa. A veteran viewer of gladiator matches, Dalir was excited, for today, a champion gladiator from Koristan would be challenging Malfoy, the champion of Capa. Talar could sense the excitement in Dalir's voice as he described the upcoming Games. He could not believe his friend could enjoy such senseless violence and voiced his concerns directly to Dalir. Dalir shook his head at Talars innocence. "You act as if they are victims, Talar. These gladiators are killers. Most are convicted criminals. Some even volunteer to fight for the money. Quit being so childish about it, Talar," Dalir said as if the Games were completely normal.

Talar quickly changed into a fresh robe, then walked to Dalir's room and began knocking impatiently. Dalir opened it with one hand and with the other handed Talar a goblet of wine. Talar accepted the drink but was startled at the offering. The youthful duo usually did not begin their drinking until after their classes ended. "Don't look at me like that, you dull northerner," Dalir quipped. "It is the Games, everybody will be drinking, it is going to be a party! Especially with this warm weather," Dalir said. Talar walked over to his usual chair, and Dalir joined him, the two gazing out over New City. Below a festival-like atmosphere filled the streets. Talar was shocked to see so much public drunkenness. While the bars and taverns of New City were usually quite livid, today, everybody was drinking right out in the streets. Dalir saw Talar shaking his head. "The Games are great times for the common folk of Capa. It takes their minds off the problems they face. Everybody will be celebrating. Just wait until we get into the Arena." Talar kept shaking his head. Not everybody would be celebrating. He was sure the dead gladiator would not be celebrating.

Talar and Dalir kept drinking in awkward silence until Talar, not wanting to spoil Dalir's mood, started asking about the Games again. Dalir immediately perked up, went back into his room for more wine, and poured Talar a glass. He then started going into detail about the Games. Dalir explained that there was more to the Games than just the gladiator matches. In an excited voice, Dalir told Talar that the Games would start with a chariot race, then acrobats and music, then finally the main gladiator match. The main match would feature up-and-coming gladiators in a massive fight or would feature the two champions squaring off, one on one. "Alright, who is the champion from Koristan? I'm sure you will be cheering for him," Talar asked.

"The champion from Koristan is Arithos. He was a slave who worked in the salt mines south of the Capital. He fights with passion and skill and has won many matches," Dalir said enthusiastically. The wine was flowing in the streets of New City below them, and both Talar and Dalir drained their goblets. Not wanting to miss their chance to leave the Keep, both boys hurried back to the main classroom. The stone walls of the Keep passed by them, and they arrived before the closed wooden doors of the classroom, where most of the class was waiting.

"Ah, here he is now. Dalir, I wager you five gold coins the champion of Capa, Malfoy, will defeat your Koristan champion," Ralphin said with a confident smirk across his face. "Of course, if you don't have the gold to wager with…", Ralphin said. Dalir produced a leather pouch from beneath his robes. The pouch rattled, and Dalir smiled before saying that he would accept the bet. Talar was not only shocked by the amount of gold Dalir carried but also when Dalir and Ralphin shook hands. Talar had only a few silver coins, not nearly worth the gold Dalir carried. After shaking hands, Dalir motioned for Talar to accompany him as the Guards opened the doors. The class proceeded to exit the academic level of the High Keep, and Talar was trying to remember the way out. Dalir and Talar were in the back of the pack of students who were now walking down a spiral staircase that was lit with candles. The candles provided little light, and the Guards escorting them urged cautioned. After a few moments, the class entered a lower level. They walked through a storage room filled with wooden barrels, then down a wide staircase which led to an open hall. The hall was decked with red carpets and various tapestries depicting Legion victories. Two rows of stone columns ran parallel down the sides of the great hall, and Talar thought that he must be close to where he had met the Emperor. The day still brought shame and rage to him, and he tried not to think about it.

Servants brought wine to the students, and Talar now had time to converse with Dalir about his bet. "So, you and Ralphin buddies now, shaking hands and all," Talar teased Dalir. Dalir rolled his eyes at the jest.

"I just can't wait to take his money. When Arithios wins, Ralphin is going to cry. Just mark my words," Dalir said. Talar shook his head at the absurdity of betting on another Man's life and voiced his thoughts to Dalir. Talar adjusted his white robe, which he hated wearing. "You are becoming more Capan than me. You look right at home in that robe Talar," Dalir said with a laugh. Talar shook his head at the thought, the two youths finished their wine, and the class started out of the hall. They passed into a wide hallway then emerged into another hall, this one smaller than the previous one. Talar glanced over and saw a pair of golden doors encrusted with red gems and realized that he was in the waiting room to the Emperor's Court. The class continued and eventually passed through a heavy set of steel doors that led them out of the Keep.

The class passed through to the outer courtyard, where the rest of their escort awaited them. Despite the wine, Talar was making a good mental map of the whereabouts of the High Keep as he looked around at his surroundings. To his right was a small barracks that the Keep's Guard used when on duty. To his left was a stone staircase that led straight up to the ramparts and the turrets above. Talar could see four torrents from his current position in the middle of the cobbled courtyard. Looking up, he could see the ballistae and the Guards manning them. Other Guards armed with crossbows stood above him as well.

Talar was mapping out the High Keep mentally when he noticed Ralphin groping Mona, who slapped at Ralphin's hands to no avail. Usually, Calbrius or Malnar would stop such displays, but they were not with the class now. The red-haired Mercium slapped Ralphin across the face. This angered Ralphin, who now picked her up in the air. Nobody was doing anything, so Talar walked briskly over to Ralphin, spun him around, and pushed him away. A second later, Ralphin's bodyguard, who Talar had learned was named Ansgar, punched Talar in the back of the head, knocking Talar downwards. Luckily Dalir was there to catch him before he hit the ground. Talar was blinking rapidly and seeing bright yellow and white stars, but after a few seconds, he gained his composure and lunged forward at Ansgar. Dalir and one of the Keep Guard's restrained Talar by the arms, but he still flailed wildly anyway. Ralphin, Tobias, Ansgar, and the rest of the spoiled Capans jeered at Talar. Talar kept trying to get free until the sargent of the escort barked at the youth to settle down. "Don't want to go back to your room now, do you boy!" the sargent growled. Talar settled down, not wanting to be reported to the headmaster.

Dalir, who had been a step behind Talar, shook his head at the Capan's disregard for Mona and was patting Talar on the back, trying to get him to settle down. Dalir looked up and saw that Mona was staring at Talar. The Mercium noblewoman was the oldest of the students, and Dalir wondered why she was still in the Academy. Mona noticed Dalir's gaze and nodded curtly. Talar had not noticed Mona's looks, for his head was pounding. An egg had formed on the back of his head from Ansgar's fist. The class and their escort kept going, crossing under the grey walls of the High Keep, across the drawbridge, and into Old City.

They began to traverse around the base of the High Keep to reach New City and the Arena. The Guards cleared a path through the commoners, who were jubilant. Dalir bought two bottles of wine and handed one to Talar, who immediately began drinking from it. The rough wine was not as aged as the wine in the High Keep, but it did help with the ringing in his ears. The people of Old City were modestly dressed in fine robes and sandals. The buildings of the older part of Capa were arranged neatly along the straight street. The class kept going and finally began entering New City, and the difference between the two sections of the city was stark. The commoners were shabbily dressed and dirtier in appearance. Some did not have sandals or any type of footwear. With the Games going on today, almost all were drunk. Some were already tipsy, staggering back and forth or leaning against walls for support. A tall Capan, who looked like a metalsmith, toasted Talar and slapped him across the back. One of the Guards leaped forward, but the smith stepped back laughing, and Talar motioned for the Guard to step down. The walking in New City was tougher as well, for the cobbled streets had ended, and the group now walked across dirt streets.

Talar could see the towering walls of the Arena ahead, but the class had to pass through a large open market before entering the giant structure. Various food vendors and merchants had their wares spread out on wooden tables or on small open carts. Wooden sticks held up linen sheets, which shielded the vendors and their wares from the sun. Dalir spotted a vendor with roasted chicken meat and bought two legs. He handed one to Talar, and Talar bit into the tender meat. Talar suspected that Dalir knew that he did not have many coins and silently thanked him for not bringing up the issue. "Figured we could use something in our stomachs besides wine," Dalir said with a sheepish grin. He tore into the chicken leg and took another swig of wine. Talar smiled in between bites of chicken and kept on going through the open market. Past the market, a row of forges for various smiths stood, and Talar could smell smelted copper. His head was beginning to feel better, and his stomach was full of the chicken Dalir had provided. Talar took a long pull from the wine bottle and stared up at the Arena, which the class was finally approaching. The walls seemed to stretch up to the skies, and Talar could now see that the columns that supported the Arena's seats were connected by concrete arches. Talar marveled at the engineering masterpiece and would have kept staring at it had he had the chance. The Guard behind Talar gently prodded him along, though, and Talar kept walking, awestruck by the Arena's size. Passing through an open set of metal gates, the class was surrounded by commoners flowing into the Arena. The Guards were quick to establish a perimeter. The commoners gave a wide berth to the cheetah cloaked stocky Guards.

As the class passed through the arched opening into the Arena, Talar looked out, for below him lay the oval-shaped floor of the Arena. The Guard behind him had to prod him again, for he was awestruck at the sight before him. A sea of humanity was already in the Arena, perched above Talar on the concrete benches that ran concurrently around the Arena. Dalir motioned for him to follow, for, with all the Capans around him, there was no way Talar could hear Dalir's voice. Talar kept up with the class as they walked up a flight of stairs, then over to where a row of red canopies was set up. The canopies were set up for the nobles of Capa, and the class took seats on the concrete benches beneath them. The commoners around the canopies nodded to the class in respect. Talar was taken back at how immodest they dressed, especially the Capan Women. Dalir was also enjoying the views of the scantily clad Women and smiled at Talar before clanking his wine bottle against Talar's bottle.

A massive horn was mounted before the largest canopy sounded, and the Arena eventually became silent. An elderly Capan, dressed elegantly in a fine white linen robe, stood by the horn, and began to speak. The Arena went quiet, and Talar felt that he could hear his heartbeat. Surprised by how quiet it had become, Talar glanced around, but the rest of the class and the commoners were transfixed on the elderly speaker. "All Rise for Your Emperor!" the elderly Capan shouted, and Talar rose slowly along with the rest of the Capan citizens. Then the Emperor himself strode forth from out of the red canopy. The Capans throughout the Arena cheered enthusiastically as the Emperor turned from side to side, waving at them. A chill went up Talar's spine at the sight of so many worshipping such a tyrant. Talar remembered how the Emperor had humiliated him in front of the others, and rage began to build up from within him. Dalir glanced over at his friend and saw the hatred in his eyes. Dalir grabbed Talar's wrist, which caused Talar to look at Dalir sharply. Dalir was smiling though and motioned for Talar to calm down. He realized that Dalir was right and took a deep breath. He would have to hide his hatred of the Emperor better.

The elderly spokesman by the giant horn spoke of honoring the New Gods and the Empire. The crowd was getting anxious now, and the elderly Capan knew it. The great horn sounded again, and the elderly Capan began to speak. "Today, we honor the New Gods, and we honor Capa with the Emperor's Games!". The crowd roared, and the elderly Capan speaker waited for them to settle down. Once the crowd settled, the speaker announced that the chariot races had been canceled. The crowd hissed with anger until the speaker announced that the chariot races were being replaced with a beast match.

As the crowd jumped up and began to cheer wildly, Talar looked at Dalir questioningly. "What is a beast match?", Talar said to no avail, as the crowd's roar drowned out his words. Fortunately, Dalir had read Talar's lips, and now he simply pointed down to the floor of the Arena below. Talar's eyes bulged in surprise as the largest Man he had ever seen in his life emerged from the entrance tunnel into the Arena. The thousands of drunk Capans roared for beast matches were rare and always bloody. The egg on Talar's head seemed to respond to the roars of the crowd, so Talar took a big sip from the wine bottle that Dalir had supplied.

Talar was now shaking his head in disbelief at the size of the Man in the Arena. The Man had to be half a rod tall, and if Talar had to guess, he probably weighed thirty stone. The Man had arms that were corded with muscles. His legs looked like upside-down tree trunks. His neck and head reminded Talar of the great bear head he had seen mounted on the wall in the tavern of Stonedom. The Man was holding the short sword common to the Capan Legions and a shield as well. The giant Man whipped the sword around with the careless ease of someone who was so strong. He flexed his muscles, and the crowd roared his name at the spectacle. "Flavus, Flavus, Flavus!!" they roared. Flavus took off his Legion helmet and raised it to the Emperor, who now stood and acknowledged Flavus. The crowd roared, for they loved Flavus. Unlike other gladiators, Flavus only fought beasts and only the deadliest of them.

The great horn sounded again, and now Flavus placed his helmet back over his long blond hair. From the same tunnel that Flavus had emerged, a loud roar erupted. The crowd was now silent, and Talar could feel the anticipation. Talar glanced over at Dalir, who was also wide-eyed with anticipation. It was once again silent in the Arena, and Talar was beginning to wonder if anything was in the tunnel when the beast made its' debut. The male lion strode confidently from the tunnel, his gaze fixed upon Flavus. Talar could hear the gasps from the thousands of Capans, for it had been years since a lion had been captured. And this lion was massive.

Talar had recognized the lion from portraits in his father's library. He had never seen one in person and now studied the foreign creature as the lion began to circle back and forth in front of Flavus. The lion's mane was dark compared to the rest of his body, which Talar figured was more than half a rod long. The Capan gamekeepers had not fed the lion for two days, and now it eyed Flavus as it continued pacing in front of him. The Arena was silent as the big cat let out another roar. Flavus was not intimidated, though and now smacked his short sword against the shield in his left hand. The lion roared back and now charged at Flavus, and Talar was shocked at the speed of the massive lion. The lion was upon Flavus in seconds and jumped up at the massive gladiator, his claws grasping towards Flavus' throat. Flavus was ready, though, and had braced himself behind the shield. The force of the lion smashing into Flavus's shield seemed to reawaken the crowd, who now screamed in amazement. Flavus was thrown back from the big cat's attack and rolled backward. The lion kept charging, perched on its' back legs as he kept swiping his paws at the rolling gladiator. Flavus was now on his knees, and he raised his shield up at the last moment as the lion jumped in the air above him. Any other Man would have been crushed by the force of the lion, but with a mighty roar of his own, Flavus flung the lion in the direction it had been going. Regaining his feet, Flavus now struck out at the lion, hitting the big cat in the mane. The thick fur and hair absorbed the sword's edge, though, and now the lion attacked again. The big cat grabbed the massive gladiator by the shoulders, and for a few seconds, Talar thought the two were dancing. Flavus' wide shoulder was now in between the jaws of the massive lion, and the gladiator shrieked in pain. The lion dragged him to his knees, but Flavus sliced his sword across the lion's chest. The lion immediately released his hold on Flavus, and both Man and beast separated.

With both Flavus and the lion wounded, the Arena's sand drank up the first drops of blood that hit it. Flavus's wound was bleeding quite badly, and his pristine muscles, which had shone in the sun now, were covered in dark red blood. The lion roared again, gathered itself, and launched another attack on Flavus. As the lion approached, Flavus swung the short sword at him, but the lion snapped his jaws and grabbed Flavus' sword arm, causing Flavus to drop the blade. Flavus fell to the ground face-first as the crowd began to worry that their favorite champion would be killed in front of them. The lion dragged Flavus by his arm for a few feet, then let go of his arm. The lion approached the motionless gladiator's head, and Talar was sure that Flavus was finished. In an incredible display of strength, agility, and resilience, Flavus reached out with his bear-like hands and grabbed the lion by his mane. Flavus was still on his knees when he threw the lion on his back and began to wildly clobber on the lion's snout. The crowd in the Arena was going wild. The lion swiped at Flavus, but the big gladiator ignored the blows as he quit punching the lion and now dove for his sword. The lion now regained his footing and jumped high up at Flavus, ready to pin the big gladiator down and bite his neck. Flavus's bloody hand grasped his sword handle, and the gladiator could see the shadow of the lion on the ground below him. Flavus turned at the last second and as the big lion landed. The lion's weight impaled it on Flavus's exposed sword.

The lions' legs kicked helplessly as he died, and the crowd again gasped collectively, uncertain of Flavus' fate. Talar found himself at the edge of the bench, all thoughts about his hatred of the Emperor far from his mind. The gamekeepers rushed over and, after prodding the lion to ensure it was dead, rolled the massive beast off Flavus, who was motionless upon the floor of the Arena. Around Talar, the commoners whispered that Flavus had been crushed. The nearest gamekeeper reached down and shook Flavus, shaking the giant gladiator back to consciousness.

The thousands of Capans who had endured the sun, crowds, and stinking streets now roared in unison as Flavus was helped to his feet. The commoners around Talar began slapping each other's backs and were screaming their approval. Talar clinked his wine bottle against Dalir, and the youths drained the contents of the bottle. "We need more wine, Talar!", Dalir stated above the cheers of the crowd. Flavus was waving to the crowd as he was being helped of the Arena. The gamekeepers were wrapping chains around the lion to drag it out of the Arena. "There are wine vendors down where we entered," Dalir said as twenty acrobats now entered the Arena.

"Ok, I'll get this round, Dalir," Talar replied, and he got up and started to make his way down the aisle to the stairway below. One of the Keep Guards who had escorted the class of young nobles to the Arena followed behind Talar.

"Hurry up, or you will miss Arithos' win," Dalir shouted from his seat.

Talar made his way down the wide steps, making his way past an assortment of commoners. Some of the commoners reeked of wine and had not washed in weeks. They were dressed in shabby brown linen tunics with a grimy rope around their waists. Some had sandals on, some were barefoot. Other commoners were dressed in fine linen tunics and dresses with embroidery, and they had sound leather shoes or boots. The better-off male commoners usually wore short trousers that ended a little bit below the knees and short-sleeved white tunics. Talar passed them all as he and his escort made their way back to the entrance, where the wine vendors had moved their wares.

Talar was waiting patiently in line, surrounded by hundreds of ordinary Capans, when someone nudged him from behind. Figuring that it was someone just trying to squeeze through the crowd, Talar ignored the nudge until it happened again. Talar turned around, ready to give some commoner an earful when he saw that it was Mona. Talar's jaw dropped at seeing his classmate. Mona grabbed Talar's arm and spun him back around.

"Act normal. Our Guards are too busy talking to each other to notice us," Mona said quietly, her voice barely audible above the crowd around them. Talar tried to turn around to find where his Guard was, but Mona tugged on his arm again, bringing his attention back to her. "I said act normal. Are you deaf, boy?" Mona asked before looking at Talar as if he was a simpleton.

"I'm not a boy, Mona!", Talar said in a low voice. He was trying to get her hand off his wrist when she asked him how he knew her name. The question caught the breath in Talar's throat, and he did not know what to say.

"Don't worry about that," Mona said while shaking her head. "We need to talk in private tonight when the Guards change shifts. Talar was completely flabbergasted and was about to question Mona when he started gazing into her large green eyes. The wine Talar had consumed was not helping him now. "Focus Talar, Focus," Mona said before pinching his wrist.

"Ahh, take it easy, Mona," Talar replied.

"I need to talk to you about your family Talar. Tonight, when the Guard changes," Mona said before releasing Talar's wrist. She abruptly turned into the crowd, vanishing out of Talar's sight.

Talar stood there dumbfounded until a commoner behind him gave him an earful for not moving forward in line. Talar mumbled an apology, purchased two more bottles of wine, and paid the vendor with one of his precious silver coins. It was not until Talar was halfway up the stairway when Mona's words began to sink in. How did she know anything about his family? Did she hear any rumors about them, and if so, from whom? The questions were still swirling through Talar's mind when he sat next to Dalir.

The acrobats had finished their performance and now exited the Arena. Dalir was about to toast Talar again when he noticed the puzzled look across the Northerner's face. "What's wrong, Talar? Did they overcharge you for the wine?", Dalir said jokingly. He stopped joking when he saw Talar's expression. "What is it, Talar?", Dalir asked, but Talar seemed to be staring at the Emperor. "Talar, Talar!" Dalir repeated, careful not to draw attention from the nearby Keep Guards. Talar finally snapped back to his senses. His mind had been wrapped around his conversation with Mona. Dalir was trying to ask him what was wrong when the Arena's speaker began introducing the visiting champion Arithos. The crowd began to jeer and hurl insults at the visiting champion. The crowd's displeasure had taken Talar's mind off Mona's words. Talar looked over the champion gladiator that Dalir favored.

Arithos was tall and athletic but not unnaturally large like Flavus. Like Flavus, Arithos had a short sword, shield, helmet, and tall leather boots. Arithos swung his sword and then raised it to the jeers of the crowd. Dalir's fist was pumping up and down, though, and the half-drunk Koristan noble was out of his seat cheering for his champion. If it were not for the Keep Guards and Dalir's proximity to the other nobles, Talar feared Dalir would have been swarmed by the crowd of drunk Capans around him. The Arena's speaker now announced Malfoy, the Capan champion of countless matches. From the tunnel below Talar, the tall Riken emerged to the screams of thousands of Capans. Unlike Arithos, who had his dark hair closely trimmed and was clean-shaven, Malfoy looked like a wild man. Rikens were known for their barbaric ways, and Malfoy fit the description. The Riken was taller than Arithos, had long straw-colored hair, and a similar blond beard seemed to cover every inch of his face. Malfoy carried no shield. Both his hands gripped the straight short swords common to Capa. His body was covered with long scars that crossed his back, stomach, and forearms. Malfoy raised both swords to the crowd, and the Arena seemed to shake. All the people in the crowd started to stand as the two champions began to circle each other. Talar could not see anything once the commoners in front of him stood. Dalir was standing and cheering wildly for Artihos, who now started the match with a quick thrust at Malfoy's chest. Malfoy easily deflected the blow with his right sword, then swiped at Arithos' shield with his left sword. Arithos spun with the momentum, and his shield snapped back in place as the two champions continued circling each other.

Talar stood now for a better view and to not look out of place. Despite the high quality of swordsmanship below him, Talar's mind kept going back to what Mona had said. The match continued below him, and the crowd around him raged. Talar could hear the blows of Malfoys' swords ringing out against Arithos' shield. A large, bald Capan in his fifties was yelling "Kill Him" over and over, his eyes filled with bloodlust. The Capan's voice was going hoarse from screaming. Another younger Capan Woman, whose body was almost completely exposed, screamed for Artihos' blood. Bloodlust filled her eyes as well. Talar turned his attention back to the match, where Malfoy was pummeling Arithos' shield with blows from both of his swords. Malfoy ducked under a blow from Artihos' shield, his long blond hair swinging wildly as he slashed at Arithos' unprotected backside with both swords. The swords sliced through the unprotected skin, and Arithos fell forward, leaning on his shield to stay afoot. The crowd around Talar screamed in bloodlust again. Talar was shaking his head in disgust as Arithos' blood stained the sands of the Arena.

Talar kept shaking his head, the reality of the situation below finally dawning on him. He had been aware that one of the champions would be killed, but to see one of them bleed and suffer in person was a different matter. Flavus's fight had been hard enough to stomach, but Talar was not sure if he could handle what he believed would happen next. Talar knew enough about personal combat to know that Arithos' wounds were serious. Dalir could sense it too, and he looked over at Talar with a desperate look in his eyes. Talar wondered how desperate Arithos's eyes looked.

The champion from Koristan was bleeding heavily. His entire backside was covered with dark red blood. Malfoy now pressed his attack, thrusting and slashing, then finishing his attack with a violent kick to Arithos' stomach that landed squarely. Arithos fell backward and screamed out in pain as his wounded backside slammed against the hot sand of the Arena. Talar shook his head in disbelief when Malfoy raised his swords to the Arena instead of finishing off Arithos. The crowd roared in approval for the stall in combat gave Arithos time to gain his feet. Malfoy lashed out at Arithos with a vicious volley from his short swords. Arithos' shield was knocked out of his hand, and he now fought back Malfoy with a maddening frenzy. Malfoy's swords slashed relentlessly, but Arithos somehow kept him at bay with only his sword. The blood from Arithos' wounds was running down his back, and Talar was beginning to wonder how much more blood the Koristan had in him.

Malfoy stopped his attacks, and the two champion gladiators resumed circling each other. Arithos suddenly dropped to a knee, and Malfoy could sense his opponent was exhausted from the exertion of defending himself. The crowd was screaming for the Koristan's life, but Malfoy did not attack the kneeling Koristan. Talar felt sick to his stomach. Malfoy had obviously bested Arithos, but instead of stopping the match, the crowd demanded blood. A lion had not been enough. Talar wanted to do something, but he could only shake his head as Arithos rose, sword high above his head. The Koristan champion cut down at Malfoy, who allowed the blade to pass harmlessly past him. Malfoy slashed down with one sword cutting Arithos' sword hand deeply and causing him to drop his blade. The now defenseless Arithos jumped back, but Malfoy had already spun around and now sliced Arithos wickedly across his bare stomach. Arithos crumpled to his knees, his hands clasping his stomach wound. His blood now soaked the sand.

The crowd was screaming "Kill" over and over in unison now. Most had their fists clenched and were making chopping motions as if they were personally going to kill Arithos. Talar felt like he was going to be sick, and he now choked down the wine which he had consumed earlier. Malfoy raised his swords to the crowd, and they roared back. Malfoy tossed one of his swords to the ground and stood behind Arithos. The tall blonde Riken grabbed the hilt of his short sword with both hands and began to slowly push the sword tip down the middle of Arithos' shoulders. Talar could see the awful look on

Arithos' face as the sword killed him, but he could not hear Arithos' screams, for the crowd around him drowned him out. Talar looked around him with disgust. The drunk, cheering Capans were all murderers, as far as he was concerned. Malfoy pulled his sword out, and Arithos fell to the sands. Malfoy picked his other sword up and now screamed and gestured for the crowd. Arithos lay motionless.

Dalir looked over at Talar, who was staring at the Emperor with the same wild look he had before. Dalir thought Talar looked as crazy as Malfoy did. Dalir looked over to his right, where Ralphin was jeering at him. He would have to pay the snobby Capan. After Malfoy had left the Arena and the elderly Capan had announced the Games over, the crowd began to slowly filter out of the Arena. Artihos was still lying upon the Arena's sands. The class followed their Guards down the stairs, and Dalir could sense that Talar had not been fond of the Games. "He chose to fight, Talar. He chose to fight," Dalir said from behind Talar.

Dalir's words brought Talar back to his senses. Watching Arithos die had put Mona's words at the back of his mind. After Arithos' had crumpled over, though, Talar began to rapidly think over what Mona had said to him. She wanted to talk about his family. There could be no positive reason why she would want to talk about Talar's family. Talar thought that his father was probably dead.

As he was thinking of that possibility, Dalir repeated the words that he had just spoken, unsure if Talar had heard him. "He chose to fight, Talar. He chose to fight." Dalir said.

Talar nodded at Dalir as the two made it down the stairs and were now level on the floor of the Arena. Arithos was being dragged out by two gamekeepers and Talar thought again of Dalir's words. He chose to fight. Talar thought of the consequences if his father was dead. Cynfor would be King, and Talar doubted his brother would kneel to the Emperor. Talar watched the Gamekeepers drag Arithos' across the sands of the Arena and he knew that he would have to make a choice soon.

Chapter XIV- Familiar Sounds

Sorel looked up as the second giant log fell through the air and fell into the Cold River in front of him. Sorel grasped his paddle and began trying to paddle the raft over to the remaining log. Sorel and Tarquin had already rigged up the first log. Sorel started paddling and realized he would not be able to make it over to the second log without leaving the eddy they were in. "You're going to have to get this one yourself, youngster!" Sorel yelled to Tarquin. Tarquin nodded and began carefully paddling over to the giant log. Tarquin secured a rope around the log and then tied it to the stern of the long canoe. Tarquin now tenderly moved to the front of the canoe with his paddle in his hand. After reaching the bow, Tarquin threw Sorel a line, and the older woodsman somehow managed to catch it on the first try.

The water of the Cold River lapped at the wooden raft Sorel was perched in as Tarquin pulled him close to the log. Sorel untied the line from the stern of the canoe as Tarquin looked on from the front. Tarquin had been a little confused about how the raft would work, but now that it was coming together in front of him, he understood how it would work. The raft would be situated between the two massive pines near the end of the logs. The rudder of the raft would give Evander a chance of maneuvering the massive pieces of timber down the river. Sorel tied the second log to the side of the raft and secured his paddle. Sorel looked over to Tarquin and smiled. The raft was all set. They were ready to go down the river and make their fortune. Sorel was about to tell Tarquin to paddle the canoe ashore so he could pick up Evander, Claudius, and Marcus along with the rest of their supplies. Before he could speak, though, Sorel spotted something flash through the sky before looking over and seeing something splash into the river behind him.

Sorel stood in the raft and looked backward and almost fell out when he saw a limp body floating in the river facedown. Not knowing who it was, Sorel awkwardly jumped off the raft, knowing that he did not have much time before the unknown woodsmen drowned. Sorel spat up water as he emerged from the cold water, and he began to swim over to the still facedown body. Sorel's boots and pants were slowing him down, but he still made it to the limp person quickly. Sorel reached out and gasped with shock after turning the body over and seeing Marcus's unconscious face. Sorel yelled out to Tarquin, but the quick-thinking youth was already paddling the canoe towards his floating friends. "Who is it, Sorel? Who is it?" Tarquin asked desperately. Sorel figured that there was a good chance that Marcus was dead, for he could not feel him breathing. Sorel knew that Tarquin and Marcus were best of friends and did not want to frighten Tarquin.

"Who is it?", Tarquin shouted as he pulled the long canoe close to Marcus and Sorel. After seeing Marcus and shouting his name, Tarquin leaned and grabbed Marcus by the shoulders. With Sorel pushing from below and with Tarquin pulling, the two managed to get Marcus in the canoe headfirst. Tarquin fell over as Marcus's legs came into the canoe. For a second, Sorel thought the canoe was going to flip. Marcus began to spit up water as Tarquin shouted out in joy at the sight of his friend breathing. Sorel sighed in relief at knowing Marcus was alive and began swimming back to the raft, which was unattended.

Sorel was wondering how Marcus had managed to fall off the cliff when he heard the screams from the direction of the camp. Sorel pulled himself up to the seat of the raft, which was one of the cross pieces of the raft. Sorel stood up and heard more screams. Deep inside, Sorel knew what was happening. Years ago, he and Evander had escaped Fort Carillon, running into the woods away from the screaming. Sorel had spent a lifetime trying to drink away those screams. Now the screaming was back, and Sorel knew it was time to run away again. Except he was in a raft, and Evander was nowhere to be seen.

Marcus woke up screaming incoherently. The fall from the cliff had scared him beyond what his senses could handle. He would have tipped the canoe if Tarquin had not held him down. "Dead, Dead, Dead, their all Dead!" Marcus shouted over and over. Tarquin's stomach sank to his knees, and a cold chill went up Sorel's spine when he heard Marcus' words. Sorel knew it was time to flee, and he yelled at Tarquin to grab his paddle. "Get out into the current Tarquin. Into the current!" Sorel yelled. Sorel looked to his right where a young woodsman, not more than three rods away, busted out of the wood line. The woodsman was Tarquin's age and was bleeding badly from a nasty cut across his left eye. Despite his wound, the boy was making good time through the maze of boulders and large rocks that dotted the shoreline.

"To Me Boy, To Me!" Sorel shouted, and the boy looked up fearfully midstride. Tarquin guided the canoe towards the shore and was about to tell him to get into the canoe when a metal-tipped spear burst from his stomach. The spear had impaled the youth, and he now fell on the ground, his legs kicking violently as his hands clutched the bloody spear.

Sorel looked over to the wood line, where he saw a Dwarf warrior standing upon one of the large grey boulders. A few more Dwarfs emerged from the wood line, and Sorel yelled at Tarquin to leave the still kicking woodsman. Tarquin was about to jump out of the canoe and drag the wounded Man in, but Tarquin had spotted the Dwarves as well. After sitting back down in the stern, Tarquin began back- paddling to escape the big eddy and the Dwarves. Sorel was paddling as well, and the left side of his giant log raft now entered the current. With his attention focused on the river, Sorel did not notice the spear flying towards him until it hit the crossbeam he was sitting on with a loud thud. A foot higher, and the spear would have killed him. With the raft now in the river and with no obstructions ahead of him, Sorel ducked down, balancing himself precariously above the river by grasping the rudder.

"GO, GO, GO!" Sorel screamed, his harsh voice bellowing across the peaceful river. Tarquin was back paddling furiously as Marcus lay in the middle of the canoe, screaming incoherently. The Capan youth's blond hair was swinging back and forth as he back paddled. A spear flew over Tarquin's head and landed in the river, floating like a piece of driftwood. The thuds of arrows embedding into the side of the wooden canoe brought Tarquin's attention back to the rocky beach. Four Dwarves were standing in a line not more than a rod away. The Dwarves were dressed in buckskin pants and knee-high leather boots. Layers of thick leather armor connected with intricate metal wires covered their shoulders and chest. Tarquin was amazed at how stocky the Dwarves were. He then noticed the tallest Dwarf pull back his bowstring and take aim at him.

Tarquin could only scream as the arrow sped towards him. At the last second, Tarquin turned his body, and the arrow flew across the canoe, mere inches away from the Capan. Knowing he was in the range of the Dwarves, Tarquin panicked and dropped his paddle. While he reached down for it, another arrow sped over his ear, and he could feel the breeze the arrow's fletching caused. Tarquin picked up his paddle and was about to put it in the water when another arrow hit the paddle, nearly knocking Tarquin over. Tarquin was shaking with fear, and he now pulled the wooden paddle through the water towards him, dramatically turning the canoe into the current.

The Cold River's current took hold of the canoe, and Tarquin kept paddling to straighten the long canoe. "Paddle Marcus, Paddle!" Tarquin yelled to his friend. The words seemed to bring Marcus out of his state of shock. The crazed look left Marcus's eyes, and he looked around as if finally comprehending the situation.

Sorel looked to his right, where even more Dwarves were running from the forest. Despite the current, the Dwarves were easily making ground on them, and Sorel looked downriver to where the river narrowed. The group had portaged around this rapid on their way upriver from Fort Carillon. A large rock formation jutted out from the right side of the river. The rock's grey surface was smooth from the river water. The Dwarves were angling for that rock outcropping, and Sorel knew they were not safe yet.

"Get Down Tarquin. Get Down, Marcus. Down Boys, Down!" Sorel screamed hysterically as the current brought him to within two rods of the rock cropping. Looking ahead, Sorel saw at least a dozen armed Dwarves waiting in ambush for them. The Dwarves were already covered in blood and were screaming their war chants. Sorel looked ahead and knew he must get the raft within a rod length's of the outcropping to stay in the river's deep channel. Sorel looked around for shelter from the Dwarves' but found none on the raft.

The Dwarves unleashed their missiles, but Sorel saw them coming. He stepped off the log crossbeam he was perched on and grasped his former seat. The river water bit at his legs and torso. Shadows from the arrows above fell upon Sorel. The old woodcutter could make out the Dwarves' war chants above the roar of the rapids.

The bloodthirsty Dwarves on the rock ledge howled as Sorel escaped past them unharmed. Tarquin's hands were shaking with fear as the canoe began to speed up as the current quickened before the rapids. "Lay down, Marcus, Lay Down!" Tarquin yelled, but Marcus did not move. Marcus' legs appeared to be useless. Despite his attempts to move them on his own, Marcus's legs did not budge. Marcus looked back at Tarquin from the middle of the canoe with a look of complete horror as he realized he was paralyzed.

Tarquin did not have time to think about his friend's injuries. The canoe was close to the rock ledge, for he had missed the deep channel that Sorel had taken. Tarquin thought about jumping overboard but did not want to leave Marcus alone in the rapids, which were a few leagues long. Tarquin steered the canoe through the opening by the rock outcropping, then dropped below the gunwale of the vessel. The Dwarves unleashed their second barrage of arrows and spears, and Tarquin ducked down as the arrows thudded into the wooden canoe once again.

Looking up hastily, Tarquin saw a shirtless stocky young Dwarf take off from the riverbank above the rock outcropping. The Dwarf flew down the short hill, bounded across the rock formation, then leaped off the rock formation with all his might. Tarquin looked on with a surprised look on his face as the Dwarf flew above the river at him. Without hesitation, Tarquin stood on his knees and swung his paddle, hitting the Dwarf mid-air and knocking him into the water. Tarquin was about to lay back down when something punched him in the shoulder and spun him around. Tarquin collapsed to the bottom of the canoe and felt something wet run down his shoulder. Looking down, Tarquin saw the fletchings of a Dwarf arrow protruding from his right shoulder and gasped out in shock and pain.

The canoe continued its course down the river trailing behind the log raft. The cold river water was making Sorel's hands numb, and the woodcutter feared he would not be able to hold onto the crossbeam for much longer. Thankfully, the recent rain had raised the river, and the log raft and canoe quickly made it down the long chute of rapids. Sorel carefully climbed back up to his perch on the crossbeam and stuck his head up to survey his surroundings. The Dwarves were on the rock outcropping still. Some were helping a bare-chested and soaking wet Dwarf scramble out of the rushing river. The boys were behind him in the canoe, but Sorel could sense something was wrong. Tarquin lay slump back against his seat, and Marcus wept uncontrollably.

Sorel used the rudder to slow the raft to allow the canoe to catch up. As the canoe came alongside him, Sorel could see the arrow protruding from Tarquin's shoulder. Sorel looked into Tarquin's eyes and could see fear. Tarquin's still shaking hands tried to remove the arrow, but upon contact, the pain was too much. "Leave it, for now, boy," Sorel said softly, only raising his voice high enough to be heard over the river. "What's wrong with Marcus?" Sorel asked Tarquin. Marcus was still incomprehensible.

"He can't move his legs," Tarquin replied, tears forming in his eyes.

Sorel nodded at Tarquin and told the youth to wrap his vest around the wound. The Dwarves were still on the formation of rocks, apparently satisfied with the blood they had spilled today. Sorel told the youths from Capa that they would be alright. Sorel told them that they would get back to Capa. They would get back to civilization. Tarquin and Marcus looked up at Sorel from the bottom of the canoe. Sorel could tell that they did not believe him. He did not believe his words either.

Chapter XV-When the Guard Changes

Talar paced nervously in his small windowless room. The lone candle on his desk provided enough light to throw his shadow against the grey stone behind him. The High Keep was quiet this time of night, and he could not hear anything except the sound of his boots on the stone below him. Talar had been thinking of all the reasons why Mona would want to speak to him so secretly. Had his father succumbed to his wounds? Had Cynfor assumed the throne of Stonedom? Was Cynfor heading south to swear allegiance to the Emperor? How would Mona know of his father's health before the news reached Capa? And why would she care anyway?

The last question was the most puzzling to him. The bump from his fight earlier seemed to only hurt more when he thought about it. Was Mona really interested in his affairs, or did the Emperor send her to test his allegiance? The questions flooded his mind, and to ease the pain from Ansgar's punch, Talar poured himself a glass of wine. He had quit drinking after watching Arithos being dragged to the pits below the Arena. The walk from the Arena back to the High Keep had all been a blur. Dalir had tried to convince Talar to join him back in his room, where he was throwing a party for the members of the class. Talar politely refused and told Dalir the wine had made his stomach upset. Dalir had frowned at that, for the two drank wine almost every day. Talar had been in his room ever since, only opening the door to accept his dinner.

Talar raised the glass of wine to his lips and sipped at the goblet. The wine helped dull the pain from the punch, and he pulled out his lone chair to take a seat. He kept thinking about Mona's true intentions. She was from Mercium, whose citizens hated the Empire. Mercium was the most recent kingdom to surrender to the Empire. The Mercium phalanxes had been a nightmare for the Capan Legions, who had trouble penetrating the long spears of the Mercium. The result was a twenty-year bloody war, but in the end, Capa had prevailed after capturing the leaders of Mercium. Mercium had surrendered ten years ago, and from what Dalir had been told, the peace was uneasy. Old wounds healed slowly, and the loss of so many Mercium citizens from battle, starvation, and disease would not be forgotten there.

Talar took another sip and considered his alternate theory about Mona's intentions. Was she a spy for the Emperor? Had the Emperor sent her on a mission to test his allegiance? To test his oath? Talar shook his head at the thought. He could not believe that she would willingly work for the Emperor. Maybe the Emperor had forced her to approach him at the Games, and maybe tonight was a trap designed to ensnare him. Maybe his father was dead? Talar considered all of this as he sipped at the wine. He was about to top off his goblet when someone knocked softly on his wooden door. Talar set the wine down, took a deep breath, and walked towards the door. He grasped the vertical wooden door handle and pulled it open. Mona stood in the hallway before the door, the candlelight from the hallway illuminating her white robe and red hair. She did not wait for Talar to invite her in, and he shut the door quickly behind her. Talar turned around to face her. Mona's face was expressionless. She was older than Talar, by at least a few years, and now her green eyes looked over the tall northerner from Stonedom.

"You should take a seat, Talar, Mona said softly.

Talar shook his head and told her he preferred to stand. "Alright, well, I'm going to sit then," Mona said before sitting in the chair. Mona looked over Talar's few possessions then looked over the barren room. "You know they kept me in here for two years before I got a room with a window... it seems so long ago now," Mona said before sighing. Her eyes were darting back and forth, unable to meet Talars.

"So, this room was yours then?" Talar asked. Mona managed to glance at him with a smile and nodded slightly. "This must be where they keep the unruly students," Talar said jokingly, trying to break the awkwardness in the room. Mona smiled again, still unable to look him in the eyes. The awkwardness in the room persisted. The light from the candle flickered and cast Talar's shadow against the wall behind him as he tried to figure out what Mona was doing in his room.

Talar was about to offer Mona a glass of wine when she began to speak. "I've come here tonight to tell you something awful. I would have told you at the Arena, but I did not think it was the right place." Talar moved closer to Mona and took a knee in front of her so that his face was even with hers. She now brought her green eyes up and looked deep into his eyes. Talar could see the pain in her eyes and the pity.

"Is he dead, Mona? Is my father dead?" Talar asked, and Mona nodded.

"Cadoc Stoneking, King of Stonedom, is dead Talar. Your father is dead. I'm so sorry, Talar," Mona said softly. Talar said nothing, his eyes fixed on the floor. He had tried to prepare himself for this moment, but now that it was here, he felt an awful sensation in the bottom of his gut, and his hands began to shake. Mona noticed his reaction to her statement, and after gently grasping Talar's shaking hands, she guided him to the seat which she had occupied. "Take a deep breath Talar, take a deep breath," Mona urged him. Talar breathed heavily as the repercussions of his father's death washed over him. He would never see his father again, never talk to him about hunting or girls, never feel his embrace. Talar's hands were still shaking, and Mona urged him to drink the wine that was in front of him.

After draining the goblet, Talar's hands quit shaking so bad, and his wits began to come back to him. Mona said nothing, but she did fill the goblet up, take a sip, then hand it back to Talar. Talar drained this glass, and the awful feeling in his stomach started to fade away. Talar's mind was overwhelmed, but after a few moments, he finally quit breathing so heavily. Tears formed in his eyes, but he did not want to cry in front of Mona, so he blinked them back. Talar's senses were coming back to him, and now he looked up, his eyes meeting Mona's.

"How do you know this, Mona? How do you know my father is dead? Talar asked solemnly. Mona looked down at Talar and replied without hesitating.

"I got a message from someone in the Resistance early this morning. Another member of the Resistance received a pigeon with the message late last night. I would have told you sooner if it was possible. I'm sorry for your loss Talar, I know the pain that comes with losing a parent," Mona said.

The Resistance? Mona? Talar shook his head in disbelief. He could not believe that Mona was a member of the Resistance. They were known for bloody assassinations and sabotage. Talar was about to question her, but Mona spoke first. "Yes, Talar, the Resistance. I joined a few years ago. It is the only thing that gets me through these days." Talar kept shaking his head in disbelief, but eventually, he asked her why she had joined the Resistance. Now it was her turn to shake her head. Mona grabbed the goblet and topped it off. She took a big swig from the goblet and looked down at Talar.

"Like I said before, I know the pain that comes when losing a parent. My father was killed ten years ago by the Capans after he had surrendered his army. My mother was killed while trying to flee to Koristan with me. The Capans kidnapped me and brought me here, to this forsaken room, within this cursed Keep. I've been here ever since," Mona said. She took another swig before handing the goblet back to Talar.

Talar looked down into the goblet at the dark red wine, his mind racing through everything Mona had said. He thought about his dead parents. His mother had died giving birth to him. He wished that he could have talked to her just once. Talar wondered if his father was with his mother. He wondered if the Druid's teachings were true.

Deep within, he knew that Mona spoke the truth about his father and about hers. Talar was not sure why she had come here so secretly, though. To spare him the humiliation of hearing of his father's death at the High Court. Talar sipped at the wine and looked Mona in the eyes. "I believe you, Mona, but why do you tell me this? Why sneak here in the middle of the night to tell me about my father's death? I barely know you," Talar said. His last sentence had barely been audible.

"Because I want to leave here, I want to leave Capa with you. I am sick of this prison," Mona said fiercely. Talar's eyes bulged at her words, and he initially thought that she was crazy. Mona was still standing before him, and she could tell that her words had an impact on the young Prince. She could tell that he was considering her plan. After ten long years of being trapped in the High Keep, Mona was desperate for her freedom. "What do you think the Emperor will do to you once he hears about your brother's rebellion? He might crucify you just to set an example to the other noble families," Mona said.

"My brother's rebellion? Cynfor has rebelled?" Talar asked, his eyes bulging again.

"Yes, after being named King, your brother proclaimed Stonedom's freedom from the Empire. He is rallying his army and heading to Thendara. Will you join your brother in battle?" Mona asked. She had asked the last question just to put additional pressure on Talar to flee with her.

Talar set his wine glass down, and now Mona saw the fierceness in his eyes. Talar had the same look in his eyes when he had thrown Ralphin off her, and Mona knew now that Talar would escape with her.

"I will escape Capa with you, and I will join my brother in battle," Talar said slowly. Mona smiled and nodded. Her plan was working.

Mona now leaned over across Talar's lap and picked up the wine glass. After taking a deep sip, she passed it back to Talar, who looked up at her with those fierce eyes of his. "How many coins do you have, Talar? Is it silver or gold? What about gems? Pearls?" Mona asked quickly. The questions were asked too quickly for Talar to comprehend, and he shook his head.

"I barely have any coins, Mona. I have no gems, pearls, or amber for that matter," Talar said. Mona now began to pace back and forth. Talar now watched her shadow behind the grey wall. He knew that they would need coin on the road back north, but he figured that the Resistance would provide them with coins. Talar could trap and fish as well. He was not worried about his lack of coins, but Mona seemed to be. After watching her pacing back and forth, Talar spoke up and informed her that he could fish and trap on their way north. The look she gave him made him feel like he was a child.

"We will have to take a ship to Badatoz. The reward the Emperor will put out for us will make it impossible for us to go across Brigantium. We will sail to Badatoz then head up the Cold River to Mercium, where my family has allies. The only problem is that I don't have much coin either, and the ship's passage for two to Badatoz will cost us at least four gold coins," Mona said quickly, making it hard for Talar to keep up. After a few moments, the gravity of their situation began to dawn on Talar. His father was dead. Cynfor was at war with the Empire. If they escaped the Keep and the city and tried to cross overland, they would be run down. If they did not escape, Talar might be killed or tortured. Or both. All the wine in Talar's stomach began to bounce around, and for a minute, Talar thought he was going to be sick.

Mona glanced at Talar and saw the pale look on his face. Maybe she should not have mentioned the crucifixion part. Too late now, she thought. Mona also thought about their lack of coins and how they would solve that. They would not have time to sneak on a ship once they ran from the Keep, and even if they did, how would they know where it was going or when? They could not hide in the city too long; someone would give them up for the reward for sure. They could steal horses and ride away, but the Emperor and Volga would send pigeons to warn every Legionairre between Capa and Mercium. How could they get coins? How?

"What about the Resistance? Can't the Resistance give you coins, Mona?" Talar asked. Mona just shook her head, though, and kept pacing.

"They just leave me notes on my desk in my room, instructions sometimes. I've never seen another Resistance member before," Mona said. Talar now shook his head in despair. Mona's visit had rocked his world, and his mind was doing its best to sort out what was going on. His father was gone, and now it was up to him to escape the Emperor. The same Emperor who had a dungeon full of torture devices just a few stories below him now. The thought of Volga leering over him made Talar shudder.

Mona kept pacing, and Talar drank the rest of his wine. The candlelight flickered, casting Mona's shadow against the wall. Finally, a thought came to Talar, and he could not believe he had not thought of it before. "I'll ask Dalir for the gold coins," Talar said. His words stopped Mona's pacing. "Dalir has plenty of gold coins. He wagered more than four gold pieces today at the Games alone. I will ask Dalir for the gold Mona. Then we will escape by the sea to Badatoz like you said."

Mona stared at Talar for a second, then kept pacing but more slowly. She kept pacing for another moment, her shadow again dancing across the grey wall in front of Talar. The silence of the High Keep was only interrupted by the soft tap of Mona's sandals on the stone floor. Mona stopped pacing and leaned against the wall next to Talar's desk. "Do you trust Dalir?" Do you trust him with your life? With our lives?" Mona asked, her eyes probing Talar's face. Talar looked down into his now empty wine glass, and after pausing for a moment, he nodded and brought his eyes up to meet Mona's.

"I do trust Dalir. With my life. With our lives. He is my friend," Talar said.

Mona nodded and accepted Talar's answer. Despite the pleasantries and luxuries of the High Keep, she longed for home, for Mercium. She had been a captive for far too long to pass up on a chance like this to escape. Mona kept looking at Talar, for there was now another element of her plan that she must launch now before Talar realized his moral dilemma. "Talar, have you seen or heard from the two guards that escorted you from Stonedom," Mona asked quietly.

Talar shook his head, and his heart sank. Alwin and Hartwin had been forced into the Legion and no doubt would suffer once word spread that Talar had fled. Talar now began to shake his head, and Mona began to mentally prepare her argument. "I can't leave Mona, I can't leave, I can't leave them. Alwin and Hartwin are like family to me. If I leave, the Emperor will surely order Volga to torture them. How can I leave? How?". Mona watched Talar turn pale with fear. She knew she had to speak now, or he would never abandon his countrymen.

"Your guards swore an oath to your family, did they not, Talar? Your father sent them down here, into the heart of the Empire, so that they could protect you. They swore to the Old Gods, did they not? To protect the line of Stoneking, to protect you," Mona stated.

"Yes, and I swore an oath of kinship to them. For they are my wards, my countrymen, and my friends. I will not abandon them to torture and endless pain just so I can play the part of the hero. I will not Mona, no matter what you say," Talars' words cut through the small chamber. Mona knew better than to argue with him now. She had thought before of not mentioning his guards but knew eventually that he would remember them and their plight. She still had one wild chance at getting Talar to help her escape. It was dangerous, though, for her, Talar, and for the Resistance.

"I might be able to get your guards out, Talar," Mona said simply, with no expression.

"How?" Talar replied eagerly. Mona now walked across to the other side of the room, and Talar shifted in his seat so he could keep looking at her.

"On the day the Resistance first contacted me, they left a letter on my desk. If I was ready to join, which I was, I was supposed to leave the reply tacked to the front door of the Academy. I crept out there one night, nervously, mind you, and tacked it up. I thought for sure that Calbrius would be waiting with two Keep Guards, ready to snatch me and drag me to the dungeon. It never happened though, and then today I found a letter on my desk, telling me to tell you about your father," Mona said.

Talar thought long and hard, but the night's news about his family was too much for him. He could not comprehend where Mona was going with her story, so he simply motioned for her to continue.

"Don't you see Talar? I can leave a letter on the door to the Academy, asking about your Guards, and asking about some gold as well!" Mona said excitedly, not picking up on Talar's gloominess. Her words, however, finally sank through to him, and he looked up at her angrily.

"Are you trying to get me killed, Mona? Are you mad? What if the wrong person reads it? What if Calbrius reads it? Or a Keep Guard? Are you mad?". Talar's outrage surprised Mona. He could be quite temperamental.

"I have thought about this before today, Talar. For a long-time, I have thought about this. I just know that someone in the Resistance will find it before Calbrius does. Then the Resistance will help us, and we will escape here together," Mona said softly.

Talar looked up at Mona and rolled his eyes. To tack a note stating their intentions on the front door of the Academy was ludicrous to him. "Your desire for freedom is blinding you, Mona. And I will not abandon my countrymen to torture and death." After hearing Talar's words, Mona knew that she was losing her argument, so in desperation, she began to slowly approach Talar from behind. Talar was sitting at the table, silent, staring at the grey wall in front of him. Mona began to slowly caress his neck. All the problems and pain that Talar was experiencing seemed to disappear. Talar stood and kissed Mona. Mona kissed him back passionately and led him by his hand to his bed.

As the two lay naked underneath Talar's only blanket, Mona whispered into his ear. "We must escape Talar. No matter what, we must escape. And we must hurry. Only the Gods know what the Emperor will do once he hears about your brother Cynfor."

Talar nodded wearily. His problems were flooding back into his mind, but Mona's soft skin pressed against his seemed to diminish those problems. "I will ask Dalir tomorrow morning, Mona."

"What about your guards? What if Dalir can't help them as well?" Mona barely whispered the question.

"I don't know Mona, I don't know…." Talar's voice trailed off. Mona smiled in the darkness, for the candle had gone out some time ago. Her plan still had life in it.

"I must leave now Talar, I will see you in class tomorrow. Be urgent with Dalir. Our time here is running out. Remember why your guards were sent here, Talar. Remember that and remember me," Mona said before kissing Talar fiercely. She slipped her robe on and quietly exited her former room. Talar stayed awake all night. He cried a little thinking about his father, then he became enraged that he had missed his father's last moments because of the Emperor. He thought of Mona and the smell of her hair and the way she kissed his neck. He thought of Dalir and of Alvin and Hartwin. All these thoughts rolled around in his head until Talar could hear the other students stirring around in their rooms as they got ready for class. Talar fell asleep then.

Chapter XVI- Written by the Victors

Calbrius's shrill voice awakened Talar. "Upon your feet, you lazy damn northerner!" Calbrius yelled. Talar was still rubbing the sleep out of his eyes when the cold water hit him. Once it did, he jumped out of bed, still naked, and was about to choke Calbrius when he slipped and fell on the slick wet stone floor. Calbrius smirked, informed him that the whole class was waiting on him, and ordered him to dress quickly. Talar did, and with Calbrius prodding him with his cane, he half walked, half stumbled down to the front door of the Academy.

Talar stumbled in, still wet from Calbrius' shower and still half asleep. His disheveled appearance drew laughs from the assembled students. Talar went over to his usual seat beside Dalir and settled in for Calbrius's morning lecture. Today, of course, was a history lesson about the fall of Mempacton. Talar visibly shook his head, for he was not in the mood for Calbrius' history lesson. Calbrius droned on anyway. Dalir had seen Talar shake his head, and with his appearance, Dalir knew something was up with his friend. Dalir poked Talar's leg and looked at him with an inquisitive smile. Talar looked at his friend, then leaned over and whispered in Dalir's ear while Calbrius' back was turned. "I'm in trouble, Dalir. I need gold coins to escape."

Dalir's smile disappeared when he saw the desperation in Talar's eyes. Dalir nodded slightly in acknowledgment of Talar's request. Calbrius's voice rang out in the background. He was describing the fall of Mempacton. Dalir looked around slowly to see if any other students had heard Talar's request. As he looked around, he locked eyes with Mona, who quickly looked back at Calbrius. Dalir now looked back at Talar, whose gaze was locked onto Mona's. Dalir knew then that something was up between the two of them.

"...their elected leaders failed to build proper defensive structures against the Troll army. But that was not the only reason Mempacton fell. The Mempactons trusted the Dwarves, they trusted the Elves, they trusted their false religion. I do not know if Master Malnar has mentioned this, but the Mempactons believed in an immortal heretic. This supposedly immortal Mempacton knight could not be killed, and their faith in his military prowess led them to that he alone could save them. Their false hope in this immortal Paladin..." at that point, Talar snapped and slammed his fist on his desk.

Silence filled the Academy until Calbrius tried speaking again. "What are you..." but before he could finish, Talar began to speak loudly and with authority.

"The Paladin is real. My grandfather rode with him when he was one of the great Knights of Mempacton. The Knights of Mempacton held off the hordes of Trolls with the Paladin leading them. His silver trumpet rallied the armies of Men and Dwarves until Capa betrayed them. Until the Emperor betrayed them!".

Silence again filled the Academy. The students around Talar stared at him like he was insane, and he looked the part, with his eyes staring straight at Calbrius. Instead of ordering the Keep Guards to remove Talar and disciplining him with his cane, Calbrius merely sat down at his desk in front of the class. Dalir looked over at Talar and thought that he was going to go after Calbrius. The tension between the two filled the room.

"So, Talar Stoneking thinks that the Emperor betrayed Mempacton. Talar thinks that this Paladin is immortal. Is that true, Talar?". After the whole class strained around in their seats to look at him, Talar nodded in response to Calbrius' question.

"The Paladin is eternal like the Elves. The Emperor betrayed Mempacton to go after the Elves." The entire class again looked at Talar like he had lost his mind, for his version of history countered everything they had been taught.

"So, if this Paladin is truly immortal Talar, then please pupil, tell me, where is this legendary Knight? Where is he?", Calbrius inquired.

The question caught Talar off guard. He had not thought of the Paladin since the Druids had last told Cynfor and him the story of the immortal Paladin of Mempacton. Talar had been a mere child then, but he remembered the Druid's deep voice describing how skilled the Paladin was in combat. Those memories were not helping him answer Calbrius' question. With all the eyes of his fellow students upon him, Talar did not know what to say, so he stayed silent instead, glaring at Calbrius instead of answering.

Calbrius now played the part of a fool, acting surprised that Talar had no answer. His facial expression changed from shock to mockery as he began to speak. "Talar Stoneking has no answer for my simple question because his mind has been warped to believe Mempacton's lies," Calbrius said loudly.

At this point, Ralphin spoke up and called Talar a stupid, superstitious northern barbarian. The class laughed at Ralphin's insult. Calbrius, however, did not laugh and quickly waved his hand to silence the laughter. "We should not insult Talar, for he has been lied to for his entire life. He simply does not know any better. We should not laugh at him; instead, feel pity for his tainted mind. He does not know any better, but hopefully, we can all teach him the truth and show him the error of his ways. For is not that the Capan thing to do? To civilize the wild Men of this world. To expose them to the lies which have defined their lives. No, pupils do not laugh at Talar. Pity him instead. Lies have clouded his judgment."

The students in the class, except Dalir and Mona, all nodded, and Talar could instantly see the pity in some of their eyes. He could see the hatred, too, especially in Ralphin's eyes. "With that, let us stop our studies of Mempacton for now and head to lunch," Calbrius said.

Chapter XVII- Downriver

Sorel tore off the bloody bandage he had cut out of Evander's spare vest. Tarquin cried out in pain, but not nearly as much as when Sorel had removed the Dwarf arrow. The process had been painful, for the arrow had punched through his shoulder with the fletchings stuck inside. Sorel had pulled out the arrow after navigating the remaining rapids. Tarquin had somehow managed to do the same despite the arrow sticking out of him. The loss of blood had taken a toll on Tarquin. Sorel could tell this, so after rebandaging Tarquin's wound, he carefully crept forward toward Marcus, checking the lines that fastened the log raft to the canoe as he did. The Cold River was slower moving here. The evergreen trees that lined the shores hid the sun from the forest floor, and the dark shadows inside the forest scared all three woodsmen now.

Sorel made his way to Marcus, who was staring vacantly at the surrounding forest. Sorel had seen numerous injuries and cuts after years of working in the woods, some quite horrific. An injury like Marcus's was not rare, and Sorel knew that paralyzed men often ended up on the filthy streets of Capa or Brigantium as beggars or worse. Sorel grasped Marcus's shoulder as he sat next to him in the low seats of the canoe. "Do not fear Marcus. I will not leave you to suffer in the streets. We will live together, wherever you want," Sorel softly said. His voice was barely audible above the soft splash of the river against the bow of the canoe. Upon hearing his words, Marcus broke out in tears again, and it was a few minutes before he was composed enough to talk to Sorel.

"You are not coming back, Sorel? You are not coming back for more timber?" Marcus asked.

"No, Marcus, I will never come up this river again. I have spent my life on this river, cutting timber and losing friends. I will never come back this way again," Sorel said. Marcus nodded, and the two men stared at the forest around them, wondering if there were more Dwarves lurking inside. "I'm going to give Tarquin a break, Marcus. You should rest as well," Sorel said. Marcus nodded and resumed his watch of the forest. A dead tree was leaning out into the water, but Tarquin easily steered the canoe and the raft around it. Sorel now took control of the canoe, and Tarquin slumped down into the bottom of the canoe, exhaustion overtaking him. Before he passed out, Tarquin asked Sorel how far Fort Carillon was. Sorel looked up at the sky, looked down at the river, and told Tarquin that they should be there tomorrow morning.

"Are there any more rapids, Sorel?" Tarquin asked for he feared if they flipped that they would all drown in their current state.

"We gotta go down through the big canyon right before Fort Carillon. It is windy, but we should be alright, Tarquin. Now get some sleep," Sorel said.

Sorel scanned the river for any obstacles ahead, and not seeing any, as he looked over the bow of the canoe. Both young men were sleeping. Sorel rubbed his temples to get rid of his headache. His best friend was dead, he had two badly wounded boys to look out for, and worst yet, he was still leagues and leagues away from civilization in hostile Dwarf country. On top of that, he had no coin, little food, and two logs worth a small fortune. He and Evander usually did not stop at Fort Carillon on their way down the Cold River. The Legionaries of the Fifth Legion who manned the remote outpost were usually the scum of the Fifth Legion, sent to Fort Carillon as punishment. The woodsmen usually bypassed the Fort. They usually headed straight to Badatoz and the shipyards there. Sorel had not set foot in Fort Carillon since he and Evander had fled from there all those years ago. He shook his head and thought over his options. Without medicine, there was a good chance Tarquin's wound would get infected. They still had two weeks on the Cold River before they reached Badatoz. They did not have food or supplies for the journey downriver. They had to stop at Fort Carillon. Sorel shook his head again and scanned the canoe for weapons.

Sorel spotted a hatchet and a small dagger lying in the canoe and made a mental note of them. For the remainder of the day, the three woodsmen remained quiet and scanned the wood line. The sky was grey and somber and matched their mood. The sun began to set, and Sorel rifled through the canoe and luckily found two blankets to keep Marcus and Tarquin warm. The thought of pulling over and stopping along the tranquil banks of the Cold River to sleep for the night was unthinkable. The three of them settled in for a long night on the river.

The red dawn stretched above the horizon as the morning songbirds played the woodsmen their melodies. An otter splashed his tail in front of the canoe and popped up just a few feet from Marcus' head, which was perched against the canoe's gunwale. Marcus did not notice the otter, and the aquatic scavenger quickly dove down beneath the water and disappeared. Eventually, the sun rose fully above the tree line, and up in the distance, a dramatic bend in the Cold River awaited them. Marcus remembered the big bend in the river. They were not that far from Fort Carillon. The thought of entering civilization as a cripple scared Marcus even more than the jump off the cliff or the vicious Dwarves. He had seen cripples in Capa and knew how poorly they lived. Sorel's words had lifted him out of complete despair, but now his entire future rested with the old drunk woodsmen. Marcus shook his head, and Tarquin saw his despair. "You can't help what happened, Marcus. It happened. We were attacked. You had to jump, or you would be dead with Evander and Claudius and the rest of them," Tarquin said. Marcus nodded in agreement and quickly looked over Tarquin. Tarquin's shoulder wound had bled through the bandage that Sorel had put on. His complexion was pale, and Marcus knew that he needed to see a healer quickly.

The canoe, the raft with the two valuable logs, and the three beleaguered woodsmen drifted around the big bend, which was halfway chocked with lily pads, and now the Men could see the cliffs that separated Fort Carillon from the wilderness upriver. Sorel had been just a boy when he had climbed that cliff and cut down the one good tree that was not windswept and twisted. He had spent most of his life upriver in the wilderness, and the stark reality that he would never be returning to this pristine land suddenly washed over him. Sitting in the back of the canoe, Sorel looked back upriver at the untouched forest, the calm, peaceful river, and the large boulders which lined the bank. A tear came down Sorel's face as he thought of leaving Evander upriver unburied. Another tear came down as he thought of never seeing the beauty of the upriver wildness again.

Sorel quickly wiped away his tears and began to prepare to run the swift current through the canyon that was approaching rapidly. "Stay easy, boys, and do not jump around when we start moving," Sorel ordered in his usual gruff voice. The sheer rocky cliffs of the canyon greeted the woodsmen, and Marcus remembered sweating like a pig as he helped pull the canoe over the top of it just a few weeks back. The Cold River's water began to become a little choppy as the riverbanks closed in as they approached the mouth of the canyon. The young Men stared upwards at the sheer cliffs above them as the water now pushed the raft and canoe surprisingly fast through the narrow canyon. Marcus looked up in awe at the sheer cliffs, and now the roar of the water rushing through the canyon filled his ears. The canyon was only two rods wide now, and white foamy water splashed against the sides. Marcus looked forward and thankfully saw the end of the canyon. A few high waves greeted the trio as they exited the canyon, but Sorel easily maneuvered around them. He had done an excellent job of keeping them above the water.

As the current brought the woodsmen out of the canyon's shadow, they began to see the stumps of trees along the river. This part of the Cold River had been cut over long ago, but the massive stumps remained as evidence of the towering pines that once stood there. On the left side of the river, the trees began to fade, then altogether disappear. High grass and cattails now filled the left side, and in the distance, on top of a small motte, stood Fort Carillon. The Fort stood about twenty rods from the river. An old rickety wooden bridge ran from the riverbank to a shabby, wooden dock. The fort was a palisade made of hand-hewn timber, and the parapets were timber as well. Marcus could spot Legionnaires patrolling along the allure behind the parapet. A guard tower jutted up from each corner of the fort.

Sorel steered the canoe and raft into the large eddy where the dock was. The wooden gunwales of the canoe tapped against the flimsy dock. Sorel quickly jumped out from the stern of the canoe and secured the vessel to the dock. He bent over and picked up the hatchet and dagger. Sorel stood up and stretched his aching back and legs. After a few minutes of stretching, Sorel walked over to the front of the canoe where Marcus and Tarquin still waited. "I have to go in there and barter for a healer and for food," Sorel said quickly. "No matter what happens, do not leave this canoe. If you see anyone rushing out here, cut the line and cast off into the current. Hopefully, these Legionnaire boys will not start any trouble, and we will get Tarquin's shoulder some healing salves," Sorel said optimistically. The young Capans looked at each other questioningly, for they were unaware of the fort's reputation. Sorel smiled at Marcus and Tarquin, then abruptly turned, and headed toward the fort.

Chapter XVIII-Fort Carillon

The scarred Legionnaire behind the parapet stared down at the scene below him. When he had heard the shouts from the other Legionnaires that a woodcutter raft was coming down the river, he had jumped out of his bunk and stumbled up the stairs to the parapet. The sight of the giant, straight pine logs made his heart leap. Those logs could be his way out of here out of this cursed fort. As the current commander of the fort, he had to decide on what to do with the ragged woodcutter walking up from the dock. After only seeing two other Men in the canoe, the Legionnaire made his mind up.

"Sargent, Sargent, do you see the size of those logs?" Legionnaire Justus asked him. Justus had been caught stealing from an officer and had been sent to Fort Carillon as punishment. His blonde hair, youthful appearance, and constant questions annoyed the Sargent and the fellow Legionnaires.

"Yea, I see them, Justus. I see them," the Sargent replied in his usual neutral tone.

As Sargent and as the current commander, he could not afford to play favorites amongst his Men. The Sargent looked down at the woodcutter and could not see any weapons on him. The older woodsmen's steps on the old walkway now reached the Sargent's ears. The woodsman kept walking until he stood directly in front of the lone gate of Fort Carillon.

"I have two wounded Men. We need a healer. We were attacked by Dwarves upriver. They killed everyone else," Sorel shouted. His heart was racing, for Fort Carillon looked to be in worse shape than ever, and he did not see many Legionnaires besides the two directly in front of him. The older of the two Legionnaires nodded and shouted behind him to someone below. The simple wooden gate to Fort Carillon swung open ominously.

"Do you have a healer? Do you have supplies to trade for?" Sorel shouted again, his rough voice echoing over the parapets.

"We've got a healer; how many Men were killed upriver?" the Legionnaire shouted back from above.

"We don't have no healer, Sargent! The healer got killed last week by that Dwarf arrow. Don't you remember Sargent?" Justus asked. The Sargent turned to the young Legionnaire with such a look of rage upon his face that Justus took two steps back.

"Speak again, Legionnaire, and I'll cut your tongue out," the Sargent whispered. Justus took another two steps back and could only nod his head and shake in fear, for he had never heard his Sargent talk to another Legionnaire like that before. His Sargent had raped the wrong woman, and her rich merchant father had seen that he be transferred here. That was thirteen years ago.

"They killed fifty Men. There were at least that many Dwarves. We barely made it out. Do you have supplies?" Sorel shouted back.

"Yea, C'mon in. We will not keep that gate open all day, Woodcutter! Now get in or be gone!" the Sargent shouted back to Sorel.

Sorel nodded and smiled grimly up at the scarred Sargent before he walked underneath him into Fort Carillon. Sorel looked around and saw the familiar sights of his youth. A small forge and woodpile lay to his left, and the stable was to his right. Ahead were the barracks, storage areas, and the lone officer quarters. In between were two abandoned buildings that used to house settlers like Sorel. Sorel walked further into the Fort and was greeted by four armed Legionnaires next to the Fort's well. One of them shut the gate behind

Sorel and barred it. Sorel heard steps above him and looked to his left as the two Legionnaires from above descended a flight of stairs to the Fort's bailey.

Sorel looked around at the motley squad of Legionnaires that was assembled in front of him. They were all dirty, their red capes were filthy, and they all had beards which were not common in any Legion. Besides that, they were all rather skinny and pale. "Who is the officer in charge here?" Sorel demanded, but the six Legionnaires all just looked at each other and laughed.

"Captain caught a Dwarf arrow to the stomach about three weeks back. Took thirty Legionnaires with him downriver and left us to hold the Fort," a dark-haired Legionnaire replied.

Silence filled the courtyard of the Fort until Sorel spoke again. "Where is your healer? Where are your supplies?" Sorel asked slowly. The Legionnaire he had been speaking to outside raised his hand as if to silence the other Legionnaires, but the dark-haired Legionnaire did not seem to see his gesture. Sorel did notice the Sargent's gesture, though.

"Healer caught an arrow to the throat while he was tending to the Captain. He is dead. Our food supplies got moldy when the roof to the storage building leaked. We have been catching fish when we have been lucky. We have not been lucky lately," the dark-haired Legionnaire replied gloomily.

Sorel now took a step back and turned around to escape the fort when he suddenly saw bright stars, and his vision blurred. Sorel turned, and as he did, the Sargent hit him again with the hilt of his short sword, this time in his face. The unexpected attack brought the weakened woodcutter to his knees. The Sargent placed the blade of his sword against Sorel's neck and bid him stand with his free hand. Sorel carefully glanced around at the other Legionnaires, but none of them moved to help him. He could not speak, for the sharp blade was still pressed to his neck.

"What are you doing, Sargent? He is a citizen of the Empire! You cannot treat him like this!" the dark-haired Legionnaire said before he attempted to pull his sword out. He did not manage to pull the sword halfway out of his scabbard before the Sargent cruelly ran him through with his short sword. The dark-haired Legionnaire clasped at the gushing wound desperately with his hands, but by the time his body hit the ground, he was dead.

Sorel was too shocked and disoriented to even attempt escaping. The Sargent wiped his blade clean on the dead Legionnaire's cloak. His blood began to pool up on the ground around his corpse. "We are taking this woodcutter's rig downriver to Badatoz. We will sell the logs and go our separate ways. The Legion left us to die here. This is how we live," the Sargent said before pointing his sword at Sorel. Sorel now came to his senses and tried to break out of the enclosing Legionnaires. He never made it. Legionnaire Justus stabbed the old, grizzled woodcutter in the back. Sorel screamed as the blade pierced him, and blood quickly began to flow from his mouth. Sorel's left hand gripped the end of the sword. His other hand pulled the small hatchet that he had concealed beneath his vest. Sorel spun and buried the hatchet in Justus's blond head. Sorel sank to his knees as another Legionnaire approached, sword drawn. Justus dropped dead.

For most of his life, Sorel had thrown hatchets at targets for fun. He had never been much of a hunter and had never thrown a hatchet at anything but a target. It was a fun hobby around camp in the cold winter when the River froze up. Sorel had always been the best hatchet tosser. Now, as he slumped down on his knees, he took aim at the oncoming Legionnaire and threw the small hatchet with all his remaining strength. The Legionnaire did not see it coming and fell dead as the hatchet thudded into his forehead with a sickening sound. The Sargent grasped Sorel's grey hair from behind, and it was then that Sorel knew he would be dead very soon. The Sargent finished Sorel off with a quick thrust of his sword, and the old woodcutter fell dead in his former home.

One of the remaining Legionnaires asked the Sargent what he wanted to do next. "I want to get on that canoe and get out of here before a band of Dwarves attack us and kill us Legionnaire," the Sargent said in his usual neutral voice. Killing was routine for a veteran Legionnaire such as himself. "What if they cast off before we reach them? That was what I meant, Sargent," a tall and slender Legionnaire named Grevix asked. The Sargent nodded and considered the question. They needed a plan, or those two in the canoe might cast off and leave them here stranded.

The Sargent looked around, and the three remaining Legionnaires could tell that he was deep in thought. None dared to disturb him. Finally, after a few long moments, the scarred Sargent spoke. "Get his vest off, get his pants off," he ordered after pointing to Sorel. "Legionnaire Randlo put them on now," the Sargent ordered. Randlo was the stockiest of the Legionnaires, and after putting Sorel's clothing on, he looked a little like the dead woodcutter. The bloodstains were visible, though.

"What's your plan, Sargent?" Grevix asked, and the Sargent went on to explain his plan. Grevix, himself, and the other Legionnaires would take crossbows and rappel over the back of the Fort's palisades. Once in the swampy high grass, they would slowly approach the canoe from cover. Once in place, Randlo would then exit the front of the Fort to distract the two in the canoe as the Legionnaires crept into shooting range.

Randlo, Grevix, and the remaining Legionnaire all nodded in agreement. "What happens when they are dead? What then, Sargent?" Grevix asked.

The Sargent did not hesitate in answering. "We go downriver. We get rid of our red capes. We sell the logs. We split the money and go our separate ways," the Sargent said confidently. "That or we rot here. Catch an arrow from a Dwarf. Get sick and fade away. I have been here thirteen years, boys, and I'm leaving today," the Sargent said. His words had the effect he wanted, for the three Legionnaires all nodded enthusiastically. "We kill those two, and we are free boys," the Sargent growled, and with that, the murderous Legionnaires set about with their plan.

Chapter XIX- A Friend's Final Gift

"He should have never left us, Marcus; he's been gone too long. Something is wrong," Tarquin said in between deep breaths. His wound had not gotten any better, and his complexion was now ghost-white. "Sorel had to leave us. We have got no food and no medicine for you," Marcus said as his eyes scanned the area around the Fort. It had been at least an hour since Sorel had departed.

"We should have never left Capa Marcus. We should have stayed in the Poor Quarter, safer there than this green wilderness. There is food in Capa too, Marcus, even if you have to steal it," Tarquin said with a sly grin on his face. Marcus nodded in agreement, for he missed his chaotic and filthy home.

Marcus saw the gate of the Fort open and alerted Tarquin. Both stared at the squat, burly figure with the white vest who was slowly approaching them. "It's Sorel!" Tarquin said with a laugh. The laughing caused him to wince, but he kept smiling, nonetheless. Marcus was not smiling, however. He was sure something was wrong with the way Sorel was walking. Something was not right. Sorel was shorter than that, or was he that tall? Marcus scanned the cattails next to the dock but did not see anything out of the ordinary. Maybe he was just skittish from the recent Dwarf ambush. He shrugged off his concerns as Tarquin stood in the canoe, waving his good arm at Sorel.

As the white vested Man came within two rods of the canoe, Marcus spotted the deep red bloodstains that covered the dirty white vest. Fear gripped Marcus because he knew then that Sorel was most likely dead. "It's not him, Tarquin. It's not Sorel!" Marcus screamed. Tarquin looked down upon Marcus with disbelief, and it was then that the Sargent and Grevix stood and discharged their crossbows. The bolts hit Tarquin squarely in the chest, only a few inches apart. Tarquin tried to scream, but only blood escaped his mouth. He looked at Marcus, his oldest friend, in complete horror as he felt death approaching.

Marcus felt and heard something fly past his right ear, and he knew that it was a bolt. He looked across the dock and saw two Legionnaires making their way toward him through the cattails. Sorel's impersonator had witnessed the ambush and now sprinted toward the canoe as well. Tarquin saw the Legionnaires as well. With his last remaining strength, Tarquin lurched off the canoe and fell upon the dock. Marcus crawled across the bottom of the canoe, screaming incoherently. Tarquin raised his head, spat out blood, and began to crawl to where the canoe was tethered to the dock. The Legionnaires ran frantically towards him, but Tarquin reached the rope before them.

Marcus pulled himself to the gunwale when Tarquin leaned over and pushed the canoe off. As the canoe began to leave the dock, Tarquin's and Marcus' hands clasped briefly, and the two friends looked each other in the eyes. Tarquin had a sad look on his face, but he could not say anything. Only gasps came out. "I'm sorry, Tarquin, I'm sorry, Tarquin!" Marcus sobbed as the current pulled him away from his dying friend. Tarquin heard his friend's words before dying.

Marcus saw Tarquin's head slump on the dock. His bright blue eyes were fixed upon Marcus. The Legionnaires made it to the dock, but it was too late. Marcus was out of the eddy, and the canoe and raft drifted away into the swift current. The Legionnaires began fighting amongst themselves, and Marcus cursed them. Tears flowed freely down his face, and Marcus vomited over the side of the canoe into the river. His body began to shake with fear. He could not comprehend what had just happened and kept mumbling Tarquin's name for the next few hours as he lay helpless in a state of shock.

Chapter XX- A Father's Decision

Dalir sat down next to Talar as the northerner ravenously ate the food in front of him. The other students around them snickered about Talar's outburst. Dalir did not pay heed to them, for they had once snickered about him as well. Talar looked over at Dalir, and Dalir could see the desperation in his face. "Can you tell me what is wrong, Talar?" Dalir asked softly. Talar nodded and stared forward. After a moment, he spoke.

"My father is dead. My brother has rebelled. I must escape Capa," Talar said before looking around to ensure no other students had heard.

Dalir's face showed no emotion when he heard Talar speak. He did not speak for a while, and Talar was about to repeat his words. "How do you know this Talar?" Dalir asked. Talar explained what had happened at the Arena, then later in his room. He left out the intimate details.

Dalir was about to reply when Ralphin, Tobias, and Ansgar all sat down across from them. Ralphin had his usual smug look on his face. "So Talar, your grandfather fought with the Paladin? Where is that Paladin anyway? I've never seen him before!", Ralphin sneered. His companions chuckled at his joke. Dalir rolled his eyes in disgust and signaled to Talar to follow him.

Talar did not reply but shot Ralphin a murderous look. Ralphin just laughed, feeling secure with Ansgar beside him. Talar followed Dalir, and the two of them sat down next to one of the large windows that overlooked the New City. The commoners below bustled about with their daily business.

"Do you trust her, Talar? Do you trust Mona?", Dalir asked quietly. Talar nodded quickly in response, and Dalir continued. "You do not have to leave Talar. You have not broken your oath yet. You can stay and prove your loyalty to the Emperor," Dalir said. Talar shook his head in response.

"The Emperor will punish me for my brother's betrayal. You saw how he berated me in front of the Court. I feel like Volga is going to come through that door any minute for me now, Dalir," Talar solemnly replied. Dalir nodded and could tell that his argument for Talar to stay in Capa was not going to sway the Northerner's mind. Talar could be right as well. While the Emperor preferred to keep at least one conquered nobleman alive to ensure peaceful rule, he also had wiped out entire families of rebellious noblemen as well. Dalir made his mind up and decided that he would help Talar.

"I will give you coin, Talar. But how will you escape? Not only do you have to escape the High Keep, but you also must escape from the streets of Capa as well," Dalir said factually. Talar shrugged then told Dalir that he was hoping that he had some ideas. Dalir nodded and stared out from the window down at the streets below. Talar looked nervously around. His future depended on Dalir's answer.

"I will talk to my father after class ends today Talar. My father has many connections in Capa, both within the Empire and from Koristan. I will do my best to convince him to help you," Dalir said and then clasped Talar's hand. Dalir could see the relief in Talar's eyes upon hearing his words.

"Thank you, Dalir. I only have one more favor, even though I have already asked for so much. I entered Capa with two loyal members of my father's court. They were forced into the Legions. Is there any way you can help free them as well?" Talar asked. Dalir nodded, then asked if there was anybody else who would be escaping with him as well. Talar smiled sheepishly.

Dalir smiled and shook his head. "Mona, correct?" Dalir asked. Talar's face turned red, and Dalir laughed at his bashfulness.

"Yes, Dalir, Mona will be escaping with us as well," Talar said, and Dalir punched his shoulder in jest. "She's older than you by at least five years. I did not know you liked the older ones, Talar!" Dalir said while laughing softly. "I will make sure there is enough room in the ship for you, your two bodyguards, and for Mona. That is, if my father can procure a ship for you," Dalir said, even though he knew his father could find a ship to provide them passage. Dalir looked around to see if anybody was trying to listen to their conversation. No one was. "I am sorry for your loss Talar. I am sorry that this has happened to you," Dalir said. He looked over Talar, trying to gauge the impact of his father's death upon him. Talar remained emotionless, but Dalir could sense his anxiety.

At that moment, Calbrius sounded the gong, and the pupils headed towards their afternoon studies. Dalir and Talar then spent the next few hours lazily swinging wooden swords at each other. Both were preoccupied with planning the escape.

Calbrius sounded the gong again, and the students began to put away their wooden practice swords. Ralphin swung his sword wildly and exclaimed he was the Paladin. The students laughed at his joke, then turned and looked at Talar to see his reaction. Talar just shook his head and put his wooden sword away.   Talar and Dalir exited the training yard. Once they were away from the other students, Dalir asked Talar if he really believed in the Paladin. "Of course, I do, Dalir. That is why I said it during class," Talar replied. He wondered why Dalir was concerned with the Paladin and not his escape, but then again, Dalir was always asking him questions about the northern territories.

Dalir was still curious about Talar's belief in the Paladin and continued with his questioning. "So, you really think that he is immortal? I mean, he does not age at all?" Not even a little?", Dalir asked skeptically. Talar was beginning to get annoyed at Dalir's questions, but he answered, nonetheless. "Why is that so hard to believe Dalir? Elves are immortal. They live forever. Why do you believe that the one Man sworn to protect the Elves cannot live forever?" Talar asked. Dalir could sense Talar was becoming agitated over his questions. Dalir also believed that Talar honestly believed in the Paladin and the Elves. Dalir could not imagine being immortal or even meeting someone who was. Dalir was skeptical of Talar's beliefs but was too respectful to question him further about them.

The two left the training yard and entered the main classroom of the Academy. Dalir pulled Talar aside to the area in front of the windows. "I will go immediately to my father and ask for his help and guidance, Talar. Be ready to flee the High Keep at any moment. Make sure Mona is ready as well," Dalir instructed. Talar nodded and shook Dalir's hand. "Thank you, Dalir. If we leave tonight and I head back north, I will probably never see you again," Talar said frankly. Dalir's kindness and companionship had made his stay at the High Keep tolerable. Dalir saw the raw fear combined with fierceness in Talar's face and knew then that his new friend was relying on him for survival.

"Maybe one day we will see each other again, Talar Stoneking, for you are a true friend of mine," Dalir said. "I must be going now, Talar, for time is working against you. Good luck, northerner. Good luck, my friend." Dalir turned and departed the Academy to find his father, the Koristan Ambassador to Capa.

Dalir went down the stairs opposite of the Academy's entrance and strolled confidently down them to where a pair of High Keep Guards stood watch. "I wish to speak to my father, the Koristan Ambassador," Dalir said. Neither Guard said a word, but the bigger one on the left did nod and gesture for Dalir to proceed. Dalir walked past the Guards and kept going until the stairs led him to the level below the Academy. Dalir kept walking passing numerous rooms until he spotted his father's bodyguards standing watch in front of his door.

Dalir smiled, for he knew his father's guards well, and they greeted each other warmly. The senior bodyguard, whose name was Carthos, teased Dalir for his partying ways, for Dalir's room was above his father's. After some more light teasing, the guards pushed the doors open into his father's large room, which was as luxurious as Dalir's. Dalir spotted his father at his large desk and called out to him warmly.

Hanno, the Koristan Ambassador, looked up from the scroll he was reading, then pushed the piece of parchment to the side and stood up to greet Dalir, his only son. Dalir was always amazed at how tall his father was, and he wondered if he was going to keep growing to become that tall. Hanno strode over to his son and grasped his hand, and pulled out a chair for him to sit down in. Hanno's long dark fingers then grasped a peculiar-looking metal pitcher. Dalir knew it was going to be water, for Hanno rarely drank wine. Dalir was surprised at how cold the water was then inferred that the peculiar metal pitcher must be keeping it cool. Hanno looked over his son and could not help but feel pride.

"So, what has brought my son down here today? Are you infatuated with another young Capan and wish for me to arrange the marriage?" Hanno teased. Dalir used to have a crush on a fellow student at the Academy, but she had been wed off to one of the Barons of Borisco, to Dalir's horror at the time.

In the years since, Dalir had forgotten about the beautiful blonde, but his father never let him forget it.

Dalir smiled, shook his head, and took a long sip of the cool water. "No, father, I am here today so that I can ask for a favor. A favor for a friend who might perish if I do not help him," Dalir said slowly and ominously. Hanno saw the seriousness in his son's dark eyes and motioned for Carthos to leave, for the bodyguard had followed Dalir into the room. Carthos shut the door, and silence filled the room until Hanno spoke again.

"Who is this friend that you speak of Dalir?" Hanno asked slowly, his eyes fixated on his son.

"His name is Talar. He is the Prince of Stonedom. His brother has been named King and has rebelled against the Emperor," Dalir said. He tried to read his father's face, but Hanno showed no emotions. Hanno stood up from his chair and walked over to the window that overlooked Capa below.

"Is this the same Prince who was practically weeping in front of the Emperor?" Hanno asked. Hanno's question surprised Dalir. "The Prince who cried and lost his honor in the High Court?" Hanno asked. Maintaining honor, even in the face of death, was quintessential to a Koristan noble.

Dalir knew that his next statements would either save Talar or leave him to the mercy of the Emperor. He thought before speaking. "Talar Stoneking is a true friend of mine, Father. He is honorable. He wishes to flee Capa so he can fight with his brother against Capa with the Dwarves." Dalir was hoping by mentioning Talar's desire to fight against Capa, Koristan's long-time rival, that Hanno would help him escape.

Hanno shook his head as he stared out the window. He never would have thought that his son would come down to him today with this conundrum. Capa was Koristan's enemy despite the recent years of peace. Hanno knew that war would once again break out between Capa and Koristan, for the Capans were constantly working on their new fleet of warships. Hanno would be rewarded back in Koristan for aiding an enemy of his country. The problem lay in not being discovered by the Capans and inadvertently provoking a war before Koristan was ready.

Hanno kept shaking his head as he walked from the window back to his seat in front of his son. Dalir did not like the look of his father's body language. "You have heard that the plague has returned in Koristan?" Hanno asked. He had whispered the question, but Dalir had heard him. Dalir nodded and thought of his mother and sister, who had succumbed to the plague almost ten years ago. Although he had been young, their deaths still haunted him.

141

"The plague has struck our sailors and soldiers especially hard. Koristan is not ready for war, Dalir. We cannot risk helping this Talar Stoneking. We cannot risk war," Hanno said quietly.

Dalir was crushed, and Hanno could tell. He told his son that Talar could stay in Capa and prove his loyalty to the Emperor. "Do you think Volga will end up torturing him, father?" Dalir had replied. Hanno shook his head again. With the Dwarf invasion soon underway, the Emperor would need to have order in Stonedom. Hanno did not know if the Emperor would keep a loyal Stonedom noble to ensure peace or kill him to instill fear amongst the citizens of Stonedom.

"I do not know Dalir. The Emperor might kill him to set an example, or he might keep him alive as a gesture of good faith to his people. Either way, you are not responsible for his fate Dalir. This Talar's brother set him upon this course, not you. Remember that Dalir," Hanno said. He had spoken the last words gently, for he could still see the hurt in his son's eyes. Hanno asked his son how he had become friends with someone who was so different from he was.

"In the beginning, he was polite to me, which is rare in the Academy. After some time, I saw that he was brave and honest, even though it brought him humiliation and ridicule. I saw that he cares for his people and for those who cannot protect themselves. Most of all, I am impressed with his beliefs and loyalty to his family and his heritage, despite its controversy," Dalir said firmly. He viewed Talar as a friend despite their differences.

Hanno raised his eye upon hearing his son's words and asked Dalir about the controversy of Talar's heritage. "Talar's convinced that the Capans betrayed the Dwarves and Mempacton all those years ago, Father," Dalir said. He smiled, thinking of Talar arguing with Malnar. "He also believes in immortal knights and Elves. But that does not mean he is not honorable Father," Dalir stated.

Hanno brought his large hand to his face and covered his eyes with it. Dalir knew his father well enough to know that he only did that with his hand when he was deep in thought.   Dalir thought that his last statement had sunk his odds of helping Talar, and he was about to say something in Talar's defense when Hanno silenced him with a sudden wave of his other hand.

"Has this Talar ever mentioned anything about the Elves to you before Dalir?" Hanno asked quietly as if he did not want anybody to hear him speak. After asking his question, Hanno rose and once again walked over to the window overlooking Capa.

Dalir was confused about his father's question, but after thinking about it for a moment, he answered. "Yes, Talar has mentioned the Elves before. He says that they are gifts from the Gods and that the Capans want to kill them all. He gets emotional when speaking of them," Dalir said to Hanno. Dalir was thinking of when Talar had gone off on a rant about the Elves while drinking on his balcony. Hanno once again was emotionless, but after a few minutes, he began to nod as if he had just come to some sort of conclusion.

Hanno walked briskly back to his chair before he sat down. Dalir knew that his words had changed his father's mind. He just did not know why. Hanno gazed into his son's eyes and smiled. "We will help your friend Talar escape. And you will be going with him," Hanno said before Dalir's jaw dropped.

Chapter XXI- A Gift from the Gods

The Elf looked at the canoe, the wooden raft, and the two giant logs. He could not believe that a Man would go through all the work of killing an ancient tree when there were so many already resting on the forest floors. His thoughts about the ancient tree that made up the raft disappeared when he spotted the Dwarf, bow drawn back, slowly moving through the high river grass. The Elf tried to hold Stripe back from following the Dwarf but was unsuccessful.

Dobervist approached cautiously, his eyes scanning the canoe for any movement. The Dwarf had spotted the canoe from the forest and was initially startled to see a vessel. His suspicions that they were being followed were confirmed then. The Men from the vessel must be the ones who he had sensed were tracking them. In the three days since the unlikely duo had departed the waterfall with the dead Troll, they had not seen anything since, but both had sensed that they were not alone.

The Dwarf now exited the high grass and awkwardly began to approach the wooden vessels, for the uneven river stone was treacherous to walk upon. Dobervist approached slowly with his bow ready but did not spot any movement within either vessel. The Dwarf checked the high grass but did not see any movement there. The only noise Dobervist could hear was the Cold River's current hitting the side of the large log raft. The canoe lay fully ashore. Dobervist approached the canoe from the stern, his eyes staring down his only arrow, which was knocked. At first, he did not spot anything until he saw a young Man stirring at the bottom of the canoe. Dobervist aimed the arrow at him but did not let it loose. The young Man appeared to be fast asleep.

Dobervist checked the shoreline again, but he did not see anything except for Stripe running towards him. Dobervist kept his aim on the young Man until he was standing right over him. "WAKE UP!" the Dwarf growled. Marcus' brown eyes popped open in shock, and he started to scream once he spotted Dobervist.

"SHUT UP!" the Dwarf hollered, and Marcus went instantly silent, shocked that the Dwarf spoke the common tongue. Marcus could not believe how human the Dwarf's countenance was. Marcus also could not believe how tall the Dwarf was. The Dwarf kept the bow aimed at Marcus until a tall figure appeared beside him. Marcus wondered how a Man could become companions with a Dwarf.

The tall figure urged the Dwarf to lower his bow, and this gave Marcus time to study the contrasting duo. The Dwarf's stocky frame was the opposite of the lean and wiry figure. Marcus again wondered why a Man would keep company with a Dwarf, but his thoughts were cut short when the Dwarf asked him a question.

"Where are your friends, boy?" the Dwarf growled again. Marcus could see the hate in the Dwarf's eyes as he leaned in and spoke.

"My friends are all dead. They died upriver. I'm the only one that is left," Marcus replied quietly. The Dwarf seemed suspicious of Marcus' answer and ordered him out of the canoe. "I can't. I can't move my legs," Marcus said.

"Out of the canoe, or I'll put this arrow through you. Now Move!" the Dwarf growled. Marcus put up his hands in defense and again repeated that he could not move his legs. "Were you injured?" the tall figure inquired. Marcus looked over the tall figure whom he had assumed to be a Man. He had high cheekbones and a square jaw, but it was his bright blue eyes and blonde hair that stood out the most to Marcus.

"Yes. We were attacked by Dwarves upriver. I had to jump off a cliff to escape. I have not been able to move my legs since," Marcus replied slowly. The tall figure just nodded, and the Dwarf and he huddled together and whispered for a moment.

"So where are your friends?", Dobervist asked, repeating his question from before. Marcus shook his head in frustration and fear.

"All my friends are dead. You and your kind killed them, Dwarf!" Marcus said, his voice filled with pain.

The Dwarf looked over to the tall, slender figure, who nodded. The Dwarf then lowered the bow, and he and the tall, slender figure approached. Marcus looked over the pair again and noted how both seemed to be dressed for the wilderness. At that moment, a small brown dog with a white stripe behind his neck jumped into the canoe and began licking Marcus.

Witnessing all his fellow woodsmen be brutally killed, watching the life fade out of his best friends' eye's along with his injury had brought Marcus to his breaking point. Stripe licked Marcus's face, and he laughed, and he temporarily forgot about his lost friends. Marcus petted Stripe, who seemed to take a liking to Marcus until Dobervist whistled and Stripe returned to his master. The tall, slender figure and the Dwarf approached closer until they were alongside the canoe. For a few seconds, only the sound of the Cold River lapping against the log rafts could be heard.

"Are you Capan boy?" the Dwarf asked. Marcus nodded. "Tell us news of Capa and the Empire. We don't get out much," the Dwarf said with a grim smile. Marcus could not believe that a Dwarf was asking him news of the Empire, and he did not know exactly what the Dwarf wanted to hear.

"What do you wish to know, Dwarf?" Marcus said softly, knowing his future depended on how he answered.

"Tell us what the Legions are up to. What Koristan, the Barons, and Mercium are up to as well," the Dwarf replied quickly.

Marcus thought for a minute, then began to answer. He told the Dwarf and the tall, slender figure about the Legion buildup in anticipation of the invasion of Thendara. He also told them of the tensions between Koristan and Capa and how Capa was building up their navy.

"That is why you and your lot cut up the trees, eh? Gonna build big ships to fight the Koristans. Is there any place you Capans do not want to conquer?" the Dwarf asked sarcastically. Marcus just shook his head, knowing it was not the time to start an argument.

The tall, slender figure now asked a question. "Do the Mercians still hold out. Do they still fight for their freedom?".

Marcus shook his head in confusion. "Mercium was conquered ten years ago. Their King and Queen were executed, and their only daughter was taken to the High Keep." Marcus figured everybody had heard of that, but apparently, these two had been in the wild for a long time. Marcus looked over Dobervist again and a sense of déjà vu hit him. It was then that Marcus realized the Dwarf's identity. "Your Dobervist!" Marcus exclaimed.

The Dwarf who had been leaning over the side of the canoe now straightened up and folded his arms across his broad chest. "It is you—your Dobervist. You escaped from the Arena ten years ago. I watched you fight when I was young. It must be!" Marcus exclaimed again before remembering his situation. The tall, slender figure seemed to look at the Dwarf in a different manner upon hearing Marcus's words.

An awkward silence followed as Marcus looked back and forth at the motionless and silent pair. Stripe jumped back into the canoe and began licking Marcus again. After another moment, the tall, slender figure asked the Dwarf what he wanted to do. Dobervist looked over the crippled youth from Capa and considered the options. He could kill him outright or leave him here on the side of the river, but to the Dwarf, the latter seemed crueler. Bears and packs of wolves roamed the riverbanks and woods, and Dobervist would rather kill the youth now than have him be eaten alive.

"I'll kill him quickly without pain. It is better than being eaten by a bear. We'll throw him in the river afterward and take his canoe downstream until we meet the Mytosis River," the Dwarf said calmly.

Marcus's heart sank as Stripe licked his face. The youth was about to start pleading, but the tall, slender figure spoke first. "There is another way. He could walk again if I want."

Marcus was bewildered by the tall blonde figure's words. How could he make Marcus walk if he wanted? There was no healer that Marcus knew of that could fix a cripple. Marcus's mind swirled with confusion until he looked over the tall blonde figure again. The blonde figure locked eyes with Marcus. Marcus stared into blue eyes and saw bright star-like shapes flash across his dark pupils. Marcus's jaw dropped in shock once he realized what the tall figure was.

"You're an Elf!" Marcus exclaimed in astonishment. The Elf nodded slowly and smiled in return. Marcus's astonishment quickly turned to fear as years of the Empire's conditioning kicked in. With a look of horror on his face, Marcus began to plead with the Elf not to cast a spell on him. The Elf and the Dwarf looked at each other, bewildered. For his entire life, Marcus had been told that Elves cast spells that cause disease, blindness, and plague. He again pleaded for the Elf not to cast a spell on him. He began to sob as he thought of Tarquin, Sorel, Evander, and the rest of his friends who had been killed ruthlessly around him. At this point, Marcus only wanted a painless death.

The Elf had spent over two thousand years of his life healing on both continents. He had not been accused of malevolent spell casting in a few centuries, so Marcus's words threw him off. The Dwarf explained the situation to him. "The Capans preach that Elves are evil and that they conspire with Trolls. They teach their young that Elves spread disease and plague."

The Elf looked at Marcus with horror on his face. Despite being hunted by the Capans for the past seventy years, the Elf was unaware of the Empire's propaganda. With a look of determination on his face, he took a few steps forward. "I will show him the truth about my kind. Then he can judge for himself," he said.

The Dwarf shook his head in disagreement. "What are we gonna do with him after you heal him, Elf. You gonna make me kill him after you show him the truth," the Dwarf said sarcastically. The Elf had stopped moving forward toward Marcus, but he was close enough for the young Capan to better study him. The Elf's face was unblemished, a rarity in Capa due to the high amount of pox. He had high cheekbones, a square jaw, and perfectly white teeth. Marcus had never seen anyone with such white teeth. His own were stained yellow due to smoking and drinking.

While still staring at Marcus, the Elf declared that he would heal the Capan. "You're insane, Elf. He will kill you for the reward as soon as he can," the Dwarf yelled, his voice reverberating off the river. The Elf just stood silently, not even looking at Dobervist. Patience was a prized virtue amongst Elves. After a long moment, in which Marcus was praying for the Elf to leave him alone, the Elf turned his head and addressed the Dwarf.

"I helped you out, Dwarf. Now we will help this boy out. But only after he swears loyalty to help me," the Elf stated.

The Dwarf looked incredulously at the Elf. "Help me out? It was me who saved you from the Trolls. How did you help me out, Elf?" Dobervist asked.

"I caught your dog," The Elf said with a smile on his face. Upon hearing the Elf's words, the Dwarf threw his head back decisively and rolled his eyes. Marcus could sense the tension between the Dwarf and Elf.

After a minute of awkward pacing on the uneven river rock, the Dwarf finally spoke. "If you are going to heal him, get it over with." At this point, the Dwarf pointed at Marcus. "If he is telling the truth, then there is someone else behind us. Which means we need to keep moving. So, hurry up."

The Elf smiled in satisfaction and resumed moving in Marcus' direction. Marcus put up his hands defensively as the Elf was now in the canoe and kneeling next to him. The Elf looked reassuringly upon Marcus, but the look scared Marcus even more. Marcus went to push the Elf away put hee easily clasped his weakened hands. "Swear to the Gods that you will aid me, not betray me and not harm me in any way, and I will heal you, Capan." The Elf's' words were slow and reassuring.

Marcus tried to pull his hands back, but the Elf held on tight. "Quit resisting. Or do you wanna pack of wolves to rip you apart. Or do you wanna end up in a Troll's belly instead," Dobervist angrily stated. Marcus thought over his situation and realized he had nothing to lose. Even if the Elf gave him plague, he would still probably die of something else out here in the wilderness.

Marcus quit resisting against the Elf. "I swear to the Gods to aid you, to not betray you, and to never harm you. On this, I swear," Marcus said. The Elf smiled in satisfaction, and the Dwarf made an impatient hand gesture to proceed. The Elf now released Marcus' hands and grasped his shoulders instead. The Elf was now almost nose to nose with Marcus, and Marcus could swear that the Elf's pupils looked like a night sky filled with stars. He kept staring into the Elf's strange pupils until he felt a tingling sensation run down his back, through his legs, then back up to the top part of his head. The Elf smiled again, released Marcus, and exited the canoe.

The Dwarf walked over, and now both stood at the side of the canoe, looking down upon Marcus. Stripe jumped out of the canoe and put his paws up on the gunwale, joining in on looking at Marcus. The Capan did not feel any different, though. "C'mon boy, hurry up, we gotta get this canoe in the water and unhitched from the trees you cut down," Dobervist barked.

The Elf nodded in agreement and gestured for Marcus to rise. Marcus could not believe that he was so stupid for trusting the Elf. He thought the Elf was playing a cruel joke on him. "Rise and join us, young Man. We must make haste; time is of the essence."

Marcus looked skeptically at the strangers who were waiting on him. He leaned forward, away from the side of the canoe, and put his hands on the gunwale. He began pushing himself up, expecting his legs to give away on him at any second. To Marcus's amazement, his legs held his body weight. He looked up at the Elf and Dwarf with a complete look of astonishment on his face. Marcus now began walking slowly, his leg muscles hurting but moving. The youth kept walking to the side of the canoe, where he gingerly lifted his legs over the gunwale and onto the ground. Tears now ran freely down his face, and the Elf smiled broadly. Even the Dwarf smiled. Marcus bent down to pet Stripe, who was jumping up eagerly. Marcus kept sobbing in relief. He could walk again!

Eventually, Marcus composed himself and began thanking the Elf relentlessly. Marcus asked the Elf what his name was, and he told the young Man that his name was Aemon. Aemon gestured towards the canoe, which was still connected to the log raft. After a few brief minutes of work, the canoe was in the water, untethered from the log raft. Marcus was in a surreal state. A few minutes before, he had been hopelessly stranded in the wilderness with no real hope of survival. Now he was in the company of an Elf and the most famous Dwarf in the realm, and he could walk.

"I'll steer," Aemon said, and Marcus and Dobervist nodded. Stripe hopped in the canoe, and the rest followed. Aemon was the last to jump in after pushing the canoe into the current. Marcus looked back at the log raft, which now lay haplessly in the eddy. His best friend had died for those logs, and his new friends had died for it as well. He had been paralyzed and almost killed numerous times for the small fortune which swirled in the eddy behind him. Marcus shook his head over his stupidity for risking his life over money. He thought about Tarquin and how he would never see him again.

Marcus gave one last look at the log raft and then turned forward, staring past the Dwarf's broad shoulders. The green wilderness surrounded them, and Marcus' ears began to pick up the sounds of the birds, which called the river their home. As he looked forward, he began to realize how precious life is and how lucky he was to be alive. Marcus concluded that life was more than money and riches. He also realized that the Empire had lied to him for his entire life, and that angered him.

Stripe jumped into Marcus' lap, and the Capan petted the dog until he fell asleep. The Dwarf and Elf were focused on paddling, and silence enveloped the vessel. Marcus thought of his vow and mentally vowed again to uphold it.

The young Man from Capa thought about all that had happened to him in the past two days and wondered what was next. He did not worry about the future, though. He was happy to be alive now.

Chapter XXII- Lies and Secrets

Dalir handed the rope to Talar. Talar looked down upon the rope with skeptical amazement. The rope was suspiciously thin, but when Talar tugged on it, it was surprisingly strong. Talar looked up at Dalir, and the Koristan could tell that the northerner was skeptical of the hemp rope. "It's just as strong as the rope you're used to, Talar. It is just lighter. And easier to hide."

"I hope so, Dalir. My life is going to depend on this rope," Talar stated quietly. The risk of capture was weighing on the northern youth, and Dalir could sense his friend's uneasiness. Dalir remembered his father's instructions, however. Hanno had warned Dalir that the odds of escaping the High Keep and Capa were not favorable. His father had also warned him not to reveal that he would be waiting for Talar, Mona, and the others at the Inner Harbor. Hanno feared if Talar was captured and tortured that he would implicate the Koristans.

"You think your father will be able to free my guards in time, Dalir?", Talar asked slowly before he set the rope on Dalir's table. The pair were in Dalir's lavish quarters.

"I believe so. He said that they were still stationed within the Old City." Talar nodded and gave Dalir a weak smile. Dalir had laid out the escape plan to Talar a few moments ago. Dalir could tell that Talar was skeptical of the plan but had stressed to his friend that no one would know of their escape until the next morning when he and Mona were absent from class. "You need to sneak out of Capa. Do not run wildly down the streets. You will never make it to the docks of the Inner Harbor. The City Guards have alarms that travel faster than you can run," Dalir had warned.

The escape plan seemed incredibly risky to Talar. It required them to repel down the High Keep, sneak through the massive Old City that he had only been through once, and then board a fishing galley that was docked in the Inner Harbor. The galley was from Koristan, and the crew had been paid to transport Talar, Mona, Alwin, Hartwin, and Dalir to Badatoz. Dalir would not be escaping the High Keep in the same way that Talar and the rest were. Hanno would not risk his son's life on such a dangerous endeavor. He also did not wish to risk a war now with Capa. So Dalir would be leaving via the sewer tunnels which happened to run under the High Keep, the Old City, and directly to the Inner Harbor.

Dalir had pleaded with Hanno to allow Talar and Mona to escape with him through the tunnels, but Hanno had refused. "Those tunnels are a Koristan secret, Dalir. Not even the Emperor knows of those ancient tunnels. War may be coming with Capa. Our country might need those tunnels," Hanno had said sternly. Dalir had felt terrible handing the rope over to Talar, knowing that a much easier escape route was possible. But he had said nothing of the tunnels or of his plan to join them at the docks. His father had forbidden it.

"Is the moon going to be out tonight, Dalir? I hope not. These white robes are going to stick out bad enough as it is."

Dalir walked over to his desk and peered over it at a chart on the wall which Talar had never noticed before. Dalir ran his finger over one of the columns and shook his head. "I am afraid it is going to be out tonight. Not a full moon, but close to it."

Talar shook his head upon hearing the setback. He had never taken to astrology, but his brother Cynfor had, and Talar was familiar with astrological charts. "We'll have to stick to the shadows and stay away from any City Guard patrols," Talar stated grimly. Dalir shook his head in agreement and glanced out his window. It was going to be dark soon. It was time for Talar to leave.

Dalir spoke Talar's name to gain his attention. The northern Prince had been staring at the floor. Dalir gestured outside. Talar saw that the sun was beginning to set and nodded in understanding. It was time to say farewell.

Talar rose from the chair and grabbed the special climbing rope. Dalir smiled and told Talar that he would walk him out. The two young Men from opposite sides of the world approached the door. A few weeks ago, they had been strangers, but now Talar counted Dalir as his closest friend. Talar was about to open the door, but he knew he had to say something to Dalir. It was probably the last time they would see each other, Talar thought.

"I don't know how to thank you, Dalir. You have done more for me than anybody else in this city, and words cannot describe how much I owe you." Dalir's heart sank upon hearing this. Lying to Talar about the tunnels was harder than he had thought it was going to be.

"You are an honorable Man Talar. I am grateful for your friendship. I wish you the best of luck. But you must be going now. A message about Stonedom may come at any time. You must focus on your escape."

Talar nodded and smiled at Dalir. He then extended his hand, and Dalir grasped it, then hugged his friend. Like Talar, Dalir wondered if he would see his friend again. He thought about telling Talar about the tunnels but did not. "Good luck Talar. I hope we meet again," Dalir said, unable to look Talar in the eyes. The lying was beginning to take its toll upon Dalir and his wished now that Talar would leave. The idea of Talar being tortured below him by Volga was going to make Dalir sick. They shook hands one more time. Talar looked over Dalir's shoulder and saw that the sun had set. He tucked the rope underneath his robe, smiled at Dalir, opened the door, and left. Dalir shut the door, then sank to his knees. He began praying to the Koristan Gods to protect his friend, but he knew that the Gods were fickle.

Chapter XXIII- Against the Empire

Talar walked through the empty stone corridor. The candles which lit the hallway were in their copper sconces, burning away. The rope bulged against the outside of his robe, so he tucked it inside more. A door to his left opened, and Ralphin emerged. Talar was surprised to see Ralphin alone. He thought now would be the perfect time to exact revenge on the portly, pig-faced noble from Brigantium.

Talar looked directly at Ralphin, but neither said a word. Talar did not want to risk his escape, and Ralphin was scared without Ansgar. Ralphin closed his door and turned in the opposite direction of Talar. Talar rounded a corner and was now approaching his room. He soon entered it and closed the door. Talar took stock of the near barren room. There was wine and bread that the servants had brought, but besides that, there was not anything that Talar could use or that he wanted. Still, Talar was not sure when he would eat again, and he knew that he would need his strength. He quickly began eating the bread as fast as he could. He washed it down with a short glass of wine and was about to stand up and leave when he suddenly stopped. He had not fully thought over his escape plan yet, and he was still worried that there would be Capan citizens on the street who would see their descent. Thinking of the descent now made his hands shake. He was not scared of heights, but he never went out of his way to climb them. And what about Mona? Would she be able to climb down the massive Spire, then down the Outer Wall, then through the streets of Capa? Would Alwin and Hartwin be on the streets waiting for them? Or would they be tortured by Volga? The questions bounced around Talar's head until he felt dizzy.

After another minute of deep thought, Talar realized that it was time to escape before Volga or the Emperor received news of Cynfor's betrayal. Talar thought briefly of his elder brother and wondered how he had been able to rebel knowing that Talar was in Capa. Talar pushed the thought out of his head, knowing that Cynfor was dealing with his father's decision and was doing what was best for the Elves, Dwarves, and people of Stonedom.

Talar stood, looked around the room, and sneered. He would not be missing it. He walked to the heavy door, opened it, and walked out of his room into the hall. Talar walked briskly towards Mona's room, having been shown the way previously by Dalir. All the rooms had identical doors. Nonetheless, Talar found Mona's door after a few moments and knocked softly. Talar looked around, checking to see if his knocking had aroused any of Mona's neighbors. It had not. Talar was about to knock again when the door opened. Mona grasped his wrist and pulled Talar into her room.

Talar was immediately struck by how beautiful Mona looked in the soft candlelight. Those thoughts disappeared when he remembered how much danger they were in. "It is time to go, Mona. I have a rope." His words had tumbled out, partly due to Mona's appearance.

"What do you mean, Talar? You have a rope? What are we going to do with that?" Mona said while shaking her head in disbelief. She had been left in the dark about the whole escape plan, and Talar realized he had to explain it to her. But he had to do it quickly. He felt like he should have already left her room by now.

"Listen, Mona, I'm only going to say this once, and then I'm leaving. If you choose to leave with me, well, that is up to you, I guess. Dalir gave me a special rope…". At this point, Talar showed Mona the rope. "…and we are going to use it to escape the High Keep. Then my bodyguards are going to escort us to the Inner Harbor, where Dalir has a ship waiting for us. I would explain more, but I have a bad feeling about sticking around here any longer. So, I am leaving Mona. I hope you go with me."

Mona nodded as the escape plan details were laid out to her. She only asked Talar one question. "So, we're going to climb down the side of the High Keep's Spire?".

Talar nodded. "Lead the way," Mona said.

Mona went to grab a red decorated linen bag with a drawstring that was filled with her belongings, but Talar shook his head. "You cannot climb with that bag, Mona. You have to leave it." Talar said quickly. Mona nodded and looked around her room for the last time. Talar walked back to the doorway and wished again he had a weapon. He had asked Dalir for a dagger or some sort of weapon, but Dalir had insisted that they should climb down unburdened, for the climb down would be long and hard.

Talar opened Mona's door and peered around outside. He did not see anyone, and he motioned for Mona to follow him. Mona and Talar walked down the hallway, side by side, their sandals making soft noises against the cold stone below. Talar had been worried about proper clothing for the journey, for winter was almost here, despite the moderate temperatures now. Dalir had assured him that the fishing ship would have all that they needed. The pair now rounded a corner and were now on the main hallway leading to the Academy's impressive wooden doors. A blonde Brigantium student hastily opened her door to the left of them. She was a quiet student, and she was a few years older than Talar but younger than Mona. She smiled at the pair, assuming they were just lovers on a stroll, which was common within the High Keep.

The pair walked a few paces more and casually loitered. Talar leaned against the wall near the entrance to the Academy. Mona, who was not sure where they were going, looked questioningly up at Talar, who now looked behind him. The hallway was empty now since the blonde student had disappeared around the corner. Talar quietly opened the heavy wooden door to the Academy and motioned for Mona to follow him, who did so with a worried look upon her face.

A few candles were lit throughout the main teaching chamber of the Academy. Talar quickly shut the door behind him and looked around, scanning the room for any Keep Guards or teachers. He spotted one. His heart sank, but he had the sense to grab Mona's shoulder to halt her advance. Malnar was sprawled across his desk. Talar realized that Malnar was asleep and had not seen or heard them. Talar released Mona's shoulder and pointed to Malnar. She nodded, for she had already seen the sleeping teacher.

Mona was still uncertain of where Talar had planned to climb down from, but as Talar gingerly tip-toed past her, she realized he was heading toward the double windows that he commonly gazed out. She knew why now; they were one of the few windows in the High Keep that were directly above the Outer Wall. Mona now looked over at Malnar, who still was asleep. The teacher's head was resting upon his forearms, and his head was turned opposite of the escaping students. Talar finally made it to the double window and took out the thin rope. He shook his head, for the rope seemed absurdly thin to hold both his and Mona's weight. Dalir had sworn upon the rope, though. Their lives would depend on Dalir now, Talar thought. Talar was not an expert with knots like a sailor, but after a moment, he had fashioned a secure double knot. Talar grabbed the rope, and while looking back at Malnar, he tugged it as hard as he could without making any noise. The rope seemed strong to Talar, and he looked back at Mona and nodded.

Talar knew what was next, and he tried to push all the fear that was in his stomach away, but it did not work. His hands started to shake as he approached the window. He pushed aside the fear in his gut and gently hopped up on the windowsill. He tossed the remaining section of the rope over the window ledge. The rope fell silently through the air, untangling as it went. After a few seconds, Talar heard the rope hit the surface of the Outer wall, and the Stonedom Prince realized he should have checked to see if any Guards were patrolling below.

After silently cursing his stupidity, Talar grasped the rope and gently leaned over the ledge and looked below. The distance below was at least a dozen rods, and then the Outer Wall was at least two rods as high as well. Talar shook his head when a strong gust of wind hit him. He could not believe he was about to climb down this tower. Talar looked back at Mona, and they locked eyes. Talar could tell she was scared, and he could not blame her a bit. He was shaking himself. Talar managed a smile anyway and motioned for Mona to join him at the window. She returned the smile and took a step forward. She was about to take another step when a croaking sound escaped from Malnar's nose.

Talar and Mona froze, not knowing what to do. Malnar rolled restlessly on his desk, almost knocking over the small candle that illuminated the classroom. Talar tapped the stone window to gain Mona's attention, and he beckoned her to join him. She quickly did, despite the noises that Malnar was making. The fear was rising in Talar, and he felt like the day in the High Court when the Emperor had embarrassed him. Except for this time, he was even in more danger. Talar was shaking now. All his weight was now being supported by the rope. Mona still held tight to his shoulders, and she could feel his fear.

Another strong gust of wind hit the two of them, blowing Mona's red hair wildly around. She knew that Talar did not trust the rope even though it seemed to be holding him. She did not blame him though, it seemed thin for descending such a height. Mona leaned over as far as she safely could.

"You must trust the rope, Talar. It is already holding you. We must get going!" she whispered in Talar's ear. The wind muffled her words, and she did not know if Talar had heard her. Talar had heard her words, and the sound of her voice in his ears was all that he needed to start making his way down.

Talar was making good time down the rope despite the bulky robe. The wind occasionally spun him around, and his arms were already hurting, but he was making it down. He was escaping! Talar's heart was racing, but he felt comfortable now to look back over his shoulder at the Old City below him. It was massive and beautiful, still visible at night due to the street torches. It briefly made Talar think of Stonedom. The overlapping red clay tile roofs oddly reminded Talar of the grey slate roofs of Stonedom. Talar pushed these thoughts out of his head and refocused on securely placing his hand on the rope before releasing the other one. He looked down and realized he was at least halfway down, and his heart raced again. He could now see the Outer Wall, and he saw no Guards patrolling behind the parapet.

Mona looked down and smiled as Talar kept descending. She knew that Talar was strong enough to climb down, but she now worried about herself. There was not much for the Women of the Academy to do in the form of exercise. Mona pushed those worries out of her head and glanced over at Malnar, who was still sleeping. She now hopped up into the windowsill and looked over, holding the rope firmly. Talar was almost to the Outer Wall, and Mona wondered if the rope could support both of them at once. Talar had not told her anything of the escape plan, and Mona wanted to scream at the Stonedom Prince for not informing her of this climbing plan. She pushed the anger out of her head. She had been locked in this Keep for years, and Talar was the reason she was escaping. Her anger should be towards the Capans, for they were her captors.

Mona looked down again and saw that Talar had made it to the Outer Wall! Her heart raced, and the thought of freedom blasted the fear out of her. Mona glanced at Malnar; he was still sleeping. She then awkwardly slid out of the windowsill, her robes bunching up and slowing her down. After a moment, her legs were dangling over the window ledge, and she reached the point where if she went any further, she would have to rely on the rope. Mona felt the wind blowing against her, but she was confident that the rope would hold her since it had already held Talar. Mona took a deep breath, then went over the window ledge.

Her hands were sweaty, and she dangerously slid down the thin rope, burning her hands as she did. After a few frightful seconds, Mona managed to wrap her legs around the rope despite her robe. She now clung to the rope desperately, her confidence gone since the near-death slide to her current point. The wind gusted again, and she bounced against the cold stone of the Spire. The wind stopped, and Mona looked down. It was a mistake. She was still almost to the top of the Spire, and the distant lights of the Old City below gave her vertigo.

Mona was overwhelmed by fear, but she managed to hold onto the rope. She continued to desperately cling to the rope until she realized that her arms and hands were burning. The pain brought her back to her senses, and she realized if she did not get moving, then she would lose her grip and fall. Mona took a deep breath, exhaled sharply, and slowly began creeping down the rope. Sweat soon began to run freely down her face, and she exhaled sharply again. She knew she was making progress, but she did not dare look down again to see how much.

Talar's feet finally hit the stone allure. He looked around fearfully, but there was no Guards in sight. The High Keep was too large to have Guards stationed everywhere. They patrolled instead. Talar looked down and saw that there was still some slack left in the rope, but not much. He looked up, and his heart stopped when he saw Mona swinging back and forth wildly so far up in the air. She did not seem like she was moving, and Talar cursed his stupidity for thinking the young Woman could do the climb down on her own. Talar was pulling on his dark hair with both hands as Mona fearfully clung to the rope. He could not believe he was so foolish. Talar spotted a torch that illuminated the Outer Wall, and he extinguished it against the Wall to help hide their presence.

Talar looked around again for the Keep Guards, but none were in sight. He looked up again at Mona, and his heart raced when he saw Mona slowly creeping down the rope. She was doing it! Talar shook his head in relief, then walked over to the parapet and looked over the side, down upon the street bordering the Outer Wall. His heart sank again. There were two High Keep Guards stationed below. Talar walked back to the rope and looked up at Mona. She was now only about four rods above him, and Talar held the rope tight to aid her descent. He looked around, expecting to see the torches of a patrol of Guards at any second. Talar wondered if he could leave Mona alone on the rope if the Guards did show up. He could jump the Outer Wall and have a chance at freedom if they did. He pushed the thought out of his mind as she slowly approached the stone walkway of the Outer Wall. She came closer to the walkway, and Talar could see that her arms were shaking. He wondered if she was going to make it without falling, but after a few more tense seconds, her feet landed squarely on the walkway. She immediately collapsed.

Talar again looked up for the Keep Guards but again saw none. He picked up Mona and half dragged her; half carried her to the parapet. Talar saw another Keep Guard racing towards the two stationed below him. The Guard running motioned for the other two to follow him, and suddenly the area below Talar was free of Guards. Talar smiled at his good luck. The young Prince from Stonedom did not know why they were leaving but was glad they were gone.

Chapter XXIV-Casus Belli

Lord Volga sat at his desk, deep within the lowest chambers of the High Keep. At this time of the night, the Emperor was asleep, and from his plain wooden desk, Lord Volga ran the Empire. Volga shuffled through the reports on his desk. He quickly scanned over reports varying from the wheat harvest, tax reports, and minor uprisings in the northern provinces. Nothing unusual, but the nightly pigeons had not arrived yet. For hundreds of years, the Men of Koristan and Capa had bred and housed the pigeons to deliver messages fast and securely through the air. They were highly efficient.

One report caught Volga's interest. The commander of Fort Carillon had abandoned the Fort and fled downriver with most of the Legionnaires after being badly wounded. Volga swore softly. Fort Carillon was vital for protecting the woodcutters who were supplying the Empire with much-needed ship masts. He would order reinforcements from the motley Fifth Legion.

Volga looked over another report, and a grim smile spread across his face. Lord Ralphunus, who was the highest-ranking lord of Brigantium, was requesting his son's future bride, Mona of Mercium, to be brought to Brigantium. Volga stood then walked over to the nearest candle, which was close to the metal gate which led to the dungeon. He lit the parchment, which burned quickly, and he let the burning ashes fall to the stone floor below. He stomped the smoldering ashes with his boot. Volga returned to his seat and smiled again. He had no intention of giving up the beautiful, red-haired, Mercium princess. He had become infatuated with her over the span of her captivity. Despite his power, Volga had no family, and since he was sixty years old, he figured it was time for him to have a wife. The Mercium princess would do fine, he thought while smiling again.

A knock on the heavy wooden door interrupted Volga's reading. He ordered the servant to come in. The servant quickly and wordlessly dropped off the day's reports. The servants knew better to speak to or look at Volga, for his brutal reputation was legendary within the Keep. Volga enjoyed his violent reputation and the power it brought him. The large, gray-haired Man thumbed through the parchments until he saw another letter from Lord Ralphunus. He lazily scanned the letter, assuming it was another complaint about Mona. The words from Ralphunus were sinking in, and Volga dropped the letter in disbelief. Cadoc, King of Stonedom, was dead and his son Cynfor had openly declared his allegiance to the Dwarves. Volga shook his head. The young northern prince would pay dearly for his betrayal. His brother was upstairs in the Academy, and Volga knew the Emperor would want justice for Stonedom's betrayal. Volga smiled; he had not had any fun torturing nobles in quite some time. He enjoyed inflicting pain on nobles more than commoners. They usually were not nearly as tough as a commoner.

Volga leaped to his feet, strode over to the door, and flung it open. "Summon Captain Tiberius and close all the gates in and out of the High Keep. Do this now!" Volga roared, and a young Keep Guard sprinted up the stairs, away from the dungeon. Volga had a suspicion that someone had intercepted one of his messenger pigeons. The news of Stonedom's betrayal should have come from Mercium, not its neighbor Brigantium. Volga had spies in Mercium, and he now worried about them. He did not fear for their safety. He feared the lack of knowledge their absence would cause. Volga walked back to his desk and grabbed his short sword, which was leaning against it. The greying Capan grabbed it, attached it to his belt, and began heading upstairs. To his next victim.

Captain Tiberius met up with Volga in the High Courtyard. He was flanked by two of his exotic-looking guards. Volga nodded curtly; he knew that Tiberius was content with his position as head of the Emperor's bodyguard. Volga knew the Captain did not seek any more power. If he had, Volga would have disposed of Tiberius already. Tiberius nodded back. Volga quickly explained the situation and asked Tiberius if the High Keep had been sealed. The Captain nodded. Volga did not waste any time and kept heading towards the Academy. After a few short moments, the four Capans had made their way up the flights of stone stairs until the double doors of the Academy greeted them. Volga did not slow down at all, for he knew the Keep like the back of his hand. Volga was standing before Calbrius' chamber in short time. His bear-like paw came crashing down on the door, awaking the Headmaster.

The look of anger in Calbrius' eyes disappeared when he saw who had knocked on his door. Volga did not waste any time. "Where is Talar Stoneking?" Volga demanded, his deep voice booming through the empty stone corridor. Calbrius had enough wits to know something was wrong, and he knew better than to test Volga's patience. The Headmaster gathered his robes about him, quickly slipped his sandals on, and strode out of his chamber with the confidence that a high-ranking Capan such as he possessed.

They arrived at Talar's room soon afterward. Volga burst through the room with such force that the door shattered against the stone wall behind it. He could not wait to get his hands on the northern Prince. As Volga strode into the dimly lit room, he did not see any movement or anybody sleeping on the small cot. There was no one there. Calbrius's jaw dropped as he stood behind Volga. Volga turned around in anger, but before he could ask his question, Calbrius was already answering it. "I don't know where he is, my Lord. He could be in another student's room. We don't lock them in like sheep, my Lord."

Volga nodded and barked for Tiberius. The Captain roughly pushed Calbrius to the side, for he could sense it was an emergency. "Gather all the students in the Academy's main classroom. Have Calbrius take stock of who is here and who is not. Awaken the Emperor as well. And bring more Guards up here now!" Volga commanded, and soon Tiberius relayed the orders. Within minutes Keep Guards had flooded the Academy floor and rousted the students from their sleep. Calbrius performed a headcount of the students as they sat in the classroom. Most were still wiping the sleep from their eyes, but some, like Ralphin, looked around in curiosity at the buzz of activity around them. The Keep Guards were clearly searching for someone.

Calbrius took stock of who was missing and went outside of the main doors of the Academy, where Volga and Tiberius were waiting. "Talar Stoneking, Mona of Mercium, and the Koristan Ambassador's son are missing, my Lord."

Volga's eyes bulged at the news, and Calbrius could tell the older Capan was enraged. He was not expecting Volga to pick him and pin him against the wall, though, which is exactly what Volga did.

"Where are they, Headmaster? This is your Academy. You are responsible!" Volga shouted, the spit from his words spraying Calbrius in a fine mist. Calbrius's legs were shaking in fear, and Tiberius thought of restraining Volga. Eventually, Volga lowered Calbrius to the floor and regained his composure. Just as he did, Ralphin spied something unusual in the main classroom. The pig nosed Brigantium noble saw something tied around the stanchion separating the double window.

Ralphin walked over to the double window. He ran his fingers over the fine, smooth rope, for he had never seen one like it. He followed the rope around the base of the double window and leaned on the windowsill. While peering over, Ralphin saw that the rope disappeared over the ledge. His heart raced, and he pushed himself back into the safety of the classroom. "There is a rope here. Rope here. Rope here," he squealed. Soon the entire class was crowding around the double window. Tiberius noticed the commotion from outside, and Volga saw him stride briskly into the classroom, and he followed behind the Captain.

Volga barked at the young students to clear the way, and they quickly did upon seeing the leering Lord of the High Keep striding towards them. Volga studied the rope, then leaned outside. He instructed Tiberius to grab his black leather coattails to prevent him from falling, and afterward, he leaned over the edge. Volga saw that the rope made it all the way down to the Outer Wall. He could not see anything, for the torch below was out. He swore viciously and pushed himself back into the classroom.

"They have made it out of the Keep. Close all the gates going in and out of Capa and alert the City Guards. Take a squad and close the Inner Harbor. Tell them to raise the chain and do it fast. Time is of the essence, so get to it," Volga ordered, and the Captain left the room running.

Volga left the Academy and began making his way to the Emperor's chambers. He was bristling with anger over losing the red-haired, Mercium beauty. The anger did not cloud Volga's mind. If anything, it sharpened it. The

Lord of the High Keep was not worried about finding either missing northerner. He was worried about the missing Koristan. If Volga's theory about the escape panned out to be true, then the Empire might be at war. Volga smiled grimly. He had longed for war with the Koristans for years, and now they might have given him a reason for it.

Chapter XXV- On the Docks

Mona collapsed against the parapet, her arms shaking from the harrowing climb down from the Academy. Talar gathered the remaining slack of the thin rope and threw it over the parapet. It made it almost to the bottom of the wall, which was vacant now. Talar heard alarm bells ring out ominously from the High Keep behind them. Their escape had been discovered!

"We must keep going, Mona. They know we've escaped." Talar exclaimed, and despite the aching in her arms, Mona stood and began climbing over the parapet. Talar assisted her, and before long, she was over the side, making her way down to the Old City below. Talar looked up and swore he could see the outline of a bunch of people in the window that he had climbed out of. It was time to leave. He crawled over the parapet, grasped the thin rope, and looked down below. Mona was already on the ground, leaning against the Outer Wall, trying to catch her breath. Talar began descending and reached the ground quickly. They were out of the High Keep!

Talar looked around. They were in a vacant lot in between the merchant tents that lined the Outer Wall. The Old City was right in front of them, the New City to the left, past the main entrance to the High Keep. Mona and Talar both looked at each other and began awkwardly running in their white robes. The robes stuck out in the moonlight. They ran along the street parallel to the Outer Wall. The houses facing the Outer Wall had been locked up for the night. Talar feared that they would be pinned in, and his fears were confirmed when he saw torch lights and heard voices behind him. They kept running until they both heard someone yell, "Stop." Talar and Mona both looked around, and from the darkness, two Legionnaires emerged. "Run, Mona!" Talar shouted as he turned to run, but just as he did, he heard a familiar voice.

"Talar, stop! It's me." Talar immediately stopped in his tracks, recognizing the voice.

"Hartwin?" Talar whispered. Hartwin and Alwin emerged from the shadows, and each took turns hugging Talar. The Prince of Stonedom was not alone any longer, and Talar's heart was filled with joy. The brothers were dressed in the garb of a Legionnaire, and they looked odd to Talar, who was used to seeing them in their dark green woodsmen cloaks. They both carried the spears common in the Legions.

Alwin seemed poised to ask Talar a question, but Mona cut him off. "We must keep going. The Guards are alerted, do you know the way?".

Hartwin nodded and took the lead, running hastily across the street until they reached an intersection. Despite the dark, Talar recognized where they were from his trip through the Old City weeks before. They rounded the corner and began making their way downhill along the cobbled streets towards the Inner harbor. The City Guard's alarms were all ringing loudly now, and lights inside of the tall Capan dwellings were beginning to appear. The four northerners kept up their fast pace, their sandals hitting the cobblestones below them loudly. Talar felt like Old City was trapping them, the rows of seemingly endless towering concrete buildings a giant maze. City Guard torches appeared in the distance, and all four of them halted.

"What do we do?" Mona asked. Talar turned around, but behind him, there were numerous torches as well.

"We'll have to fight our way through. Alwin and I will lead the way. You two run around us and don't stop." Hartwin said grimly. The elder brother tightened his grip on his spear and turned back towards the advancing Capans. Talar could not believe that it was going to end this way after just meeting up with Hartwin and Alwin. Fear began to overwhelm him like the day at the High Court. As the fear settled in, Talar's hands began shaking. If the Guards took him alive, he would be ruthlessly tortured. These thoughts froze Talar, and he felt like he was going to collapse when he spotted something familiar in the moonlight. Blinking through the fear and the night's darkness, Talar spotted the aqueduct that had fascinated him on his journey to the High Keep. A wild idea popped into Talar's head, and suddenly the fear vanished.

"There is another way," Talar said forcefully, stopping the other three. "Look," Talar pointed at the aqueduct, which because of the slope of the hill was only a few feet above their heads. The four of them ran over to the aqueduct. Alwin handed his brother his spear and immediately grabbed Mona by the waist and picked her up. Mona's hand grasped the top of the aqueduct, and she pulled herself up despite the burning in her arms muscles.

Alwin now cupped his hands together, and Talar placed his left foot in his hands. He quickly rose through the cool air, and his hands grasped the edge of the aqueduct. Mona helped pull him up. Alwin and Hartwin followed suit after handing up their bulky spears. Hartwin was about to start making his way down the aqueduct when Alwin tapped his shoulder. The patrol they had seen in the distance was now approaching. The four of them wordlessly dropped down into the aqueduct, which was about three feet high. Talar was lying in cool water that was flowing steadily, but it was shallow enough not to impede his breathing. He could hear the footsteps of the patrol stop. He thought that they must be right underneath him.

"I don't see them, Sarge." The voice speaking the words was deep and crude. "Let's turn back boys, they must have ducked into a house." The Sargent's voice was even deeper, and he had a thick Brigantium accent. Talar heard the patrol's footsteps fade into the distance, and he carefully raised his head to look around. The patrol was out of sight, and the cobble street was empty.

"Let's go Hartwin, this aqueduct should bring us close to the Inner Harbor. The ship waiting for us has three golden fish painted on it." Talar added the last part in case he did not make it to the Inner Harbor the others would still have a chance. Hartwin did not reply, but he did start making his way down the aqueduct. His Legionnaire sandals splashed in the shallow water. Alwin, Mona, and Talar followed, with Talar in the rear.

The aqueduct cut across the street then continued downhill on top of houses. The four of them ran down the aqueduct, the water splashing around their feet. Talar occasionally could hear voices from inside the houses, for the aqueduct sometimes ran right past open windows. After a few more minutes, the four of them came to an intersection of the aqueduct. Three different aqueducts lay before them, with the one straight ahead plunging downhill in between houses. Talar immediately knew that the aqueduct ahead would lead straight down to the harbor, for the other two veered out back into the Old City and New City. Hartwin seemed hesitant.

The elderly brother, who had recently collapsed numerous times during the harsh Legionnaire recruit training, was beginning to feel his age. He had been awakened by a young servant girl and handed a letter stating that Talar was escaping tonight. He had also been given the key to the main barracks gate. Half an hour later, he and Alwin had met up with Talar and Mona. With his aching bones and sore back, the elder brother shook his head in anger. He had no idea where the aqueduct ended or if it continued running straight. Talar spoke up from behind and urged him forward.

"To be young again," Hartwin muttered, then stepped forward to the edge, his toes dangling off. The aqueduct was pitched almost straight down. Hartwin shook his head again. "C'mon Hartwin, we must make haste," Talar said in his youthful voice. Hartwin shook his head again. He was getting too old for this.

Hartwin sat down and pushed himself forward until gravity took hold of him, and he began sliding down. He held the spear over his shoulder, and Talar watched him disappear soundlessly into the darkness. The two Capan buildings perched overhead towered over them, and Talar saw someone on a balcony up above them drinking from a goblet. They must keep going, Talar thought. Alwin followed his brother and Talar watched him disappear after a few seconds. He had not heard Hartwin scream out, so he thought the aqueduct must be safe.

"C'mon Mona," Talar whispered, but Mona was already at the edge. She sat down, looked back at Talar with a smile, and pushed herself forward. At least she was not scared, Talar thought. Talar now moved forward and sat down. He could feel the drop before him, despite the darkness. Talar pushed off.

Water-soaked Talar's robe, and he felt cold air hitting his face. For a few seconds, Talar thought he was falling straight down, for he was going incredibly fast. The aqueduct's pitch lessened, and Talar felt himself slowing down a little. He looked up and saw the outlines of columned mansions and lights from the adjacent houses fly by. His feet tapped Mona's back. Mona grabbed his sandals and pulled him closer until they were sliding down together. She was laughing wildly, and her long red hair brushed against the side of her face. Talar began laughing too, for he could now smell the scent of the ocean. They were getting close to the harbor!

"I love it," Mona yelled, for they were gaining speed again. Talar began to laugh too. He quickly remembered sliding down the creeks back home with Cynfor, but this was much better. They continued sliding, descending through the Old City at an alarming speed. Mona kept laughing, but Talar was now looking out ahead more, the initial dazzle of the passing city lights gone now. He could not see Alwin, and he had not heard any warnings. But how did the aqueduct end? Talar thought back and tried to remember what Captain Tiberius had said.

The aqueduct went back in between two tight houses, and Talar noticed the houses were wooden and looked shabby. He looked back up ahead and saw that the aquifer seemed to disappear entirely. His heart sank. "Mona!" Talar shouted before he hugged her.

They plunged together over the end of the aquifer. Talar saw cobblestones and briefly saw the ocean before he was submerged in cold water. His feet hit bottom, and he stood in water that was higher than his waist. He was unharmed. Talar looked around and saw Mona standing up. She was unharmed as well. He looked to his right and saw Alwin and Hartwin. He looked to his left and saw a handful of Capans roaring with laughter. "Two more!" a skinny sailor said laughingly, and the Capans around him joined in. They had landed in a public fountain that was in a middle of a row of taverns. The tavern patrons laughed at the young nobles, for only nobles wore white robes. Some of the disheveled fishmongers and sailors leered at Mona, but Hartwin walked over and escorted her out of the fountain. Talar waded through the fountain and hopped out into the street.

The openness of the Inner Harbor washed over Talar. For the past few weeks, he had felt caged in, first in the High Keep, then in the maze of towering buildings during their flight. Now looking around, he could see far down the wharf in both directions, and a sense of freedom coursed through him. He was brought back to reality by the sound of Mona's voice. "Do you know where the ship is, Talar? The harbor is huge."

Talar just shook his head, for he did not know the location of the ship Dalir had told him about. The plan was to sneak down here then walk the docks until they found the ship. Mona saw that he did not know, and she was not surprised. Hartwin spoke up and suggested that they split up and search for the ship separately. "We can't, Hartwin. We don't have time. There will be patrols down here soon." Talar said as the four huddled together.

"I have an idea," Mona said, and she turned around, still dripping wet, and approached the group of tavern patrons who had jeered at them just before. The skinny sailor smiled from ear to ear at the sight of Mona.

"Why hello, beautiful. See, you've come to your senses and wanna come to be with a real Man!" he slurred while slapping his buddy's back.

Mona just smiled. "I'm looking for a fishing ship for Koristan. The ship's ready to launch. Any idea you can tell me where it is, friend?" Mona said innocently. The skinny sailor just shook his head as if he did not comprehend the question. "A fishing ship from Koristan...?" Mona inquired again, stepping closer.

"Of course, I know where that ship is. I am the helmsman for the harbor pilot. Brought every ship into this harbor." The helmsman slurred his words, but Mona knew they had gotten lucky. She stepped even closer, and she could see pockmarks from the plague had scarred half the man's face.

"Alright then, point me in the direction of the ship," Mona asked, smiling as hard as she could at the drunk.

"Why should I? What is in it for me?" the drunk helmsman replied to the delight of his fellow tavern patrons, who had increased in number since Mona had walked over. Mona thought quickly, knowing that the City Guard patrols were closing in on her.

"If you describe the fishing ship and its location...I'll kiss you. I promise." Talar's jaw dropped to the amusement of the tavern patrons. Alwin and Hartwin shook their heads as they walked over behind Mona.

The drunk helmsmen staggered from side to side, but he finally nodded in agreement, to the delight of his friends. He leaned in closer to Mona and smiled. Mona could see his rotten, yellow teeth, and she could smell the rancid odor of stale wine mixed with fish. She wanted to gag.

"Not yet. First, you must describe the ship." Mona ordered. The helmsman leaned back and grabbed his chin with his thumb and index fingers as if in deep thought. He was playing to the crowd, Mona realized. She was about to start complaining when he spoke. "

"It is not a ship built for the open seas. It is a fishing galley for the Shimmering Sea. Twenty oars, two beams. Small cabin in the back with three goldfish painted on it. Can't leave the Shimmering Sea with that one," the sailor said with a smile. Mona smiled and asked again where it was. "Not so fast, pretty girl. First, my kiss!" The sailor said, and the crowd roared again with laughter. They could sense Mona's discomfort. The sailor leaned in, and Mona knew that she had to kiss him to get away. The sailor was expecting a kiss on the lips, but Mona grabbed his pock-marked face and kissed that instead to the delight of the crowd. Mona pushed the sailor back afterward. "That was hardly a kiss, my dear." The sailor pouted.

Hartwin and Alwin stepped forward, and Alwin grabbed the drunk sailor by the collar. "You made a deal. Where is the ship?" Alwin growled. The drunk sailor knew better to mess around with an angry Legionnaire, and he began rapidly pointing down the docks.

"That way, that way, towards the end of the docks. Across from the Broken Oar," the sailor said frightfully. Alwin released him, and the four sprinted in that direction. Talar hoped the drunk sailor had not lied to them.

Various sailors, merchants, and beggars passed by Talar as he ran behind the others. Like his companions, he was searching fervently for the Broken Oar as he ran. Different taverns passed by the four northerners; The Thirsty Dog, The Big Barnacle, The Eighth Mate, the Shallow Surf, but none of them were the ones they were looking for. Hartwin smacked into a fish monger's pushcart, and the little old lady pushing it angrily hit him with a long stick she used for thieves. After receiving a few blows, Hartwin grabbed it and threw it at the old lady. They kept running through the crowds, who were mostly drunk tavern patrons.

After pushing his way through a throng of tavern goers, Talar looked up and saw a weathered wooden sign. The sign's fainted white paint showed a single oar, broken in the middle. Talar knew that he had found the tavern and yelled at the others to come back. Talar pointed at the sign, and the three others all ran back and looked it over. Talar was already walking over to the dockside, looking for the fishing galley.

He spotted it quickly, for the drunk helmsmen had described it accurately. The fishing galley's three golden fish stood out against the galley's dark brown wood, and Talar could see two beams standing out against the moonlight. He ran over to the ship and heard the sea hitting against it. He saw a Koristan fisherman coiling a rope and yelled to gain his attention. The Koristan looked up, dropped the rope, and yelled for the Captain. A tall Koristan with a red sash and short sword appeared and quickly looked over the four companions.

His instructions were to give passage to four northerners. They matched the description he was looking for, and he motioned for them to come aboard. Before Talar could jump aboard, he saw a flurry of movement as the Koristan sailors sprung to action. Oarsmen assumed their positions, and the Captain was shouting orders.

"Prepare to shove off!" the Captain shouted as Mona, Hartwin, and Alwin climbed aboard. Talar let out a deep sigh of relief, for he finally felt safe. He smiled at Mona, who walked over and hugged him.

The Koristans had their feet on the dock, ready to shove off when a loud metallic noise suddenly burst out above the hum of the tavern patrons who filled the taverns lining the docks. Talar looked around but could not figure out where the noise was coming from. But from the look on the Captain's face, he knew it was not a good sound. The Captain walked across the ship, and Talar followed, ducking under the sails of the two main beams. The noise continued, and now Talar could tell what was causing it. A giant rusty iron chain was being lifted out of the sea's water. At each end of the crescent shape Inner Harbor there was a metal crank that two men turned to slowly raise the chain. When the chain was raised, no ship could enter the Inner Harbor of Capa. And no ship could leave.

Talar's heart sank, for he realized that all the danger they had endured had been for nothing. They were trapped! The thought of Volga leering over him as he lay haplessly in the High Keep's dungeon made Talar's hands shake with fear. The Captain turned around slowly. "They have raised the chains. There is nothing more we can do for you, my Lord. For the safety of my crew, you and your friends must leave my ship now," the Captain stated. Talar nodded, knowing what would happen to the Koristans if they got caught by the Capans. They were so close! There must be something they could do to stop the chains, and with his hands still shaking, Talar saw that there were only a few of the City Guard standing watch over the laborers who were raising the chain.

"If we lower the chain, will you bring the ship forward, so we can jump on?" Talar asked the Captain. The middle-aged Koristan Captain rubbed his chin and looked over to the small stone building which housed the metal crank. He had nothing to lose by waiting to see if the northerners could lower the chain, so he nodded at the young Lord standing in front of him. He also offered his short sword.

Talar grabbed the short sword and went back towards the stern of the ship and began explaining the situation to his companions. The rusty chain scraping sound had ceased, and Talar knew the chain was up now. They must lower it. "We will attack the crank house and lower the chain, then jump aboard as the ship leaves." Alwin and Hartwin nodded. Hartwin reached out for the short sword, and Talar exchanged it for Hartwin's short spear. The three Men from Stonedom jumped off the ship.

Mona attempted to join them but was held back by the Koristan Captain. Talar shook his fist angrily and yelled at her to stay put. She quit resisting the Captain. Talar shifted his focus back to the crank house, which lay ahead.

"Stay behind us, Talar. We will use our disguises to our advantage," Hartwin said quietly, but the words just passed over Talar. The spear was shaking in his hands, and he was glad that Hartwin and Alwin could not see his nervousness. His battle with the Goblins seemed so long ago, and that fight had been almost spontaneous, for the Goblins gave no warning of their attack. Tonight, was different. Talar knew a fight was coming, and he tried to steady his breathing and focus. As the three of them approached the crank house, Talar's heart raced with each step, and he wondered briefly if he would die soon.

Talar looked past the brother's shoulders and saw that there were only three City Guards standing watch at the crank house. The two laborers, their work completed, were leaving the crank house. Talar looked over the City Guard's, who was dressed like the Legionnaires, except with white cloaks. Each Guard had overlapping leather plate armor over their shoulders which connected to an iron breastplate. High leather boots rose to their shins, and they wore long white shorts, which made long days of patrolling the streets of Capa tolerable. They stopped right in front of the Guards, and Talar did his best to stop the spear from shaking. He waited for Hartwin to make the first move. Hartwin did not wait long.

The eldest City Guardsman did not notice that the Legionnaire had his sword unsheathed. He had been told to look out for a pair of nobles in white robes. Not noticing the unsheathed sword would cost him his life, for Hartwin ruthlessly slashed him across the neck. The City Guardsman's blood covered Hartwin, but that did not stop the veteran swordsman. Hartwin lunged with the short sword in the direction of the next Guardsman, who fell trying to escape the northerner's attack. Hartwin kicked the Guard in the face and grasped the short sword with both hands, ready to finish off the fallen Guardsman. The last Guardsman had gained his composure from the initial attack and drew his short, wide dagger. He was young but had been in enough fights to know that it would take longer to draw his sword. The young Guardsman leaped forward, dagger in hand, ready to slay this false Legionnaire.

The aging Hartwin had not noticed the young Guardsman attack and would have been stabbed if not for his brother, who lunged with his short spear at the slender young Guardsman. The young Guard knocked the short spear aside with his dagger and drew his sword with the other. Hartwin plunged his sword down, killing the fallen Guard. The brothers cornered the remaining Guard in the entrance of the crank house.

"Watch our backs!" Hartwin barked, and Talar realized that Hartwin was yelling at him. Talar's senses were sharpened now, his training was kicking in, and he spun around, spear ready. The citizens of Capa stood aghast, not knowing what to do. Talar heard a scream behind him. He looked back quickly and saw that the remaining Guard had been stabbed in his side by Alwin's spear. The remaining Guard dropped his weapons and fell to his knees, clutching his wound desperately. Hartwin grabbed him by the back of his head, and Talar turned back to the crowd, not wanting to watch what happened next.

"Get out of here while you still can, boy!" Hartwin barked, and Talar watched the young Guard stagger off into the crowd. There was a moment of silence before the watching crowd began yelling out.

"Murder!" some shouted, while others yelled, "Traitors!". Talar looked back at the brothers, but they were in the crank house already. The crowd closed in on Talar, who stood alone, his back to the crank house.

"Hartwin!" Talar shouted nervously and was instantly relieved when the elder brother appeared.

"Get back and help Alwin," Hartwin said calmly as he wiped the blood off his face with his Legionnaire cape. He then picked up the dagger that the wounded Guard had dropped and ordered Talar to give the sword on the ground to Alwin. Talar did as he was commanded, for taking orders from Hartwin was nothing new to him.

Talar walked into the crank house, and he saw Alwin straining against the giant metal crank, which used intricate metal gears to lower and raise the massive chain. He dropped the sword and spear and threw his weight against the crank. It slowly began to move, the metallic noise reverberating through the night air. They kept turning the crank together for another moment until Hartwin called for his brother from outside the crank house.

"We've almost got it, Hartwin! Another moment!" Alwin responded, but when he looked up from pushing the crank, he saw why his brother had called out. Alwin stopped pushing and bent over to pick up the sword that Talar had brought in. Talar protested against Alwin leaving until he too turned around and saw what was outside.

Captain Tiberius and ten fellow members of the Emperor's Guard stood outside, surrounding the crank house. The two torchlights that were attached to the crank house illuminated their shiny breastplates and bright yellow cloaks. Alwin stood next to his brother, guarding the entrance. "Keep lowering the chain Talar," Alwin said, his eyes not leaving the Guards in front of him. Alwin could see that the fishing galley had heard the chain being lowered and was now slowly approaching. Talar was about to protest when he spotted the galley as well. He went back inside and threw his weight into the crank. The chain began to lower, but Talar's muscles burned from the excursion. Talar heard swords ringing out and heard Hartwin curse. He tried to look up over the crank, but that only slowed him down.

The Guards had attacked together at once, hoping to overwhelm the brothers. Hartwin had thrown the dagger underhand, killing the most eager Guard, which slowed down the rest. Hartwin and Alwin retreated to the crank house entrance and began fending off the slashes from the Guards. Hartwin parried a thrust from a dark-haired Guard, then a slash from another, but he could not avoid the short spear which cut open his face. Alwin had already slashed one Guard by then, and he leaped to his brother's defense after hearing him curse. Hartwin wiped the blood out of his eyes as Alwin slashed viciously at the attacking Guards. His blows were fended off. Tiberius whistled, and the Guards took a step back. He was not aware of the galley's approach and wanted the Stonedom Men to tire and bleed before he finished them off.

Hartwin tried to wipe the blood out of his left eye, but he had been badly cut. Alwin picked up a spear and grasped his sword with his other hand. He thought briefly of the young barmaid in the tavern back in Stonedom whom he had considered marrying. He knew that would never happen now, and for a moment, the anger from combat subsided within him. He breathed deeply and thought if Talar escaped, then word would spread about his and Hartwin's actions. Songs would be sung about his bravery. The Druids would speak his name. He would enter the next life, and the Old Gods would not punish him. A thin smile crossed Alwin's face.

"To the death, little brother. Do not let them take you alive," Hartwin said after spitting up blood. His mouth filled with more blood, and he spat again on the cobblestones. Alwin nodded. The Emperor's Guards advanced again, and battle broke out. Hartwin grabbed an attacking Guard's sword arm and ran him through with his sword. The act left him exposed, and this time Alwin could only watch as Hartwin was cut down by a screaming Guard. His heart sank, but he fought on, thrusting the short sword into the Guard who had killed his brother. Alwin released the sword's handle and swung the spear, back and forth, in a vain attempt to ward off the remaining Guards. He looked down upon his brother, who stared at the night sky with vacant eyes.

"Get out of here, Talar. Get out!" Alwin shouted over the metallic noise of the crank, before the Guards charged for the last time. Alwin managed to stab one Guard before being overrun. He fell back into the crank house, his spear gone, his fists and hair swinging wildly.

Talar watched the commotion unfold around him, but he kept pushing the crank. Alwin fought on, using his forearms to defend himself. He cried out when the Guards' blades sliced him, and blood soon covered the crank house floor. Talar kept pushing until, finally, the metallic noise stopped. The chain was lowered! Talar looked back in time to see Alwin being pushed into him. Talar almost fell out of the opening, and he felt something warm and wet run down his waist as Alwin touched him. Talar knew it was Alwin's blood, for the tall Stonedom Guard had been sliced numerous times. Alwin barely stood on his own.

"Jump Talar, Jump. I'm done." Alwin said, the last words being muffled by blood. Talar stood in the opening and watched as the Guards rushed again. Alwin lunged into them, and they quickly threw him down, stabbing him repeatedly. Talar knew he was dead and jumped out, but he felt a pinching sensation before he hit the water below him.

The cold salt water of the Inner Harbor shocked Talar as he rose to the surface. He looked back at the Guards, who were hesitant to jump after him in their armor. It would not have mattered if they had anyways, for, at that moment, Talar heard Mona's voice from above him. Talar turned in the water to see the fishing galley as it cut through the water right in front of him. Talar reached up to grab the gunwale but could not reach it. For a second, he thought they were going to pass right past him, but suddenly, powerful hands grabbed him, and he felt himself being lifted through the air. Talar fell into the fishing galley as it exited the Inner harbor, and the fall knocked the wind out of him. He heard Tiberius scream in frustration, and he knew that he had escaped Capa. Talar tried to stand, but he felt something warm coursing down his side. He thought it was Alwin's blood before he went unconscious.

Chapter XXVI- Tension

Marcus bent over and picked up another piece of wood for the fire. With his arms full of wood, Marcus turned and headed back to their campsite. He eventually made his way out of the majestic pines, which offered him a view of the campsite along the Mytosis. Grey boulders, the size of cows, covered the beach, but the trio had found an open area big enough for a campsite. Dobervist emerged from the waist-high water with a trout that he had speared. He tossed the fish on the ground then cursed at Stripe, who was licking at it.

They had made their way down the Cold River until they had spotted the convergence of where the Mytosis River met up with the larger Cold River. Marcus had thought that paddling upriver would have been much harder than going downriver. After Dobervist fashioned another paddle with the hatchet, the three of them had made decent progress, though. They stuck to the shoreline, when possible, to avoid the current and portaged around the rapids. Marcus was in good shape from cutting timber, but his arms still burned from their first day up the Mytosis River.

As Marcus approached the campsite, he let out a deep breath and thought of Tarquin. His friend's death still stung deeply. Marcus mentally vowed to never forget Tarquin or his bravery. He also vowed not to die like Tarquin. Not to die for nothing. Looking back at the whole timber cutting expedition, Marcus realized greed had gotten his friend killed, and nearly himself killed as well. Marcus dumped the firewood on the ground, and Aemon looked up. The Elf had a small fire going, and he leaned over, grabbed another piece of wood, and kept tending the fire. Dobervist was finishing cleaning the trout, and Stripe went over to greet Marcus before he sat upon the moss-covered riverbank. Marcus petted Stripe and looked around at the towering pines around him. All he could hear was the soft bubble of the Mytosis River and the occasional popping of the campfire. The tranquility and peacefulness of this wilderness camp were so different than the New City neighborhood that Marcus called home. After being in the wilderness, Marcus wondered if he could live in Capa again.

The fire had taken hold, and the Elf leaned back out of the smoke. "Were lucky it is not spring, or the black flies would be on us," Aemon said softly. Marcus nodded, not really appreciating the absence of the pesky flies. "We haven't had much time to talk. When we first met you on the beach, you mentioned your friend's deaths. I am sorry you lost your friends, Marcus. I'm sorry for your loss," the Elf said.

Marcus smiled at the Elf for his kindness and thought for a moment before he spoke. When he did, he spoke slowly. "And I am sorry for your loss, Elf. My people wage war upon yours. I am sorry for what the Empire has done to you," Aemon's eyebrows shot up, for the statement surprised him. Dobervist just snorted.

"If you are so concerned about the Elves, why did you not do something about it. You could have joined the Resistance," the Dwarf said mockingly. Dobervist did not trust Marcus, and he was not shy of showing his discontent for the Capan. Marcus considered the Dwarf's words. He could have joined the Resistance. He thought of the reasons why he had not.

"I should have joined the Resistance, Dwarf. If I had known the truth, then I would have. I have been told lies my entire life—lies about the Elves, about the Empire, about everything. I am angry at the Empire for lying to me, but I am angrier at myself for believing their lies," Marcus said softly. Dobervist considered his words and looked the young Capan over. If the Capan was lying, he sure was good at it, the Dwarf thought. Silence engulfed the camp except for the crackling of the fire and the river's noise. Marcus looked over at the famous Dwarf, who was cooking the trout in an iron pan across the fire. The Dwarf had masqueraded as a Man, his unusual height fooling the Capans into believing he was not a Dwarf. When his identity had been revealed, Dobervist's status as Champion had been revoked and his death arranged in the Arena. The Emperor had wanted to make an example of the Dwarf, but he had escaped. His fame had grown even more since then.

The trout was done cooking, and the Dwarf gestured for Marcus to grab his share of the meal. Aemon, like all Elves, did not eat any meat and instead had dined on a handful of berries that he had gathered earlier. After retrieving his dinner from the stern-looking Dwarf, Marcus sat back down and started eating. The trout was delicious, and he fed the trout's skin to Stripe. The sun had already begun setting, and Aemon rose to tend to the fire. Stripe curled up to Marcus and fell asleep.

"Looks like he's got a new friend," the Elf said jokingly, but the Dwarf snorted again. "He likes anybody who'll feed him."

Marcus and the Elf glanced at each other as Dobervist rolled over as if to go to sleep. It would be dark soon, and sensing the Dwarf's grumpiness, the Elf and Man went to asleep as well.

Marcus awakened to the sound of the Dwarf and Elf breaking camp. Stripe licked his face as he stood up, and the young Man gently pushed the dog away. The sun had not crested the evergreen-covered hill in front of them yet, but it was light enough to break camp. The three companions guided the canoe back into the water and proceeded to paddle upriver again. The sun crested the hill behind them, and the shadows disappeared along with the cold temperatures. Autumn had come to the north country, and Dobervist and the Elf knew that snow would soon cover these hills. They kept paddling throughout the morning, spotting beavers and otters, ospreys and eagles, and other wildlife. Marcus felt a sense of peacefulness after his recent mishaps. The sound of a rapid up a head meant that the companions would soon have to exit the river. As they pulled the canoe out of the water, Marcus spotted movement upriver on the opposite side.

Something was moving through the rhododendrons that lined the bank. Marcus froze, and the Dwarf and Elf looked behind. They saw Marcus point across the river and looked over. A large creature was emerging from the darkness of the thick hemlock forest. A long black snout pushed through the glossy green rhododendrons, and two yellow eyes followed behind it. The creature kept moving, and Marcus's jaw dropped as a massive black bear plowed through the rhododendrons. The three were still waist-high in the cold river, with Dobervist perched against a jagged boulder in the lead. Marcus thought Stripe was going to bark and draw the bear's attention, but the Dwarf clicked his tongue, and the small dog remained motionless in the canoe. The pair had hunted together for years, and Stripe obeyed Dobervist.

The bear slowly made his way over the uneven boulders lining the riverbank until he came to the smooth moss-covered boulder. The bear looked around, and Marcus was sure the bear was going to charge into the river after them. The bear looked as big as a horse. Instead of jumping into the river, he simply bent his neck and began lapping water from the river. Marcus looked ahead at Dobervist, who was already looking at him for some reason. The Dwarf did not say anything to Marcus, so the Capan instead turned around and looked at Aemon. "Stay still," the Elf whispered above the sound of the river.

Marcus nodded, but his curiosity got the best of him, and he slowly turned his head back to the bear, which was still drinking. Marcus studied the bear and saw his ears twitch before he pulled his head up and look around. The bear started making his way back to the forest. The bear stopped again, looked back at the trio as if he knew they had been watching, then peacefully entered the dark forest. The bruin was soon swallowed up by the thick rhododendrons, and he passed out of sight.

Marcus let out a deep breath and looked back at Aemon. The Elf was smiling at the Capan's uneasiness. Marcus looked forward to Dobervist to see if they were going to portage now. The Dwarf was already looking at him, and Marcus had the feeling he was being studied by Dobervist.

"Let's go," the Dwarf quietly said in his deep voice. In quick time the trio portaged around the rapid and was back paddling upriver. Their paddles propelled them upriver as the midday sun beat down upon them. Not much was said, as all three focused on paddling. Marcus took note of how Dobervist's head was always swinging back and forth, like a pendulum. It was tough for Marcus to forget that the legendary Dwarf was right in front of him. He had been hunted by the Empire for the past ten years, and Marcus had grown up seeing his bounty posters across New City. When he was a child, Marcus had seen Dobervist fight in the Arena. Marcus knew that here, in the wilderness, he was at the Dwarf's mercy.

They paddled throughout the afternoon, and the young Capan's arms began to tire. He knew better than to complain and risk the Dwarf's wrath, though. The sky above quickly began to change. The endless blue sky had disappeared, and a dark rain cloud was bearing in on them from the east. All three of the paddlers knew it was going to rain, and Dobervist pointed with his paddle to a cove on the right side of the river. They paddled into the cove, which was protected by a rock outcropping. Driftwood covered with white foam greeted them. The cove was lined with large sheer boulders. Marcus had no idea how they were supposed to get out of the canoe here. Dobervist was looking around as if he was contemplating going back out into the river. Aemon whistled, and Marcus and Dobervist turned towards him. The Elf pointed to an overhanging hemlock branch and began paddling in its direction. He steered the canoe along the overhanging branch, which was a rod's length above them and only half an arm's length wide. The Elf did not even bother stopping the canoe before he reached up, grabbed the tree branch, and gracefully pulled himself onto the hemlock branch, which swayed with the additional weight of the Elf.   The Elf stood and twisted his body through the tree branches until he reached the sheer boulders. Standing above Marcus and Dobervist, the Elf motioned for the tethering rope, which the Dwarf tossed up. The Elf tied the rope to the hemlock branch and motioned for the Dwarf and Marcus to repeat how he had ascended. Dobervist picked Stripe up, who scrambled across the branch until he was jumping up to greet Aemon and explore the forest past the Elf. Dobervist followed, and the stocky Dwarf almost broke the tree branch when he pulled himself up. Marcus was alone now in the canoe, paddle in hand, the current of the Mytosis River right behind him. Dobervist tossed the rope at Marcus, and the Capan youth caught it. He looked up at the Dwarf, bewildered.

After a few seconds, Marcus realized the Dwarf was testing him. He had the canoe to himself, and he could escape the Dwarf and Elf by backpaddling into the current. He could probably be out of the cove before either Dwarf or Elf could jump in. He could paddle down to Badatoz. Down to the Empire. Marcus paddled over to the hemlock branch instead. He pulled himself up onto the branch while holding the rope. He stood and looked up at the Dwarf and Elf, who was on the sheer boulders above him. The Dwarf was hard for Marcus to read, for his eyes never seemed to blink, and he showed no emotion. Aemon waved at him to come to join him, though, and Marcus soon made it ashore after tying off the canoe. Cold drops of rain began to fall, but the thick canopy of pine needles above caught most of them.

"We need to get the canoe up here. We can use it for shelter," Dobervist said before he walked back down to the vessel. Marcus did not think that the three of them could pull the heavy canoe up the sheer rocks at that angle. Dobervist grabbed the tethering line, braced himself, and began pulling the line up. The Dwarf's muscles bulged, and Marcus began pulling at the slack. Aemon leaned over the ledge and pulled the bow over. The Dwarf kept pulling, and Marcus was amazed at his strength. After another minute of work, the canoe made it up the sheer rocks to level land. Dobervist flipped the large canoe over on its side and collapsed, exhausted by the effort. Stripe ran over and jumped on his lap as the rain started to fall more steadily.

"We need firewood," the Dwarf said. Marcus offered to gather it. Marcus did not have to walk far to find firewood. By the time he was back, Aemon and Dobervist had constructed a crude hemlock bough shelter around the canoe. Aemon quickly got a fire going, and the three of them sat in silence around the small, smokey fire. The rain now began to fall heavily outside. They had not stopped to fish today, and Marcus's stomach growled with hunger. He wondered if the others heard it.

The hours passed by as the rain continued steadily. At some points, it rained so hard, Marcus thought that their crude shelter would collapse, but it held up. The three sat in silence, and despite his hunger, soreness, and emotional stress, Marcus knew better than to complain. He instead thought of his lost friends and of Capa. Life in New City was chaotic. Stabbings, beatings, rape, drunkenness, and thievery were so common at night that City Guard did not even try to stop them. Any time Marcus had tried to save coins, they had been stolen from him. Most of his friends he had grown up with were dead, drunks, or in the Legion. As he lay under the canoe, Marcus knew if he went back to Capa, he would probably never make it out again.

"We need to talk," the Dwarf said. His words were audible above the heavy rainfall. The Capan and the Elf scrambled from under the canoe to join the Dwarf at the smokey fire. They were running out of firewood, and soon the darkness of the night would swallow them whole. The Dwarf leaned over the campfire; his scarred face lit up by the small flames. "With all this rain, we are not going to be able to paddle upriver tomorrow. Maybe for two days, if it keeps raining. I think we should ditch the boat. Start making our way across land. Get some distance from the river."

Aemon nodded, and the thought of leaving the canoe behind saddened Marcus. "We have to talk about our destination, Elf. Who are we meeting up with? Where is he? You mentioned Oakbridge before but are you sure?" the Dwarf said respectfully. The Elf did not answer right away, and silence filled the camp. The Dwarf's question had surprised Marcus, who had assumed that the Dwarf and Elf both knew their destination.

The campfire popped and sizzled when some raindrops hit it. Stripe licked Marcus's hand, and he scratched the dog's ears to calm him. Eventually, the Elf spoke. "Our destination is Oakbridge, but I am not exactly sure where in Oakbridge." The Elf leaned over, closer to the fire. "I am looking for a dear friend of mine. A relative. I must try to bring him back."

Both Dobervist and Marcus could detect the sadness in the Elf's words. Both had numerous questions for the Elf, but neither said anything. The campfire hissed again, and for long moments an anxious silence filled the camp. Dobervist leaned over and threw the last of the firewood on. It would be dark in an hour. The rain kept pouring outside.

"I do not know where my friend is. He is sick, and I must help him. I have heard from other travelers that he was spotted around the old farms just north of Oakbridge," the Elf said. His words washed over his companions, answering some of their questions.

"Who's chasing you, Elf? The Capans?" Dobervist asked. Aemon nodded.

"Every time I try to make it to Oakbridge, I run into the Capan's hunters. I usually lose them after a few days, but they always chase me back into the wilderness. The hunters buy horses when they need them. I cannot outrun them in the open." Dobervist nodded and then gave Marcus a quick look of disgust. Marcus felt disgusted. He had known about the Emperor's hunting parties, but he had never realized they were hunting Elves. He had never seen an Elf in the Arena before. Marcus wondered what the hunting parties did with the Elves.

Silence again filled the campsite, and Marcus wondered what other lies the Emperor had tricked him into believing. Lightning erupted in the distance, and a boom of thunder followed behind it. Dobervist leaned over the campfire again. "Alright then. We will hide the boat in the morning after we cross the river. After breakfast, we will make our way over the ridgeline, make sure the Capans behind us lose track. Then we will head north out of the mountains to Oakbridge. Take us a few weeks longer than paddling, but I will feel safer off the river. I cannot hear anything around the river, and it would be easy to ambush us in the deep water," Dobervist said. The Dwarf looked at Aemon, who nodded in agreement. To his surprise, Dobervist looked at Marcus as if he were wondering if he agreed with his plan. Marcus did not say anything, for the Dwarf's fierce blue eyes unnerved him. "What say you, Marcus. Do you agree with my plan?" the Dwarf asked in his deep voice. Marcus nodded, shocked that the Dwarf had addressed him.

Dobervist smiled when the Capan nodded. He had been skeptical of the boy's loyalty. Dobervist had studied Marcus all day, and after passing Dobervist's test with the canoe earlier, the Dwarf felt certain that the boy was not a Capan spy. He knew he was not a Capan warrior, for Marcus did not have the look of a fighter. He still did not trust him, though. It was not as if the Dwarf had not trusted Capans before. Capans in the Resistance had helped him escape the Arena. Dobervist stared into the dying fire and sighed. He would not trust Marcus until they fought together. If they ended up fighting, Dobervist knew the untrained youth did not stand much of a chance. Dobervist felt like another fight was coming up. Oakbridge was not big enough for a full-time Capan garrison, but patrols often passed through. There were also looters who raided the Mempacton ruins to the north, hold out farmers and a few new settlers. There were also Troll raiding parties that came down from the rugged peaks of the Cloudy Mountains. Dobervist began to settle in for the night. He looked over at the young Capan, who was playing with Stripe again. The Dwarf hoped that Marcus fought bravely and proved himself. He would hate to watch the gentle boy die.

Chapter XXVII- The Shimmering Sea

Mona walked up the narrow wooden stairs from below deck. She stepped up onto the deck then turned to the east. The sun was just beginning to crest the horizon. The sun's rays pushed back the shadows that covered the galley. It was the first sunrise she had seen since she had been taken by the Capans. The sight of it overwhelmed her. Memories of her childhood flashed through her mind. The last sunset she had seen had been with her mother before her capture and eventual execution. Tears formed in her eyes, but Mona quickly wiped them away. She turned as she did, not wanting the silent Koristan oarsmen to see her.

The oarsmen continued their trade, propelling the galley swiftly through the glass-like water of the sea. Mona took a deep breath and exhaled slowly. She felt like it was her first breath of freedom. Dalir walked down from the small bridge where the Captain and helmsmen were steering the galley. He asked how Talar was doing.

"He's sleeping. The ship's doctor said he will wake later today," Mona said briskly. She had become angry upon finding out that Dalir had escaped the High Keep without them. She became even madder when Dalir would not tell her how he had escaped either. That had been hours ago after Talar had collapsed, and now she had regained her composure. Until she got back to Mercium, she would have to be cordial to Dalir, whose ship she was on. Her arms ached from the climb down from the High Keep, and she began to massage them.

"Are you in pain? Should I send for the doctor?" Dalir inquired, but Mona smiled softly and declined his offer. She looked down at her hands. Talar's blood had dried in spots. Dalir saw the blood on her hands and walked away to find soap and water. Talar's wound had been sewn shut by the ship's elderly doctor. The oarsmen had quit rowing to allow the Koristan doctor to work. The doctor had told Mona that the wound would heal quickly. He had given Talar a sleep elixir to prevent him from breaking the fine stitching. The doctor promised that he would check in periodically.

The sun had finally driven the shadows away, and now Mona gazed upon the Shimmering Sea. On both sides of her, there were small islands in the distance. Some of them were grass-covered. Some were just grey rock sticking out from the sea. Further, in the distance, Mona could see a shoreline, and she realized she was looking at the Koristan continent. Dalir returned with a bowl of soap and water. Mona began cleaning Talar's blood off. The pair were silent as the oars hit the water in rhythm. Dalir finally spoke. "I know you think I wronged you by not telling you about my escape plan. It is you who is wrong, though. I could not risk war upon my people just to save you and Talar. My father forbade it, and I understand why he did so."

Dalir's words hung in the air. Mona did not respond. She could tell from Dalir's tone that there was no point in trying to shame him. She admitted to herself that risking open war between Empires just to save Talar and herself was foolish. But she would not admit it to Dalir.

"Why are you here, Dalir? Why did you risk getting captured in the Inner Harbor? The Capans are going to notice your absence. Won't that start a war?" Mona asked while staring out at the distant Koristan shoreline.

"In other times, it would have Mona. Luckily for me, the Capans have already started amassing their Legions for their upcoming invasion of the Dwarf lands. The Capans do not want to fight wars on two fronts. The Emperor will question my father about my absence, and my father will lie to him and tell him I am with illness. He will tell the Emperor that I was sent back to Koristan, and I will travel north with you and Talar," Dalir said without pausing. Mona was overwhelmed by his statement. Silence filled the morning air.

The galley's captain walked down from the raised bridge and approached Mona. He introduced himself formally and commended her for her bravery. Mona smiled in return and thanked the tall, weathered captain for his service. She was still processing Dalir's previous statement and had a hundred questions for him. The captain adjusted his maroon vest, which was standard on the ship, along with baggy white pants that stopped just below the knees. He bowed to Dalir, who bowed in return. The captain shouted encouragement to the oarsmen and returned to the bridge.

"We'll have to get new clothes in Badatoz. I will have the captain send someone ashore for us to find something suitable for the three of us. Weapons too. I imagine Talar will want a long sword, probably a shield as well," Dalir said quickly. "I can't wait to get rid of these awful robes. I should have secured proper attire for us before our escape, but everything happened quickly. We will need a rowboat as well, I would think. To head north up the Cold River. The captain can buy that for us," Dalir said without pausing. Mona was overwhelmed by Dalir's rapid-fire statements, and she waved her hands at Dalir to slow him down. Her anger at Dalir was disappearing as she saw how enthusiastic he was about helping them on their journey north.

"Slow down, Dalir, slow down," Mona said. She turned her back to the Shimmering Sea and looked down the galley. The oarsmen toiled underneath the shade the twin sails offered. "You still haven't answered my question. Why are you here? Why did your father approve your plan?".

Dalir shook his head and leaned against the bulwark. "You honestly do not know, do you? I knew Talar was clueless when it came to politics, but I thought you would know better, Mona," Dalir said evenly. Mona said nothing, so Dalir continued. "The Capans have just secured their northern flank with their defeat over the Riken tribes. Now only the Dwarves and Borisco oppose them on their side of the Shimmering Sea. The Boriscans are divided and weak. The Capans have defeated all their real enemies over the past one hundred years. First Brigantium, then Mempacton, then Mercium, your homeland." Mona was intrigued by Dalir's words. "The Capans depend on war. Their economy revolves around it. They depend on expansion. If the Dwarves fall, where will the Capans turn to?" Dalir said. He had based this lie in truth as his father had instructed him to. Mona remained silent. The tense peace between Koristan and the Capans had existed for her entire life. She had never been schooled in Koristan politics and had not realized how fearful the Koristans were of their northern neighbors.

"They will head to Koristan, Mona. That is where! With all the gold and jewels from the Dwarves, the Capan coffers will be filled. The defeated Rikens will be drafted to create new Legions. The massive galleons they are constructing will transport these Legions to Koristan soil—my homeland. So, I will aid you and Talar. Hopefully, Capa's Legions will be destroyed during the war with the Dwarves," Dalir said angrily. Mona nodded. Dalir's words made sense. She looked up at Dalir and saw the anger in his dark eyes. She felt the same way about the Capans. Neither said anything for a while until Dalir spoke up.

"I bet we ruined the Emperor's day," the Koristan said with a smile, his bright, white teeth contrasting with his skin. Mona threw back her head and laughed. She turned and looked back over the Koristan coastline. The feeling of freedom was starting to build up within her, replacing her anger that the Capans caused.

"Yea, I bet we did," she replied, and both she and Dalir started laughing.

Chapter XXVIII- Death Warrant

The High Court was silent. None of the Capan senators, generals, or admirals present dared to make a noise. The rage seething from the Emperor radiated throughout the room. None dared to speak now. Some of the senators seemed to stop breathing as if that would conceal their presence. Captain Tiberius had just given his report of the Inner Harbor fight. He was still covered in Alwin's blood, and his short sword's sheath had blood trickling down it. Alwin had bit his left cheek deeply as Tiberius had finished him off. Tiberius stood at attention still, not worried about the Emperor. He had personally wounded the Prince of Stonedom and had killed his two guards. He felt that warranted him reprieve from the Emperor's wrath.

The Emperor leaned back on his throne and scratched his chin. His anger was starting to diminish after hearing Tiberius' report. His father had taught him as a child how his anger could lead to his downfall. He took a deep breath and tried to clear his mind. He looked over the High Court, and the Emperor smiled. He had not even said anything, and all the scheming senators and generals around him were shaking with fear. Despite the Prince of Stonedom's escape, the Emperor still instilled fear in both foes and friends.

The Emperor looked to his right, where his father was seated with the other Legion commanders. General Initium met his gaze, nodded slightly, and scanned the room. The Emperor looked back down upon Tiberius, who had assumed his usual position at the bottom of the throne. He was pleased that his personal bodyguard had wounded the Prince of Stonedom and killed his two bodyguards. He would be even happier when the Prince was captured. The Emperor looked over at Lord Volga, who seemed eager for the Emperor's upcoming question. Volga had briefed the Emperor in his private quarters before the High Court started their early morning session. Volga informed the Emperor about the death of Cadoc Stoneking, the rebellion of his eldest son, and Talar's escape. They both had quickly concluded that someone was aiding the young Prince. The Emperor saw that the hulking Lord Volga was enraged at the Prince's escape. He had a wild look in his dark eyes, and his long gray hair was unkempt, which was unusual for Volga. "I'll find them, and when I do..." Volga had muttered after giving his initial report. The Emperor had to ask him who else had escaped before Volga remembered to tell him about Mona. The Emperor was surprised that she had made it down from the Academy's tower without falling. He was even more surprised when Volga told him that the Koristan Ambassador's son was also missing.

"Summon the Koristan Ambassador, Lord Volga. Bring him to me," the Emperor said, and his words seemed to hang above the High Court. Volga instantly turned and motioned to two Keep Guards, who took off running. The tension in the High Court began to build up as all the high-ranking Capans waited for their Emperor to confront the Koristan Ambassador. Rumor had already spread that the Koristan's had provided a ship for the northerner's escape. Others whispered that the Koristan Ambassador's son was missing. If so, the two egregious acts combined could lead to war against Koristan. Many of the high-ranking Capans hoped so. They felt their true enemy was to the south, across the Shimmering Sea. Not to the desolate and barren north, where the Dwarves lived. The Legions were prepared for war in the upcoming spring. The senators and generals now hoped the Emperor would abandon the foolish expedition north and focus on Koristan instead.

The Keeper of the High Court entered through the large golden doors. His robe was a little disheveled due to the early hour. His loud voice carried through the High Court clearly, though. "Hanno, Ambassador of the Koristan Emperor."

All the waiting Capans now looked eagerly at the golden doors before Hanno walked through them. He was wearing the dark magenta robes that all the upper nobles of Koristan wore. Carthos and the other bodyguard flanked Hanno, but Hanno's height and appearance caught all the Capan's attention. Hanno walked down the main entrance toward the Capan Emperor, seemingly unaffected by the ill looks the angry Capans gave him. Hanno strode past the massive columns, his height almost as impressive as the columns themselves. Hanno waved at his bodyguards to linger back as they approached the Emperor. It was a court custom.

Hanno confidently approached the Emperor, who gazed upon him from his perch on the throne. Tiberius gently put up his hand, palm out, as a sign for Hanno to halt. Hanno bowed after he stopped, then looked into the Emperor's eyes. Hanno could feel the anger permeating from the Emperor, and he knew he had to tread lightly. He chose his next words carefully. "I, the Koristan Ambassador, am here to serve you, Emperor. How can I help you at such an early hour?" Hanno's words reverberated through the High Court. The quip about being summoned at such an early hour did not seem to go over well with the Emperor or the rest of the Capans. Hanno did not want to appear weak, so he had decided to add the quip.

The Emperor was in no mood to play verbal games, so he got right to the point. "You were summoned here at this hour to explain your son's absence. So, start explaining...Ambassador," the Emperor ominously said. All the Capans now peered intensely at Hanno, knowing that his response would dictate the future.

"My son, Dalir, has left Capa due to an illness. He told me he visited a Koristan fish vendor yesterday and afterward felt ill. By the time he visited me yesterday, he was quite sick. I ordered a Koristan merchant galley to take him home, to be treated by my personal doctor," Hanno said calmly. The tall Koristan looked around him at the white-robed Capans who seemed to be digesting his story. Hanno looked back up at the Emperor fearlessly, hoping his lie was being believed.

"And when were you going to inform me of your son's departure and of his illness? The disease can spread quickly, and yet, only now am I learning of it," the Emperor replied to Hanno.

"Dalir left yesterday afternoon. I was going to inform you of it today, Emperor. As for my son's illness, I do not believe it is contagious. My guards and I are in good health. My son, however, has always had a weak constitution, and as such, is prone to frequent stomach illnesses," Hanno replied coolly.

The mood in the High Court was mixed. Hanno's ability to keep calm under the Emperor's scrutiny nulled some of their previous convictions of Koristan's aid to the Stonedom Prince. The Emperor looked over at Volga, who seemed skeptical of the Ambassador's story, then over to his father. The youthful General Initium blinked his eyes and nodded calmly, and the Emperor took it as a sign to believe the Ambassador. The Emperor knew his father's judgment was biased, and he remained silent as he thought over the Ambassador's fate. Initium wanted more Elf blood, so risking a war with Koristan did not make sense to him. The Emperor, who did not rely on the Elf blood nearly as much as his elderly father, could not shake the feeling that the Ambassador was lying. It was just too great a coincidence that the Stonedom Prince would escape the same night that the Ambassador's son went ill.

The Emperor looked at Hanno, exhaled sharply, and finally made his decision. "So, you sent your son home over a tummy ache Ambassador?" the Emperor asked. The Capans in the High Court all sneered at their lieges' question. Daylight began filling the High Court through the high windows that ringed the ceiling. Servants began putting out the torches to reduce the heat in the Court.

Hanno smiled at the Emperor's insult. In normal times, an insult such as that could lead to trade embargos and the removal of the Ambassador from Capa. But the Koristan nation was in havoc due to the plague that afflicted the southern part of the continent. Hanno knew any trade interference with Capa now would cause further pain amongst his people. He also had to avoid outright war, but he was beginning to feel that all the Emperor's attention was on the Dwarves. Besides that, Hanno knew for a fact that the Capans still did not have enough warships to invade Koristan properly.

"Yes, Emperor, I did not raise my son to be a warrior, like I was. I knew upon his birth that he was destined to be frail, so I set out to educate him. Luckily, Emperor, I was appointed to Capa, where you allowed his entrance into your prestigious Academy. I hope that once he has recovered from his illness, that you will allow him to return to the Academy," Hanno said before bowing.

The Emperor's upper lip curled upwards after hearing Hanno's words. He covered his mouth with his hand to help conceal his disgust. The Koristan had not taken the bait; the insult to his son should have provoked a stronger response. The Emperor wondered why the Koristan had retreated towards diplomacy so quickly and wondered what was going on in the continent to the south. His navy still had not built enough ships to invade the neighboring shoreline cities of Koristan, but soon they would. The Emperor had a feeling from Hanno's reactions that something internally was conflicting with the Koristans. He made a mental note to instruct Volga to investigate further. For now, the Ambassador would stay in Capa.

"I would like to thank the Ambassador for arriving so promptly this morning," the Emperor said with a jest of his hand. Hanno smiled at the Emperor, then quickly gazed around the High Court. Most of the Capans were disappointed in their Emperor's tone. Still, some of the noble Capans had small smiles peaking from the corners of their mouths. He made a mental note of those favorable to Koristan. "Your son will always be welcome in Capa. He will be allowed to return to the Academy once he is fully healed. Which I hope is soon. We would not want him to miss any more schooling now, isn't that right, Ambassador?" the Emperor asked. Hanno nodded and smiled. The Emperor smiled in return before locking eyes with the Ambassador. Both Men knew the other was up to something.

The Emperor made a sweeping gesture in a kind manner, and Hanno and his bodyguards bowed before taking place amongst the Capan nobles. Hanno was expressionless as he watched the Emperor rise. But inside, he was ecstatic that he had avoided trade and physical conflict with the Capans. If war had broken out now, Dalir's mission would have been pointless.

The Emperor stood in front of his throne and looked out at the nobles assembled before him. "Let it be known, here and now, that the Empire of Capa is at WAR with all the dirty, mangy dogs from Stonedom who declare allegiance with the Stonekings! If a Stonedom citizen remains loyal to my Empire and to me, then they will not be harmed. Their families will not be harmed. Their homes will not be burned...," the Emperor paused now, catching his breath. "...but any Stonedom citizen who joins the Stonekings will be put to the sword. Along with their families and homes!" the Emperor said dramatically before bringing down his fists. The assembled nobles, thankful that their Emperor's wrath was not unleashed upon them, began to yell, and scream. The Emperor let the rage and anger build up amongst the nobles for a few minutes. To Hanno and his bodyguards, the Capans seemed engulfed in bloodlust.

After a few minutes of blood-thirsty screaming, the Emperor raised his hands and restored order to the High Court. An obscenity about a young

Stonedom woman made the Capan nobles laugh and the Emperor smile. Eventually, the nobles settled back down, and the Emperor beckoned at Volga, who stepped forward from the Emperor's side.

"Lord Volga send messenger pigeons to all the Lord Commanders in the east. Instruct them to form search parties for the fugitive Prince of Stonedom and for any who accompany him. Tell them to kill Talar Stoneking and his companions. I will not risk him escaping me twice," the Emperor said before looking down at Hanno. The Koristan Ambassador was not smiling anymore. The nobles cheered at hearing the Prince of Stonedom's death warrant. The Emperor let them go back into a blood-thirsty frenzy. He looked down at Hanno, saw the Ambassador's expression, and smiled. Despite his best efforts to conceal it, he knew the Koristan Ambassador was afraid.

Chapter XXIX- Awake

Talar's eyes fluttered as he dreamed about his escape from Capa. He was sweating profusely and shaking as he re-lived Alwin's death and his chaotic leap onto the Koristan galley. Talar's eyes suddenly snapped open. The dark wooden planks that made up the galley's deck greeted them. Talar craned his neck in confusion. He quickly spotted Mona, who was looking out a circular window. She was dressed in the white robes of the Academy still, and Talar's heart began to race as he feared that Tiberius had captured them. The slight rocking of the ship and the smell of the sea quickly made Talar's fears disappear. He began to push himself up out of the Captain's bed.

Talar's movement caught Mona's attention, and she rushed over to Talar's side. "Don't move Talar, you are still too weak," Mona said before he collapsed back into the bed. He hit the feather mattress, and a sharp pain streaked through his right side. Talar gasped in pain. "You are going to open your stitches up Talar, you must rest for now," Mona said softly before she eased Talar's head back onto the pillow below.

"Are they dead?" Talar asked, his voice dry and raspy. Mona looked into his eyes and nodded. Talar felt sick to his stomach, and Mona thought he was going to wretch. Mona reached for a clay pitcher of water and poured Talar a cup. Talar's hands were shaking when he grasped the cup that Mona had offered. He drank the cool water and began to shake his head over and over. "I can't believe they are both gone, Mona. Alwin was stabbed so many times. He threw himself against me, he gave me time to escape...". Mona took the shaking cup from Talar and set it back upon the small desk by the bed.

"They died saving you, Talar. They died saving us. We would not have escaped without their courage. Without your courage Talar," Mona said softly. Talar had a wild look in his hazel eyes, and Mona was worried that he would re-open his wounds if he went into a rage.

"My courage?", Talar asked. He was shaking his head, and his eyes were beginning to tear up. Alwin had been like an older brother to Talar. Hartwin had been like an uncle. Talar had taken his first boar with Hartwin in the wild forest south of Stonedom when he was just a boy. He had been barely old enough to pull back the bow. Thinking of that hunt made Talar's stomach churn. Talar did not want Mona to see him like this, and he asked her to leave him alone. Mona looked down upon Talar and shook her head at his foolishness. He had risked his life to save her. He had climbed down from one of the highest towers in the world. He had been stabbed. Yet, he was afraid to shed a few tears in front of her. Mona smiled at Talar, leaned over, and gently kissed him upon the lips.

The kiss surprised Talar, but he did not turn away from it. For the moment, his attention was fixed upon Mona as she began to speak quietly. "Take the time to grieve the deaths of your friends Prince of Stonedom. Remember all the good times that you had with them. That is how I got through the death of my mother and father, Talar. Instead of dwelling on their horrible deaths, I picture all the moments that I had with them. I suggest you do the same, Talar." Talar nodded and tried to reach out to grasp Mona's hand, but he found that he was weak. Mona noticed the movement and grasped Talar's hand. "No matter what, Talar, do not blame yourself for Hartwin's and Alwin's deaths. You did not cause their deaths Prince, the Emperor, and his minions did. Never forget that Talar."

Talar began to fill with rage as he realized Mona was right. He had been feeling guilty about their deaths, but now rage began to fill him. Mona saw this and knew that something within Talar had been released. Before the flight from Capa, Talar had strongly disliked his captors. Now he hated Capa. Mona nodded, released Talar's hand, and began to walk around the bed. She did not need a sweet northern Prince. She needed a cold-blooded swordsman to escort her back to Mercium. She wanted Talar in the right mindset before they started heading north. Mona looked like she was going to exit the Captain's small cabin, but she stopped before speaking again. "You must know one more thing, Talar. Dalir is on this ship. He escaped the High Keep by some other route."

Talar's jaw dropped. He could not believe it. Dalir was on the galley! A hundred questions swirled through his head. "How did he escape Mona?". Mona shrugged and told him she did not know. "Why would he risk his life for us? Risk war with Capa?" Mona again shrugged and told him that she did not know. Talar's grief had temporarily disappeared, his mind filled with questions about Dalir's presence on the galley. Mona stood and opened the door to leave, but she turned back and looked at Talar.

"Remember Talar, we are still far from the north. We still need Dalir's help to get back home. Rest easy now, Prince of Stonedom. I will have food and water sent down." Mona shut the door, and Talar was left alone with his thoughts. He thought about the barmaid that Alwin had been courting and how she would mourn his death. He thought about how Cynfor would react. Alwin had been one of Cynfor's close friends, for they were of similar age and had grown up together. Talar thought of his father. He thought of Dalir's escape. He thought of Mona. Mainly he thought of Capa. When he had first glimpsed the massive city, he had been awestruck by it. The massive city was unlike anything he had ever seen. Talar thought of Capa's grandiosity. He thought of Capa's disdain for the Elves and Dwarves. He thought of Calbrius lecturing him about the Paladin, about his beliefs. Talar seethed with rage as he laid helpless in the bed.

He thought of the massive fires that the Druids started on the summer solace. The Druids would construct massive bonfires around the sacred stone pillars on the southern part of Stonedom. The embers would burn for days afterward. Talar laid in the bed, and he thought of Capa on fire, on how massive that fire would be, on how long those embers would burn for. Talar envisioned the streets of Capa burning before he drifted off to sleep.

Chapter XXX- Sailing and Waiting

Dalir awakened to the sound of bells. The bells rang to notify the crew when it was their shift to row. Dalir pulled on the white, baggy short pants that he was becoming fond of and a red vest that was standard attire for the ship's crew. It had been two days since Talar had awakened and three since they had left Capa. Dalir slipped his feet into his sandals, and he left the small cabin room that was adjacent to the Captain's main room where Talar still slept. He ascended the ladder to the deck then was greeted by the cool early morning air. He then walked up to the aft of the gally. In the elevated rear deck, the Captain was conferring with his navigator. Not wanting to interrupt the busy Captain, Dalir instead looked around and took in his surroundings. To the north, he could see the coast of eastern Capa and the fertile plains that fed the Empire. To the south was Koristan, his homeland. Now Dalir turned to the east and smiled as he watched the sun slowly begin to crest the horizon. The sun's brilliant orange and light red rays penetrated the darkness around Dalir. Dalir could feel the sun's warmth already, and he knew it was going to be a warm day.

The Captain started issuing orders, first to adjust the sails, then to the ship's carpenter, and lastly to the head oarsmen. Dalir was staring at both coastlines when the sun rose in the east, and the last shadows of the night disappeared. Mona appeared with two cups of hot tea and handed one to Dalir. Dalir thanked her, and Mona smiled in return. Dalir had been worried about breaking the news to Talar that he had escaped by a different route. Fortunately for Dalir, Mona had told Talar, and from what she said, Talar did not blame Dalir for his actions.

"Is he still asleep, Mona?" Dalir asked quietly, not wanting to disturb the Captain who was back to conferring with his navigator. Mona nodded, and Dalir exhaled loudly. The ship's doctor had assured them that Talar's sleep was normal and that he would awaken soon. Dalir hoped so. The Captain had informed Mona and himself over dinner last night that they would be approaching Badatoz around midday. He had requested a list of weapons, clothes, food, and other supplies that the three northern bound fugitives would need. Dalir had no idea what to expect once they started heading north. He had read about the north and had asked Talar what his homeland was like, but besides that, he did not know what to expect. He did know that once they started north from Badajoz, they could not buy supplies again until Oakbridge. The Captain would want the list before he departed from the ship for Badatoz. He had informed Mona and Dalir that they would be staying in a small Koristan cove across from the main port of Badatoz. After buying supplies and a small oar boat, the trio would begin their journey the following morning.

Dalir motioned for Mona to follow him, and they made their way forward, past the sitting oarsmen to the elevated front deck. It was not crowded here, and Dalir sat down after pulling out the list, and Mona joined him. He presented the list to her, and she began to read it aloud. "One small rowboat. Three pairs of leather boots. Six pairs of wool socks. Two pairs of pants. Two dresses. Four wool shirts. Three heavy cloaks. Three packs. Two swords. One shield. Food." The list ended, and Mona looked up at Dalir and shook her head as if he was a child.

"What?", Dalir asked defensively.

"First, why am I regulated to wearing dresses? We are heading into the wild land of the north. We will be traversing through a wilderness filled with bears, wolves, Trolls, angry Dwarves, and malicious Capans. And you think wearing a dress is a good idea?" Mona asked. She rolled her eyes, and Dalir was taken aback. He mumbled an apology, and Mona just shook her head again. "So, you will have to change your list to six pairs of pants and six wool shirts. You also forgot about blankets, soap, and cooking utensils. What do you mean by food?" Mona asked, and Dalir shrugged his shoulders. "I don't know how much we should bring, Mona. The map I have says it is two hundred leagues to Oakbridge, and I do not want to run short or bring too much. We must paddle UP the river, and I do not want to get caught out in this wild land in the middle of winter. I do not know what food to bring either. I know meat will spoil, and bread will mold. So, I was thinking blocks of cheese, apples, maybe some other fruit if the Captain can find it."

This time Mona did not roll her eyes, for she could tell that Dalir had put some thought in the food that they would need. "Tell the Captain to purchase salted pork, salted beef, and some hard-boiled eggs as well. The salt will help preserve the meat." Mona said. Dalir nodded, heard the cry of a seagull, and looked up as the bird flew overhead. Mona looked down and silently re-read the list. "Three swords, Dalir. Change the list to three swords."

Dalir's head snapped back from the seagull to Mona. "Three swords?" He asked hesitantly. "You think Talar will want two because I only need one," Dalir stated. Mona shook her head in frustration.

"It's for me, Dalir. In case I need it when you two are not around." Dalir began to object, but he saw the fiery look in Mona's eyes.

"I will add it to the list Mona, but we will be there to protect you," Dalir said. Mona smiled, patted Dalir on the hand, and told him that she knew that. Her mother had bodyguards much bigger and stronger than Dalir and Talar, and they had died defending her from the Capans all those years ago. As a child, she remembered those brave bodyguards making similar promises. She would not be fooled again.

"Try to get a sword that isn't too big for me," Mona said before she stood and turned towards the aft. She gazed ahead, and she thought she could see a bit of land along the horizon. The wind blew her hair, but she did not care. She felt good being free. Dalir announced that he was going below deck to amend the list, and he quickly departed, leaving Mona alone. The morning sun had burned away the coolness of the morning, but the wind was steady enough to alleviate the heat. Mona thought about the future trip and her return home to Mercium. Her occupied homeland was close to Oakbridge, which was their destination. She wondered if any of her countrymen remembered her. It had been years since she had been taken captive. Did any Merciums know about her? Did they care? Being locked away in the High Keep had kept her deprived of such information. She wanted to know the truth.

For the next two hours, Mona enjoyed the sun and cooling winds as she thought about the journey ahead and her homeland. She was trying to remember the names of her family's allies, but it had been so many years since she had heard them that she could not remember. Deep in thought, she did not hear the elderly doctor approach. "He has awakened, young Lady," the elderly ship doctor said. Mona turned, thanked the doctor, and began to make her way below deck to the Captain's chamber. On her way to the Captain's chamber, she informed Dalir that Talar was awake. Dalir had finished amending the list, and he brought it along for Talar to inspect. Mona gently opened the door, then peeked inside to see Talar staring out the window. She motioned for Dalir to follow her.

Talar smiled weakly before he shook Dalir's hand. Mona poured Talar a cup of water and asked him if he was hungry. Talar sheepishly nodded, and Mona quickly left the chamber to find the ship's cook. Talar looked back at Dalir, who was holding a piece of parchment. "What do you have there? The list of Women you have slept with," Talar hoarsely whispered to Dalir. Dalir was not sure how Talar would react upon hearing how he had escaped the High Tower, but now all thoughts of conflict between the friends disappeared.

"Not big enough for that tally," Dalir jokingly replied before he took a seat next to Talar's bed. Talar drained the cup of water and clumsily tried to pour himself another. Dalir poured the water instead and gently handed the cup over to Talar.

"What is the parchment for Dalir?" Talar asked, his voice barely audible above the waves hitting the side of the galley.

"It is a list of supplies for us. For our journey north. The Captain will be going into Badatoz tomorrow morning, and we will be leaving tomorrow evening. Would you like to look the list over Talar?" Dalir asked. Talar nodded and began looking over the list. After a few moments, Dalir asked him what he thought of it.

"Your penmanship is remarkable. I scribble like a child compared to your pen marks, Dalir!" Talar stated. Dalir laughed at the joke and was once again relieved that Talar did not harbor ill feelings towards him for not allowing him to escape with him.

"What do you really think, Talar? Mona and I have been waiting for your input all morning already."

"The list is fine; except we are going to need a bow and arrows. Fishing lines and hooks would be a good idea as well. Add on a few pieces of flint for fire-starting, too," Talar replied, and Dalir got up to again change the list. "Leaving me already?" Talar asked, and Dalir shrugged and told him he would be back shortly. Mona returned just as Dalir was leaving and nearly dropped the plates and bowls of food that she was carrying when Dalir bumped into her.

"WATCH IT!" Mona barked, and Dalir jumped back, allowing her to enter the narrow doorway. Talar laughed again, but this time a slight pain jumped up his back, and he clutched his side. Mona rushed over and began loading a big plate of steaming fish, salted potatoes, and fresh bread that was a little burned. The white chunks of fish were covered in a thick white sauce, and after the first bite, Talar began to eat as if he was starving. Dalir and Mona looked at Talar devouring the plate of food, looked at each other, and shook their heads. Talar looked up, smiled, and slowed down his chewing. Dalir left to alter the list, and Mona restocked Talar's plate with more food, this time adding fresh limes and oranges. Talar ate it all.

Talar finished eating, and Dalir entered the Captain's quarters. He took a seat beside Mona. Talar handed the empty plate over to Mona and drained the clay cup of water again. He felt better since consuming the meal and expressed his desire to go above deck to Mona and Dalir. Mona began to object, but when Talar told her that he had never seen Koristan, the debate was settled. Talar began to gingerly pull himself out of bed, and he was surprised at how weak he was. Dalir took Talar's arm and placed it over his head, allowing Talar to gain his footing. Talar and Dalir slowly made their way out of the Captain's quarters, past the other chambers, and up the steep stairs to the top deck. When the pair came up onto the main deck, Talar immediately felt better upon breathing in the fresh sea air. Talar was breathless, so Dalir helped him down on the step separating the main deck from the foredeck. Talar looked around and smiled as his eyes drank in the bluish, green Shimmering Sea. The galley was full of hustle and commotion as the oar rowers worked in unison. The other members of the galley were busy scrubbing the decks and trimming the sails. All the activity in front of Talar allowed him to forget Alwin's, Hartwin's, and his father's deaths. For a moment, a smile crossed his face as he watched the strange actions of the galley crew in front of him.

The ship's doctor slowly made his way across the galley, and he shook his head when he got closer to Talar. The elderly Koristan began speaking in his native tongue before he lifted Talar's arm and inspected the wound. "He says that the stitches have not been broken and that the fresh air will be good for you," Dalir said as the doctor finished his examination. The doctor patted Talar's shoulder and said something to Dalir. Dalir shook the doctor's hand, and the elderly doctor headed below deck.

For the next hour, the three of them lounged around at the front of the ship, joking about Headmaster Calbrius' hubris, Malnar's monotone voice, and Ralphin's pig nose. "You were going to marry him, Mona. I bet you were looking forward to the wedding night," Dalir said jokingly. The joke cost him a punch to the arm and a threat to be cast overboard. All three of them were upbeat now that they were free from the Academy and from the Emperor's henchmen. From time to time, Talar would stare out over the Shimmering Sea, not saying anything to anyone. In these moments, Dalir and Mona knew he was thinking of the loss of Hartwin, Alwin, and his father. Eventually, Mona or Dalir would crack a joke or make a comment about the sea, and Talar would return from his thoughts of the dead brothers and his dead father.

Dalir was pointing out a lone dolphin to Talar and Mona when one of the galley crewmen in the rigging above yelled, "LAND AHEAD." Dalir and Mona immediately spun around, but it took Talar longer to turn, for his side was still sore. Up ahead, far in the distance, the shoreline of the Badatoz peninsula rose from the sea.

The three youths were gazing at the peninsula and did not hear the Captain approach them from behind. His voice startled them. "The tailwind has increased our speed by a few knots. It is not even mid-day."

Although startled and wounded, Talar managed to stand and shake the Captain's hand. He introduced himself and thanked the Captain for his service. The Captain nodded and inquired about his wound and the cook's cooking. Talar told him the wound felt better and that the cook's food had reinvigorated him. "Good, I am glad to hear this. Your quick recovery and this tailwind have altered our plans. Do you think you are ready to start the trip upriver today? I think it would be best if you rowed past the Capan towers along the river at night," the Captain said.

"I do not think I will be able to row without opening my wound, Captain. I am sorry for having to endanger you and your crew for a minute longer than necessary," Talar said, his head slumping in shame. The Koristan Captain shook his head at his foolishness.

"I do not expect you to row, young Lord. I know of your wound; you almost bleed out on my deck. I am amazed you are already up and walking! No, young Lord, I will command one of my oarsmen to accompany you upriver until you are fit enough," the Captain replied.

"This crewman that you plan to send with us will be stranded in a foreign wilderness once I regain my strength. Unless you plan to have him accompany us all the way north to Stonedom? And what of the extra provisions that he will need? We must think this through, Captain," Talar said, shaking his head after he sat back down. The Captain seemed ready to argue with Talar, but Mona spoke up instead.

"How many people do you need to row one of these boats?" she asked the Captain. The Captain answered by raising two fingers from his clenched fist. Mona laughed at the Men's foolishness. "Well, I got two arms. I can row if Dalir is up for it," Mona said before looking at Dalir. Mona's statement had left the Captain and Talar speechless. Dalir, who prided himself on his physique and appearance, simply nodded at Mona, for he too was shocked by her bold manner.

"Well, it is settled then. Dalir and I will row the boat while Talar heals. Dalir, you should give the Captain the list that you have diligently worked on. I think I am going to visit the cook for some of that fish. Thank you, Captain," Mona said before bowing slightly to the Captain. The Captain nodded in return and looked back at Dalir and Talar, who was still seated.

"She is a bold one. Hopefully, her courage does not get her in trouble," the Captain said softly before taking a seat next to Talar. "I have read your list of provisions and will do my best to purchase them at the market before the market closes today. I believe haste is warranted since the Emperor could have alerted the Lord of Badatoz about your escape," the Captain said.

"So, what is your plan, Captain? How do you propose we go upriver unnoticed?" Dalir inquired.

"We will dock right at the main wharf, close to the river's outlet. You two and the bold one downstairs eating will remain below deck, out of sight. My crew will be on guard in case anybody tries to board the ship while I go to the market. By the time I return with the provisions, and we outfit the boat, it will be close to dark. Luck is on your side tonight, young Men," the Captain said softly.

Talar smiled, for the older Captain's confidence gave him some reassurance about traveling unnoticed past the towers of Badatoz. Dalir asked the Captain what he meant about luck being on their side tonight. "The moon is hidden tonight, Dalir. It will be a dark night. The Capans will not be able to see our ship once we leave the light of the harbor. We will row upriver, past the dangerous currents, so that you will be in calm waters once you start off," the Captain said with a smile.

Talar and Dalir looked at the Captain then nodded. They both thought the plan was sound, and they both trusted the Captain with their lives. The Captain told Talar to rest, then turned away to tend to the galley, for the coast of Badatoz was approaching. Mona returned from her meal and rejoined them. Dalir informed her of the Captain's plan, and Mona agreed that it was a good plan.

"So, Mona, I don't want to upset you, but...do you really think you can row up the river? Along with all the provisions. It is not going to be easy," Talar asked cautiously, not wanting to upset her.

Mona coolly looked at Talar, then at Dalir. "I climbed down the Spire by myself. In case you have forgotten. I would like to see Dalir do that," she said briskly. Dalir rolled his eyes and looked at Talar as if telling him to drop the subject. Talar picked up on his body language and instead talked about what lay in store for them during their trip ahead.

"From what I have read in my father's library, the Cold River lazily meanders through the Fertile Crescent. Fort Carillon is upriver, but we will be leaving the river before then. Once we leave the boat, we will have a ten-day trek over the foothills of the Stone Mountains and the Stone Plateau. From there, we enter the river valley of the Capulus, where Oakbridge and the Great Road will take us to Stonedom," Talar said quietly.

"Have you been through this country before Talar?" Dalir asked.

Talar shook his head. "I have hunted in the Stone Mountains, but I have never been in the hills that surround the Cold River," Talar replied calmly. Mona and Dalir looked at each other hesitantly. Neither was comfortable with the thought of traversing the unknown wilderness with just Talar to lead them, but that was the only option. Talar could sense their uneasiness. "Look, there is plenty of game and fish around the river, so we will not starve. I will use the sun and the stars to keep us heading north once we leave the river. We will be in Oakbridge in no time. Probably within a week or so," Talar said calmly.

Dalir exhaled loudly. Mona tried to remember the last time she was in the north. She was young then, but she remembered how cold it was. "What about the cold Talar? What about the snow?" Mona asked. Talar brought his head up slowly before he answered Mona's question.

"We must beat the winter. We must beat the heavy snow and the deep cold. We have four or five weeks before the snow usually comes. Late autumn storms are common though...", Talar trailed off, the fear in his eyes evident to Dalir.

"Talar, you sound worried. We will have the proper clothing, won't we? And look how warm it is now. Why worry?" Dalir asked. Talar looked at Dalir as if he were insane. Mona had a similar look on her face as well.

"Dalir, have you ever seen the snow? Slept outside in the cold? The weather can kill us and will if we do not make it to Stonedom and shelter before winter sets in!" Talar exclaimed. Dalir was shocked at his outburst. Hailing from the much warmer southern continent, the farthest north Dalir had traveled was Capa, which enjoyed the warm breezes from Koristan. He had heard about the snow, read about snow, had seen paintings of snow, but he had never experienced it himself. Now he wondered if he was truly ready for this journey he was about to embark on.

Talar began to apologize, but Dalir waved his apologies away. He had been completely unaware of the danger that the weather would pose, but he was glad Talar had informed him. "How will we cope with the cold Talar?" Dalir asked.

"The foothills of the Stone Mountains are much higher in elevation than the valley of the Capulus. Once we drop down into the valley, we should be warmer. Until then, we have a fire at night when I feel it is not dangerous. Hopefully, the weather stays warm, and we do not encounter any snow," Talar said.

Dalir and Mona both nodded, feeling a little better about their prospects. Both were still nervous about the upcoming trip, though. The galley's crewmen continued to row, and as Badatoz approached, the three turned to look upon the fortress city. The grey stone of Badatoz rose bleakly from the coast. Its' towers and walls were coming into focus as the crewmen rowed away. Talar eagerly gazed upon the famed fortress. Badatoz was the Empire's latest fortress, designed to defend the only waterway to the Emperor's coveted Fertile Crescent.

Talar finally could see Badatoz, and he was immediately impressed at the engineering that had gone into building it. The outer battlement was only a rod from the rocky coast, offering a would-be attacker little ground to fight on. The towers had arrow slits throughout them and had massive ballistae pointed out over the harbor. The town and market seemed to be in between the outer battlement and the inner battlement, which was situated higher up on a hill than the outer battlement. Within the inner battlement, Talar could see a Great Hall and a Keep that rose above the rest of the towers. He shook his head in amazement, for the fortress was comparable to Capa's High Keep. It dwarfed Stonedom's Keep.

"It is impressive, isn't it?" Dalir asked. Mona and Talar shook their heads in silence. "Let us hope we do not see the inside of it," Dalir said softly. The Captain then came and told them that they should head below deck to avoid detection. Talar was able to walk below deck on his own, but by the time he made it to his bed, he was exhausted. Mona had the cook bring him and Dalir plates of food. Both young Men devoured the food. Talar was amazed at how hungry he was despite his earlier meal.

After the meal, time seemed to slow down as the galley rowed into Badatoz's harbor. The three fugitives from Capa could hear voices coming from the wharf from the cabin's lone window. All three tried to hide their anxiety and fear as they waited for the Captain to return from the market. They were back in Capan territory now.

Chapter XXXI- A Late Night Departure

The cool night breeze brought the sound of laughter and singing into the cabin through the open window. Merchants from around the world mingled with farmers, trappers, tree cutters, smiths, and craftsmen. Badatoz's strategic position and security allowed the economic worlds of Capa and Koristan to mingle, setting up a vibrant atmosphere to do business in. The joyous singing from the wharf taverns caused Talar to wake from his slumber. "How long have I been sleeping?" Talar asked, and Mona told him he had been out for a few hours. "I don't even remember going to sleep," he said quietly. Dalir smiled uneasily, for neither he nor Mona had heard anything from the Captain since he had departed the ship hours ago. Talar adjusted the white robe that he had been wearing since the escape from Capa. Neither he nor Mona had changed their robes, and both were longing for new clothes to wear.

Dalir stood up and began to pace back and forth. He was getting worried about the fate of the Captain. He did not know what he would do if the galley was boarded by Capans. He looked at the window and thought that he could squeeze through it. From there, Dalir figured he could hang on to the galley's rudder until the Capans left. Dalir suddenly realized that his plan did not include Mona and Talar. He stopped pacing and looked out the window again. He felt ashamed, but deep inside, he knew that his escape would prevent a Koristan-Capan war and the deaths of thousands.

"What are you looking at, Dalir?" Talar asked. He was feeling much better since his second meal and slumber, and now he was eager to get out of his Capan robes and start the journey north.

Dalir shook his head and was about to speak when a flurry of commotion erupted above deck. The three could hear orders being shouted and footsteps. Besides that, they were clueless as to what was happening above them. Dalir's heart began to race, and he looked again at the window when suddenly the door to the chamber burst open. It was the Captain! With a wide grin on his face and an armful of wool clothes, the Captain strode into his quarters. Mona, Dalir, and Talar immediately began asking him questions. The Captain tried to answer all their questions but did not manage to answer any of them. Before they knew it, the Captain was gone, and the wool clothes were in their hands. They heard the oars hit the water, and the galley was soon moving.

The familiar sound of the oars rhythmically hitting the water made all three of them smile and hug each other. "I am going above deck to check out this boat and our other provisions," Dalir said. Mona said that she was going to the other chamber to change out of the Capan robes, and Talar looked eager to change as well.

A half-hour later, Mona, Dalir, and Talar stood on the deck of the galley. They were going through the supplies that the Captain had obtained for them. All the supplies were lying in the middle of the flat-bottomed skiff. The skiff was outfitted with two sets of wooden oars and took up a large portion of the galley's deck. Dalir was looking over the beautiful hand-crafted ash bow and the bristling quiver of arrows that the Captain had purchased. Mona was checking over the salted meats and getting used to the brown pants that she had exchanged with her robes. Talar sat on the deck, his back resting against the galley's wooden rail. His eyes were fixated on a long broadsword that sat in the skiff. The broadsword was resting against a wooden shield with a metal boss in its center. The sword had a small circular pommel with a matching circular iron guard. A leather sheath covered the wide blade. The blade was shorter than what Talar would have desired, but he could not complain about it. The sword was well made. What made the sword unique was the copper wire that was wrapped around the grip of the sword, giving the sword's grip a red hue.

Talar stared at the sword knowing that one day he would have to wield it against the Capans. He wondered how he would act standing in front of the hordes of Legionnaires as he defended Thendara. He hoped that he would be as brave as Alwin and Hartwin. Thinking of their brutal deaths made Talar's stomach turn, but he forced himself to keep looking at the sword. The upcoming battle of Thendara was all Talar could think about. He did not know how the Men of Stonedom, and the Dwarves would stand up to the might of Capa. Talar then realized that if he and Cynfor lost at Thendara, then his people would be wiped out. His family name would become forgotten, along with the culture it ruled over. Talar realized this and knew that only the Gods could prevent the destruction of his people, the Dwarves, and the Elves.

Dalir walked in front of Talar, disrupting his thoughts about the future. "How does everything look, Dalir?" Talar asked. His wound prevented him from inspecting the boat and the supplies, but he trusted the Captain's judgment.

"Everything is in good order, Talar. Do not worry. The skiff looks well built. I am excited, Talar! The north awaits!" Dalir exclaimed. He had been in Capa for five years, and he was elated to finally see some of the vast northern continents.

Talar laughed at Dalir's excitement, and Dalir's enthusiasm broke through Talar's somberness. "How long before the sun rises? Dalir inquired.

"Just a few hours. That should give us time to get away from here," Talar said. The Captain appeared and informed them that they would be sitting the skiff in the water soon. That meant that they were already in the mouth of the river. The oarsmen brought in their oars, and Talar tried to feel if the current was moving them. He could not feel a current nor any waves. He looked overboard, but he could not see anything. The clouds still hid the moon. Four crewmen then lifted the skiff and lowered it overboard. A wide rope ladder was secured to the railing of the galley. The crewmen turned and looked anxiously at Mona, Dalir, and Talar. Their simple lives had been turned around by the three of them, and now they yearned to go back to their normal routines. Nonetheless, they all smiled, for they were all proud to have served their country. The crew's smiles were illuminated by the small oil lamps that dangled from the two masts.

Mona did not need any other indications. She had been waiting for this moment for years. Mona turned and shook the Captain's hand. Then she gave the Captain a kiss on his cheek for his bravery, twirled around, and bowed to the crewmen before she walked towards the rope ladder. The crewmen tried to stifle their laughter when they saw the Captain's bewildered face. They bowed in return to Mona in dramatic fashion. Mona deftly leaped on top of the rail and began climbing down. Within seconds she was out sight. Dalir now turned and walked towards the Captain, whose face still showed his shock at Mona's kiss. "Thank you for your service. How much do I owe you for the skiff and the supplies?" Dalir asked as he fumbled for his pouch of gold coins.

The Captain shook his head. "I am sure your father will repay me generously, Dalir. Stay safe on your travels," the Captain said before he shook Dalir's hand. Dalir thanked the Captain then he walked over to the railing. Dalir looked over but could not see anything. A sudden burst of fear struck Dalir, but with all his countrymen looking at him, he managed to pull through it, and hoist his leg over the rail. He gave the Captain and Talar an uneasy smile and began climbing down into the darkness below.

Talar walked carefully over to the Captain. He was still sore from his wound, but he was feeling remarkably better. "Give my thanks again to your doctor. Thank you, Captain, for your bravery and honesty. You saved our lives," Talar said.

The Captain nodded and shook his hand. "Let me assist you over the rail. You do not want to re-injure yourself now," the Captain said. Talar nodded, and as he walked across the wooden deck of the galley for the last time, he thought of everything that had happened to him since he had left his home. Before the hunt, he had thought that nothing bad could happen to him. He had heard and read about bad things happening to other people and other families. For some reason, he did not think that they could happen to him. Now, Talar stood in front of the railing, peering into the darkness below with a sword wound in his side and dead friends left behind. The harsh realities of the world had nearly killed him.

Talar began to try to raise his leg over the rail, but he felt strong hands lift him up instead. He grasped the rail as he stood precariously over the water below. He looked over at the galley, the crewmen, and the Captain for the last time. "Fight well, Prince of Stonedom. They cannot take your honor nor your pride," the Captain said. Talar nodded, but he did not have time to think of the words' meaning, for his focus lay upon getting into the skiff below. Talar gingerly climbed down the rope ladder. Pain shot up through his right side. Swearing softly, Talar kept climbing down until his feet hit the side of the skiff.

"Help him in Dalir," Mona instructed from the front of the skiff. She had leaped in and taken the position in the front, her hands on the oars, ready to take off from the galley. Dalir's hands grasped Talar's waist, and Talar swore again as the pain jolted through him. Dalir guided Talar into the skiff, and both collapsed upon the heap of supplies in the middle of the skiff. The skiff buoyed alarmingly, but Mona steadied the small vessel with her oars. "Carefully get into the back, Dalir. Carefully! And stay low!" Mona ordered, and Dalir complied.

"Untie the mooring ropes and cast off. Good Luck, you three. Good Luck!" the Captain ordered from above. The excitement and near darkness made Dalir and Mona's fingers tremble, but they both managed to undo the crewmen's knots. They both threw the lines off, and using their right arms, pushed off from the galley. Dalir could see the three golden fish that were painted on the galley's side slowly disappear in the darkness.

"Are you ready, Dalir?" Mona asked, and when he answered yes, the two of them began rowing. The water was smooth, and the skiff quickly headed away from the lights of the galley. After a few minutes, the galley's lights were gone, and the three of them were left alone in the darkness. "How are you feeling, Talar?" Mona asked. She had heard Talar swear on his way into the skiff and was worried about his wound. Talar told her that he was fine. The pain had subsided once he had settled down in the middle of the skiff.

Talar thought of the Captain's last words to him. The words reaffirmed Talar's belief that he could not escape the wrath of Capa. His decision now was how to live with this new reality. He thought back to the night that Hartwin and Alwin died, and he remembered how scared he had been. Despite this, he realized that he had acted well, had done what Hartwin had ordered, and had survived the fight. He had overcome his fear that night. Talar used the silence to prepare himself for the next time he would have to fight the fear back. The oars hitting the water and his companion's breathing were all Talar could hear. From behind him, in the darkness, Dalir spoke up. "We are on our own now," Dalir stated, and Talar knew his new friend was right.

Chapter XXXII-Upriver

Mona's arms were starting to burn, but she vowed to keep rowing until Dalir asked to stop. The sun was just starting to crest the horizon. The darkness was fading slowly, and Mona looked around uneasily. Rowing blindly in the dark had been unsettling to her. The water was cold, and the river was wide. Mona squinted, and through the fading darkness, she could see the banks of the river. They were paddling in the middle of the river, where the current was strongest. "We should head to the side of the river. The current is not as strong there," Mona said softly. Dalir voiced his agreement from the back. Mona and Dalir steered the skiff towards the shoreline. Dalir asked if she wanted to take a break.

"If you want to stop Dalir, we can stop," Mona said. Her arms and shoulders were burning.

"Yes, I could use a break," Dalir replied. "We can take a break up ahead," Dalir stated. Mona looked ahead and spotted a small pool off the main river.

They pulled the skiff in the pool, and Dalir exited first. He began pulling the skiff to the sand bar. He was still wearing the short white pants he had borrowed from the galley sailors, so he did not get too wet. Mona stood and exited the skiff. She turned and looked down on Talar, who was fast asleep.

"It's good for him to get some rest, Mona. He needs it," Dalir said. Mona nodded and informed Dalir that she thought it would be easier going for them now that they could see. Dalir nodded in agreement. The sun's first rays brought the chatter of songbirds into the willows behind them.

"Yea, I think you are right, Mona. Look how strong the current is in the middle of the river compared to where we are now," Dalir said optimistically. His words and the bird's lullabies caused Talar to awaken.

Talar wiped the sleep from his eyes and looked backward at Mona and Dalir. The two grinned at his awkwardness, for he was wedged between the provisions and the bench that Mona had sat on. Talar tried to stand, but his feet were asleep, and his side was still sore. Once he gained his footing, he staggered out of the skiff. He joined Dalir and Mona, who had taken seats on the sandbar. The three gazed out at the river as the sun continued its morning ascent. Badatoz was out of sight, and Talar realized he could not smell the sea anymore.

"We did it. We escaped," Mona said. She fell back laughing while reaching her arms out to the sky. "We are free!" she exclaimed, and her lively spirit washed over the other two beside her. Dalir looked down upon her and smiled. He then stood up and started skipping stones in the river. Talar spotted a slender tree limb on the bank behind him and thought that it would be good for fishing. He tried to stand, but Mona grasped his arm before he could. "Thank you, Talar. You risked everything for me. Now I am free," she exclaimed. Talar looked into Mona's eyes, and for a second, he thought she might kiss him. Instead, she patted his arm and smiled. A little disappointed, Talar stood and retrieved the fishing stick he had spotted. The wound in his side was sore, but it was not emitting the shooting pain like before.

The three agreed that it was time to go. Dalir motioned for Talar to enter the skiff first. Mona followed, and Dalir deftly jumped in after pushing off. They made good time along the bank of the river, and after a little while, Mona and Dalir fell into a comfortable rhythm. Talar felt bad for just sitting there in the middle of the skiff. He found the line and hooks from the sack of provisions, and he fashioned a crude fishing rod with them. With no bait, he could not use it, however.

With not much else to do, Talar took in his surroundings. The riverbank that they were closest to him stood at least half a rod above him. Blue and orange kingfishers flew into the small holes that they had previously burrowed in the side of the riverbank above the water. Small groves of trees littered both riverbanks. The autumn sun was just starting to turn their lush, green leaves yellow and red. The massive branches of ancient silver maples and willow trees draped across the sides of the river, providing some respite from the sun. The skiff continued upriver, and in between the groves of trees, Talar could spot vast fields of wheat and barley. The fields stretched as far as Talar could see.

Occasionally a stone mansion with small barns around it would come into view. These were the homes of the rich Capan landowners. The stone mansions were surrounded by fig plantations and orchards of apple, peach, plum, cherry, and pear trees. Workers frantically toiled in the hot sun as the farm bosses overlooked from the shade. Laborers stacked ox pulled wagons high with the autumn harvest.

By midday, Dalir and Mona desperately needed a break. They pulled the skiff into a shallow pool that was underneath a massive willow tree. Mona tied the skiff to one of the tree's exposed roots and then collapsed on the rocky beach below her. Dalir joined her, and it was up to Talar to dig up food for lunch. He found some of the salted beef and a few apples and distributed it amongst the others. The three of them ate quickly. Dalir suggested they rest until the hot noonday sun passed over. Mona, whose shoulders were aching, quickly agreed. Talar volunteered to take watch so Mona and Dalir could rest.

A few hours later, Mona and Dalir awakened, and they started upriver once again. The afternoon passed quickly, and they made good progress. Talar had found a few worms at their last stop, and he lazily cast the line into the water. A golden eagle soared above them briefly for a moment, but besides that, the afternoon passed without incident. The sun began to sink below the horizon, and Talar suggested that they find a place to sleep for the night. There were no spots ahead, so they kept rowing. Luckily, Mona spotted a secluded glen off a side channel. They wearily pulled the skiff up onto the ground. Dalir handed out some of the salted pork, and the three ate and prepared for sleep. It was a brisk, clear night but not cold enough to warrant a fire. The three did not talk much, for they had been up before the dawn and were exhausted from rowing all day. Sleep overtook them soon.

The next three days passed, as the first day of their trip. The trio awakened early, ate quickly, and rowed for much of the day. Talar was becoming increasingly bored, but Mona forbade him from rowing. The only thing that changed was the scenery. The vast flat plains of the Fertile Crescent were slowly being replaced by the round foothills of the great Stone Mountains. The current was also increasing. Talar assured Dalir and Mona over lunch that this was the last day of rowing.

"How will we know when to leave the river Talar? I cannot wait to stop rowing. I feel like my arms are going to fall off!" Dalir exclaimed. His complaints caused Mona and Talar to laugh. After hiding his smile, Talar informed Dalir that they would leave the Cold River once they spotted Deaf Falls. "Deaf Falls? Why do they call it that?" Dalir asked.

"My father told me it was because only a deaf person would not be able to hear it. I have never seen it before. I am looking forward to it, though. Being stuck in this boat with the two of you is the most bored I have ever been!" Talar exclaimed.

Mona was about to agree with Talar when she spotted movement in the distance. They had not seen anyone besides the workers in the fields for the past four days. Now on the opposite side of the river, a fleet of barges emerged from around a bend in the river. The square, flat-bottomed barges were loaded high with bales of wheat, barley, and bushels of fruit. Dirty, bare-chested laborers pushed the barges downstream with long wooden poles. A burly, bald Capan farm boss stood in the leading barge and was glaring menacingly at them. He wore a short white robe in the Capan style, and the trio's presence seemed to upset him.

"What's his problem?" Dalir asked. To the Koristan, the Capan seemed to be staring right at him.

"He probably doesn't like Koristans, or he is jealous that we are with Mona, and he is not!" Talar replied. All three of them laughed as the sour Capan floated harmlessly by. A little while later, they passed the stone dock where the flotilla of barges had departed. Talar spied another Capan farm mansion on a knoll overlooking the river. They kept paddling, but the river's current was getting stronger.

It was late in the afternoon when Dalir and Mona were both about to give up for the day. The current was consistently strong now, and progress had slowed considerably. Mona was going to suggest that they call it a day when she heard a low rumbling noise in the distance. Mona looked behind her at Talar, who was motioning for her to keep rowing. The skiff rounded a bend in the river, and all three smiled in amazement at the sight ahead.

Deaf Falls crashed into the Cold River on the river's left side. The Falls was at least a Capan city block wide and fell at least four rods into massive boulders. The trio stared in amazement at the waterfall and felt the sound of the rumbling deep within them. Out of the three of them, Dalir was the most amazed at the waterfall. Having lived in one large city or another for his entire life, the city dwelling Dalir was enthralled by the natural beauty that lay before him. The thundering of the falls drowned out all the other thoughts in Dalir's head. He gazed in wonderment as the white water fell gracefully over the drop. Talar waved his hand to get his attention and motioned for them to continue.

They rowed on past the falls. The falls' massive swirling eddy, which was filled with driftwood, logs, and heaps of yellow foam, passed by them. Once they got past the overwhelming noise of the waterfall, they pulled over to the left side of the bank. They managed to awkwardly scramble out of the skiff, and Dalir secured it to a skinny willow tree. "It is magnificent, Talar!" Dalir said loudly, for the waterfall was still audible. Talar nodded, and he motioned for them to huddle together so that they could hear each other better.

"I think we should get the skiff into the woods and hide it. Then we can set up camp for the night," Talar said before looking into Mona and Dalir's face to see if they agreed. They nodded at the navigator of the trip. Dalir began hoisting the skiff by its' lead rope up onto the bank. Mona assisted, and soon the skiff was up on top of the riverbank. Talar began unloading the skiff, and the other two followed his lead. Talar reached down into the skiff and pulled out the broadsword. It was the first time he had handled it. They continued to unload the provisions until the skiff was empty, then they hid it underneath some brush further into the woods. They walked back to their supplies and began to settle in for the night.

A cool breeze blew up from the waterfalls. Talar began to build a campfire ring. He found the flint in one of the provision sacks and quickly made a fire out of the abundant kindling that surrounded them. The trio gathered around the small fire and began to prepare dinner. They were steadily consuming their supply of salted beef and salted pork. Talar began to fashion snares for rabbits with rope from the skiff. Dalir watched curiously, for he had never trapped or hunted before. After creating the snare, Talar motioned for Dalir to follow him. The two young Men left for the woods beyond the campsite. Talar quickly found a game trail, and Dalir studied how he set the trap. Talar slapped Dalir on the back after he set the snares, and they went back to the fire. The night was quickly approaching, and the sounds of crickets filled the air. Dalir and Talar came out of the woods and settled down by Mona. She was tending the fire and cooking some of the salted pork and beef up. They had eaten most of the fruit and bread already and were down to meat, hard-boiled eggs, and water.

Talar informed Mona that he had set the traps and that he would fish tomorrow around the waterfall. Nodding in relief, Mona took a deep breath and went back to cooking dinner. She was famished from rowing all day. She finished cooking the food, and they all ate vigorously afterward. Mona began preparing her bed for the night, and Talar was going to do the same when Dalir spoke.

"Now that we are leaving the river, do you think we will encounter any Trolls or Goblins?" Dalir asked.

Talar shook his head. "We are too far south. Goblins and Trolls do not venture south of the Stone Mountains. I am more worried about bears and Dwarves," Talar replied.

Dalir's eyes shot up at this, and he looked down at the sword that the Captain had purchased for him. It was a scimitar which was the weapon of Koristan's cavalry. Dalir felt reassured that he was armed with a familiar weapon in case some wild beast tried to attack him. His lack of knowledge about his surroundings intrigued him and frustrated him at the same time. The night's darkness surrounded them, and Dalir figured he should start working on the task that his father had given him.

Dalir stood up and carefully made his way through the darkness to where the supplies were piled up. He had made sure that the other two had not spotted the three bottles of wine that he had told the Captain to purchase for him. His hands found their way around the bottles, and he hauled his prizes up towards the campfire.

"Look what I got!", Dalir said loudly while holding a bottle in the air. Talar laughed, and Mona shook her head, but soon all three were drinking. The fire roared in front of them and illuminated the Cold River for them to gaze out. Talar drank deeply and stared up at the bright stars of the night. A wave of emotions and thoughts washed over him, and he looked back at the fire, then at his companions. He thought of Hartwin and Alwin and how he would break the news of their deaths to his brother. He thought of Stonedom and his father. He wished to speak to his quiet, tempered father now, but he knew that it was impossible now. He thought of the Capan legions and the upcoming war.

"What else might we encounter once we start off tomorrow?" Dalir asked Talar. The question brought Talar's attention back to the campfire and his friends. Talar shook his head and took a swallow from the bottle of wine. The heat from the fire was intense, so Talar moved back until he could rest against a giant cottonwood. Dalir was still looking at Talar liked he expected an answer.

"I do not know Dalir. Hopefully, something we can eat," Talar said with a coy look on his face. Mona laughed at the joke, and finally, Dalir did too. Dalir thought carefully about how to phrase his next question.

"What if we come across an Elf? The Capans have told me that they are evil and are like witches," Dalir said slowly. Talar looked down and then shook his head. He slowly brought his head up and stared at Dalir with an intense look in his eyes.

"Do you believe the Capans Dalir?" Talar asked dryly.

Dalir shook his head and took a long swallow from the bottle in his hand. "I'm just asking in case we run into one Talar," Dalir said evenly, not trying to upset the temperamental Prince. Talar nodded and saluted Dalir with his bottle. He took another swallow from the bottle and looked at Dalir.

"The Capans hunt the Elves, so I doubt one will stop to talk to us since we are Men," Talar said. Dalir nodded. Talar's words reaffirmed what his father had told him. Now Dalir needed Talar to tell him the exact location of the Elves so he could talk one into traveling back to Koristan. The plague was sweeping through Koristan, leaving the country weak and exposed to Capa. Hanno had instructed Dalir to find an Elf and persuade the Elf to travel to Koristan to help his people. Dalir did not know why his father believed in Elves. At the time, he was glad to agree to his father's plan so that he could render aid to Talar and Mona.

Dalir stood and approached the fire. He stared into the flames until Talar spoke. Talar felt bad about being coarse with Dalir. "The Elves live just outside of Thendara. They have retreated from their sacred groves. Now only in the far north, on the other side of the lake, can you find those who can heal all…" Talar's voice trailed off.

Dalir's jaw dropped, and he looked at Mona and Talar to see if they had noticed. Neither had! Dalir felt like he had struck gold and guzzled more of his wine down before sitting back down. Mona took a sip from her bottle and gazed at Talar. "Do you really believe those old legends, Talar? About the Elves and the Paladin of Mempacton? About his silver horn? Healing the blind and living forever? I was told those legends when I was young, too Talar. I quit believing them long ago," Mona said.

"I believe in them, Mona. Everyone in my family and in Stonedom believes it. The Druids taught me to believe in them. Alwin and Hartwin believed in them when they died," Talar said. Silence fell upon the camp except for the crackling of the fire.

"Then where is this immortal Paladin Talar? In the stories, I was told he was to protect the Elves forever. Yet now, only you and the Dwarves are going to fight. Have you ever seen an Elf, Talar? Have you ever seen one heal anybody?" Mona asked. Her questions cut through the night's silence. Dalir was surprised by her tone towards Talar, but he was eager to hear the Prince's answer.

"I do not need to see something to believe in it, Mona. The fact that you have lost your belief in the teachings of your ancestors is sad to me. It is sad to see that Capa has changed you," Talar said before looking at Mona with pity.

Mona just shook her head in disagreement, not wanting to push the issue and upset Talar. Mona offered Dalir her bottle, which was still mostly filled. Happy with the information he had gleaned from Talar, and with the extra wine from Mona, Dalir took the bottle and jumped over Mona to be closer to Talar. Mona shook her head in frustration with her two younger companions, and she prepared for sleep.

Talar and Dalir continued to drink until the fire's embers were barely glowing. They drank their own bottles first, then took turns drinking from Mona's. With the last bit of wine in the bottle, Dalir motioned towards Mona, who had been asleep for hours. "You two should be together, Talar. You argue like an old Man and his wife!" Dalir whispered giddily.

Talar slowly shook his head. "I would gladly marry Mona if she would have me Dalir. It is not destined to be, though. The Legions of Capa await my brother and me now," Talar said resolutely. Dalir could not argue with Talar's logic. He could sense the somber mood that his remark had caused and tried to cheer Talar up.

"The Dwarves have a legendary fortress. Even I have heard about it, Talar. You and your brother will fight the Capans from there. I am sure you will be victorious, Talar," Dalir said optimistically. The northern Prince just shook his head.

"We are badly outnumbered, Dalir. The Capans will come in the tens of thousands. We will be crushed, and everything I know and believe in will be lost," Talar despaired. The wine and his future struggles had made him sullen.

Dalir did not know what to say, so he handed his remaining wine to Talar. "Well, I still think you should be with her. You two have been through a lot together. It is meant to be," Dalir stated before he stood and prepared for sleep. The light from the fire was fading quickly, and Talar drank the last of the wine up.

Talar rubbed his face with his hand and looked up at Dalir. "Mona will change her name and cut her hair once we get into Oakbridge. Then she is off to Mercium to live with some Mercium lord. Which is good, Dalir. She deserves better than to be a widow. Dalir, I do not believe I will be alive by this time next year. I am preparing myself for this. There is no need to bring Mona into my war," Talar said. Dalir thought for a minute and then told Talar that they would discuss it tomorrow. They both found level spots around the dying fire and went to sleep.

Mona wiped the tears from her eyes once she heard her companions sleeping soundly. She had been awake during their conversation and had heard everything. Mona stared up at the stars and thought of Talar's words. She knew she had a decision to make once they reached Oakbridge.

Chapter XXXIII- The Searchers

Marcus woke up shivering. The field he had slept in was covered in a thick frost. Aemon was already awake and was tending the fire. Dobervist was still asleep with Stripe sprawled out beside him. Marcus brushed off the green wool tunic that Aemon had bought him. They had bartered with a traveling merchant outside of Oakbridge after coming down into the Capulus Valley. That had been two weeks ago.

Marcus's movement caused Stripe to wake up, which caused Dobervist to wake up. Cursing the cold, the Dwarf stood and joined Marcus and Aemon around their small campfire. The Elf had foraged earlier and returned with an armful of apples and large orange mushrooms. Dobervist looked at the mushrooms doubtfully.

"They taste like chicken. Or so I have been told," Aemon said before taking a bite out of the large mushroom. Dobervist nodded and followed suit. He looked around and scanned his surroundings. The overgrown field had long ago been abandoned by the Mempacton farmers who had worked the land. Now the once productive field was overgrown with thorn bushes, short bushy pine trees, and tall native grasses. Behind him was a tree-lined hedgerow. The Dwarf did not see anything and finished his morning meal.

Dobervist wiped his beard clean. "Do we continue our search for your friend? Or do we do the sensible thing and get you up to Thendara before winter sets in?" Dobervist asked quietly. He did not want to give away their position.

Aemon was already stomping out the small fire. He shook his head in frustration. "We must keep searching for now. Once it snows, though, we will head to Stonedom. We cannot risk being caught out here in cold winter with no proper shelter," Aemon said. Marcus looked relieved. The young Man from Capa had never been so cold in his life. He was grateful that Aemon had purchased him the green tunic. Marcus could not imagine it getting any colder, but apparently, it would.

The three took off again, bushwhacking through the overgrown and abandoned farms that had once supported the vast population of Mempacton. The small rolling hills were bucolic, especially with the trees turning colors and the Stone Mountains jutting up in the distant horizon. The difficulty in walking around varied. Sometimes, Dobervist had to break through the dense thorn bushes with a large stick he had found. Other times they found old farm lanes and animal paths to walk upon. Run-down farmhouses and collapsed stone barns were common. The evidence of their previous inhabitants was apparent. Busted wagons, rusty scythes, and hammers, and rotting pitchforks dotted the landscape. To Marcus, it seemed like everybody just decided to pack up and leave at once.

Two weeks ago, when they had climbed down from the Stone Mountain Plateau, Aemon had told them that the friend he was looking for rode a tall, black horse and had black hair and blue eyes. Besides that, he had not given any more of a description. Marcus figured it did not matter since they had only seen the one merchant in all their travels around the area.

They walked off the top of the hill and started walking through a hillside apple orchard. The apple trees had been left unattended and had spread. The walking looked difficult, so they started to go around the overgrown orchard. Stripe spotted a rabbit and took off after it but quickly returned after losing sight of the rabbit. They now descended off the hill towards a bubbling, stony creek below.

Stripe lapped at the water, and Marcus and Dobervist began filling their waterskins. The Elf cleaned his hands and face with the cold water and scratched Stripe's ears. Aemon spotted an old farmhouse with only one wall standing and suggested they head in that direction. Dobervist just nodded and took the lead again, heading out of the gulley. The Dwarf had thought that this search was futile from the start, and the last two weeks had only confirmed his belief. Marcus was content to serve and assist the Elf, and he enjoyed seeing the red, yellow, and orange leaves erupt in color all around him.

They walked through a wet meadow that was chocked with dying dandelions. The sun was starting to burn off the morning's frost. They arrived at the one-walled farmhouse. A barn owl flew out of the structure, startling Dobervist, who shook his head. There was nothing around except an iron wheel from an ox cart. Marcus picked up the wheel and started to play with it, which drew Stripe's attention. Over the past few weeks, the dog had become fast friends with Marcus. Their friendship had at first angered Dobervist. After seeing how Marcus cared for Stripe, the Dwarf quit being so harsh with the Capan.

The Dwarf now shook his head and spat on the ground. He was getting tired of gallivanting around the hills of Oakbridge. So far, they had gotten lucky. No Trolls or Capans had been spotted. The Dwarf looked at Marcus and rolled his eyes. He whistled, and Stripe ran over obediently, leaving Marcus alone with the metal wheel. Dobervist walked over and leaned his bow against the farmhouse's lone wall. He did not think it wise to wait until the snow arrived to start their trek to Stonedom.

"What is so important about finding this Man? Why do we waste our time and risk our lives, Elf? I have been patient with you over the past two weeks. I will not look further until you explain why we should keep looking," Dobervist said quietly.

Marcus dropped the wheel. From Dobervist's tone and the look on his face, Marcus figured he was serious. Marcus was worried. They relied on the Dwarf for protection. Aemon solemnly shook his head and walked over to where the Dwarf stood. Marcus and Stripe followed behind.

"We are not looking for a Man. We are looking for one of my family members. He became lost long ago, and I have been searching for him for many years. He is needed now. Now more than ever..." the Elf trailed off.

Dobervist looked at Aemon as if he had spoken a riddle. The Dwarf blinked, shook his head, and asked Marcus if he understood what the enigmatic Elf had said. Marcus just shrugged his shoulders, and the Dwarf threw his hands up in frustration.

"Speak plain, Elf. How can a Man be related to an Elf? And years? You have been looking for this Man for years? How many years have you been looking for him?" the Dwarf asked, becoming impatient with the Elf.

"Seventy years. I have been searching for him for seventy years," the Elf said. Marcus' and Dobervist's jaws dropped. Seventy years! Marcus could not believe it. Seventy years was longer than most Capans' lifespans! Marcus just looked at the Elf in amazement. The fact that the Elf was immortal was just starting to sink into the young Man from Capa.

Dobervist was dumbfounded. Seventy years! The Dwarf was about to ask another question when he spotted movement in the gulley that they had just left. Whatever it was was large and was now motionless. Dobervist's heart began to beat. He squinted, but his eyes could not pierce through the bright foliage of the small trees and honeysuckle. He did not think that it was an animal, for they had just passed through the area. The Dwarf did not hesitate.

"Do not look. We are being followed. Do not look around," the Dwarf said in a matter-of-fact tone. Aemon's and Marcus's jaw dropped. Neither looked around, though, and the Dwarf was grateful for that. It gave him a few moments to see if there were any other trackers around them. The Dwarf now felt like he was being watched. Years and years of being alone in the wilderness had honed his primal instincts. Marcus's hand was shaking with fear, and Dobervist ordered him to pet Stripe. "Just act normal for now, lad," the Dwarf said while looking down at Marcus. The Dwarf's calmness was helping Marcus from being overwhelmed with fear. The Elf began to speak, but Dobervist's eyes made him go quiet. The Dwarf needed silence to see if there were others out there. He put his right arm out against the farmhouse's remaining wall and acted like he was stretching. Twisting his back slowly, the Dwarf carefully scanned the brushy field before them. Anything could be lurking behind one of the tall bushes, and the Dwarf would never know. The Dwarf did not see anything in the brushy field before them, and now he turned back to where he first saw movement. As Dobervist scanned the gully and the tree line, he spotted a hulking figure, who quickly hid behind a tree. Dobervist's heart pumped even faster.

The Elf could sense the Dwarf's consternation. He calmly walked over and leaned against the wall as well, as if nothing were out of the ordinary. "What is it, Dwarf? What do you see?" the Elf asked, trying to act normal. Marcus' hands were shaking hard now, his memories of his friend's horrible deaths coming back now, like never before. He held Stripe, who licked his hand nervously.

"There is a large Man hiding in the gulley we just came out of. The field we are about to walk into is a perfect spot to ambush someone. I feel like I am being watched," the Dwarf said quietly. Aemon remained calm. He had been in hundreds of dangerous situations through the span of his long life. He knew the importance of keeping a cool head.

"What do you propose, Dwarf? How do we get out of this mess?" Aemon asked.

The Dwarf thought of his options. Below him was another overgrown orchard of thorny apple trees. Above them, the overgrown field tapered off as it went up the steep hill. It would be slow going that way. In front lay the field that Dobervist was worried about. That left only one option.

"We go back and head down the gulley," the Dwarf answered, and Marcus' heart sank. The Elf looked surprised but did not argue.

"If the large Man catches up with...?" the Elf asked, his voice trailing off.

Dobervist looked down at his hunting knife and tapped it twice. The Elf nodded. "Back to the gulley then," Aemon said. The Elf noticed how scared Marcus was and walked over to him. He threw his arm around Marcus's back and began slowly walking towards the gulley as if they were old friends strolling through a park. Dobervist picked up his bow, whistled at Stripe, and took the lead.

Dobervist slowly walked through the dandelion field, his boots crushing the faded yellow flowers. He was walking towards the corner of the field, away from where the Man was hiding. Aemon and Marcus followed behind, the youth from Capan breathing heavily from his fear. The three of them and Stripe were about three rods away when the large Man burst out of the gulley's tree line. Dressed in brown woodsmen's clothes and carrying a large crossbow, the Man was one of the largest that Dobervist had ever seen. "RUN! RUN!", Dobervist shouted as he waved the other two forward toward the corner of the field. Dobervist kept his eyes on the big Man and watched as he knelt and took aim at Aemon with his crossbow. Dobervist grabbed Marcus and Aemon by their tunic collars and shoved them down. The cross bolt whistled harmlessly above them.

Dobervist looked up and saw the big Man pull a long dagger from his belt. The Man was scarred, bald and his neck was as thick as a bull's. With a sneering grin, the Man began to run toward them. Dobervist did not hesitate and pulled Marcus and Aemon to their feet, ushering them to the corner of the field. The three took off sprinting and now entered the gulley. Their feet slid down the steep embankment, and only Aemon was able to land gracefully. Dobervist landed on his bow, and he heard it crack as he landed. He threw the broken bow in the stony creek bed and looked up. The big Man was leering down at them from above and looked as if he was contemplating sliding down as well. "THIS WAY!", Dobervist shouted, and he took off down the creek bed, his boots kicking up the clear water. Aemon and Stripe quickly followed, and Marcus realized he better get going. Marcus' heart was racing, and he was almost surprised to look down and see his feet moving. Marcus risked falling and glanced in the direction that their attacker had come. To his horror, he saw the big Man running parallel to them through the woods above them.

The embankments on either side of them were becoming shorter, and Marcus spotted brushy fields on both sides of the creek. Dobervist chose the fields opposite of their attacker and was about to leap out of the creek bed when Axios erupted from the thicket opposite of them. Luckily for the three of them, one of his massive boots slipped on the wet creek stones, and he tumbled headfirst into a small boulder. Axios cried out in pain and rolled into the creek. Stripe began biting him in his neck, his sharp teeth drawing more blood. Dobervist drew his knife and bent over, ready to finish Axios off. The pounding of horse hooves made him stop and look up. Three more horsemen were racing towards them along an old cart path.

"RUN!", Dobervist shouted, and he pulled Stripe off Axios and scooped up the panting dog. They took off running through the brushy field, the high grass making their progress slow. Dobervist looked behind, expecting to see galloping horsemen behind him. Instead, Axios' large frame was blocking the old cart path where it crossed the creek. The three horsemen were shouting at him in rage to move, but Axios was having trouble standing up.

Dobervist, Marcus, and Aemon took advantage of their attacker's misfortune and disappeared into the brushy field. The large viburnum and honeysuckle brushes provided cover. Dobervist quickly directed them back into the direction that they had come. They were soon in the woods. Dobervist spotted a moss-covered pile of rocks, placed there decades and decades ago by some Mempacton farmer who had cleared the plot for crops. He slid behind the pile of rocks and set Stripe down. Marcus and Aemon crouched beside him, and all three looked through the young saplings, their eyes scanning for any sign of their attackers. Long, intense minutes passed until Ameon finally whispered to the Dwarf.

"Here comes one," Aemon whispered. Through the orange and yellow leaves Cyprian carefully followed the trio's tracks through the blanket of bright maple leaves. Cyprian stopped when he spotted the pile of moss-covered rocks. Dobervist looked at Aemon, and they both knew it was time to run again. Dobervist picked up Stripe, and the three of them took off running. Cyprian blew a hunting horn, and the shrill trumpet cut through the air. As Dobervist was sprinting through the sapling forest, he heard two more calls in the distance. Dobervist looked behind, but Cyprian was having trouble negotiating his horse through the maze of think saplings. The trio burst out of the sapling forest and emerged in the field that they had slept in the night before.

This cat and mouse game continued for the next few hours. Dobervist would try to lead them away from their attackers, but no matter what direction he took, they always came into the sight of one of the horsemen. Then a horn's blast would pierce through the countryside and would quickly be answered by more horn blasts.

After being sighted trying to cross a field, the trio ran back into another sapling forest and leaned against the remains of a falling-down barn. They all were becoming exhausted from the constant running. Dobervist knew what the experienced hunters were doing. They were slowly pushing the three of them out of the brushy hills around Oakbridge and down into the flat, open valley fields which were still farmed.

The hunting horns blared again. They were getting closer and closer. "What is the plan, Dwarf? They are getting closer," Aemon coolly asked. The Dwarf considered their options. The sun would be setting in a few hours. The darkness would be their only chance to escape.

"We keep this up until night and escape in the darkness," the Dwarf stated. Aemon only smiled and shook his head.

"Full moon tonight, Dwarf. They will spot us in the moonlight," Aemon said flatly. Marcus's heart sank. His legs were burning from the constant running. On top of that, they had been eating meager meals that they had been foraging, and the lack of a proper diet was catching up to him.

The Dwarf knew the Elf was right and only shook his head. "I guess we will have to fight it out with them. I will ambush one of them. I cannot fight them all at once with only a knife," the Dwarf said quietly, and Marcus preyed that the Dwarf's success. Aemon shook his head, though.

"These Men are hunters. They will be hard to ambush. There is another way. We head to Oakbridge," the Elf said. His eye scanning the woods around them for any Capans. Dobervist shook his head in confusion. He did not understand why the Elf wanted to go to Oakbridge, and he voiced his question to Aemon.

"We have no other options," Aemon replied.

"There are Men in Oakbridge, Elf. I am still a fugitive from the Empire in case you have forgotten. You want to be hanged by the townsfolk instead?" the Dwarf asked.

Aemon shook his head again. "Have faith in me, Dwarf. Not so long ago, the people of Oakbridge fought with your kind. Maybe we should remind them why they fought," the Elf said whimsically. Dobervist shook his head, for the Elf's words confused him once again.

Aemon stood up and began walking downhill towards the valley, where the Capan hunters wanted him to go. It would be dark around the time they arrived in Oakbridge. It was the sixth day of the week, and Aemon figured Oakbridge would be busy. Dobervist thought the Elf had gone mad and remained motionless alongside Marcus.

Aemon noticed that the others had not followed him. The Elf stopped and turned back, looking at the others. "You two must trust me. This is the way. The time has come," the Elf said with a smile.

"The time has come for what," Marcus asked, his stomach growling as he did so.

"The time for me to reveal myself once again. Let us go to Oakbridge, my friends," the Elf said before turning downhill. Marcus and Dobervist could only shake their heads and follow the ancient Elf down into the valley, which was filled with danger.

Chapter XXXIV- Through the Wild

The loon's echoing call reverberated across the Cold River, awakening Talar. The Prince from Stonedom looked around and saw that Mona and Dalir were still wrapped in their blankets and were sleeping. The embers from the fire had faded away. Talar pulled his blanket off and quietly stood up. He looked around to ensure they were still alone. Seeing nothing but the tranquil river and an empty forest, Talar headed to his trapline.

Talar held his breath as he approached his first trap. He let out a sigh of disappointment at finding it empty. He kept going along the game trail, not as confident as before. The light from the morning sun filtered through the weeping willows which loomed all around him. The sound of the river hid his footsteps, and Talar walked quickly to his next trap.

To his surprise, a large rabbit was ensnared in the neck trap, and Talar quickly picked it up and along with the trap. He checked the other snare, but it too was empty. He returned to the camp with one rabbit and his three snares. Mona and Dalir were already awake, and Talar unceremoniously threw the rabbit on his blanket. Dalir and Mona looked surprised to see Talar and the dead rabbit.

"One of you dress it. I'm going down to the river to fish," Talar said as he rummaged around for the fishing hooks. The Captain had supplied them with three fine silver barbed hooks. The Captain had told Talar that silver would attract any fish and advised him not to lose them.

Talar cut a strain from his wool blanket and pulled an even thinner strain from that. After tying the strain of wool around the hook's eye loop, Talar wrapped the remaining length of wool around a large tree branch. He then took off towards the waterfalls. Dalir looked at the dead rabbit, then at Mona. Dalir did not know how to butcher a rabbit, and he did not want to watch either. Dalir took off after Talar, leaving a disheveled Mona, who had just awakened, with the dead rabbit.

Dalir ran carelessly into the glen. It felt good to stretch his legs after being in the skiff for three days. He felt even better on not having to row anymore, and he massaged his sore arms. Dalir looked around at the strange trees with their strange bright colors. He had never been in such a wilderness. The massive willows and sycamores did not allow much of the morning light to penetrate where he walked. He pushed through waist-high ferns, their green fronds smooth and forgiving. Dalir realized that he could not spot Talar. He was about to call his name when Talar appeared from beneath the green ferns. He held an exceptionally large white grub in his hand and smiled triumphantly. Dalir caught up, and the two went through the ferns to the banks of the massive waterfall. Deaf Falls once again impeded their ability to communicate, so Dalir watched intently as Talar prepared to cast. They were standing on a large flat boulder, and the swirling eddy in front of them occasionally spat out a froth of yellow foam down the river to their left.

Talar baited the fine silver hook with the white grub and carefully tossed it into the swirling eddy. The swirling current took the hook and grub with it. Talar held the wool line tightly as it drew tight from the swirling current. Dalir looked on in interest. Talar felt a sharp pull, and he yanked the line quickly. A short struggle ensued. Talar gripped the sturdy wool line as the massive trout he had hooked pulled him from side to side. Dalir thought that Talar was going to fall into the dangerous water, so he stood up and pulled Talar back. The two of them fought the massive trout, their four hands gently pulling the trout in after he had tired himself from the fight.

Dalir stared in amazement at the massive trout and its rainbow-colored scales. His heart was racing, and he and Talar grasped hands in joy at hauling in the trout. Talar began to clean the trout out, and Dalir now watched, eager to learn from his experienced friend. Still not being able to hear each other, Talar quickly showed Dalir how to clean the fish. They headed back to the camp afterward with their catch.

Mona shook her head and smiled at seeing the giant trout. She preferred fish over pork and beef and had been getting sick of their diet. The rabbit still lay on the ground undressed, and Talar looked at Mona questioningly. "I've been in Capa for most my life. How many rabbits do you think I butchered there, Talar?" Mona asked.

Talar nodded, not wanting to start an argument over a minor issue. He passed the trout to Mona and asked if she could cook it. "I can cook Talar. Cook better than you," she said laughingly. Talar seemed more mature to her now. She figured that the fight at the wheelhouse had matured him. She had thought of Talar's words all night. A life of servitude awaited her if she did leave them at Oakbridge. If she were lucky enough to find a Mercium Lord to harbor her and eventually marry her, she doubted the Lord would treat her as well as Talar did. She shook her head at remembering Talar being smacked by Ashgar before the Arena. He had been the only one to stand up to Ralphin. Now he was standing up for her again. She thought over her options as she prepared the trout for breakfast.

Talar smiled and was glad that she was still in a good mood. He had seen Dalir massaging his arms, and he knew that Mona was hiding her soreness. "Well, I'm a horrible cook, so as long as you don't burn it, we should be good!". They all laughed, and Talar grabbed the rabbit and told Dalir to follow him. Not wanting to disappoint Talar, Dalir followed and watched Talar butcher the rabbit. After watching, Dalir figured he could do it without emptying his stomach's contents. They returned to the campsite, and Talar poured some salt from their other provisions over the rabbit to help preserve it.

The trio ate half the trout. The tender meat was a welcome change from the salted pork they usually ate for breakfast. After eating, Talar salted the remaining fillet. The three then began preparing for the overland trek. Mona and Dalir were especially eager to be away from the skiff, the oars, and the river. Talar cut three saplings for the trio to hang their provisions off. They tied the sacks of provisions over the end of the tree saplings and placed the other ends over their shoulders.

Dalir and Talar strapped their swords over their shoulders. Talar picked up his shield and handed Mona the long dagger that the Captain had purchased in the Badatoz market. "Be careful with it, Mona," Talar warned. Mona nodded and placed the dagger in her belt. She was content that Talar had not tried to withhold the weapon from her. Talar looked around for the last time at their simple campsite and the river behind it. The massive forest that lay between the Cold River and the Great Road lay before them. Talar asked his companions if they were ready.

Dalir nodded. His heart was racing at the thought of the journey ahead. He had already learned a great deal about the Elves, and he intended to travel to Stonedom to find one. That meant that he would continue with Talar.

"I'm ready, Talar, lead the way. I'm ready to be away from the river," Mona said confidently. Dalir nodded in agreement with Mona, so Talar turned and started walking towards the ridge that would take them above Deaf Falls. Mona and Dalir followed Talar through the glen that they had camped in. They passed through the weeping willows and started climbing towards the Falls. Talar did not feel any pain in his side, but his legs were burning from the climb. They climbed the ridge through a maze of small boulders and spotted Deaf Falls through the trees. Talar pushed through the brush with his shield, and Mona and Dalir followed behind, careful not to get their provisions snared in the thick brush.

The trio stood on the flat ground above the wide waterfall. Deaf Falls again hindered their ability to speak, but they all smiled in amazement at the beautiful sight before them. The elevation they had gained by climbing up to the massive waterfalls granted them a memorable vista of the vast Fertile Crescent. After staring for a few moments in awe, Talar waved his hands, got the other two's attention, and started heading up the unnamed waterway that spilled over Deaf Falls. Talar had spent hours of his youth staring at the large colored map of the north that was in his father's library. He felt confident that he could bring them out of the wilderness and into the Capulus Valley. He had been hunting and exploring the Stone Mountains since he was old enough to walk. This was his first time leading an expedition, and he knew it was up to him to lead the other two out.

The trio set off up the river, their provisions bobbing up and down below the saplings that they had been tied to. The going was slow for an hour as they navigated the slippery stream bank. After surveying the stream for a shallow spot to cross, Talar finally spotted one and stopped the group.

"Quite the view back there!" He said with a smile. Mona and Dalir nodded in agreement.

"We could see all of the Fertile Crescent! It is massive!" Dalir grinningly stated. It was the first time the group had stopped, and they all took a drink from the sheep waterskins that the Captain had supplied. They refilled the waterskins, and Mona asked which direction they were headed to next.

Talar pointed across the creek. "We go across. The terrain on this creek will become steep and will slow us down. It will be easier to climb the Stone Plateau from the other side," Talar said. Dalir nodded, but Mona looked at the stream and its' current skeptically. The water would be up to her waist, and she feared being washed downstream. Talar told her that they would lock arms. She nodded hesitantly.

Before she could object, Talar and Dalir were in the water, and they motioned for Mona to follow them. The autumn air was warm, so the cold creek water surprised her when she stepped in. She locked her left arm around Talar's right arm and her left arm around Dalir's left arm. Talar started leading them across the creek, and Mona's breath was taken away by the cold clear water. Talar carefully found his footing, and he led them across the river. He and Dalir practically carried the shorter Mona across the river, and she was soaked from the waist down. Dalir asked if she wanted to stop to start a fire, but she refused.

"I've been wet before, Dalir. I will dry off," Mona said and motioned for Talar to lead on. Talar smiled and admired her toughness and bravery once again. He would have been enamored with under different circumstances. The looming war shattered all those ideas, though, and Talar did not speak to Mona as he led her and Dalir on towards the looming Stone Plateau.

The trio continued as the sun rose, and Mona's clothes were dry by the time they stopped for lunch. They sat on a fallen oak tree as other giant oaks around them dropped their nuts. The nuts hit the crunchy yellow and orange leaves with loud thuds. To Dalir, the strange symphony of the nuts made him feel like he was on another planet. Koristan had few areas as lush and vibrant as these massive forests that seemed to stretch forever. Dalir took his sword and quiver off from his back. He placed the bow against the oak log and stretched his legs out. His feet dangled from the fallen tree.

Dalir spotted a strange creature covered in what he thought was some sort of needle. It was slowly crawling headfirst down an oak tree. Dalir pointed out the strange creature to Talar.

"It is a porcupine Dalir! The spikes on it are quills. They use them to keep other animals off it. They are harmless, my friend," Talar said. Dalir nodded and kept looking at the strange animal. They finished eating the other part of the trout, this time eating the fish cold. The trio took off after their lunch, and Dalir and Mona occasionally asked Talar about the forest around him. They did not pester Talar with questions about the upcoming war or his life in Stonedom. Both of his companions knew that Talar was reeling from the death of his friends and father.

They continued through the afternoon, always heading uphill. The oak and maple trees eventually quit growing as they gained elevation. The deciduous trees were replaced with towering pines and spruces. The forest floor where they walked was darker now. The needles of the softwoods allowed less light to come through. This eliminated much of the undergrowth, which had slowed them down before, and their progress increased considerably.

The sun began to set, and Talar searched for a flat place to sleep. He could see none. He did spot a large grey boulder with a flat top and directed his companions over to it. They had not seen anything other than porcupine and the occasional bird overhead, so Talar figured it was safe to start a fire. The trio sat against the boulder, exhausted from another long day. After eating the rabbit, the trio climbed on top of the boulder and stared up at the stars in the sky.

"We are making good time. If we keep this up, we will reach Oakbridge much sooner than I expected," Talar said. Mona and Dalir could only nod. The days of rowing and now walking had taken a toll on both. After laying out their wool blankets, all three quickly fell asleep on the cold, uncomfortable stone.

The hooting of an owl awakened Dalir. He pushed himself up and immediately felt the soreness in his muscles. The owl's yellow eyes stared down at Dalir. Dalir watched as the large brown owl spread his wings and took off into the forest below them. He rolled over and drank from his waterskin and began to roll up his blanket. Talar and Mona were awake at this point, and in no time, the three resumed their journey towards the Stone Plateau.

Their morning passed quickly, and it was after lunch when Talar spotted an opening in the woods just below them. He could hear water moving, and he figured the opening must be spring. They needed water, so he led them down to the clearing. Talar spotted a small pool of water that fed a babbling stream. The water emerged from the ground above the pool, and it was there that Talar bent down to fill his waterskin.

"What is that Talar?" Dalir whispered, and Talar looked up to see what Dalir was whispering about. Talar spotted what Dalir was pointing at. In the small opening before him, with his head towards the babbling brook, lay a Man like a creature with its' leg propped up against a large pine.

Talar stared in disbelief as his waterskin overfilled with water. He had read of such creatures in one of his father's books. The creature looked like a Man and had a buckskin loincloth for clothing. His hair was brown and long. He had an unkempt beard. He snored loudly, and Mona, Dalir, and Talar all jolted at the loud noise. His Man like appearance ended at the waist. For propped up against the pine tree was a single massive leg with a proportionally large foot shading the Man-like creature from the sun.

The single large leg looked like a Man's, but it was much larger and corded with muscles. The large foot was covered with calluses, and dirt was embedded in the skin. Talar spotted a large spear by the strange sleeping creature and motioned for the others to step back.

Dalir took a step back, and a dry tree branch snapped underneath his foot. The massive leg swung off the pine tree, and before the companions could react, the Man like creature stood before them on his single leg. He looked down at the three of them, and to Dalir, the strange Man-like creature looked curious. Before any of the companions could speak, the one-legged creature picked up his spear, swung his long arms, and in a single leap, he bounded into the thick young spruce trees that surrounded the opening.

The trio heard the one-legged creature crash through the forest below them for a few moments before the noise faded away. Before anyone could say anything, Dalir burst out with laughter. Talar and Mona did too, and for a few moments, they laughed in amazement at the creature that they had startled.

"Are you going to answer my question, Talar?" Dalir asked, trying to catch his breath from laughing too hard.

"I do not know Dalir! I have read about creatures such as those, but I do not know their names," Talar said.

"You do not know his name Talar?" Dalir asked skeptically. Talar shook his head. "Oh, I thought he might be related to you. One of your cousins, perhaps?" Dalir asked, trying to keep a straight face. He failed, and the three of them burst into laughter again. After regaining their composure and filling their waterskins, the trio took off again. Talar explained what little he knew about the one-legged creature, which was not much.

"From what I read; they are great warriors. They are supposed to live around the mountains of Borisco, which I hear are nearly as big as the Stone Mountains. I have no idea what one is doing around here," Talar said, telling the other two all he knew about the strange creatures.

The next few days passed without incident. The provisions the Captain had bought them were dwindling, but the traps that Talar and Dalir set provided plenty of fresh meat. They also came upon patches of blackberries that grew in areas where the giant trees had toppled over. Overall, they were well-fed but weary by the time the trio could see the end of the massive forest.

The trees had gotten progressively smaller by the time they settled down for the night. Now a ridgeline up to the top of the Stone Plateau lay above them through a maze of boulders. The three collapsed for the night and ate the last of their salted provisions. They had plenty of berries for the next day, but beyond that, they had no food. Talar knew they had to cross the Stone Plateau and enter the fertile valley beyond it by tomorrow. It had rained briefly yesterday, but now it looked clear.

Too tired to talk, the three weary travelers bundled up for the night at the tree line. Mona thought of her future once again as she looked up at the stars. Soon they would be in Oakbridge, and over the past few days, she had made up her mind. She would not run away from Capa's tyranny. She would not flee to Mercium and marry some stranger. She would stay with Talar and travel to Stonedom. She would fight with the Dwarves and with Talar. She would fight for her lost family.

When they woke up in the morning, dark clouds lingered above them. In the distance, darker clouds slowly headed towards them. All three dug their wool cloaks out of their packs as large cold drops of rain began to pour steadily upon them. They took off up the hill, skipping breakfast. Talar found an animal trail up the ridgeline, and they slowly made their way up the steep escarpment. Talar and Dalir slipped often. They were burdened with the shield and bow, and their weapons weighed them down as they climbed up. The rain kept pouring, and the wind whipped the cold drops into their faces.

The storm worsened, and thunder and lightning erupted above them. They kept slowly climbing, fighting the wind, rain, and slippery rocks. After a few hours of slow travel, they reached the final ascent to the top of the Stone Plateau. A narrow animal trail used by the mountain goats that inhabited the harsh rocky landscape was flanked on both sides by sheer cliffs. The trio could not see anything around them when the storm clouds blew in. For a moment, Mona thought she was going to be blown off her feet. Talar grabbed his companions, and the three hunkered down beside a moss-covered boulder as the rain poured even harder. Thunder and lightning erupted above once again, and the wind made it impossible for any of them to even lift their heads up. After a few moments, the storm finally abated, and Talar cautiously raised his head.

The brutal storm raged further down the Stone Plateau and the morning sun peaked through the clouds when the last of the raindrops ended. The trio's wool cloaks had not kept them dry, and all three were soaked to the bone. Knowing that there was nothing to do but to get off the mountainside, Talar started off. He took his time as he crossed the dangerous passage upheld, using his shield against the wind. The storm clouds were gone, and as he looked down on Mona and Dalir, he was once again filled with awe at the sight before him.

Mona and Dalir joined Talar after making it past the cliffs. They stared out at the land that they had traversed. The Cold River lay far in the distance and the Fertile Crescent beyond that. Dalir shook his head in amazement when he spotted the stream above Deaf Fall's where they had crossed days earlier. It seemed so far below now. The trio took the sight in and smiled at each other despite their wet clothes.

The sun's rays shown bright as the three walked on level ground for the first time since they had left the glen by the Cold River. They followed the animal path across the top of the Stone Plateau. Their progress increased once again as morning turned to afternoon. The wind was strong at times, and the short junipers along the Plateau offered little protection from the wind. They ate their lunch of berries as they walked across the Stone Plateau.

It was a few hours after reaching the top of the Plateau when they rounded a corner in the worn animal path that they had been following. Small white boulders the size of a pumpkin littered the ground around them along. For the past few hours, the junipers had limited their view. Suddenly on their left, the junipers ended, and a new vista lay before them.

The Capulus Valley lay before Talar, Dalir, and Mona. A sea of orange, red, and yellow leaves lay below them as thousands of chestnut, oak, maple, elm, and cherry trees swayed with the wind. The abandoned farms along the hills opposite them seemed far below as well. Dalir spotted a narrow river snaking back and forth in the middle of the valley and knew it must be the Capulus. He saw cleared, green pastures dotted with boulders below them, past the orange and yellow leaves. Past the green pastures, Dalir could see buildings clustered together in a grove of trees along the river.

Dalir was filled with excitement and was about to hug both Mona and Dalir when he saw their faces. Both seemed on the brink of tears. Neither had thought that they would be back here in this spot where the lands of Mercium met the lands of Stonedom. Now they looked at each other, and both smiled. They had both endured humiliation and pain at the hands of the Capans, and now, finally, they were back home in the north.

"Is that Oakbridge below?" Dalir asked. Talar grasped Mona's hand. He looked into her green eyes, and she knew then that Talar would always fight for her. She knew then that her destiny lay with Talar. With the Prince of Stonedom.

"Yes, Dalir. That is Oakbridge," Talar replied.

"Do you think we can reach it before nightfall? I am starving Talar," Dalir said, his stomach growling. Talar and Mona laughed.

"Yea Dalir, we might make it before dark. As long as your stomach does not attract any bears!" Talar said. He let go of Mona's hand and gave Dalir a playful push with his shield. Dalir's stomach growled again, and they all laughed.

"Let us see this Oakbridge. I have heard enough about it," Dalir said before he followed Talar and Mona off the Stone Plateau.

Chapter XXXV- The Tavern by the River

Dalir's stomach growled despite the blueberry in his mouth. The large blueberry patch that Mona, Talar, and Dalir had walked into as they descended the Stone Plateau was a blessing. The three of them took a break and plundered the blueberry patch for every berry they could find. The afternoon sun-dried their clothes, and a slight breeze blew the stunted spruce trees around them. After filling their bellies with berries, the three kept walking downhill.

Talar used his shield to push through the stunted spruce trees that the trio encountered. The short sharp needles of the spruces scratched their bare arms. Eventually, they burst through the short spruce trees and entered a dark evergreen forest. The forest floor was open and clear of brush, and the three emerged out of the dark evergreens and into hardwoods. Their legs were starting to wear out from the long journey from Badatoz, and Talar now doubted they would reach Oakbridge before dark.

The three kept walking down the steep plateau until the sun started to set and darkness overtook them. They collapsed against an old tree trunk, completely exhausted. Talar wiped the sweat from his brow and looked around. He could not see anything around them. Too tired to start a fire, Talar informed the others that he was going to stand watch.

"That is fine with me, Talar. I'm too hungry to fight off the one-legged Man anyway," Dalir muttered before he pulled his wool blanket up to his shoulders and closed his eyes. The memory of their encounter with the strange one-legged creature made Mona and Talar smile. The moon was beginning to rise. Talar looked up and gazed at the moon. The moon was almost full, and Talar figured it would be a full moon the next night. The moonlight allowed Talar to survey his surroundings. He turned his head and scanned the woods but saw nothing. An owl hooted in the distance, and Talar turned his head in its direction. Mona was sitting by Dalir, her eyes locked on Talar.

Mona stood and gently stepped over the now sleeping Dalir. She sat down next to Talar and offered her hand. Talar accepted it, and the two sat in the moonlight for long moments, too tired to speak. After a while, Mona put her head against Talar's shoulder, and she fell asleep. Talar looked down at Mona through the moonlight. Talar thought that she was the most elegant woman he had ever seen, despite her shabby wool tunic and unkempt hair. His heart stirred with emotions when he thought of Mona. Ever since he had first glimpsed her fiery red hair and her green eyes, he had known that there was something special about her. Now, after everything they had been through, he desperately wanted to tell her that he wanted her as his wife. His father had married by the time he was Talar's age. A Woman as old as Mona who was not married was a rarity. He thought of a life with Mona. He thought of raising children with her and growing old beside her. After a few moments, though, he came back to reality.

Talar looked down upon Mona. He knew deep in his heart that he would never have that life now. The Emperor and his Legions would never allow it. Talar thought of Alwin and Hartwin and let out a deep breath. He knew a similar fate awaited him, and he hoped he would show the same courage that the dead brothers had shown. Talar gently eased Mona's head down to the ground and covered her up with his wool blanket. He walked away and looked out into the valley below. He could see the lights from the houses in Oakbridge. Talar leaned against a tree and looked out over the woods, determined to stay awake and keep guard.

The robins' morning chorus awakened Talar. He shook his head as he realized he had fallen asleep standing up. There was a thick blanket of fog around them, masking the valley below. Talar gently shook Mona's shoulders to wake her up. Her eyes opened, and she smiled up at Talar. He smiled back and helped her to her feet. Mona brushed the dirt off her pants, and Talar kicked Dalir's feet gently. Dalir woke up, and immediately his jaw dropped. He had never seen fog like this, and he could not believe the valley below was invisible now. They wrapped their wool blankets and cloaks around their waists and discarded the saplings that they had previously been using to tote their provisions. Dalir's stomach growled loudly. "Let us go to Oakbridge before I end up eating one of these trees," Dalir said, and Mona and Talar shook their heads in agreement.

Talar led the way down the plateau through the thick fog. Occasionally, they would encounter a ravine that was too steep to walk down, but Talar would navigate around them. The morning wore on, and the sun began to burn off the fog, allowing the trio to catch glimpses of the valley below. Their pace was quick despite their lack of energy. Their feet flew down the steep terrain, and it was mid-morning when Talar looked up and spotted the end of the forest. Ahead, the large oak and chestnut trees ended, and a green boulder-strewn field started. Talar slapped Dalir on the back and pointed ahead. Dalir let out a shrill yell of victory once he spotted the green pasture and took off, running towards the field. Despite his growling stomach, Dalir ran out of the woods and into the green pasture. Below him, only one or two leagues away, lay Oakbridge. Talar and Mona walked out of the woods and joined Dalir. They all looked down at the cluster of houses and barns that made up Oakbridge. Dalir shook his head in awe once he spotted the three massive oaks which gave the town its' name. The trees were massive. Even from this distance, Dalir knew they were bigger than any tree he had ever seen. Dalir shook his head again in amazement at the strange land he had journeyed into.

The walk through the lush green pasture was uneventful, and within an hour, the three of them were standing on the outskirts of Oakbridge. Talar had been observing the town on the walk down through the field and had not spotted any Capan calvary. Dalir, Talar, and Mona jumped over a small ditch that ran below the field. For the first time since they had left Capa, their feet felt the smooth cobble of a proper road. The Great Road lay underneath them now, and Talar looked back away from Oakbridge. Stonedom was only a two-day walk from here. Talar knew he was close to home.

Talar looked back to Oakbridge and led his companions to the famous bridge which the town was named after. They walked down the Great Road, the clear water of the Capulus rushing beside them. Dalir's jaw dropped again when he spotted the famous bridge. Long ago, during a brutal winter, a powerful storm had come down from the far north. The storm caused one of the massive oaks to snap in half. The top half had fallen across the Capulus, and the Men of the village had quickly set about turning the massive piece of timber into a bridge.   Dalir followed Mona and Talar up a wooden ramp, and he stood looking over the rushing waters of the Capulus. Dalir figured that he, Mona, and Talar could all lay down, head to toe, and they still would not cover the bridge's width.

"How do these trees grow so big? It is a miracle!" Dalir stated.

"The Elves planted them, long ago Dalir," Talar replied. Dalir shook his head with amazement again, and Dalir followed his friends and entered the town of Oakbridge.

The two remaining massive oaks stood opposite of each other, and their canopies provided shade for the market below them. Farmers, smiths, and merchants all haggled with their customers, and it was strange to Dalir to see so many people after being in the wilderness for so long. Dalir looked to his right and saw a side street with a row of two-story stone and thatch houses facing the Capulus. More stone and thatch houses stood behind the market, and Dalir wondered if there were any taverns in the town. He was about to ask Talar this when he looked to his left.

The Oakbridge Tavern's large wooden sign, which hanged from chains over the entrance, swayed in the breeze. The sign depicted a fish drinking from a tankard. Talar led his companions to the only tavern in Oakbridge. Dalir could not believe what he was seeing. The Oakbridge Tavern had been built out of the massive oak tree that had created the bridge. Three stories of windows loomed over Dalir. He looked through the tavern's windows during their walk to the massive tavern's entrance.

Talar swung open one of the heavy doors of the Oakbridge Tavern, for the winters were brutal this far north. A heavy door was needed to keep the chill out. He gestured for Mona and Dalir to enter, and Dalir looked around the tavern with curiosity once he entered. Immediately the smell of roasted potatoes, meat pies, and fresh bread greeted his nostrils. Dalir grabbed his stomach to try to keep it from making any more noise!

Dalir looked around the brightly lit tavern and marveled at the craftsmanship that had gone into creating the place. The entire inside of the tree had been meticulously hollowed out, and Dalir could only guess how many years that had taken. The effort had been worth it, though. The tavern was huge and could hold at least a hundred people. Dalir could see a horseshoe-shaped bar surrounded by circular tables and benches. On each side of the tavern, a fireplace stood, and above each fireplace, deer skulls and antlers adorned the walls along with a large metal chandelier that provided light. Two staircases met the floor of the tavern behind the horseshoe bar, and Dalir saw an elderly Man dressed in a fine-dyed red wool tunic descend the stairs and sit at the bar.

Talar walked past Dalir and motioned for Mona and him to sit at the bar, which was a thick slab of wood supported by empty barrels. Talar pulled out a stool for Mona, and after she was seated, Dalir and Talar sat down. The rough wooden bar stools did not have any cushions, but the trio did not care. It felt wonderful to all three of them just to sit down. The barkeep poured the old Man in the red wool tunic a copper tankard of hard cider, then turned around and walked over to the trio.

The barkeep eyed all three of them suspiciously. From their dirty, disheveled, and ragged appearances, he doubted they had coins for drink or food. They did have weapons. Once he reached the trio, the barkeep reached underneath the bar and put one of his large hands on a metal cudgel he used to keep the peace in the tavern.

"My name is Madoc. I own this place. How can I help you, youngsters, today?" the balding barkeep asked. Madoc was middle-aged and had worked in the tavern his entire life. He had seen enough to know that the harsh landscape around Oakbridge could drive people to do desperate things. He gripped the cudgel underneath the bar top, ready to defend his life and his tavern, if necessary.

Mona and Talar looked over at Dalir. It was then that Dalir remembered that neither had any silver or gold coins on them. Realizing they were waiting on him, Dalir spoke up. "Yes, thank you, Madoc. First, we would like three plates of whatever you have cooking in the kitchen. And a bottle of wine," Dalir said with a smile. Madoc did not smile back.

"We do not have wine. This is not Capa. We do have hard cider. Best hard cider in the land," Madoc said proudly. Dalir nodded and informed Madoc that three tankards of hard cider would be fine. Madoc nodded and crossed his arms. He looked down upon Dalir as if expecting something.

Dalir did not know what the barkeep wanted, so he kept awkwardly smiling at him. Finally, Madoc spoke up. "Do you have coin to pay for this? I accept copper, steel, and bronze coin if you have them, Young Sir," Madoc said evenly. Now that he was closer to the three youths, he could tell something was off about them. Their wool tunics were dirty but intricately woven. Their weapons were of high quality too.

Dalir assumed that he would pay for the meals after eating them, which was custom in Koristan. Upon hearing that the barkeep would accept copper, steel, and bronze for payment, Dalir smiled and fished out a gold tenpenny from his coin purse. Madoc's eyes widened when Dalir dropped the small gold coin in his hand. Madoc turned around and yelled into the kitchen, which was tucked between the ends of the bar beneath the twin staircases. Madoc looked down at the gold tenpenny and smiled. If the three youths decided to spend the night, he figured more gold would be coming his way. The barkeep tucked the gold into his pant pocket and started pouring three tankards of hard cider for his guests.

Madoc brought the three tankards over, and all three waited in anticipation for Madoc to set them down. Once he did, all three grabbed the tin tankards and took a long swallow of the sweet hard cider. After days and days of nothing but water, the cider's sweetness was a treat for the three of them. After taking another pull from the tankard, the three of them leaned back in their stools and waited for the food. They did not know what they were going to eat, but to the three famished companions, any hot food would be welcome.

After sipping on their cider for a few more moments, the batwing doors leading from the kitchen to the area behind the bar swung open. Dalir's jaw dropped when a tall Woman about his age strode through the batwing doors with their plates of food. When she set the steaming plate of potatoes and fish in front of Dalir, he forgot about his hunger. The usual libertine Dalir was speechless in the presence of the beautiful barmaid, and Mona was going to laugh at his slack jaw when she noticed Talar was in a similar state.

Mona's face began to turn a little red with jealously, and she could not believe that she felt that way. Nonetheless, neither one of her companions should have been ogling the tall barmaid with blue eyes and dark hair. Not wanting to seem impolite, Mona used both her hands to punch Talar's and Dalir's kneecaps. Talar and Dalir let out a moan and looked at Mona, who sat between them.

"Eat your food, Dalir. You have been complaining for days about how hungry you are. Now the food is in front of you, and you're sitting there like a slack-jawed fool!" Mona said with a smile before she began to eat her food. She thanked the tall barmaid, who had laughed at the boy's loud moans.

"Sigrid! Bring them three more glasses of cider!" Madoc ordered, and the former Queen of the Rikens picked up the three empty tankards. She walked over to the large oak barrel by the batwing doors and began filling them. Her people had chased her off after their horrendous defeat at the hands of Clavis' Third Legion. She had been pelted with rocks, hit with clubs, and had arrows shot at her before she escaped through the mob of angry Rikens. With no food or supplies, she had wandered through the wildlands north of Oakbridge for weeks and weeks. The Trolls constantly hounded her, and it had been hard for her to gather food while they hunted her. She had spotted Oakbridge after climbing the ridgeline that overlooked the Capulus valley. Not knowing what to expect, she had wandered into Oakbridge looking even worse than the three companions did.

Sigrid finished pouring the cider and brought the tankards over to the companions. Madoc smiled at the young Woman's proficiency. She had stumbled in the tavern a few weeks ago, half-starved and looking rough. She did not speak the common tongue, which was prevalent from the north to the Capital. Madoc knew that a Woman as beautiful as her would draw in more customers, so he had offered her a job, and a place to stay, despite the difficulty in communicating with her. Once she understood what he was offering, she had agreed. She slept in the room next to where Madoc and his wife and young child stayed in the third story of the hollowed-out oak.

The busy schedule kept Sigrid's mind off the slaughter that she had witnessed. Her military failure haunted her dreams, but her people's mutiny against her hurt even more. She doubted that her people would ever accept her back, and she had come to peace with that. She had accepted her new life in Oakbridge and viewed it as a blessing. The lonely and desperate weeks in the wilderness had almost broken her. Now she was surrounded by the amicable people of Oakbridge, and she enjoyed the lively ambiance of the tavern.

Dalir came back to his senses and hastily pulled out another gold tenpenny. He put the gold coin on the bar counter and pushed it towards Sigrid, who looked at Dalir curiously. She put the gold coin in her green trouser pocket and smiled at the Koristan nobleman. She turned back to the kitchen, and Dalir watched her leave, his heart beating rapidly as she did.

"I can't say that I have ever seen you so flustered around a Woman before Dalir," Mona teased, and Dalir's ears burned with embarrassment. The three companions finished their potatoes and steamed fish, and they all took a deep breath after their last bite. Dalir waved at Madoc, and the owner of the Oakbridge Tavern walked over and asked how their meal was.

"It was excellent, Madoc. The white sauce on the fish was particularly tasteful. My compliments to the cook," Dalir said. Madoc nodded in reply and asked Dalir if there was anything else he wanted.

"Yes, we will need three rooms for the night, and we will be having dinner later on here as well!" Dalir said cheerfully. Madoc seemed a little shocked at the young Koristan's request. The balding barkeep scratched his head. "Is there a problem with that Madoc?" Dalir asked.

"No problem, Young Sir. The only thing is, I only have two rooms available. Is that an issue?" Madoc asked, and Dalir shook his head. "Excellent, it will be six more ten pennies for the rooms. Plus, one more tenpenny for tonight's dinner, which is boar. Fair enough, young Sir?" Madoc asked, and Dalir nodded. Dalir produced the coin from his purse and passed it over to Madoc, who was smiling. Once he stuffed the gold coins in his white apron, the barkeep ducked underneath the wooden bar and gestured for the three companions to follow him.

They followed Madoc to the back of the tavern and up to one of the twin winding staircases. A polished wooden handrail helped them ascend the spiral staircase, and before long, they were walking on the second floor. Madoc led them down the hallway that overlooked the tavern common area to the last two rooms. He pulled out a large metal keyring and opened the two doors. Madoc handed two keys to Dalir, then smiled and turned back towards the stairway.

After glancing into the small room and finding it satisfactory, Dalir turned to Talar and Mona. "Which room do you want, Mona? I'm exhausted and am going to sleep," Dalir said wearily.

"Talar and I will share this room," Mona said, pointing at the last room in the hallway. Dalir's eyebrows shot up, for he expected that Mona would want her own room. Dalir smiled at Mona, but her expression quickly wiped the smile off his face.

"Alright then, I'll take the other room, I suppose," Dalir said, trying to hide his smile. "I guess I'll see you two later for dinner then..." Dalir said awkwardly. Talar was going to reply when Mona grabbed his hand and pulled him into the last room.

"Thank you for paying for everything, Dalir. Enjoy the afternoon," Mona said after taking the room key from Dalir. Then she abruptly shut the door.

Dalir shook his head. He had not expected that, but he was too tired to think about it. Dalir entered his room and collapsed on the feather stuff mattress, not bothering to take off his dirty clothes. Soon he was dreaming of the beautiful barmaid downstairs.

Chapter XXXVI- Miracles and Murderers

The sunlight shining through the lone window slowly made its' way down Dalir's head until it was shining in his eyes. Dalir awakened and blocked the strong sunlight with his hands. He stood up and stretched, feeling better after sleeping and eating a proper meal. Dalir walked over to the crude-looking wooden table that was next to the window. He washed his hands and face in the clay pot of water and looked out the window. The market was filled with townsfolk and traders. Dalir noticed that there were more merchants and people shopping than before. After looking down at his own clothes, Dalir figured he could use a new outfit. His woodsmen's clothes were dirty and ripped in spots. He did not want to look shabby when he met Talar's brother, the King of Stonedom.

With his mindset on purchasing better clothes, Dalir was about to leave his room when his eyes fell upon his scimitar. He wondered if he should bring the weapon into the marketplace. Dalir walked back to the window and looked out again. He did not see any Legionnaires, and hardly any of the townsfolk below carried swords. Dalir turned around and walked out of the room, leaving the scimitar inside the room. After locking the room, Dalir walked over to the wooden railing and looked down over the common area of the tavern.

The tavern was starting to fill with sixth-day customers. Townsfolk and travelers alike came in for food, drink, and each other's company. Dalir spotted Sigrid bringing two tankards of cider towards what looked like a table of Boriscan merchants. He was once again dumbfounded by her beauty, and he watched her walk back into the kitchen before he walked down the stairway. The crowded tavern was filled with merry laughter. Sigrid came out of the kitchen again, this time bringing plates of food to the Boriscans. Her eyes briefly met Dalir's, and his heart raced. She set the food upon the table and returned to the kitchen, paying no attention to Dalir. Dalir sighed and kept walking towards the tavern's twin doors. To his right, an intense game of dice was being played out between what looked like a local townsman and a merchant from Mercium. To his left, two more townsmen in drab brown tunics were loading their pipes with free tobacco that Madoc left along the fireplace mantle.

Dalir opened the heavy door and took a deep breath of fresh air as he looked over Oakbridge. He did not see any Capans. He looked over the two towering oak trees. A few of their red and orange leaves came off and fluttered down to the market below, resting on the cobbled square. Not wanting to block the entrance to the tavern, Dalir walked down to the cobbled square below. Merchants quietly haggled with the townsfolk over prices. Dalir strolled through the market. He saw copper merchants from Brigantium peddling cookware, a Boriscan merchant selling glass windows, and a spice merchant from Badatoz. Dalir spotted a weapons merchant who had an array of daggers and knives laid out on a red blanket. Dalir bent over and examined a small, slender knife with a deer horn handle. He thought the small knife would be practical for cleaning fish and rabbits. He purchased the knife from the elderly man who was selling them. Dalir slipped the knife into his pocket and looked around for a clothing merchant. He did not spot any around him, and for the next hour, Dalir walked around the large marketplace. Dalir finally spotted bolts of cloth spread out on the grass underneath the massive oak that was furthest from the river. A Woman in baggy green pants and a bright blue vest bid him to inspect her fares. Dalir smiled after he reached down and ran his fingers over a bolt of red camel wool. The camel wool was considerably finer than the lambswool he had on. Dalir asked the Woman if she could make him a tunic of the fabric. She nodded, and the two of them negotiated a price. The female merchant had a thick Badatoz accent, and she did not budge on her price. Dalir desperately wanted to be out of the rough tunic he wore, now so he succumbed to her demands. After paying her in gold, the middle-aged Woman took Dalir's measurements with a string and began preparing him a tunic.

Dalir took a seat against the massive oak and looked eastward towards the Stone Mountains. He had not really looked at the massive mountain range when they had descended the Stone Plateau, for his eyes had been on Oakbridge. The snowcapped peaks of the Stone Mountains seemed to touch the clouds. Dalir looked up at the Stone Plateau, which he had just climbed down from. The Stone Mountains looked much taller. Dalir shook his head at the thought of climbing up one. Dalir had never seen a mountain range like this. He looked upon the magnificent peaks in silence while he waited for his tunic. After a few moments, Dalir noticed a peculiar object closer to the river, and he got up to investigate it. As he got closer, he saw that the object was a stone monolith, about half a rod high. The monolith was covered with bizarre ruins that Dalir could not decipher. He studied the monolith for a few moments, then headed back towards the oak. The sun began to set behind him, and the merchant called out to him that his tunic was done.

Dalir walked around the base of the oak and smiled when he saw the merchant Woman hold up his red tunic. She told him to try it on, so Dalir stripped the dirty woodsmen tunic off and slipped on his new tunic. The soft camel wool was a welcome relief to the scratchy woodsmen tunic. Dalir thanked the merchant. The rest of the merchants around him were starting to pack up their wares and were heading towards the tavern. The town lamplighter began his duties. He slowly raised the long metal lighting pole to the large candles that were encased in red-tinted glass.

Dalir walked with the crowd underneath the red hue of the streetlights that hung above him, to the tavern's entrance. He kept his right hand on his gold pouch, for the stagnant crowd was a pickpocket's dream. Dalir waited patiently in line until he entered the packed tavern. The lively tavern was filled with patrons, and Dalir looked around for an open table. He spotted one in the back corner of the tavern, opposite the side where he had his lunch earlier. Dalir began to weave through the crowd towards the open table. He squeezed between two tables full of rowdy townsfolk and made it to the back corner table. He threw his old woodsmen's tunic on the bench and sat down.

Before him, the jovial crowd clinked their tankards together and drank down the delicious cider. A young Woman in a plain rectangular brown tunic began playing the flute. An elderly Man who looked like a farmer joined her with his fiddle. The townsfolk began dancing in pairs, and it was not long until most of the tavern started clapping and tapping their feet to the rhythm. The song ended, and the dancing townsfolk cheered in appreciation. Madoc and Sigrid walked through the common area, dispensing cider and handing out plates of steaming roasted boar. Dalir's stomach began to growl, and he raised his hand to get Madoc's attention. The tavern owner spotted Dalir, and with years of practice, he quickly weaved through the crowd and set a plate of roasted boar in front of Dalir.

Dalir smiled upon seeing the plate of food and was going to thank Madoc when the flutist and fiddle player began another tune which drowned out his thanks. Madoc nodded, turned, and headed back towards the bar. He directed Sigrid towards Dalir. The tall barmaid approached Dalir with a tankard of cider. Dalir tried not to stare at the barmaid as she walked over to him. Dalir looked up at her and smiled, still unable to talk because of the rowdy music and dancing. She looked down at him as if she had a question, and Dalir froze when her hand reached out. Her fingers felt the soft red camel wool of his tunic, and she shook her head. She laughed after she felt how soft they were. To the former nomadic hunter, the thought of a Man wearing such fine clothes was funny to her. She kept laughing as she walked to the kitchen.

Dalir shook his head, not knowing why Sigrid had laughed at his fine red tunic. He took a sip from his tankard of cider and was pondering why the barmaid had laughed when some commotion and shouting at the front door drew his attention. A short, stocky fellow dressed in buckskin trousers and a buckskin tunic burst into the tavern. His long, dark, wild, unkempt beard flung from side to side. He pushed back those who he had knocked into on his way in. The music abruptly stopped, and Dalir stared in wonder at how wide the short fellow's shoulders were compared to the rest of his body. Behind him, two more Men appeared with a small dog. All three of the newcomers stood back-to-back-to back as the angry tavern goers who had been pushed aside cursed at them angrily. The short, stocky fellow waved his arm at them to back up, then headed towards the bar.

The short fellow's younger companion did not draw Dalir's attention. His older companion did. His blonde hair almost seemed silver, and he walked gracefully despite his dirty green wool trousers and ripped brown tunic. The three of them walked towards the bar as the silent tavern goers looked over three of them. Dalir noticed that quite a few of the people in the tavern were looking at the three newcomers then looking at him. Dalir did not want to be associated with the trouble-making newcomers and put up his hands defensively. A merchant from Stonedom in the table in front of him shook his head and pointed to the corner of the tavern besides Dalir. Dalir looked over and saw on old, faded parchment tacked to the tavern wall. The parchment had turned yellow from hanging there for ten years.

The parchment depicted a short, stocky figure with long hair and a long beard. Below the picture, in the common tongue, the words 'Wanted Dead or Alive' were printed. Above the picture, one word was printed on the parchment: DOBERVIST. Dalir gulped down the cider in his mouth and turned back to the three newcomers. The tavern goers around Dalir began to whisper, and he could feel the mood of the tavern change.

The taller newcomer with the silver-blonde hair produced three large gold coins and ordered food and drinks. Madoc looked into the tall newcomer's eyes when he placed three tankards of cider in front of him. Madoc gasped in shock once he saw his pupils. Madoc was left speechless after seeing the starry night eyes of the tall newcomer. The tavern owner almost forgot to take the gold coins. The whispers around Dalir were growing louder. Dalir heard the word 'Dobervist' being spoken softly amongst the crowd.

Dobervist grabbed the tankard of hard cider from the bar top and drained it. He had been parched from the constant running that they had endured all day. They had made it into Oakbridge just as the sun was setting. The Dwarf was eager for Aemon to get on with his plan. They had not seen their pursuers for some time, but Dobervist knew they would be searching this tavern sooner or later.   The Dwarf could hear the townsfolk whispering his name, and he knew it was a matter of time before one of them acted.

Dobervist slammed his empty tankard on the bar and pointed at Madoc to fill it. "What is the plan? They know who I am. If you are going to do something, then now is the time!" the Dwarf whispered urgently to the Elf. Aemon nodded and scanned the tavern. He found what he was looking for and walked over to the fiddle player. The elderly fiddle player looked up at Aemon and was about to ask what he wanted when the ancient Elf pointed to a young Man behind the fiddle player. The young Man was leaning against the hearth of the fireplace, a wooden crutch by his side. Aemon motioned for the young Man to join him, and the red-haired youth slowly limped out. His left foot was dragging on the tavern floor as he did. The boy was the son of the fiddle player, who was not going to allow some stranger to embarrass his disabled son.

The fiddle player stood up suddenly, causing his chair to be knocked over. The tavern went silent, expecting fisticuffs. "What do you want with my boy?" the fiddle player demanded, but he too was shocked when he looked into the Elf's eyes. His temper abated, and the fiddle player asked the Elf again what he wanted, but this time in a softer tone.

The tavern was silent except for the crackling of the fireplace. After a long moment, the Elf gently put his hands on the fiddle player, who was in awe of the constellation he saw in the Elf's eyes. Aemon guided the fiddle player away from his son, and the Elf stood in front of the youth who was leaning on his crutch. Aemon smiled and reached out and placed both his hands on the youth's bare neck. The red-haired youth cried out, not knowing what the tingling sensation coursing up and down his spine meant. A few of the Men in the tavern stood up, ready to defend the crippled boy. After a moment, Aemon withdrew his hands and stepped back.

The red-haired youth looked at Aemon in shock. He looked down at his left foot, which he had never been able to move. He could feel the blood pounding through the foot's veins, and he tried to move it. To his surprise, his left foot moved. The boy let out a whoop when his left foot moved into its normal position. Most of the tavern goers were standing now, and Dalir tried to look over them. Dalir heard a collective gasp from the crowd when the red-haired youth cast his crutch to the tavern floor and walked over to the bar. He turned back with tears of joy in his eyes and walked over to the Elf.

The boy's father rushed to his boy's side and looked on in disbelief as his son walked in front of him. The boy looked at his father and smiled, and both father and son were ecstatic and overcome with joy. The mood in the tavern turned to shock as the tavern goers looked at each other in disbelief. Dalir heard the word 'Elf,' and his heart raced. Dalir studied the tall blonde newcomer. The father hugged Aemon then began shaking his hand and thanking him. The tall blonde newcomer humbly accepted both the father's and son's praises and advised the boy to give the foot time to gain strength. The boy nodded, hugged Aemon again, then hugged his father before Aemon walked back over to Dobervist.

The shock and silence of the tavern evaporated as the red-haired youth began to dance to one of his father's tunes. Suddenly noise filled the air, and everyone present looked on in awe at Aemon and his companions. Aemon took a sip from his tankard of cider and looked over at Dobervist, whose face was still grim. "That was very nice of you, but our hunters are still after us," the Dwarf said while looking worryingly at the tavern entrance. Aemon nodded and, without warning, leaped dexterously onto the bar top. Usually, Madoc would clobber the offending patron's feet with his cudgel, but the tavern owner was too enthralled by the Elf to move.

Aemon put his hand palm out to silence the crowd before him. All the patrons of the tavern looked on in shock as the Elf began to speak. "My name is Aemon, good people of Oakbridge. I am an Elf from Thendara. I come here tonight to heal your sick and lame. To heal your cripples and infirmed. Bring them to me now, and I will help them, my friends," the Elf said loudly. An audible gasp once again came out of the tavern patrons. A middle-aged Man in a grey tunic and black pants pushed through the crowd in front of Aemon. His right arm was paralyzed from falling off a horse ten years ago. He looked up at Aemon with hope in his eyes. Aemon jumped down from the bar and put his hands on the injured man's neck. He, too, cried out as a tingling sensation engulfed his body. The crowd roared and whooped in joy when the popular townsman raised his right arm and began swinging it around.

Over the next hour, Dalir and the rest of the patrons looked on in awe and shock as Aemon healed one after one of the Oakbridge townsfolk. The blacksmith's blind mother regained her vision, a sickly child regained her strength back, and dozens of more townsfolk lined up for the miracle healing that Aemon offered. Toothaches disappeared along with sore backs and arthritis. An old farmer who was constantly coughing took a clear, deep breath for the first time in years. Aemon remained gracious the entire time he was healing, never asking for anything from the Oakbridge townsfolk. The line of townsfolk who needed healing dwindled to nothing, and after healing the last sick child, a loud roar of joy rang out through the tavern. The townsfolk slapped Aemon's back. They bought Dobervist tankards of cider and shook Marcus's hand. A few fed Stripe scraps of their boar meat.

Dalir stood, ready to walk over to the Elf and introduce himself. His father had told him to bring an Elf back to Koristan to heal his people from the plague before Capa could invade. Now against all the odds, an Elf was standing right in front of the Koristan noble. Dalir was determined to convince the Elf to join him. Dalir was about to go over when the tavern's twin doors were flung open, causing the tavern patrons around the doors to be knocked to the tavern floor.

Silence gripped the tavern. Four heavily armed Men stepped over those who they had knocked over. Dalir's jaw dropped when he spotted the unnaturally large Axius. Dalir had never seen a Man this big besides Flavus in the Arena. Cyprian drew his sword, and his fellow hunters followed suit. Cyprian pointed the sword at Aemon and motioned for him to come over.

Aemon shook his head. Stripe began to growl. Axius shook his head once he saw the small dog. His neck still bore the dog's teeth marks.

"Come with us NOW! You do not want to spill any blood now, do you?" Cyprian shouted, knowing of the Elf's disdain for violence. The Elf shook his head again. Dobervist slowly began to draw his knife, and Ragonious smiled at the Dwarf.

"You think your little knife is going to save you, Dwarf!" Ragonious said loudly. The Capan's words confirmed the tavern patrons' suspicions, and a few began to murmur about the fugitive Dwarf. Dobervist remained silent and held his knife by his side. Marcus, who was unarmed, looked behind him for another exit, but he only saw a pair of staircases.

"There is nowhere to run!" Cyprian said loudly. "Now come with us, Elf! Drop the blade, Dwarf, or we will kill you!" Cyprian shouted.

Dobervist let out a deep breath and looked over the Capans in front of him. He had been on the run for years, and he always figured that the vast reach of the Capan empire would eventually catch up with him. The Dwarf figured he could keep the four Men in front of him busy while the boy and the Elf escaped. "It took you imbeciles, ten years to find me. Now you expect me not to fight?" Dobervist growled. Everyone in the tavern froze, expecting violence to break out.

Dalir was one of the tavern patrons who were frozen. The sudden change in events had overwhelmed him with shock. Dalir could only watch as the Capans began to slowly advance towards the Elf, Dwarf, and young Man. The Elf grabbed his companions and began to back up, away from the Capans. The crowd of patrons split apart, allowing the three desperate companions to drawback towards the stairway opposite Dalir. Dalir looked across the bar, over the shoulders of the patrons seated in the barstools. He heard the Elf's voice cry out to the crowd. "Step forward, Men of Oakbridge. Defend me. I healed your sick. I healed your old. Save me!" the Elf pleaded.

The four Capans waved their short swords menacingly at the patrons of the tavern. "Stay back, Oakbridge peasants! We are Capans. We have Legions! They will be here next spring! Do you want your town burned? Do you want to be slaves in the mines down south?" Cyprian shouted. His words caused the patrons to remain frozen. The Elf's healing had healed the cripples and injured of Oakbridge. The Capan's words now paralyzed all the patrons. They all had heard of the Capan's cruelty to their Mercium neighbors to the west. They had heard the stories of slaughter, rape, and enslavement. They had heard that Stonedom had rebelled and had hoped to remain neutral. A few in the crowd who were armed thought of attacking the Capans. None of them wanted to make the first move, though.

The Capans advanced towards Dobervist, Marcus, and Aemon again. The three of them were against the bottom step of the stairway. "Step forward, Men of Oakbridge. Step forward!" the Elf pleaded. No one in the crowd moved, and Dalir was on the far side of the tavern. Cyprian looked around at the tavern patrons, who cowered from his grimace. He smiled, and his nose reared up in disgust over the commoners. He looked at the Elf and knew that his hunt was soon to be over. Cyprian took another step forward, and his comrades followed his lead.

"Help us! Aemon pleaded in disbelief. He had been certain that after healing the sick that the townsfolk would defend them. "Is there anyone who will defend us? Anyone?" Aemon cried out.

Silence greeted the Elf's pleas. Cyprian took another step forward, and it looked like the Capans were about to rush the Elf. It was then that Dalir heard his friend's voice. It resonated through the silent tavern, and everyone in the tavern looked towards the loud voice.

"I WILL DEFEND YOU!" Talar shouted. He brandished his broadsword, lifted his shield, and descended the stairway towards the Capans.

Chapter XXXVII- Aemon's Other Gift

Talar spotted the bed when he entered the small sleeping chamber. He sat down on the bed and was about to put his feet up when Mona chided him. "At least take your boots off Talar!" she exclaimed, and Talar obliged her request. They were both too tired to talk, and after Mona locked the door, they both fell fast asleep.

A few hours later, Talar heard a door shut in the room adjacent to his, and the noise brought him out of his afternoon slumber. He pulled his legs out of bed, his muscles still sore from their journey. Talar stood and walked over to the small table in the room and washed his face in the clean water provided by Madoc. Talar walked back over and looked down upon Mona, who was just starting to wake up. She sat upright in the bed, her long red hair unkempt by her slumber.

"We need to talk Talar about our future," Mona said and instructed Talar to sit by her. She looked at the youthful Talar and shook her head when she remembered when she had been Talar's age. Back then, she had hoped for a handsome, strong, wealthy nobleman to rescue her from the High Keep, but her wishes never came true. She looked at Talar now and questioned if her feelings about Talar were love or respect. She had read about true love while at the High Keep. She had read about how people fell in love at first sight and could not live without each other. She knew in her heart that she did not feel this way about Talar.

She did respect Talar, though. She respected his courage and bravery that he had shown against the Capans. Against the Emperor who had murdered her family. She respected his determination and grit. Besides that, he was kind and thoughtful, and she admitted that he was attractive despite his youth. Some Women could afford the luxury of waiting on true love. Mona knew she could not.

"I heard you talk to Dalir. On our last night on the Cold River," Mona said after taking Talar's hands into hers. Talar blushed and started shaking his head, not knowing what to say. Mona smiled, then gently kissed Talar on the lips.

"I accept Talar Stoneking. I accept your proposal for marriage," Mona said, her words leaving Talar speechless. He finally came to his senses and shook his head again. "I go to war, Mona. I fear I will not return. You should go to Mercium," Talar said quietly.

"Mercium? Mercium, Talar? Who do I know in Mercium? I have not been there since I was a child. Who will shelter a fugitive from Capa? From the Emperor?" Mona asked. Talar did not reply, for he had no answers.

"No, Talar. I shall be your wife. You have proven yourself to me time and time again. We will fight against the Capans together. For my family and for your people, we will fight Talar!" Mona said fiercely, and it was then that Talar fell in love with Mona. He had been on his own since his arrival in Capa, and now that loneliness vanished when they kissed each other passionately. Talar pulled the blankets back over the two of them.

Sometime later, Mona looked down on her sleeping lover and smiled. She looked out the window and saw that the sun had set. She stood and began to wash. Talar woke and began dressing. He looked at Mona's slim figure and shook his head. "I do not wish to upset you before our marriage ceremony Mona," Talar said, and from the tone of his voice, Mona knew something was up. She quit washing and looked over at Talar, who was putting on his boots.

"I know you want to fight against the Capans, Mona. You are not a warrior, though. You have never been trained. I think it best if you stay with the Elves when the battle does come. You can assist them," Talar said quickly, hoping Mona would agree.

Mona rolled her eyes, and from her expression, Talar knew that she was not in agreement. "I'm not planning on swinging a sword at the Capans, Talar. I am not daft. I will shoot Dalir's bow," she said briskly to Talar's surprise. Mona could sense Talar's doubt about her archery abilities.

"If you do not believe me, go to Dalir's room and fetch it for me," Mona said. Talar nodded, now pondering if Mona truly did have the strength to pull back the bow. She had climbed down from the High Tower and rowed up the Cold River after all. Talar left their room and walked over to Dalir's room. Alwin had used his key to enter Talar's room on their journey south when they had stayed in the tavern, and Talar was not surprised that his key opened Dalir's room. Talar spotted the bow and quiver of arrows next to Dalir's scimitar and grabbed them. He returned and presented them to Mona. She smiled, set the quiver down on the table, and brought up the bow.

She tossed her red hair back and grabbed the bow string. Talar looked on in silence as Mona slowly drew back the bowstring. Soon the bow was at the full knock, and she slowly let off, bringing the bow to its resting position. Talar grudgingly nodded, and Mona laughed at his skepticism. She set the bow down and was about to speak when above they both heard shouting from downstairs.

Talar looked at Mona inquisitively, then walked over to the door. Talar unlocked it then stepped out into the hallway, the voices from below getting louder as the shouting escalated.

"There is nowhere to run!" Cyprian said loudly. "Now come with us, Elf! Drop the blade, Dwarf, or we will kill you!" Cyprian shouted.

Talar looked down and was in shock. Below him, three figures were in a stand-off with four heavily armed Men. Talar's attention was on the tall blonde figure with silver hair. He was an Elf! Talar saw the four Men advance towards the Elf, and he knew he had to act. Talar turned then bolted back into the room.

"Capans! Downstairs! They are going to kill an Elf!" Talar exclaimed before he grabbed his sword and shield. Mona's jaw dropped in disbelief, and before she could ask a question, Talar was already out of the room and was striding down the hallway. Talar heard the Elf cry out for aid, he saw the townsfolk of Oakbridge hesitate, and he saw the four Capans advance. Talar pulled the leather sheath off the broadsword and tossed the sheath to the floor. Talar took a deep breath and began to descend the stairs. He rounded the bend in the stairway, and Talar marveled at how steady his hands were. The fear was pounding through him, but he pushed it out of his mind.

"Help us! Is there anyone who will defend us? Anyone?" Aemon cried out. Talar saw that no one in the crowd was going to aid the Elf. Talar knew it was up to him.

"I WILL DEFEND YOU!" Talar shouted, his voice startling him by loud it was. Everyone in the tavern turned their eyes towards Talar. He raised his sword and shield and walked down the final flight of stairs. Cyprian and Talar locked eyes. The Capan was surprised with the hatred he saw in the tall, young Man's eyes. Talar looked into Aemon's star-filled eyes and knew he was an Elf instantly. Talar nodded at Aemon as he walked past the Elf. Dobervist smiled at Cyprian. His odds of survival were increasing.

"Who are YOU, peasant? How dare you threaten a Capan!" Cyprian hissed, his words breaking the tavern's silence. Talar smirked at the Capan's arrogance.

"I am Talar Stoneking, Prince of Stonedom, and I do NOT trade words with Capan SCUM!" Talar shouted at Cyprian. His words stunned the tavern goers. The four Capans looked around nervously. The townsfolk began whispering Talar's name. The Stonekings were known as just and fair rulers and were well respected in Oakbridge. Now the Prince of Stonedom was in a standoff with four Capans, and the simple townsfolk could not believe what was happening. Talar knew the power of his family's name, and now he spoke to the townsfolk.

"Fight with me, Men of Oakbridge!" Talar shouted, pointing his sword at the crowd around him. "I am a Stoneking! Fight with me!" Talar roared, and some of the townsfolk now pushed towards the Capans. Cyprian sensed that the crowd was getting bolder.

"Stay back! Remember, our Legions will be here soon. They will burn Oakbridge if you disobey. They will burn Stonedom. They will destroy Thendara! Back off and let us have the Elf!" Cyprian hissed.

"Do you not believe in the Old Gods? Cannot you remember the Druids' teachings? Do you not pray at the stone pillar to the Gods?" Talar said, his voice chiding the townsfolk. The townsfolk and travelers in the tavern from the north began to nod. Their religion was ancient and widespread in these territories.

"Then what is wrong with you? The Gods have sent you a blessing. A healer. Yet you fail to defend him!" Talar kept up his scolding tone. "The God's will judge you in the next life, Men of Oakbridge. Remember that!" Talar shouted. More townsfolk began to push towards the four Capans. Cyprian was about to hiss another warning when Axius started laughing. The big Man's deep guttural laughs scared the townsfolk back, and Axius advanced towards Talar. He was sick of hearing the boy's voice. Talar brought up his shield, ready to defend himself as Axius advanced towards him. Axius raised his sword, ready to crush Talar when an arrow sliced through the air. The arrow landed in the tavern floorboard in front of the giant ex-Legionnaire's right foot.

The arrow halted Axius' advance. All eyes in the tavern turned towards the stairway. Mona stood there, bow in hand, and was now knocking another arrow. Madoc's wife, whose father was the blacksmith, picked up her husband's cudgel from below the bar. She thrust the club in Madoc's arms and glared at her husband. Madoc, who feared his wife's wrath, started to move forward, but a scowl from Cyprian stopped him.

The thud of the arrow hitting the floorboard jolted Dalir out of his state of shock. He was not going to stand by and abandon Talar. Dalir slipped through the crowd in front of him. He stole a cue from Aemon and flamboyantly jumped up onto a bar stool, then stepped onto the bar. Dalir cursed his stupidity for leaving the scimitar in his room. He drew the small knife from his pocket. All eyes now were locked on Dalir as he gingerly stepped around tankards of cider towards the Capans. Tadius backed up to Cyprian, keeping his sword up. The angry townsfolk were ready to mob them, and he did not want to die in the tavern.

"We need to go, little cousin. We will get him on the Road," Tadius whispered urgently. Cyprian shook his head in frustration, refusing to heed his cousin's demand. Dalir saw them whispering and now spoke up over the crowd.

"Take your friend's advice and leave Capan. Leave while you can, or you will never leave!" Dalir warned ominously. Cyprian wondered who the young Koristan was. Ragonious and Axius started to back up as the angry crowd crept forward.

Dalir was about to speak when he saw someone jump up to the bar counter beside him. It was the barmaid! She flung her long black hair back and brought up the cudgel that she had grabbed from Madoc's hands.

"Make room. Let them leave!" Dalir ordered. He knew the heavily armed Men would not die easily, and he did not want to see bloodshed. The crowd obliged, and Tadius and Ragonius saw that now was the time for them to escape. They looked over at Cyprian, who looked ready to hack his way to the Elf. They each grabbed one of his arms and started pulling him out of the tavern. Axius walked backward, waving his sword menacingly at the crowd until all four of them exited the tavern.

The door of the tavern slammed shut, and when it did, the tavern patrons cheered in victory. Townsfolk and out-of-town merchants alike began swarming Talar, Marcus, Dalir, and Aemon. They thanked them, shook their hands, and promised to buy them drinks. No one dared approach the Dwarf, and he and Stripe took up residence at the end of the bar. When an older Man with a large gut leaned in to kiss Sigrid, she hit him with the butt end of the cudgel. He cried out in agony, and the tavern patrons laughed as he staggered back to his seat.

Mona unknocked the arrow and returned it to the quiver at her hip. After Talar had flown out of the room, she had rushed to the stairway after grabbing the bow and arrow. Now, she stepped out of the shadows of the stairway and down into the tavern common area. Her movement caught a few of the crowd's attention, and soon all eyes in the tavern were now on Mona. She walked through the crowd towards Talar, and those in front of her made room for the red-haired woman with the bow.

She looked at her future husband with pride, for he had fearlessly stood up to her enemies. Talar saw Mona approaching and smiled when she neared. "That was a good shot, Mona. Beginners' luck, I suppose?" he asked jokingly. His words silenced the crowd, for all wanted to hear the Prince's words.

Mona threw back her head and laughed. Many Men in the crowd marveled at her beauty, despite her bleak clothing. "Good shot, Talar? I was trying to hit that big bastard!" Mona said. Her response drew a roar of laughter from the crowd.

After the crowd's laughter died down, Aemon spoke up, and all in the tavern heard the elegant Elf's words. "Who is your companion Prince of Stonedom? Who yields the bow which has saved my life?" he asked, coming closer to Talar and Mona as he did. The young Woman looked vaguely familiar to the Elf.

"She is Mona of Mercium. She is to be my wife once we reach Stonedom," Talar said loudly. His words brought a gasp from many in the crowd. Dalir started coughing on the cider that he was drinking when he heard Talar's words. Sigrid started slapping his back, and it took Dalir a few minutes before he could get his breath back. Throughout the crowd, the traders from Mercium and Stonedom began whispering. Talar could not make out what they were saying. Madoc's wife spoke up as Madoc returned from the entrance doors after locking them. Her family originally came from Mercium, and she could remember when the Capans had kidnapped the royal family of Mercium. The King and Queen of Mercium had been publicly executed, but all had wondered what had happened to the lost Princess. Madoc's wife could not resist asking the beautiful young Woman about her heritage.

"You are Mona of Mercium, my lady?" she asked Mona, and Mona nodded. "Was your father the King of Mercium, my lady? Are you truly Princess Mona?" she asked hopefully. Years and years of doubt and anxiety now evaporated from within Mona when she heard Madoc's wife question. After all the years away from her home, she had wondered if anyone remembered her. Tears of joy began to build up in Mona's eyes, and she walked over to Madoc's wife. She set the bow down upon the bar top and reached over, gently grabbing her shoulders. All in the tavern watched in silence.

"It is. I am Princess Mona. I was held in the Capital by the Emperor. Talar Stoneking helped me escape," Mona said emotionally. Madoc's wife beamed with happiness, and she took Mona's hands from her shoulders and held them in her hands.

From behind Talar and Aemon, an older Mericum trader spoke up. "You are not our Princess anymore," he said, and his words drew all the patron's attention. Mona looked back at the trader despite the sting from his words. "You are not our Princess," the trader repeated, but then to Mona's surprise, he bent over and kneeled on one knee. "You are our Queen. The Queen of Mercium! Queen Mona," he said loudly, then bent his head in respect. Both of his sons had died fighting the Capan Legions. He would never consider himself a Capan.

Mercium traders throughout the tavern kneeled in respect, and all in the tavern shook their heads in wonder. This night would be talked about for decades to come. The night that the Elves and the Queen of Mercium returned. Most of the tavern patrons would never forget what they saw. A few, however, would never remember, for Madoc offered free cider to all. The crowd swarmed the bar, and Mona returned to Talar and hugged her future husband.

A familiar tingling sensation now started to climb up Aemon's spine as he looked at Talar and Mona. He only felt the sensation when he first saw someone or something that would impact his future. He had felt it when he had met the Dwarf and when he had met Marcus. The sensation was another gift that the Gods had given him. Now the sensation coursed through his body as he looked at Talar. He had only felt the sensation this strong once before, hundreds of years ago. When he had first met the Paladin.

Chapter XXXVIII- An Oath Fulfilled

Dalir awakened to the noise of someone pounding on his door. The loud noise caused him to groan, and Dalir lifted his head off his pillow. He became nauseous and collapsed back on the bed. His mouth felt as dry as the deserts back home in Koristan. Dalir tried to roll over but found that someone was lying on his arm. He pulled the blanket back, and to his surprise, he saw a young Woman with blonde hair sleeping on his arm.

"Wake up, Dalir! We have to get going," Dalir heard Talar say from the hallway outside. Talar kept pounding on the door. Dalir took a deep breath and vainly tried to remove his arm from underneath the blonde Woman. He gave up and looked up at Talar as he entered his bedroom. Sunlight strewed through the lone window illuminating Talar. He shook his head at the sight before him. Dalir's fine red camel hair tunic and the rest of his clothes were scattered around the room. Amongst Dalir's clothes, Talar could see a Woman's dress. Half-empty tankards of cider filled the room. Talar accidentally knocked one over when he pulled the curtains open. Sunlight now filled the room, and Dalir groaned again.

"Quit your whining, Dalir. The Elf and the Dwarf are waiting for us downstairs! Hurry up and get dressed," Talar said, before throwing Dalir's clothes at him. Talar's words inspired Dalir. He heroically pulled his arm out from below the strange Woman in his bed. His actions caused the blonde Woman to awaken. She rolled over and began kissing Dalir. Dalir tried pushing her off him, but he could not summon the strength. Talar shook his head and wondered how to get Dalir on his feet. After chasing the Capans out of the tavern, the hard cider had flowed all night. The Elf had asked to join Talar's party to Stonedom, and other patrons of the tavern wished to travel with them as well. Now they all waited downstairs.

"C'mon Dalir, everyone is waiting for you!" Talar said. The drunk young townswoman kept kissing Dalir. He had only one tankard of cider last night, but Dalir had gone wild after a few tankards. He had gone to sleep only a few hours ago. Mona now entered the room, the bow slung over her shoulder, and she looked down at Dalir. She was not impressed. Mona grabbed the pot of water used for cleaning and threw the cold water on Dalir and the blonde woman.

The blonde woman shrieked and recoiled back underneath the blankets. "How dare you!" she said when her head popped up from underneath the blankets. When she saw that it was Mona that had doused her, she retreated underneath the blankets.

Mona smiled and looked at Dalir, who was still moving slowly for his clothes. "Do you want another one, Dalir? Hurry up!" Mona said sternly.

"Please no," Dalir whimpered as he clumsily pulled on his trousers and red cloak. Dalir checked his coin pouch and found that it was still full. He smiled, patted the blonde Woman's side, and stood up. Talar grabbed him to keep him from falling. Mona grabbed Dalir's knife and scimitar and handed them to him. Talar grabbed Dalir's rain cloak and steered him out of his room. Mona and Talar guided Dalir down the hallway and down the stairway.

Dalir looked over the tavern's common room as he pulled out a barstool to sit on. Aemon, Dobervist, and Marcus were sitting a few seats down from him. They all grinned when Dalir asked Madoc for some water. The tavern owner smiled and disappeared back into the kitchen. Madoc returned with the tankard of water. Dalir tried drinking, but his stomach was stirring relentlessly. He was not used to the hard cider, which was stronger than the wine he usually drank. Aemon took pity upon Dalir and walked over to him.

Dalir was staring miserably at the bar counter when he saw Aemon out of the corner of his eye. The Elf was leaning against the bar next to him. Remembering the oath he had sworn to his father, Dalir told Aemon that he needed to speak to him privately.

"Yes, I know Dalir. You told me this several times last night. We will speak later today, that is, if you can keep up with us today," the Elf said. Dalir shook his head in confusion. Dalir could not remember talking to the Elf last night. He could not remember much now that he was thinking about it.

"I will keep up, my Elven friend. I just have to catch my second wind," Dalir said weakly. Aemon shook his head in dismay, and Madoc came back with another tankard. The stout tavern owner pushed the tankard in front of Dalir, and the smell of the purple concoction caused his stomach to boil.

"By the Gods Madoc, what have you assaulted me with, on this fine morning?" Dalir asked. His question drew laughs from Aemon, Marcus, Mona, and Talar. Even Dobervist was smiling.

"Cure for any katzenjammer, my friend," Madoc said with a smile as he nudged the tankard closer to Dalir.

"What's in it?" Dalir asked, confused by Madoc's use of the Mempacton language.

"Radish juice, cumin, crushed hot mustard seeds, pepper, and a pinch of dill," Madoc replied as he leaned over the bar, curious if the foreigner would drink his concoction.

Dalir withdrew from the foul-smelling brew, and the others in the tavern tried not to laugh. He had never even heard of most of the ingredients. He was too weak to inquire about them. Unbeknownst to him, Sigrid was watching from the kitchen to see if he had drunk the brew that Madoc had instructed her to make.

"You will feel right as rain in an hour, young Lord. That concoction has been healing ill stomachs for forty years in this tavern," Madoc said in his northern accent. The rest of the tavern patrons looked on with anticipation. Dalir slowly brought the tankard to his lips. Dalir slowly began to drink, and to his surprise, the purple liquid was better tasting than it smelled. Dalir downed the tankard and dropped it on the bar top to the cheers of those in the tavern. He grabbed his stomach and let out a deep breath. He took another breath and smiled at Madoc. His stomach was feeling better. To the surprise of all those in the tavern, Dalir pulled a silver tenpence from his purse, tossed the coin on the bar, and started heading towards the exit.

As Dalir passed Talar, he stopped and whispered in his friend's ear. "Let us be gone of this place, that Madoc is trying to kill me, I swear." Talar laughed again. Talar picked up his sword and shield and led the party out of the tavern and into the mid-morning sunlight. Dobervist, Stripe, and Aemon were following Mona out of the tavern when Madoc's short wife handed Marcus a basket of food. Marcus was about to thank her when she hushed him out the tavern, pointing at his departing companions. Marcus nodded, grabbed the basket of food, and yelled out a quick thanks before he left the tavern.

Marcus looked out over Oakbridge and spotted the party to Stonedom in the market. A small crowd of townsfolk and merchants had formed around them. Marcus walked down the tavern steps and now marveled at the giant oak trees. He had not seen them when they had sprinted through the marketplace last night on their way to the tavern. He stared at the trees for a long time, overwhelmed by their presence. They were even bigger than the pines that he had cut. Marcus looked back at the tavern and realized it had been one of the oaks and that its broken top had formed the bridge. Marcus smiled, for now, he finally knew why Oakbridge was called Oakbridge. He almost blushed at his ignorance.

Marcus heard the townsfolk offering their thanks to Aemon and his friends. After joining his companions, a few of the townsfolk slapped his back in appreciation. For the first time since Tarquin's death, Marcus was at peace. He saw that the party to Stonedom was starting to leave. Marcus followed Dobervist and Aemon away from the townsfolks to the bridge over the Capulus river. Stripe playfully jumped on his leg, and Marcus bent over to scratch the dog's ears as he followed Aemon. Marcus saw that several townsfolk and merchants had joined the Prince of Stonedom's party. Marcus figured that altogether they would number about twenty. A Stonedom fur merchant had loaded supplies from the townsfolk onto his two-wheeled, ox-driven cart. The party to Stonedom waited for the Elf, Dwarf, and Marcus to cross the bridge. Marcus hoisted the basket on his shoulder and was about to set off across the bridge when Aemon suddenly turned. The Elf stopped, and his actions caused Dobervist to stop as well. Aemon walked up to Marcus and put his hand on his back and instructed him to place the basket of food down. Aemon guided Marcus over to the bridge's rail, and Marcus remembered the last time the Elf had laid his hands on him. He remembered how destitute he had been.

Aemon took his hand from Marcus's back and grabbed the rail of the bridge. The ancient Elf and the former street boy from Capa stared out over the roaring waters which flowed down the Capulus Valley. In the distance, the Capulus River cut through the seemingly endless rolling hills of northern Mercium.

Aemon looked up at Marcus and smiled. "I believe that you have upheld your oath to me, young Marcus," the Elf said gracefully. Marcus was taken aback by the Elf's words and remained speechless. "You risked your life helping me look for my friend. You bravely stood with me last night, Marcus. You could have died back in that tavern," Aemon said, gesturing at the Oakbridge tavern. Marcus nodded slightly, not knowing what to say. Aemon stepped back from the rail and threw his arm around Marcus's shoulders as if they were old pals.

"Now I head to Stonedom, and from there to Thendara. I have given up on my search for my lost friend. I must now prepare for war. War with your countrymen Marcus. You heard what they said last night. They will be coming in the spring," the Elf said softly. Marcus nodded and looked over at Dobervist. The bearded Dwarf was bent over, petting Stripe, but he had heard the Elf's words.

"I do not think it is wise for you to follow me any further. Like I said, you have upheld your oath to me," Aemon said. He did not think it practical to bring the young Capan into Thendara before the war. Aemon pointed out to the rolling hills of Mercium before them. "You are free from your oath Marcus. You are free to do as you wish. The world awaits you, young Man!" the Elf said excitedly. Marcus was dumbfounded by the Elf's words. Dobervist saw that Marcus was upset by Aemon's words. The Dwarf stood, and he and Stripe walked over to Marcus.

"The Elf is right, Marcus. You have fulfilled your oath. You stood with us last night when no others would. This Road here," the Dwarf said, pointing towards Stonedom, "only leads to war. War with Capa. Do you wish to fight your countrymen, Marcus?" the Dwarf asked solemnly. Marcus had not thought of any of this, but he knew the Elf and Dwarf's words were true. Marcus looked down at the running river below him, not knowing what to say or do.

After a moment of silence, Aemon reached into his trouser pocket and pulled out his purse of coins. He grabbed Marcus' wrist with one hand, and with the other, he placed the leather purse in Marcus' hand. Marcus knew the Elf's purse contained a small fortune of old Mempacton gold coins. He shook his head in wonder at the weight of the purse. Marcus looked into Aemon's starry night eyes and tried to push the purse back into the Elf's hands. Aemon playfully leaped away, and the Dwarf laughed.

Dobervist slapped Marcus on the back and shook his free hand. The Dwarf was crushing Marcus' hand, but Marcus did not show his discomfort. "You are a good Man, even if you are Capan. Hopefully, the Gods will look over you. Good luck, kid!" the Dwarf said gruffly. Dobervist released Marcus's hand, then turned and walked down the bridge. Aemon walked over to Marcus and shook his hand. Marcus stared in amazement at the stars moving in the Elf's pupils for a moment before releasing his hand. The Elf smiled and pointed out towards the rolling hills of Mercium again.

"You know, the coasts south of Borisco stay pretty warm in the winter Marcus. I have heard that Boriscan Women are quite friendly. If I were a young Man, with a purse full of coin, maybe I would head there," the Elf said. Aemon smiled, patted Marcus' shoulder, and turned to join the party to Stonedom.

Marcus remained mute, shocked at what was happening. He realized that the Elf was not stopping, so he called out to the Elf just as Aemon was about to step off the bridge. "Thank you, Aemon. Thank you for everything. I will never forget you!" he called out. The Elf stopped.

"Promise me you will not cut any more trees down, Marcus. Especially those," the Elf said, pointing at the two giant oaks. "I planted those. Leave those alone, Marcus!" the Elf said jokingly. Aemon turned away and started down the Great Road towards Stonedom.

"I won't cut any more trees down, Elf! I promise!" Marcus yelled. He shook his head at the sight of the ancient Elf walking away from him. Stripe jumped up onto Marcus's leg, and Marcus bent over to him. Marcus scratched his ears until Dobervist whistled for him to join him. Stripe looked up at Marcus, expecting him to join him. Marcus scratched his ears again. "I'm going this way, little buddy. You head to that Dwarf! He needs you more than I do!" Marcus said before he urged Stripe towards Dobervist. Stripe barked once as if he was saying goodbye, then raced over to Dobervist. A tear formed in Marcus's eye, but he was quick to wipe it away.

Marcus watched the Stonedom party for half an hour until they disappeared out of sight. He turned back and grabbed the rail where Aemon had stood. Marcus looked over the rolling hills of Mercium, and a sense of freedom washed over him. He was rich! He was alive! He was free! Marcus shook his head in wonder. For the first time in his life, Marcus could do whatever he wanted. The feeling of freedom made him start pumping his fist in joy. After a moment, Marcus realized that any of the townsfolk could be watching him. He looked around in embarrassment. None were, and Marcus looked back down the Capulus valley over Mercium. He could see the Great Road running alongside the Capulus, and he looked to his right where the Great Road met the bridge.

Marcus looked to his left. Stonedom lay that way, and Marcus knew he would not be welcome there since he was a Capan. He felt terrible about leaving his friends, but he knew that the Dwarf would look out for the Elf. Marcus looked back towards his right, picked up the basket of food, and took his first steps towards Mercium. Goosebumps went up Marcus' spine as he walked past the Oakbridge Tavern and down the Great Road towards Mercium. The roaring water of the Capulus drowned out the noise his boots made against the cobble.

Marcus looked out at the valley before him. The orange, red, and yellow leaves rustled due to the morning breeze. Marcus wished that Tarquin could see the sight before him now. Marcus looked up to the sky and yelled out. "I will never forget you, Tarquin! You are my brother! My friend! I will never forget you!" Marcus yelled, knowing that none would hear his voice over the roaring water. Marcus knew that Tarquin would not want him to succumb to grief, so Marcus pushed the thoughts of his deceased friend out of his head.

Marcus turned and looked back at Oakbridge one last time. The quaint village stood peacefully underneath the looming Stone Plateau. Marcus tried to etch the image in his memory. Marcus turned back and headed towards Mercium. Marcus spotted an eagle flying over the Capulus. "I am as free as you are, my friend!" Marcus said to the soaring bird. He pumped his fist in celebration as his feet kept moving down the Road.

Chapter XXXIX- A Hunter's Wrath

Tadius and Ragonius threw Cyprian towards the horses. Axius watched the Oakbridge tavern doors to see if any of the townsfolk were going to follow them. Cyprian turned towards them, his arms shaking with rage. Tadius had never seen his cousin in such a state. "That bastard Prince is going to die! Mark, my words cousin, mark my words!" Cyprian seethed. He was still holding his short sword, and now he pointed it at Axius. "If that big bastard could remain still, we would already have that damn Elf! We had them, Tadius, we had them!" Cyprian whined in frustration. Tadius and Ragonius looked at each other worryingly. They had never seen Cyprian lose his composure before.

"Calm down, Cyprian. We will ambush them further up the Road," Tadius said, pointing towards the bridge. Ragonius nodded and sheathed his sword. The former gladiator champion began untethering the horses they had purchased in Oakbridge two weeks ago.

"That Elf and that Prince will have an entourage to Stonedom. I guarantee you that we just made him a hero by running out of there. We should have grabbed the Elf while we had him in that tavern," Cyprian sneered angrily.

"We will ambush them all, little cousin, past the Lakes up the Road. Saddle up for now and let us set off. We accomplish nothing by standing here!" Tadius admonished. Cyprian shook his head in frustration, but he knew Tadius was right. He sheathed his sword, mounted his horse, and slowly rode to the bridge. Cyprian waited for the others to mount, especially Axius, whose horse was barely big enough to support his large frame. Ragonius rode over to Cyprian, and both hunters stopped halfway across the bridge, looking east towards Stonedom.

"Your cousin is right, Cyprian," Ragonius said softly. Cyprian said nothing and just stared out into the valley that was lit up by the full moon. "It does not matter how many swords the Prince rallies tonight. We will put a few volleys of arrows into them and let Axius rush them. That is why we keep him around, right?" Ragonius said coldly.

Cyprian nodded in agreement at Ragonius' plan, and some of the anger within him began to subside. Ragonius could sense that his words had some effect, and he looked over at Cyprian, ready to comment on how joyous it would be to see Axius fall in combat. Before he did, his eyes spotted campfires further down the Capulus Valley. Cyprian noticed Ragonius looking past him. He looked downriver, down the Capulus Valley, and spotted the campfires as well.

The two hunters looked at each other, and both smiled. The campfires were spaced out equally and symmetrical. Only a Legion would set up their camp like that. Tadius and Axius rode up to their companions, the noise of their horses' hooves alerting Ragonius. Ragonius pointed out the campfires to them. All four hunters stared down into Mercium at the fires. After a moment of silence, Cyprian spoke.

"Tadius, you will remain with the Elf. Stay out of sight and keep track of him. We cannot be certain that he is headed towards Stonedom just because he was with the Prince. Do you have your signaling mirror? Cyprian asked.

Tadius nodded and produced the small mirror from his knapsack. "Will you be getting more swords, cousin?" Tadius asked. Cyprian nodded in the moonlight.

"The three of us will head down the valley and bring back more swords. We should be able to reach that Legion by morning!" Cyprian said excitedly. With a Legion so close, the hunt was back on, and Cyprian was again full of enthusiasm. "Stay out of sight, Tadius, and use the mirror twice an hour to signal your position. Look for my reply!" Cyprian said to his cousin. He then wheeled his horse around and took off down the Great Road towards Mercium. Ragonius and Axius spurred their horses and took off after their leader. Tadius rode forward, planning to hide out in the forests overlooking Oakbridge until the Elf departed.

Cyprian urged his horse on at breakneck speeds, and Ragonius and Axius followed behind. The moonlight above illuminated the deserted Great Road in front of them. They did not speak or slow down, and Cyprian knew they would need new horses when they reached the Legion. For hours they rode like this, their horses covered in sweat, blood dripping from their noses as the hunters rode them to death.

 The sun rose over the Stone Mountains in the east. Cyprian and his hunters rounded a bend in the Great Road and spotted smoke below them in a field close to the Capulus. Cyprian did not stop and kept riding hard towards the field. He spotted a patrol of sentries and stopped his horse. He climbed off, and when his feet hit the ground, the horse collapsed, desperately panting for air. Cyprian ignored the horse and started walking towards the startled sentries.

Ragonious and Axius dismounted from their horses and joined Cyprian. The three hunters walked towards the Legionnaires, who had raised their javelins in defense. "We are Capans! We are scouts! What Legion is this, and who is the commander?" Cyprian growled. The senior Legionnaire in charge of the patrol hesitated before answering Cyprian. The three horsemen's sudden appearance perplexed the Legionnaire, for his commander had told him nothing about incoming scouts.

"There are no scouts coming from your direction!" the Legionnaire shouted. His commander had warned the Legion about Riken infiltrators, and now he pulled his short sword out and pointed it at Cyprian. Cyprian shook his head in frustration. He began unbuttoning his tunic, and the Legionnaire wondered what he was doing. Cyprian eventually pulled out a ring on a thin silver chain. Cyprian broke the chain and put the ring on. He brazenly walked over to the senior Legionnaire, and he flashed the ring in the Legionnaire's face.

When the Legionnaire saw the ring, he immediately lowered his sword and fell to his knees. His comrades followed suit, and the Legionnaire begged for forgiveness. The Legionnaire had seen a ring exactly like the one on Cyprian's finger only once before. That had been when he had joined the Third Legion and kneeled before Commander Clavis. It was Capan tradition for Legionnaires to kiss the skull ring on his Commander's finger before officially joining. Every Legionnaire knew that only the ten Legion commanders and the Emperor's personal henchmen carried the silver skull rings. From the looks of the four horsemen, the Legionnaire guessed they were the latter.

"Answer my question, Legionnaire, and do it quickly," Cyprian said coldly. The Legionnaire informed the hunter that it was the Third Legion and that Clavis commanded it. Cyprian nodded, then ordered the Legionnaire to take him to his commander. The morning sunlight had chased away the pre-dawn shadows. Cyprian could see that most of the Legion had already broken camp. The senior Legionnaire led them through the company of engineers that was breaking down the officer's tents. One large red tent remained standing, and the senior Legionnaire brought the horseman with the skull ring to it. He saluted the senior guard at the red tent and went back to his duties. A few of the engineers working around the four hunters wondered who they were, but they kept their questions to themselves. Their campaign had been successful but long. The Rikens had regrouped into small bands after their massive defeat, and it had taken several weeks to bring them all to heel.

"Who are you?" the tall guard outside of the tent demanded. Cyprian showed him the skull ring, and he too fell to his knee before the hunter. The guard's movement caught Clavis's attention, and he walked out of the tent to see what was going on.

Clavis caught sight of the skull ring on Cyprian's finger before they locked eyes. Clavis remained silent, for he was caught off guard, and he did not like the feeling. He had heard ill rumors of the Emperor's mysterious hunters, and now they were in front of him. Clavis's bodyguard emerged from the tent and stood behind the kneeling guardsmen.

"Who are you?" Clavis asked calmly, for he had heard that these Men were used to dispose of unruly Legion commanders.

"My name is not important. Time is, though. What you do now is more important than any battle that you have won. The Emperor himself will hear about your decision. I need as many Legionnaires and horses that you can spare. I need them now," Cyprian said respectfully, not trying to provoke the Legion commander. Over the years, Cyprian had met more Legion commanders than he could count. He had learned that the most flamboyantly dressed commanders were usually the worse to work with. Luckily, this one was attired in the Legion's standard officer uniform, along with his skull ring.

Clavis took a moment to consider Cyprian's words. Most of the Legion had left before dawn, his officers eager to return to their homes in Capa. Clavis had stayed behind with his bodyguard to oversee the breakdown of their camp. Only the engineers, the sentries, and his guards remained. They all had horses, though.

Clavis nodded before speaking. "I can only spare thirty of these engineers. They have fresh horses. Where are you taking them?" Clavis said cautiously.

"That is not important, Commander. How long before they are ready to ride? We must be leaving soon!" Cyprian said impatiently.

Clavis nodded and saw the frenzy in Cyprians' eyes. Clavis looked over to his Riken bodyguard, whose name was Gunther. "I will see to it immediately, Commander!" Gunther said before saluting. Clavis nodded in appreciation when his useful bodyguard left to organize the engineers. Gunther had been the first Riken chief to ally with the Capans, and his knowledge of the Riken lands had helped the Legions win. As a reward, his son Ashgar had been sent to Capa to become a Capan lord. Now Gunther began barking orders at the engineers, his thick Riken accent sometimes making his words unintelligible to those around him.

Clavis offered Cyprian breakfast inside the tent, but the hunter refused. He did not eat much anymore, maybe some berries or an apple now and then. Neither did Ragonious or Tadius. The Elf blood kept them strong, not vittles. Clavis heard the large hunter's stomach growl, so he brought out a few hard-boiled eggs and handed them over to Axius.

By the time Axius had swallowed down the last egg, the thirty engineers were mounted and in formation behind the hunters. The morning sun was shining, and Clavis looked up and thought it was going to be a warm day. So far, the northern snows had stayed away, and he was thankful for that. Gunther returned to the tent's entrance and informed Clavis that the company of engineers was ready. Clavis looked at Cyprian and gestured at the engineers behind him. "These Legionnaires are yours. Tell the Emperor that I live to serve him!" Clavis said before kneeling on one knee. Gunther followed his lead, and Cyprian was pleased with the commander's obedience and display of respect.

One of the sentries brought three fresh horses to the hunters, and they quickly mounted. "The Emperor will hear of your loyalty, Commander, I promise you that. I will send your Legionnaires back when I am done with them!" Cyprian shouted. He then dug his heels into the horse's flanks and took off. His fellow hunters and the engineers followed them. Their horses' hooves thudded loudly through the field. Clavis stood and watched his Legionnaires and the strange hunters ride towards Oakbridge. He wondered what they were up to. He did not like sending his troops off out on their own into enemy territory, but he knew better than to risk the Emperor's wrath.

After they had ridden out of eyesight, Clavis ordered his remaining bodyguards to assist in taking down the rest of the Legion's camp. He told Gunther to walk with him as his tent began collapsing behind him. "I have a task for you, my old friend," Clavis said to Gunther. They had fought together for five years, and Gunther was the closest thing to a friend that Clavis had. Gunther nodded, and Clavis had the feeling that the clever Riken knew what he was going to be ordered to do.

"Take a horse and keep an eye on my Legionnaires, Gunther. Keep out of sight and observe those strange hunters. See what they are up to. Do not be seen, Gunther! Do you understand?" Clavis asked, and the greying Riken nodded. Gunther was older than Clavis but was still in astounding shape for being fifty years old. He placed his helm over his brown, greying hair and set off for his horse. Soon Gunther was speeding through the field, his horse throwing up clumps of dirt as he galloped. Clavis watched his bodyguard disappear behind the tree line and shook his head. He had never let an enemy force catch him on his flanks before, but now he felt like he had. He did not know what that skull bearer was up to, but he did not like it.

One of the remaining sentries informed Clavis that they were ready to debark and join the rest of the Legion. Clavis nodded and looked up the valley in the direction of Oakbridge. When he had woke up a few hours ago, he had been looking forward to leaving. Now he wanted to stay, but he could not leave the Third leaderless. He knew something foul was amok near Oakbridge. He desperately wanted to know what was happening. Clavis sighed. He would have to be patient. The sentry brought over his mount, and Clavis mounted the pinto-colored horse.

Clavis waited for the rest of his Legionnaires to mount their horses and supply wagons. He had been caught off-guard in enemy territory, and he vowed to himself not to let that happen again. The sentry rode next to him, awaiting his commander's orders. "We are done with this country Legionnaire. We are headed towards Capa. I bet the Women are waiting for a Legionnaire like you, my friend!" Clavis said to the young Legionnaire. He smiled at his commander's joke. "To Capa!" Clavis shouted, and his Legionnaires followed him across the field towards the Great Road.

Chapter XL- Old Friends

Talar smiled at Mona before she playfully punched his arm. His gaze returned to the familiar landscape that lay around him. Clear, blue lakes and ponds filled the far northern end of the Capulus valley. They were the source of the river. The Great Road gently snaked its way upward around the lakes. Copses of birches and aspens overlooked the bodies of water, and the party to

Stonedom passed through one now. The golden and yellow leaves of the birches and aspens fell upon the party due to a light breeze.

It had been a few hours since their departure from Oakbridge, and with every step, Talar took he felt more at ease. They were getting closer to Stonedom, and Talar wanted to see his brother and friends. One of the wheels of the cart hit a pothole in the road and became stuck. Talar and two of the Oakbridge townsfolk threw their shoulders behind the cart, and it quickly became free. The Oakbridge townsfolk had armed themselves with wooden staves and spears. Only the blacksmith's two sons carried swords. The townsfolk used the staves and spears as walking sticks as they casually strolled along the Great Road.

Dalir looked up through the golden leaves of the overhanging aspens at the snow-covered Stone mountains. Rocky ledges were visible when the clouds parted, and Dalir thought of climbing the mountains that were even higher than the Stone Plateau. The party rounded a bend in the Road, and a large heron was startled and flew over them, back towards Oakbridge. Dalir turned to gaze at the strange long-beaked bird, and when he did, he saw someone behind them on the Great Road.

Dalir walked around the two-wheeled cart and informed Talar of the unknown figure behind them. Talar ordered the party to halt, and now all those bound for Stonedom turned to watch the figure approach. As the figure grew closer, all could see that the person was running briskly along the Road. Dalir's jaw dropped in astonishment once he saw Sigrid's black hair bouncing back and forth. She had left her barmaid outfit at the tavern and was adorned in buckskin trousers like Dobervist's. She slowed down when she came within speaking distance to the party. She bent over to catch her breath. Besides her buckskin trousers, she was wearing a red tunic that looked like Dalir's. "Your fashion choices are becoming quite popular, Dalir," Mona teased. Dalir tried to hide his embarrassment. His heart was racing at seeing Sigrid again.

Sigrid regained her breath and began speaking in her native tongue. Talar and Dalir looked at each other and shrugged. Neither spoke Riken, and neither had a clue what she had said. Talar was about to ask if anybody in the party spoke Riken. To his surprise, Aemon began conversing with Sigrid in her native tongue. Despite not knowing what she was saying, it was obvious that Sigrid was upset about something. After a moment of conversing, Aemon nodded and motioned for Sigrid to join them. Sigrid walked over to Dalir's side of the ox cart, and he handed her a waterskin from the cart. She drank from it and handed it back to Dalir with a smile.

"What did she say, Aemon? She seemed upset?" Talar asked. The cart and everyone around it resumed their journey along the Great Road.

"She says that she was a Queen among the Riken. That she led her people in a great battle against Capa and that they lost. She was expelled from her tribe. She hates the Capans and wants to fight against them," the Elf said.

Talar and Dalir were stunned by Aemon's words, but Mona started laughing. She walked behind the cart, then hugged Sigrid. Sigrid looked at Mona with surprise but did not retreat from her gesture of kindness. "I think I've met my new best friend!" Mona exclaimed and then began introducing her companions.

"You have already talked to Aemon, and that tall, lanky fellow is Talar. This is Dalir, of course," Mona said, seemingly oblivious to the fact that Sigrid could not understand her. Mona introduced Dobervist as "the Dwarf" before he sulked behind the Elf. All the townsmen and merchants had stayed clear of the infamous Dwarf so far, not wanting to upset the former gladiator. Being around Princes, lost Princesses, and a legendary Dwarf and Elf was something that none of the common folk had ever expected in their lives. To the common folk escorting Aemon, they seemed to be living in a tale or fable, something that people would speak about for centuries after.

Sigrid nodded and clutched Mona's left hand as if they were old friends. Dalir shook his head as the two women chatted incessantly, despite not knowing what the other was saying. He rolled his eyes and walked over to Talar and Aemon. They each nodded at Dalir as he fell in pace with them. Dalir looked over at Dobervist, who returned his friendly smile with a grimace. Dalir fell back in line, and Aemon shook his head at the Dwarf's unfriendly attitude. Stripe ran over to Dalir and began jumping up on him, and Dalir bent over and tossed a stick for the dog to fetch. Stripe bounded through the yellow leaves and grass, picked up the stick, and returned it to Dalir. Dobervist cursed and shook his head.

"What is your problem now, Dwarf? I have met hundreds of your kind, but you are by far the grumpiest Dwarf I have ever met!" Aemon stated.

"I've had that dog for ten years, and he has never brought the stick back for me!" the Dwarf exclaimed loudly before looking up at Aemon. There was a moment of silence, and Aemon, Talar, and Dalir looked at each other. The three of them all laughed loudly at the Dwarf's expression. Dalir threw the stick again, and when Stripe brought it back again, there was even more laughter. Even Dobervist started laughing a little.

After the laughter stopped, Aemon looked over at Dalir, who did not notice the tall Elf studying him. The young Man from Koristan had pestered the Elf repeatedly the night before in a drunken manner. The rowdy tavern crowd, coupled with Dalir's inebriated state, had prevented the two of them from communicating. Now on the open road, the Elf thought it would be a good way to pass the time.

"You wanted to talk last night, young Dalir, well now is a good of a time to talk as any," the Elf said. Dalir saw that none of the commoners were close enough to hear him, but he was not sure if he wanted to unveil the true intentions of his journey north to Talar. Dalir kept silent for a moment, and Aemon was about to ask if he had heard his words when Dalir began to speak.

"My father, the ambassador to the Emperor of Koristan, sent me north to find an Elf," Dalir said, and his words shocked Talar. Dalir turned his eyes away from Aemon and looked over at Talar regretfully. "There is an awful plague afflicting Koristan, and we seek the help of your race to overcome the malady," Dalir said carefully. The news shocked Talar, for he had heard of no plague in Koristan before this. Along with Mona, he had suspected that Dalir had been sent north with them for some additional reasons, but he had not expected this.

The two young Men, Elf, Dwarf, and dog kept walking alongside the cart, the only noise being the wooden wheels creaking as they passed along the Road. Aemon thought over Dalir's request in silence. Hanno had taught Dalir enough about negotiations that Dalir knew better than to press the ancient Elf for an answer immediately. He had also taught Dalir that you did not have to negotiate an entire deal at once.

Aemon thought over Dalir's request as he looked up at the snowy Stone Mountains. There were no snowy mountains in Koristan, only deserts and fertile farmland along the great rivers. He and his kind had once established a small colony in Koristan until the power of Elf blood had become known. Aemon shook his head as he thought back to that fateful day three hundred years ago in the palace of the King of Koristan. He had been summoned to heal the elderly Queen by the King and had accidentally cut his finger on a piece of parchment. The old Queen had dabbed her finger in his blood then raised it to her mouth. Before Aemon could stop her, she had put her finger in her mouth and instantly turned fifty years younger. Aemon would never forget the King's face when he saw what a few drops of Elf blood had done to his wife. He had ordered Aemon and his companions into chains. For years, Aemon had been captive in the King's dungeon, his blood drawn daily. Eventually, the Paladin rescued him. Aemon had never returned to Koristan. The Capans had become aware of the power of Elf's blood somehow, and Aemon suspected it was from the blood the Koristans had taken from his body.

Now there was an Emperor in Koristan, and Aemon wondered if this Emperor knew of the power of Elf blood. The nations and tribes of Men were constantly collapsing, and when they collapsed, technology, ideas, and traditions were lost. He wondered if the knowledge of Elf blood had been lost to the rulers of Koristan.

"Who rules Koristan now, Dalir? How long has this Emperor's family been in power?" Aemon asked, and the question surprised Dalir. The young noble had assumed the ancient Elf would know, but he answered diligently, nonetheless.

"The House of Malichus has been in power for over a hundred years, Aemon the Elf," Dalir replied. Aemon shook his head, then darted around a pothole in the road.

"How old is this Emperor? How did the last Emperor die? Do you know these things?" Aemon asked, and Dalir nodded. Talar and Dobervist remained silent, but both were keenly listening to the conversation.

"The current Emperor is a young Man, only thirty years old. His father died due to chest problems. He had coughing fits for years before he succumbed to it, and his son became Emperor. It was a peaceful transition of power," Dalir stated with pride, for lesser countries were constantly bickering over leadership.

Aemon nodded, for it seemed to him that the power of Elf blood had been lost to the Koristans. He walked on in silence, thinking about the future and the upcoming war. After a few moments of reflection, Aemon spoke.

"If I survive the upcoming war, I might consider returning to Koristan and helping your people, young Dalir," Aemon stated. Talar looked at Dalir, curious to see his friend's reaction. He could tell Dalir was analyzing something.

"We share a common enemy, Aemon. My father told me that if you help Koristan, then the Emperor will declare war on Capa!" Dalir said proudly. Talar and Aemon stopped in their tracks at hearing Dalir's words. Dalir had to urge them on to keep up with the rest of the party. Dalir's words bounced through Talar's mind as he thought of the consequences of Koristan declaring war on Capa. The Capans would have to keep most of their Legions around Capa to defend it, making the defense of Thendara much easier. He might not die in the war! He could live with Mona!

Aemon thought over Dalir's offer. If the young Koristan words were true, Aemon knew that he or one of his kind must begin the journey to Koristan and soon. He remembered Marcus' warning of the invading Legions that were preparing for war. The Elf knew they were not enough warriors between Stonedom and the Dwarves to fend off such an army. He knew he needed another army to help his people.

"I will give you the answer once we return to Stonedom and I confer with my people," Aemon told Dalir. Dalir nodded upon hearing the Elf's answer. Talar wondered why the Elf would hesitate at accepting such an important deal but did not risk offending the Elf by asking him.

The next few hours passed without interruption, and the party made good progress on top of the cobble-lined Great Road. As the sun began to set in the west behind them, Talar began to look for a good spot to rest for the night. The party walked past several small ponds that were full of water lilies, and Talar felt happier now than at any time in recent memory. He was close to home, he was set to be married to a beautiful Woman, and he finally had hope about the upcoming war since Dalir's revelation.

The party had not passed any old farms for quite some time, so when Talar spotted the ruins of a stone farmhouse and barn on a knoll overlooking the Road. He told the party that would be where they would set camp for the night. The party walked up the small knoll, and the orange ox that pulled the cart protested. The Mercium merchant on top of the cart used his whip, and the ox stubbornly pulled the small cart up the hill and behind the single-story farmhouse, which was mostly collapsed.

The townsmen and traders began setting up for the night in the flat area. Talar looked around the abandoned farmstead and shook his head in disgust. Capa's betrayal seventy years ago had caused Mempacton to fall and all these farms to be left to ruin. Now the forest was slowly taking over the farmstead. Grass grew throughout the farmhouse, and vines snaked up along its remaining walls. The two-story barn had a large hole in its roof, and a maple tree had grown through it, its orange leaves covering the farmyard.

Aemon joined Talar, Dalir, and Dobervist as they scouted around the large, decaying barn. They walked around the side farthest from the house. Talar examined a grindstone, its wooden crank handle, and frame still in good shape. Dobervist leaned back against the barn, weary from his constant travels. Dalir picked up an old rusty scythe and tried it out on some of the weeds growing up around the barn. Aemon laughed at Dalir's futile attempts, but he quit laughing when he rounded the barn's corner and looked out.

A large, black horse neighed loudly and walked over to greet Aemon. The horse's neighs brought Talar, Dalir, and Dobervist to the back of the barn, and all three looked on in shock as the tall, black steed lowered his head into the Elf's arms. Besides being familiar with the Elf, the horse appeared to be decrepit and old. Most shockingly, the horse was covered in rusty chain mail, and he neighed again as Aemon fumbled with the rusty metal straps that held the chain mail in place. The Elf unstrapped the chain mail and pulled it off the horse, leaving a cloud of rust in the air after the chainmail hit the ground.

Talar looked at the black horse and could see tufts of greying hair. He also saw long, white scars across the horse's body. Talar wondered if the large horse was a warhorse. He was big enough to be one. Talar had only seen draft horses as big as the black steed in front of him.

"Is it you Plumo, is it truly you?" Aemon cried out loud, and the horse neighed and again muzzled the Elf, who hugged him.

"It has been too long, my friend. Too long," Aemon said as he stroked the old horse's mane. "Bring me to him, Plumo, bring me to him," Aemon said softly. Dalir, Talar, and Dobervist's jaws dropped when the horse neighed and slowly turned. The horse looked back at Aemon, then to Talar's surprise, the horse looked at him. Talar stared into Plumo's dark eyes until the horse snorted and led Aemon to the other side of the barn.

The aging horse stopped and neighed once more after he reached the opposite side of the barn. Aemon spotted a keg of cider leaning against the barn and walked over to it. Past the keg, under a rotting wagon with one wheel, lay his friend, whom he had been searching seventy years for.

Talar and the others spotted the Man lying underneath the wagon. He was covered in rusty plate mail, a form of armor that had gone out of style long ago. Talar shook his head and held his nose. He could smell the Man's rancid body odor. He could also smell vomit, and Talar spied where the Man had gotten sick. Talar shook his head and asked Aemon the question that was on his, Dalir's, and Dobervist's minds.

"Who is that Aemon? Do you know him?" Talar asked. Aemon shook his head, and for a moment, Talar did not think he was going to answer him. Finally, the Elf spoke. "That is the Man I have been looking for, Talar Stoneking. He is my friend and a family member," the Elf said as he began to pull the Man by his legs out from underneath the cart. The Man groaned and flapped his arms helplessly.

"Who is he, Aemon? Who is he?" Talar asked again. The Elf stopped pulling on the man. Aemon pointed down on the passed-out Man, then looked at

Talar. "He is my brother-in-law, Talar. He is also the Paladin of Mempacton," the Elf serenely said. Aemon's words stunned Talar.

"THAT is the Paladin of Mempacton?" Talar asked incredulously. Aemon nodded, and the armored Man rolled about before vomiting on his armor.

"That is the Paladin of Mempacton, Talar. Now give me a hand and let us get him up," Aemon said calmly. Talar was shaking with disbelief as he helped the lost Paladin of Mempacton to his feet.

Chapter XLI- Family Revelations

Aemon and Talar got the heavily armored Man to his feet, but they strained underneath his weight and his armor's weight. His stench was nearly unbearable, and both the Elf and Prince gasped for fresh air as they brought him around the barn. All three of them fell when the armored Man tripped on a vine. Dalir rushed over to give aid. With his help, the three of them helped the Man to the barnyard.

Dobervist lagged behind the others, not bothering to help the drunk Man. Like Aemon, he had spotted the keg of hard cider. Dobervist picked up the half-empty keg with ease and drank the warm, bitter cider. Dobervist set the keg down and was about to follow the others back to the barnyard when the horse that Aemon had called Plumo suddenly walked in front of him.

Plumo nudged the Dwarf backward, towards the one-wheeled cart where the Man had slept. Dobervist backed up, not wanting to spook the old horse. Like most Dwarves, he did not like horses, who towered over him. "Easy boy," Dobervist growled, ready to punch the horse in the mouth. Plumo kept advancing, gently pushing Dobervist back until he stood next to the broken cart. Plumo neighed and looked at the Dwarf expectantly. "What is it?" the Dwarf asked, raising his hands in confusion.

Plumo neighed again and began pawing the ground with his hoof. The horse's hoof struck something metallic, which got the Dwarf's attention. Plumo neighed again and lowered his head to the ground where he had been pawing. The Dwarf shook his head and bent over by the old horse. Dobervist brushed away some leaves and twigs until his hands touched smooth metal. Dobervist kept brushing away the leaves until his eyes could make out the outline for a large metal shield. He picked up the kite-shaped shield with both hands and studied it. Plumo remained silent and looked on as the Dwarf admired the old, rusty metal shield. The kite-shaped shield was a style that the Dwarf had never seen before, but he could tell the rusty shield was well crafted despite its current shape. The shield's round top tapered down to a point and was nearly as tall as the Dwarf. Dobervist ran his fingers over the face of the rusty shield, and he could feel intricately interwoven patterns on the shield.

Plumo neighed again, and the Dwarf stopped admiring the shield and looked at the horse. Plumo was staring at the spot where the shield had been, and now Dobervist looked there. Poking up through the orange and yellow leaves, he could see another piece of rusty metal. Dobervist set the shield against the broken cart and bent over again. He used his hands to brush off the leaves, and this time the outline of a sword became visible. Dobervist shook his head as he picked up a rusty sheath with a smooth, round pommel sticking out. The sword was longer than the short swords Dobervist had used in the Arena. Dobervist pulled on the sword, expecting it to be rusted shut inside the rusty sheath. To his surprise, the sword easily pulled away from the sheath, and Dobervist held the sword up to inspect it. To his astonishment, the sword's blade was rust-free. He smiled at seeing the craftsmanship and wondered how a drunk could have acquired such a weapon. He took a few swings with the sword and was surprised at its balance and light weight. He sheathed the sword, picked up the shield, and with Plumo trailing behind him, he walked back to the barnyard.

Aemon, Talar, and Dalir had just dragged the unconscious Man into the barnyard, and there was confusion amongst the party once everyone had spotted them. Sigrid had been instructing Mona on how to use the bow that she carried. She handed the bow back to Mona. They walked over to the armored Man, who was laid down against the cart. The rest of the townsmen and merchants who had joined them walked over as well, creating a cluster around the cart. Questions filled the air, but neither Talar nor Aemon answered.

"Give me some room to talk to him, Talar. I cannot focus with all these people around me. I wish to speak to him alone," Aemon said before he bent over his lost friend. Talar nodded and began instructing the party to step back. They listened to Talar and began to disperse. Mona grabbed Talar by the arm and asked him who the stranger was.

"I do not know Mona. Aemon claims he is a kinsman to him. We found him behind the barn," Talar said as Dobervist now entered the barnyard. Talar saw the sword and shield that the Dwarf was carrying and walked over to inspect them. Talar walked ahead of Mona, giving Dalir a chance to confer with her.

"The Elf says that rank Man is their Paladin! The one that got Talar in trouble back in the Academy," Dalir said to Mona. Mona rolled her eyes and looked back at the dark-haired, disheveled Paladin. His long, black hair was covering his face, and the Elf was shaking him, trying to bring him out of his drunken stupor. Mona shook her head in disgust.

"That is the knight that Talar revers? A drunk wandering the wilderness?" Mona said sadly. She was worried about the disappointment that Talar would have to deal with once he realized his hero was a drunk.

Dobervist presented the sword to Talar first, and Talar ran his fingers over the hilt of the sword. Talar pulled the sword from the sheath, and like Dobervist, he was shocked to see that the blade was not corrupted. Talar held the sword up with one hand, inspecting it in the fading evening light. The blade was wide at the base, in the old Mempacton style. An inscription in Mempacton was inscribed on the blade, but the fading light prevented Talar from reading it. Talar sheathed the sword and handed it back to Dobervist. Dobervist showed Talar the kite shield, and the Prince shook his head as his eyes inspected the relic. There were a pair of kite shields like the one that the Dwarf held now hanging in the library within the Stonedom Keep. He had often spied his father looking up at the shields, but he never had paid them much attention. Talar's thoughts about his father made him realize that tomorrow he would be visiting his gravesite, and that realization now washed over Talar.

Plumo walked past Dobervist and Talar, and the old horse's presence was noticed by a few of the Oakbridge townsmen. One of the blacksmith's sons stood in front of the greying horse, and Plumo neighed angrily at the Man.

"My Lord, it is not right to make a lame horse suffer like this. I will take the horse behind the barn and relieve him of his misery," the blacksmith's son said. The young blacksmith's thick fingers grabbed Plumo's mane, and he tried to pull the horse. Pluto reared back suddenly and bit the blacksmith's hand, causing the young blacksmith to cry out in pain. Talar rushed over and pushed the young blacksmith back. He then began to soothe Plumo, who was wild-eyed.

"Easy boy, easy," Talar said quietly, looking into Plumo's dark eyes. Talar slowly moved closer to the large horse and slowly brought up his palm, allowing the horse to inspect it. Plumo huffed loudly, then moved closer to Talar, and Talar began scratching the area between Plumo's eyes. Talar turned back and looked at the young blacksmith and the other townsmen.

"The Elf is familiar with this horse. We will await Aemon's decision on what to do with him," Talar declared. The townsmen nodded and walked over to the campfire that the others had started. Talar motioned for Mona, Dalir, Dobervist, and Sigrid to follow him and the five of them set up their own campfire away from the townsmen and merchants. Plumo followed behind and slowly sat down behind them, towards the run-down farmhouse.

The old timbers that Dobervist had torn from the side of the barn burned quickly, sending flaming embers up into the evening sky. The setting sun was quickly disappearing behind the distant hills of Mercium, and Mona looked back at her homeland. She wondered if she would ever return there. Since being recognized by her countrymen back in Oakbridge, she had felt a sense of relief. She no longer wondered if her family was still remembered. She no longer wondered if her people remembered her. She watched Talar throw another timber on the fire, and he smiled at her from across the flames. She no longer felt alone.

Aemon had removed the armored Man's breastplate and dragged him over to the cart, which was in between the two campfires. He walked towards the cart and grabbed a waterskin. Aemon walked back to the hapless Man and began pouring cold water over Man's head. The Man shrieked and began wildly swiping at Aemon, but the Elf easily dodged his hands. Talar stood and was going to assist Aemon, but the Elf motioned for him to sit down. Aemon kept pouring the cold water over the Man's head until the waterskin was empty. The Man shook his head like an angry bear, but the Elf's trick had worked. The man was out of his stupor.

The Man pulled his long dark hair away from his blue eyes, and he stared up at Aemon. "Is that you, Aemon?" the Man said weakly, his voice as dry as one of the leaves that blew in the wind around him. He had spoken in Mempacton, a language only the Elf and Talar understood.

"It is me, Brimhilt. It is me, my friend," Aemon said before kneeling in front of the Man. Brimhilt hid his eyes with his hands, not believing that the Elf was actually there.

Brimhilt began weeping, tears flowing freely from his eyes. "I have failed you, my brother. I have failed. I have failed. I have failed," he repeated over and over until Aemon leaned in and embraced his brother-in-law. "I am sorry, Aemon. I am sorry for everything. I failed you and your people," Brimhilt said, his voice breaking with emotion. He had not seen Aemon since the fall of Mempacton and had assumed that his wife's brother had died in the chaos. "I failed to protect your sister, Aemon. It is my fault that she became what she is now," Brimhilt said sobbingly.

"What she is now? She is not dead? Gweneth is alive?" Aemon asked, his slender Elf hands shaking Brimhilt's shoulders. The adjacent campfires' light cast a faint glow upon Brimhilt's face as his emotions overwhelmed him again. He looked down, unable to look Aemon in the eyes.

Aemon grabbed Brimhilt's chin and brought it up, so he could look his brother-in-law in the eyes. "Is my sister dead, Brimhilt? What happened to her?" Aemon asked, and he could see the pain in Brimhilt's eyes as he began to answer.

"When the Capans attacked the Dwarves, I had my knights charge into the Trolls, but it was too late by then," Brimhilt said, his eyes feverishly bouncing back and forth as he re-lived the worst day in his long life. Aemon nodded, and released Brimhilt's chin, then sat down in front of him.

"Gweneth ran across the Silver Bridge to give aid to some wounded knights. She was fearless that day, as always," Brimhilt said, wiping tears from his eyes as he thought of his bold wife. "The Trolls swarmed both sides of the Bridge, and she was cut off, Aemon. I tried to reach her, but Plumo was pushed off the bridge by the Trolls, and the current took us away. I saw her swinging a sword, Aemon. I saw her with a sword before I was swept away," Brimhilt said, his eyes swelling with tears again.

Aemon had turned white as a ghost upon hearing the Brimhilts' words. Elves did not commit violence because they were unable to do so. They were peaceful because violence would alter their state of being. If an Elf committed a violent act, such as murder, even in self-defense, then that Elf would change immediately. The violent act would corrupt the Elf's soul, and the evil Gods would take possession of the Elf. To Aemon, death was much better than becoming violent.

"You always warned me, Aemon. You always warned me what would happen if one of your kind became violent. I have seen what happens. Not a minute goes by now that I do not hate myself for not listening to your words. She should not have been out there. Gweneth should not have been there..." Brimhilt said, his words trailing off.

Brimhilt's words had stunned the ancient Elf, and now Aemon lowered his head and wept upon hearing of his sister's fate. He had mourned her death seventy years ago and had thought she had died when the Trolls had razed Mempacton. Death was much better than becoming what had befallen Gweneth. Only a few Elves had ever turned over to the evil Gods, and it had taken great alliances to defeat them in the past. Aemon shook his head, unable to handle his sister's fate. Both Elf and Paladin wept until Stripe ran over and began to lick the Elf's face. Aemon petted the dog and tried to regain his composure. Around both campfires, there was silence as the Elf and Man spoke in the strange language, but all knew the Elf and armored Man were mourning someone.

"You said you saw what happens. What do you mean by that Brimhilt? Have you seen Gweneth since the battle?" Aemon asked softly. Brimhilt nodded, and Aemon's jaw dropped in disbelief.

"You saw her then? Where is she, Brimhilt? When was this? Aemon asked with a spark of hope in his voice. Brimhilt shook his head and raised his head, looking Aemon in the eyes.

"She is gone, Aemon. Gweneth, as we knew her, is gone, my brother. I am sorry, she is gone," Brimhilt said before his head slumped back down on his chest.

"Where is she, Brimhilt? Answer me!" Aemon demanded loudly. The Elf's loud words broke the silence around the barnyard as all watched the emotional exchange between the Elf and Man. After a long moment, Brimhilt answered. He looked Aemon in the eyes, his blue eyes meeting the Elf's star-filled ones.

"She is in Mempacton, Aemon. She sits on the King's throne. She commands the Trolls now. She is evil, Aemon. She is not your sister any longer. She is not my wife. Gweneth is gone. I am sorry for failing you, Aemon. I will always be sorry," Brimhilt said. Aemon shook his head and brought his hands to his face.

"When was this, Brimhilt? When did you see her? Aemon asked quietly, trying to ignore the impact of Brimhilt's words.

Brimhilt shook his head again and threw up a hand derisively. "I do not know, Aemon; it was long ago. I have been drinking. Every day is the same. It never ends. I am an abomination. My kind should have never been created," he said miserably.

"When was it, Brimhilt? When did you see her?" Aemon asked again, raising his voice.

Brimhilt looked down at the ground, trying to sift through his hazy memories. "It was about fifty years ago, Aemon. She came to me in my dreams. She told me to find her in Mempacton. So, I rode Plumo to the outskirts of the city, and I walked in. The Trolls just looked at me, Aemon. They did not attack me. One of them led me to her. It was awful seeing her like that, Aemon. She is not your sister any longer. You must trust my words, my brother," Brimhilt said softly.

"What did she say to you, Brimhilt?" Aemon asked. His hands were shaking as he thought of what had happened to his beloved sister.

"She asked me to lead her army of Trolls. She fears the Capan Legions and wishes to destroy them before they destroy her. She did not like my answer, but she refused to kill me. She wanted me to suffer. To suffer forever…," Brimhilt said.

"So, she allowed you to leave? Even after you refused her?" Aemon asked, trying to understand what had transpired.

"You do not understand, Aemon. Gweneth is gone. Your sister is gone. That thing I talked to in the King's courtyard was pure evil. There were corpses everywhere, Aemon. She feasts on them with the Trolls. She made me watch as she tortured a family that the Trolls had captured. Then she had her Trolls beat me and thrown in the river. She is not your sister anymore, Aemon," Brimhilt said. His words were too much for the Elf to hear.

Aemon stood and started screaming. "No, No, No!" he repeated loudly. He rushed away from Brimhilt, whose head was once again slumped on his chest.

Aemon rushed past Talar's campsite, visibly shaken by the conversation he had with the armored Man. Dobervist lept up and took after the Elf. He caught up with Aemon, who was bent over, vomiting.

The Dwarf patted the Elf's back to consul him. He told Aemon that he was not alone, and to the Dwarf's surprise, the Elf straightened up and hugged the shorter Dwarf. Dobervist awkwardly returned the Elf's embrace as the Elf wept. After a few moments, Aemon regained his composure and thanked the Dwarf. Aemon tried to push thoughts of his sister out of his head as he thought of the needs of his people. With his people in his mind, Aemon wiped the tears from his eyes and walked back towards the campfires. He did not look at Talar or any of the others as he walked past them to rejoin Brimhilt.

Brimhilt raised his head and nodded at Aemon, who sat down in front of him once again. "We are heading to Stonedom. A Capan army will be invading next spring. My people need your sword, Brimhilt. It is time to quit drinking and honor your oath. Like you said, brother, Gweneth is gone. We must prepare for the Capans," Aemon said softly.

"Quit drinking?" Brimhilt said cynically. "I live to drink and drink to live, Aemon. Your sister haunts my dreams. I see her when I shut my eyes, I hear her voice. No, Aemon, I will keep drinking," Brimhilt stated.

"You took an oath, Brimhilt. All those years ago, you swore an oath. To fight for the Elves, to the death. Well, my friend, you are still alive. My people need your sword once again," Aemon said pleadingly. Brimhilt shook his head angrily and stood up groggily. He stumbled towards Aemon and pointed a finger down at the sitting Elf.

"I have failed, Aemon!" he shouted. "I have failed. I saw the corpses of hundreds of your kind lining the streets of Mempacton! I have failed. I am cursed. I have failed!" Brimhilt shouted in Mempacton.

Like the others around the campfires, Talar saw Brimhilt towering over Aemon. Unlike the others, only Talar could understand what the Elf and the stranger were saying. The Druids had insisted on him and Cynfor learning the dead language. Brimhilt's conversation with Aemon had been heartbreaking for Talar to hear. Nonetheless, Talar now knew he was in the presence of a legend. He had thought before that perhaps the Elf had been mistaken about the stranger. Talar did not believe that the drunken stranger could be the legendary Paladin until he had heard him converse with Aemon. Talar also heard Brimhilt speak of the fall of Mempacton in such detail that despite being mind-boggling, it had to be true. Talar looked on in anger as the drunken Paladin shouted at the grief-stricken Elf.

Talar rose and strode over to the Paladin, placing himself between the armored Paladin and the prone Elf. "You are a hero to my people! To me! We need you, Paladin. The Elves need you! We face countless Legions!" Talar yelled in Mempacton. Brimhilt looked down at the young Man, then looked back at Aemon.

"Is it you, Tomlin? Did you make it out of Mempacton as well, my friend?" Brimhilt said before shaking Talar's hand. Talar did not pull back but was stunned by the sudden shift in the Paladin's tone. Talar did not reply, and Brimhilt asked him again if he was Tomlin. Talar's grandfather's name was Tomlin, and now Talar looked in Brimhilt's blue, feverish eyes. Talar shook his head slowly and looked down at Aemon, who was also shaking his head.

"He is Tomlin's grandson, Brimhilt. He is the Prince of Stonedom, his name is Talar. He and his brother wage war against the Capans. To defend my people and the Dwarves," Aemon said. The Elf's words had a visible impact on Brimhilt, and the Paladin turned back to his resting spot against the cart. Brimhilt shook his head, confused by the Elf's words.

"So, Tomlin escaped Mempacton? He must have if he has a grandson. It would be good to see Tomlin again. The only Man I could train swords with..." Brimhilt trailed off. Aemon shook his head, sad to see his friend's state of mind. While Aemon could heal the body, he could not heal the mind.

"We need your sword, Brimhilt. Your presence will boost morale. Give us some hope before aid arrives. Besides that, do you not want revenge on the Capans? They stole everything from you. Where is your anger? What about your honor?" Talar demanded. Brimhilt looked Talar up and down. The boy looked just like Tomlin, and Brimhilt shook his head again at the resemblance.

"You need a heart to produce anger, young Talar. I lost my heart when I saw what happened to his sister," Brimhilt said, pointing at Aemon. "I have failed to uphold my oath. I am cursed. There is no hope. You will be better off without me. My people are gone. My knights are gone. Everything is lost!" Brimhilt said before breaking down once more. Tears streamed down from eyes. He stood up again, looking around for his keg of bitter cider.

"No! Everything is not lost! We fight on still! You must join us! You MUST!" Talar shouted before he grabbed Brimhilt's wide shoulders. Brimhilt only shook his head and wept. After a moment, Talar knew it was futile trying to recruit Brimhilt. Brimhilt pushed Talar's hands away and mumbled as he walked away from Talar.

"I am a failure. I lost everything; I am of no use. Leave me alone, Tomlin's grandson. Your face haunts me." Brimhilt stumbled out into the darkness, heading to the back of the barn. Talar turned to go after him, but Aemon called out.

"Leave him, Talar, let him go," Aemon said quietly in Mempacton. Talar nodded and sat down in front of the Elf.

"I am sorry for your loss, Aemon," Talar said. Aemon smiled at the Prince's kindness. For seventy years, he had searched for Brimhilt, and now after finding him, he wished that he had not. He looked over at Talar, surprised that the young Man spoke Mempacton.

"How did you learn Mempacton, Talar? It has not been spoken in decades," Aemon asked, trying to get his mind off his sister's fate.

"The Druids taught me and my brother the language. They said it was the language of our ancestors. The Druids said that the Common tongue was a southern language, and not ours," Talar replied. Aemon nodded and looked up at the night stars for a moment. Talar did not want to interrupt the Elf's thoughts.

"Brimhilt is lost, Talar. The Paladin is lost to us. I will try convincing him in the morning to join us, but I doubt he will. He has hidden for seventy years. If he wanted to fight, if he wanted revenge, he would have done so by now," Aemon said sadly. Talar nodded and wondered how Aemon had known that Brimhilt was still alive. He asked Aemon the question, and the Elf did not hesitate when he answered.

"When the first Paladin, Henrik, was created, we linked his spirit to my spirit. This had never been attempted before, and I was the only Elf to volunteer. After the ritual, I found that I was linked to the Paladin. I felt that Brimhilt was alive, that his spirit was still in this physical world," Aemon said pragmatically. Talar nodded, trying to understand the archaic ritual. After a few moments of silence, Talar suggested that they go back to his campfire. Aemon nodded and followed Talar.

The mood was somber when Talar and Aemon sat back down. Dalir attempted a few poor jokes to break the mood, but they drew few laughs. Bread and cheese from Madoc's kitchen were passed around, and after eating, all were ready for sleep. The day's trek had been long, and all were looking forward to entering Stonedom. Dobervist stated that he would take the first watch, and the others nodded before they quickly prepared for sleep. The light from the campfire slowly burnt out, and the party fell into a deep slumber.

Aemon looked up at the night sky, studying the stars. His people had come from the stars, and upon leaving this physical world, they would return to the stars, to their home. Only Elves that turned evil, like Gweneth, would remain in this realm. Aemon left the campfire and walked into the ruined farmhouse. He wept and grieved for his sister for hours until he heard doves singing their morning songs. Their melody brought him some reprise from his grief, and he left the farmhouse to greet the morning sun. The sun's rays had awakened a few members of the party, and Aemon bid them good morning as he walked through the barnyard.

Aemon walked around to the back of the barn and found Brimhilt passed out by the now empty barrel of cider. Plumo was standing guard over him. Aemon rubbed the horse's head as they greeted each other. Plumo neighed and looked down at Brimhilt as if there was something wrong.

"I cannot do anything for him, my friend. His love for my sister has shattered his honor. You must look after him, Plumo. He will need you," Aemon said to the old horse. Aemon looked over the old horse, who had fought with Brimhilt for over five hundred years. Like so many times before, Aemon gently touched Plumo's neck and healed the warhorse. Within seconds, Plumo's grey hair disappeared, and his muscles regained their strength. He neighed loudly as he regained the strength of youth, and now, he playfully tussled with the Elf. Aemon smiled and patted the horses' back. Aemon looked down at the sleeping Brimhilt and shook his head sadly. He had hoped to find the old Brimhilt, his friend and protector. Instead, he had found a shell of his former self. He had found a Man overcome with grief and despair.

"I hope you find peace, my brother," Aemon said to the slumbering Brimhilt. "I hope that one day you find peace," Aemon said before turning away. He scratched Plumo's nose one more time before heading back to the barnyard. He did not look back at his friends as he walked away.

Talar saw Aemon entering the barnyard and walked over to him. He had roused the party out of slumber, and now they were preparing to depart. "Do you want me to bring your friend, Aemon? We could put him in the cart. I do not think that his horse will make the trip to Stonedom, though," Talar stated quietly in Mempacton.

"There is nothing that we can do for him, Talar, and there is nothing that he can do for us. Let us go to Stonedom. There is much to prepare," Aemon stated, and Talar nodded. His entire life, he had read the stories about the Paladin, about his courage and bravery. Now, after meeting him, he felt that he had been tricked. Aemon saw Talar's despair and put an arm around the Prince.

"Do not let Brimhilt break your spirit, Talar. I know you and your people have revered him for his bravery. Do not judge him in the state that he is. The loss of my sister broke him Talar. You should have met him before Mempacton fell," Aemon said, and Talar nodded. The rest of the party were ready to travel, and now all the members of the party looked at them expectantly.

"To Stonedom!" Talar shouted, and the party began to leave the abandoned farm. Aemon lingered behind as the others walked down towards the Great Road. He had searched for Brimhilt for so long only to find horror and disappointment. He had placed most of his faith in the Paladin, but now he realized that only the Dwarves and Men of Stonedom could save his people. Aemon looked down at Talar and Dobervist as he left the run-down farm. He hoped that their bravery would hold out in the face of the upcoming battles. The Elven race depended on it.

Chapter XLII- Blood on the Road

Stripe ran ahead of the party on the Great Road, occasionally looking back at Dobervist to check if he was still following. The morning sun was near its zenith, and the Dwarf was enjoying the warmth upon his bare neck. Dobervist walked ahead of the rest of the party, content to be away from the Men who traveled behind him. He thought of Thendara and his upcoming reunion with his people. He wondered if the Dwarf King would accept him. He had unwittingly murdered three of his brethren as a gladiator in the Arena. They had been dressed up as Goblins and drugged to mask their strength. His reaction upon learning their identity had given Dobervist away as a Dwarf. Before that, his Capan owners had assumed he was a short, stocky, Man, not a Dwarf.

During the ten years since his escape from the Arena, Dobervist had often wondered if his fellow Dwarves would accept him. Having been captured by the Capans as a child during the aftermath of the fall of Mempacton, Dobervist did not know any other Dwarves. He wondered if the Dwarves of Thendara had heard of his deeds. He wondered if they would punish him.

Dobervist and Stripe made it to a high point along the Great Road, and both Dwarf and dog looked out at the countryside before them. A long, narrow lake filled with cattails obstructed the southern side of the Great Road. On the opposite side, the Great Road skirted a stand of birch and aspen, their golden leaves covering the stone cobbles of the Road. Not seeing anything out of the ordinary, Dobervist turned and signaled to Talar to keep advancing the party.

Stripe ran on ahead, down the hill, and waited patiently for Dobervist to catch up. Dobervist slowly walked down the hill as a stiff breeze blew his wild, dark hair around. He heard the wagon's wheels clanking against the stone cobble behind him as he looked over the dark, murky water of the narrow lake. Dobervist made it to the bottom of the hill and scratched Stripe's ears before the dog ran off in front of him. Dobervist kept walking, and he watched Stripe disappear into the woods ahead of him.

Stripe yelped out in pain, and Dobervist's heart sank as he feared the dog had been bit by a viper. He rushed forward, looking for the dog, when suddenly three red caped Legionnaires burst up through the leaves. Dobervist saw their metal-tipped javelins flying towards him, and he dove to the ground, his shoulder hitting the hard cobble of the Great Road. Before he could get up, he felt the sharp point of a spear point pressing into his neck. "If you move Dwarf scum, you will DIE!" a voice said in a thick Capan accent.

Dobervist's neck was turned back towards the party, and the Dwarf helplessly watched in horror as a volley of arrows and javelins hit the party behind him. The blacksmith's son was hit in the chest with a javelin, and he fell off the cart, mortally wounded. The orange ox was hit with a few arrows, and it bellowed out in pain before falling to its knees. Another volley flew, and more townsmen and merchants fell to the ground, screaming out in pain. Red caped Legionnaires streamed out of the woods, running at the hapless members of the party. Dobervist saw mounted Legionnaires gallop out of the woods and surround the wagon. They swung their short swords, and more townsmen fell. Dobervist tried to get up, but the Legionnaire above him pressed harder against his neck, drawing blood.

Dobervist saw the Prince of Stonedom savagely slash a Legionnaire across the face with his sword. His action drew the rebuke of the Legionnaires around him, and he was forced back towards the wagon, blocking their spear and sword thrusts with his shield. He saw Aemon leap off the wagon, dodging arrows as he ran towards the narrow lake. He saw the massive Capan from the Oakbridge tavern riding towards Aemon, and the Dwarf shouted at the Elf. His warning was not heard over the roar of the battle. The large Capan lept from his horse on top of Aemon's back, forcing the lanky Elf to the ground.

The Dwarf watched the Koristan fend off a Legionnaires' sword thrust before the Legionnaire punched him with his free hand. Dalir fell, and two other Legionnaires jumped on him. Sigrid grabbed his scimitar, but before she could raise it, she had a spear point at her throat. Talar fought on, his back against the two-wheeled cart. Mona crouched under the wagon, desperately trying to load her bow as the screams of the dying rang out around her. Talar ran a Legionnaire through with his sword, then blocked a spear thrust with his shield. He then parried a sword thrust with his sword before thrusting his sword tip through the attacking Legionnaire's throat.

Ragonious saw the Prince slaying the Legionnaires in front of him and ran over, pulling the other Legionnaires back. The former gladiator champion smiled at Talar, and Talar recognized him from the tavern. They both swung their swords, and sparks flew when the blades met. Talar thrust with his sword at Ragonious's throat, leaving his right side exposed. A Legionnaire saw the opening and stabbed Talar with his spear. Talar screamed out in pain and dropped his sword. He tried to pull out the spear, but the Legionnaire pushed the spear down more, driving Talar to his knees. Talar screamed out in horrible pain.

Mona leaped out from beneath the wagon and tried to give Talar aid as his blood stained the cobbles below him. Ragonious grabbed her long, red hair and slapped her, almost knocking her unconscious. Dobervist now felt more spear tips pressed against his neck.

"You move, and you will die, Dobervist!" Cyprian shouted. He ordered the Legionnaires around him to bind the Dwarf's arms. Dobervist resisted, but another poke from the spear tip at his neck made him stop. Dobervist felt course, thick rope being tied around his wrists before being hauled to his feet. As he rose, he saw that he was surrounded by even more Capans. Cyprian turned the Dwarf around and squatted down so that they were eye level.

"The Arena is going to go wild when I drag you in there," Cyprian said. Dobervist struggled against the rope binding his wrists to no avail. "Capa will celebrate while you are torn piece by piece in front of them!" Cyprian said gloatingly. Dobervist spit in Cyprian's face and the Capan quickly wiped the saliva off his face. He then hit Dobervist on the cheek with the round pommel of his short sword, causing Dobervist to fall and bleed.

"Get him up and follow me," Cyprian ordered before heading towards the wagon. Wounded townsmen and merchants cried out in agony. "Kill all those wounded! Leave him for me!" Cyprian shouted as he pointed at Talar. Dalir, Sigrid, and Mona looked on in horror as the Legionnaires carried out their orders. The wounded townsmen and merchants raised their hands and pleaded for mercy. The Legionnaires showed them none. They emotionlessly plunged their swords and spears through the wounded, quickly silencing their screams and moans.

An unnatural silence followed the end of the wounded townsmen's screams. Cyprian looked around in satisfaction. The townsmen and merchants all lay dead. The arrogant Prince was withering in pain. Dobervist was captive, and only a few Legionnaires had been lost. Now Cyprian looked around for Tadius and Axius, who he had ordered to catch the Elf. He did not see his cousin or the massive ex-Legionnaire until he walked around the wagon and looked towards the murky lake. Axius was carrying the motionless Elf in his arms. Cyprian's heart raced as he feared that Axius had killed their prize.

"Did you kill him, you simple bastard?" Cyprian roared, causing Axius to look at him in confusion. Tadius appeared behind Axius and the motionless Elf and told his cousin to calm down.

"The Elf is alive. Axius knocked him out to keep him from squirming away. That Elf is like a snake. Get the chains, little cousin. We GOT HIM!" Tadius cried out triumphantly. Cyprian smiled and motioned to Ragonious, who was already turning to go to Cyprian's horse. Inside his haversack was a set of metal wrist and leg chains.

Axius brought the Elf over to Cyprian, and the skull bearer looked over his prize. Aemon was bleeding slightly from a cut above his eye, but his breathing was steady. Cyprian smiled when Ragonious returned and locked the chains around the Elf's wrists and ankles. After locking the Elf up, Axius set him down, and all four hunters slapped each other's back and shook each other's hands. Their hunt had been long and hard, but now they had achieved success.

"All you Legionnaires will receive one hundred gold coins as a gift from the Emperor!" Cyprian shouted, and the Legionnaires shouted with joy. A hundred gold coins could buy a large farm, a big house in Capa, or plenty of pleasure in Capa's brothels. The Legionnaires smiled and celebrated. Cyprian walked over to Talar, who was still being pinned down by the Legionnaire who had speared him. Cyprian slapped the Legionnaire on the back and took the spear from his hands. He pressed the spear deeper into Talar's side. Talar screamed out in pain again and almost blacked out from the pain. Mona tried to break free from the Legionnaire holding her, but she failed.

"Looks like the Prince has a lover, boys!" Cyprian shouted after seeing Mona's response. Cyprian pointed at Mona and Sigrid, then pointed to the woods. "Take them into the woods, boys! Have fun with them! Let the Prince hear his lover scream as he bleeds to death! Cyprian said laughingly. The other Capans joined Cyprian, and all laughed at Talar as he helplessly watched Mona and Sigrid being dragged to the woods.

Dalir broke free of the Legionnaire holding him and tried to free Sigrid, but the Legionnaires swarmed him and beat him down. Cyprian allowed the Legionnaires to kick the Koristan for a minute before ordering them to stop. He motioned for Axius to raise Dalir's head from the ground. Cyprian knelt and looked at the bloody Koristan, whose face was bleeding and swelling profusely from the beating. "I think a life in the salt mines is the fate for you, my finely dressed friend!" Cyprian said sarcastically. Dalir did not reply. His mouth was clogged with blood. The Legionnaires laughed at the rich Koristan and bound his wrists behind his back. The Emperor did not allow slaves within the cities or farms of Capa. They were allowed in the mines, though, which were far from the cities. The Legionnaires hauled Dalir to his feet, dragged him over to Aemon, and tossed him to the ground. They then grabbed Mona and Sigrid, and the company of Legionnaires started heading towards the woods, dragging the two screaming Women as they went.

Cyprian walked back over to Talar and looked down at the bleeding Prince. He nodded as his eyes met the green eyes of the Prince. There was no fear in those green eyes, and Cyprian smiled at his fallen foe. "Funny how things work out, Prince," Cyprian said as he wiggled the spear sticking out of Talar. Talar screamed out in pain again. Talar had both of his hands on the spear, trying to keep it from moving and causing more pain. His eyes were filled with rage, and Cyprian wiggled the spear again to his amusement. Talar tried to stifle his screams, desperate not to give the Capan any more satisfaction.

"You bastard!" Talar cursed, spitting up blood on his brown tunic. Cyprian nodded and looked over Talar's wound. The spear was imbedded deeply within the Prince, and Cyprian knew it was a fatal wound. He released the spear and sat down next to the wounded Prince, whose strength was failing.

Talar desperately tried to keep the spear upright as the spear point sent flames of pain through his body.

"You are right, young Prince. I am a bastard. A real mean bastard, but because of what happened today, young Prince, I will live forever. Mean bastards like me rule the world, Prince. Good Men like you do not stand a chance! Just the way it is," Cyprian said. He patted Talar on the back before standing up. He admired the Prince's courage and skill in battle and would not torture him anymore. Cyprian stood and walked away from Talar, ready to leave once the Legionnaires were done with the Women. Cyprian stood in front of Ragonius, Tadius, and Axius. He was about to speak when he saw all their eyes drawn to something behind him. Cyprian turned and spotted a lone horseman above them on the hill. The Man sat on a big, strong, black horse and was covered in rusty plate mail. A rusty square helmet enclosed the Man's head, and Cyprian stared in wonder at the strange sight.

"Who is that?" Cyprian said aloud, pointing his sword at the armored Man on the hill above him. The black horse was pacing back and forth, pawing the ground angrily. Cyprian walked over to Talar and grabbed the spear again, causing Talar to scream out in pain. "Who is that Prince? Who is it?" Cyprian asked. A chill went up Cyprian's back. The armored Man and the black horse looked eerily familiar. "Who is it?" Cyprian shouted, his tone alarming his fellow hunters.

Talar looked up at the hill, then looked back at Cyprian. He smiled as he looked into Cyprian's dark eyes. "That is the Paladin!" Talar shouted. Blood flowed from the corners of his mouth. "That is the Paladin!" Talar shouted, and he saw the fear in Cyprian's eyes. The fear in Cyprian's eyes confirmed Talar's beliefs. All morning he had questioned everything he had been taught as a child. Seeing the Paladin reaffirmed everything Talar had been taught. Talar thought of the Druid's lessons. He knew if he died soon, he would go to the next life for judgment. Talar started laughing hysterically, for he saw the fear that his words had caused.

Chapter XLIII- The Lost Paladin

Brimhilt swiped at the fly that had landed on his face. The sun immediately blinded him, and he raised his hand to block the sun's rays. His head was throbbing from the bitter cider he had drunk last night, and his throat was dry. He rolled over onto his stomach and took a deep breath once his stomach had quit churning. He slowly rose to his feet and surveyed his surroundings. The events of last night were re-playing through his mind.

Breaking the news of Gweneth's fate to Aemon had been worse than he had imagined.

Brimhilt staggered over to the empty keg of cider. He shook the empty keg then angrily threw it in the bushes behind him. He had been married to Gweneth for nearly four hundred years, and now the memories of their long marriage flooded Brimhilt's mind. He took another deep breath and leaned against the side of the barn, trying not to weep. Only drinking dulled Gweneth's memories. Brimhilt regained his composure and set off to find something to drink.

Brimhilt stumbled around the back of the barn then out into the barnyard. Plumo saw Brimhilt and trotted over, nuzzling Brimhilt and snorting loudly. Brimhilt grabbed his reins and looked over his old warhorse. Plumo's grey hair had vanished, and his sleek, black coat glistened in the morning sun. Brimhilt had seen the effects of Aemon's healing more times than he could remember. He shook his head as he looked at the five hundred- and twenty-two-year-old horse. They had ridden into battle together for almost all those years, usually with Aemon behind them, ready to heal either if they were wounded.

Brimhilt smiled at Plumo's regained youthfulness. He had dreaded his horse's death. Plumo was more than his steed. The two had fought together for centuries, and both had saved each other's lives on numerous occasions. Plumo neighed and turned his head towards the ruined farmhouse. The warhorse then trotted over, stopping to look back at the trailing Brimhilt from time to time. Plumo walked over to where the cart had been the previous night. He started pawing the grass, and Brimhilt patted the horse's neck when he spotted his rusty breastplate, shield, and sword. Brimhilt had kept the armor out of habit. It had proved useful when he was forced to slay a bandit or Troll that he encountered from time to time.

Brimhilt picked up the thick breastplate and fumbled with the dry leather binding that secured it to the plates covering his arms. After a moment, he secured the breastplate then looked down at his sword. He shook his head upon remembering Talar's scolding. The boy thought that he was a coward.

"Do you think I am a coward, my friend? Do you think I have abandoned my oath?" Brimhilt asked Plumo. The warhorse snorted and pawed the ground again. Aemon's voice was echoing in Brimhilt's mind as he looked down at his sword. For over five centuries, he had fought as the Paladin, as the protector of the Elves. The King of the Dwarves had forged the sword as a wedding gift when he had been wed to Gweneth. The Dwarven King had folded the sword ten thousand times. He thought of his wedding, and he remembered kissing Gweneth on the Silver Bridge as the people of Mempacton cheered wildly.

Four centuries later, he had lost his wife on the same bridge, and he tried to force the memory from his mind.

Brimhilt bent over and picked up his sword. He pulled the sword a few inches out of its' rusty scabbard. Three words written in Mempacton were engraved across the round guard. He had shouted those words before leading his knights into battle. Brimhilt thought of the meaning of those words. He thought of the oath that he had taken all those years ago. The oath was written on his sword's guard. Henrick, the first Paladin, had whispered the words to Brimhilt as he lay dying from a Troll wound. He had then whispered the words that Brimhilt could not remember before dying. Brimhilt had transformed into the immortal Paladin immediately afterward, immune to aging and disease. He read the three words and sheathed the sword.

Brimhilt looked around the ruined farm and shook his head. Thousands of farms like these had been lost along with the great city of Mempacton. It had been Brimhilt's duty to protect his people, and he had failed. The ruined farm was a reminder of his failure, and Brimhilt looked down into the valley below, eager to escape the area. He did not have enough gold left to purchase another keg of cider in Oakbridge, so Brimhilt turned his eyes east towards Stonedom. He knew Aemon was heading to Stonedom, and he figured his brother-in-law would supply him with drink.

Brimhilt turned and looked at Plumo. The warhorse was missing his mail coat, and saddle and Brimhilt tried to remember where he had put them. Plumo snorted and began trotting towards the back of the barn. Brimhilt followed Plumo to the broken cart behind the barn. When he spotted the busted cart, Brimhilt recognized it from his hazy memory. He walked over behind it and spotted his old leather saddle, haversack, and helmet. He grabbed the rusty helmet and dragged the saddle over to Plumo. The warhorse was standing by his mail armor.

Brimhilt took the old blanket that he had wrapped around his saddle and placed it over Plumo, who remained motionless. He then gently strapped on the chain mail coat then strapped on his saddle and haversack. He led Plumo by the reigns around the side of the barn and stopped when he saw the old grindstone wheel. Brimhilt pulled his sword out of its scabbard and ran his finger along both edges. Like usual, the unique Dwarf sword was sharp. The sword never went dull. Brimhilt pushed the blade back into the scabbard and kept walking out into the barnyard, Plumo following behind. He walked over to his shield and picked it up. He ran his fingers over the rusty dents in the shield before mounting Plumo.

Plumo took off at an easy trot once Brimhilt had mounted, not waiting for Brimhilt to urge him forward. Brimhilt smiled at Plumo's eagerness, and he figured the horse wanted to see Aemon again. They rode down from the farmhouse as the morning sun continued its climb. Brimhilt looked up at the snowcapped peaks and ridges of the Stone Mountains once they reached the Great Road. Plumo's hooves clunked on top of the grey cobbles of the Great Road, and Brimhilt urged him on at a faster pace. The wind blew Brimhilt's black hair away from his eyes as they quickly made their way towards Stonedom.

For the next hour, Brimhilt rode Plumo east along the winding Great Road, past the ponds that lined the road. He thought of Gweneth and what she had become, and he cursed the Gods for making him suffer. He thought of the thousands of Mempactons who had died under his watch. He had heard the city wailing in terror when the Trolls sacked it. He wondered what he had done to deserves such misery.

Brimhilt rode up a steep hill while wondering if he would be cursed forever. He pulled Plumo's reigns sharply, stopping the big warhorse suddenly. Brimhilt spotted the dead bodies of the Oakbridge townsmen and merchants below him. Their blood stained the grey cobbles of the Great Road. He saw two young Women being dragged into the stand of birches and their screams drifted up to him. He saw Aemon in chains and saw the Prince of Stonedom being tortured. A horrible rage began to fill Brimhilt as the red-caped Legionnaires spotted him and began pointing at him. He had not seen a Capan since the fall of Mempacton. Since he had lost Gweneth. His hands shook with rage as he looked down at the Capans. Down upon the Men who had betrayed Mempacton. Brimhilt took a deep breath and reached behind to unstrap his shield and helmet. He placed the square, rusty helmet on his head and stared out from the horizontal slit. Brimhilt had been a warrior for over half a millennium and knew he had to restrain his rage. He took another deep breath and slid his forearm through the kite shield's vertical handle. He secured the kite shield then reached back into his haversack.

Brimhilt's hand searched through his dusty haversack while the Capans below scurried from the woods to the area around Aemon. He grasped the handle of what he had been looking for and brought it out. Plumo sensed what was going to happen and began pacing back and forth, pawing the ground with his large front hooves. Brimhilt looked down at the silver trumpet that he had pulled out. He had not looked at the trumpet in many years, except when he had thought of selling it for drinking money. The trumpet had been a wedding gift from Aemon, who had received it from his father thousands of years ago.

Brimhilt stared down at the trumpet and thought of Gweneth and his lost city. For seventy years, the Gods had punished him, but now Brimhilt figured they were giving him a chance to end the suffering. He patted Plumo's neck a final time before bringing the engraved silver trumpet to his lips. Brimhilt took a deep breath and blew on the trumpet.

A cloud of dust erupted from the trumpet along with a muted horn sound. The Capans below burst out laughing at the spectacle above them. Brimhilt cursed loudly, the anger inside him building relentlessly. Plumo reared back, ready to charge, but Brimhilt restrained him. He emptied the dust from the silver trumpet and brought it to his lips again. He blew the trumpet, and the Capans ceased laughing. None of the Legionnaires had ever heard such a crisp, resonating sound. The trumpet's clarion tone was joyous to hear but almost overwhelming. The Legionnaires looked at each in wonder. Two of the Capan's below had heard Brimhilt's enchanted silver trumpet before. Cyprian turned and looked at his older cousin, his face contorted with anger and disbelief.

"You told me you killed him, cousin! You told me he was dead!" Cyprian raged at Tadius. Neither Ragonius nor Axius had ever seen Cyprian become so angry at his kinsmen before. They looked at each other with worried expressions. Tadius shook his head in disbelief. Brimhilt raised the trumpet to his lips, and its crisp noise seemed to reverberate off the cliffs of the Stone Mountains. The Legionnaires looked at each other, wondering if northern magic was causing the noise.

"I saw him fall, Cyprian! I saw him die!" Tadius pleaded, shocked at hearing the legendary horn of the Paladin of Mempacton. Tadius had watched Brimhilt be pushed into the flowing currents that ran under the Silver Bridge. He had ridden through the chaos of the battle, watching the armored Paladin struggle against the currents until he had eventually sunk. Tadius could not believe that it was Brimhilt. "It cannot be," Tadius said softly, and Cyprian angrily shook his head. He ordered the few Legionnaires who had remounted to charge the lone horseman.

Brimhilt raised the silver horn to his lips for the third time, and its tune bounced off the cliffs of the Stone Mountains. The Legionnaires trying to mount their horses were thrown off by the animals, who feared the echoes that Brimhilt's trumpet caused. Brimhilt placed the trumpet in his left hand and brought his shield up to protect his left side. He unsheathed his sword, and it made a screeching noise as it left its scabbard. Brimhilt brought his sword up in front of his face so that he could read the words inscribed into the hilt.

Brimhilt lowered the sword and secured his feet in the stirrups. He leaned forward and spoke into Plumo's ears. "Today is the day, my friend. Today is the day," Brimhilt said, and Plumo snorted loudly. Plumo spun around and pawed at the ground again, ready to charge. Brimhilt raised his sword then pointed it at the Capans.

"FOR MEMPACTON! TO THE DEATH!" Brimhilt shouted. The last words that he had shouted were the ones inscribed onto his sword. Centuries ago, Brimhilt had sworn to defend the Elves to the death. He planned to keep his oath today. Brimhilt dug his heels into Plumo's side, and the warhorse charged down the hill.

Plumo's hooves rang out as he thundered down the Great Road towards the Capans. The rejuvenated warhorse sprinted towards the Capans, who nervously stepped back from the approaching impact.

"Stand your ground! Use your javelins!" Cyprian shouted at the Legionnaires. Years of drilling took over, and the Legionnaires obeyed, quickly forming a spear line. They did not carry their rectangular shields, for they were too bulky to ride with. Brimhilt and Plumo raced down the Great Road, and Cyprian gave the order for his Legionnaires to volley.

Brimhilt saw the arrows and javelins arcing through the air, and he brought his shield forward. The shield protected Plumo's head from the arrows. A javelin hit Brimhilt's shoulder, but his thick armor caused the projectile to bounce off. A cloud of rust flew up from the impact on the shield and armor. A few arrows hit Plumo's chest, but his rusty chainmail stopped them from penetrating. Plumo charged on, oblivious to the arrows that were embedded in his armor. The Capans were approaching quickly, and Brimhilt raised his sword, ready to swing at his enemies.

Plumo burst through the line of Capans, his massive frame throwing Legionnaires aside. Brimhilt swung his sword at a Legionnaire's face. The Dwarf blade sliced through the Legionnaires round helm and across his face. Brimhilt brought his bloody sword up as the wounded Legionairre fell to the ground screaming. A javelin hit Brimhilt's shield, and he urged Plumo forward with his feet, not wanting to be swarmed. Plumo sprung forward, then bit a Legionnaire's arm and flung him back to Brimhilt, who efficiently stabbed him through the throat. Plumo galloped forward, leaving the shattered Capan line behind. After running almost half a furlough, Brimhilt urged him to stop and turn.

"Form line again! Cyprian shouted, pulling up the Legionnaires who had been tossed aside. He was covered in blood from the Legionnaire that Brimhilt had slashed. "Get over there! Kill him!" Cyprian screamed at the three Legionnaires who had mounted their horses. The Legionnaires drew their short swords and galloped towards Brimhilt. They formed a line across the Great Road, and their red capes blew back from the speed they had attained. Brimhilt raised his sword and urged Plumo forward towards the charging Capans. Brimhilt did not need to guide his seasoned warhorse to the flank of his enemy. Plumo turned deftly before hitting the charging Legionaries, and Brimhilt swung his sword violently, beheading the Legionnaire nearest to him. Plumo kept charging, leaving the mounted Legionnaires behind him. Brimhilt raised his sword again as Plumo galloped wildly towards the Capan line.

A few arrows harmlessly flew past Brimhilt before he and Plumo crashed into the Capan line for the second time. Brimhilt slashed downwards with his sword, felling two more Legionnaires. A Legionnaire tried to spear Plumo's rear flank, and the warhorse started kicking madly. The big horse's rear hooves hit the spear wielding Legionnaire square in the face, killing him instantly. The other Legionnaires fell back from Plumo. Brimhilt parried a sword thrust and returned the gesture by killing the attacking Legionnaire. The Legionnaires started to swarm around him. One brave Legionnaire jumped up, trying to drag Brimhilt off Plumo. Brimhilt's feet strained against his stirrups. He used all his strength and raised his shield, which the Legionnaire was hanging onto. Brimhilt stabbed the Legionnaire and urged Plumo forward away from the mob of Legionnaires.

The two-remaining mounted Legionnaires had turned around by this point, and they galloped behind Brimhilt. Brimhilt viciously swung his sword at the lead Legionnaire's horse. His blade hit the horse's head, sending the Legionnaire headfirst under the falling horse. Plumo made it to the top of the hill where they had first charged. He turned Plumo around just in time to meet the charging Legionnaire. Brimhilt saw a long scar across the big nose of the middle-aged Legionnaire who swung his short sword at him. Brimhilt raised his shield, and a cloud of rust flew up in the air. He then simultaneously turned Plumo and swung back with his sword, and his blade met the Legionnaires throat. The Legionnaire rode for a few seconds before dropping his sword and clutching his throat. He then fell off the horse and hit the ground.

The Legionnaires below watched their two comrades be killed, and Cyprian could feel their fear. A third of their comrades were dead. The mounted knight and his devil horse seemed invincible. Cyprian looked around, unsure of what to do. He spotted Axius, who was getting up on his feet from the impact of Plumo's last charge.

Cyprian spotted one of the large wooden staves that the Oakbridge townsmen had carried. He picked up the oak stave and handed it to Axius as the rest of the Capans looked on. "Axius, knock him off next time!" Cyprian roared. Their commander's anger rallied the remaining Legionnaires. Cyprian had them form a double line, and he, Axius, Tadius, and Ragonius stood behind. All the Capans stared up at the Paladin, who galloped back and forth.

Mona emerged from the wood line as Plumo and Brimhilt charged down the hill once again. She shook her head in awe as the giant warhorse slammed into the lines of Capans. Talar had been right, after all, she thought. Plumo ran over two Legionnaires and savagely brought his hooves down repeatedly on them as he had been trained to do. Mona heard the ring of steel upon steel as Brimhilt's sword, and shield met the Capan's swords and spears. She ignored the battle and ran across the Great Road to the two-wheeled cart. She slipped on the bloody cobbles and felt blood covering her arms. The Capans had held her down, ready to rape her, when Brimhilt's trumpet had sounded. Sigrid had been knocked out, her ferociousness delaying the Capans until the trumpet had drawn them away. Mona grimaced, gagged, and wiped the blood off her. She stood and marched determinedly over to Talar as Brimhilt battled the Capans behind her. She spotted Talar lying against the cart's wheel. She cried out when she spotted the pool of blood that he lay in.

Mona rushed over to Talar, who somehow managed to smile at her. His hands were locked around the spear, which still protruded from his body. Mona's stomach sank when she saw the pain in Talar's eyes. She gently grasped the spear, and Talar cried out. "Please, Mona, let it be. The pain is too great!" Talar pleaded, tears filling his eyes. Waves of throbbing pain filled his body. Talar had turned white as the snow on the Stone Mountains behind him.

Mona held the spear and looked into Talar's eyes. She had to remove the spear if Talar was to survive. She placed his left hand on her shoulder and looked into his youthful green eyes. "I am sorry, Talar. I am sorry," she said before quickly pulling the spear out of the side of Talar's stomach. Talar howled in pain, and he kicked his legs uncontrollably. Blood poured from the wound, and he tried to stop the flow with his hands. Mona looked around and spotted a dead Legionnaire. She ripped his red cape off and wrapped it around Talar's wound. Talar was not moving, and Mona looked up at him. His eyes were closing, so Mona shook him. "Wake up, Talar. Wake up," Mona pleaded, and Talar opened his eyes and stared at Mona. He smiled, and Mona saw blood dripping from his lips.

"Run, Mona. Run. I go to the next world. Run to Stonedom," Talar muttered before his eyes shut, and he slumped back against the cart's wheel. Mona screamed helplessly in desperation. She shook Talar to no avail. Mona looked back as Brimhilt continued to wheel Plumo around the desperate Capans. She saw Aemon in shackles and figured she could drag him over to Talar. She also saw a Capan dressed as a woodsman standing guard over Aemon. The Capan had a bow drawn and was waiting for a shot on Brimhilt. Mona looked to her left and saw her bow lying under the cart. She grabbed the bow and quiver and knocked an arrow. She looked down at Talar, who was still motionless, before taking aim.

Capans fell and staggered away from the battle against Brimhilt. Some were missing hands, some noses, some ears. They were all covered in blood. Mona aimed at the Capan guarding Aemon, waiting for the wounded Capans to fall or stagger out of her line of fire. A Legionnaire with a horrible cut across his face collapsed, giving Mona the chance to release the arrow. She remembered Sigrid's words and aimed high at the Capan. She released the arrow, and it flew, hitting Tadius in his ribcage. Tadius dropped his bow and fell to his knees, screaming loudly. Cyprian turned from the battle and saw his cousin lying on the ground. He cried out and rushed to Tadius's side. Blood was pouring from Tadius' side. He looked up at Cyprian fearfully and tried to speak. His words were garbled by the blood, and Cyprian watched in horror as his cousin and friend died in his arms. Tadius's eyes rolled back, and Cyprian set Tadius on the ground. Ragonious rushed over, a vial of Elf blood ready, but it was too late. Tadius was dead. Cyprian's head snapped back and forth as he searched for Tadius' killer. He shouted furiously when he spotted Mona holding the bow.

Dalir watched Cyprian charge Mona, sword raised. "Run, Mona, Run!" he screamed before Ragonious kicked him. Dalir struggled against his bonds, but he could not move. The kick from Ragonious had knocked the wind out of him, and he looked on as Mona raised her bow at the charging Cyprian.

Mona heard Dalir's warning, but she would not leave Talar to Cyprian's wrath. She knocked another arrow and took a deep breath as Sigrid had taught her. She let the arrow go as Cyprian raised his sword. The arrow hit his shoulder, but Cyprian did not drop his sword. Before Mona could react, Cyprian closed the distance between the two of them. He grabbed Mona's shoulder and stabbed her in the heart. He screamed in rage at Mona, who grabbed her chest and fell. She landed next to Talar, and Mona squeezed Talar's hand before dying. Dalir saw Mona fall, and he screamed out desperately.

Cyprian turned to survey the battle against Brimhilt after breaking the arrow protruding from his shoulder. The Paladin had successfully kept moving amongst the Capans. His sword lashed out, and when it did, Capan blood flew. Cyprian saw that over half the Legionnaires were dead or wounded. The look on Tadius's face shook Cyprian as he walked past his fallen cousin. "I will take Tadius," Cyprian said, his voice shaking with grief. He would not leave his cousin here on the Road. "Put the Elf on your horse. Then kill the Dwarf," Cyprian instructed Ragonious. Ragonious nodded, sheathed his sword, and started dragging Aemon away. Cyprian turned to Axius, who held the long wooden stave. He had restrained Axius from the fight, waiting for the right time to unleash the massive ex-Legionnaire upon Brimhilt.

The Legionnaires continued their attack against Brimhilt, who saw that Aemon was being dragged away. He felt and heard the Capan's blows fall upon his shield, helm, and armor. He slashed down at the Capans, screaming defiantly as he did so. Plumo moved from side to side, forward and backward, never standing still. Cyprian saw his chance when Brimhilt turned away from him and pushed Axius towards the fray. Axius rushed at Brimhilt, who was parrying and blocking spear thrusts with both his sword and shield. Axius raised the stave like an ax, and with all his strength, he hit Brimhilt, knocking the Paladin off Plumo. The Legionnaires rushed around the fallen Brimhilt as Cyprian shouted out gleefully. Plumo saw that Brimhilt had fallen and now rushed forward, standing on his back hooves, kicking at the encroaching Capans. Plumo's bravery gave Brimhilt time to regain his feet and bearings. It also exposed Plumo's unprotected underside, and two Legionnaires stabbed him with their spears in that area. Plumo screamed in pain, and Axius now hit the warhorse in the head, driving the warhorse to his knees. A Legionnaire was about to cut Plumo's throat when Brimhilt charged forward.

Brimhilt cut the Legionnaire's arm off, and the Capan screeched as blood flew from his arm. Brimhilt blocked a spear thrust from another Legionnaire, then slashed his attacker's hands. The Legionnaire fell to his knees, and Brimhilt swung his sword at his face, killing him. Plumo thrashed on the ground, mortally wounded from the blows. Plumo's fall had separated the Capans into two groups giving Brimhilt a chance to fight despite being so outnumbered. Another Capan slashed at Brimhilt, but he blocked the blow and thrust immediately with his sword, stabbing the Capan in the stomach. The Legionnaire fell, and Brimhilt felt a sword hit his backside. Another cloud of rust flew up as Brimhilt's old plate armor saved him again. Brimhilt turned as his attacker was raising his sword. Brimhilt slashed at his knees, dropping the Legionnaire, before reversing his sword to finish him off.

Brimhilt backed away from Plumo as the separated group of Legionnaires joined the party that Brimhilt had devastated. He looked over and saw Aemon being tied down across a horse. He raised the trumpet, which he still held in his left hand, and blew the horn one final time. The silver trumpet's tune filled the valley once more. The horse Aemon was being tied to panicked from the sound and threw Aemon off. The unconscious Elf hit the ground hard before the horse bolted. Brimhilt turned back to the Legionnaires, who cautiously crept towards him, weapons ready. Brimhilt raised his sword and advanced, eager to engage his enemies before they surrounded him. The Legionnaire in front of Brimhilt dodged his sword thrust but not his shield. Brimhilt whipped the kite shield around, knocking the Legionnaire to the ground. Brimhilt plunged his sword down into the fallen Legionnaire's neck before fending off another sword strike with his shield. He dodged a sword thrust from his opponent before hitting him in the head with the pommel of his sword and cutting his throat with his sword's blade.

Brimhilt looked up just in time to see Axius swing the wooden stave at him. He swung his sword, and the Dwarf blade cut the oak stave in half, leaving Axius stunned. Axius clumsily fended off Brimhilt's sword thrusts, backing up as he did. He slipped on the bloody cobbles, and Brimhilt leaped after him, impaling the big Capan hunter as he scrambled backward on the slippery cobbles of the Great Road. A Legionnaire sneaked up behind Brimhilt. He swung his sword from above his head with both hands, and the blade hewed into Brimhilt's helm, driving him to his knees.

Other Legionnaires sliced and hacked at Brimhilt, their blows sending more rust into the air. Their swords did not penetrate the Paladin's armor, and he ignored the throbbing pain from the back of his head as he rose, knocking some of his attackers down. He parried a sword thrust with his own sword and then whipped his blade back towards the Legionnaire's face, cutting his eye and face. The Legionnaire screamed in agony and stumbled away from the fight. Brimhilt turned and swung his sword after feeling another blow across his back. His blade decapitated another Capan before the remaining five Capans surrounded him, driving him to his knees from their relentless strikes. Brimhilt's old armor finally broke down from the abuse, his backplate falling to the ground. He felt a sword slice his back, and he cried out before trying to swing his sword. A Legionnaire grabbed his sword arm, so Brimhilt grabbed his leg and brought him to the ground. Brimhilt climbed on top of the fallen Legionnaire as his comrades desperately hit Brimhilt with all their strength. Brimhilt slashed at the Legionnaire, who raised his bare arms against the blade. Brimhilt slashed his arms, then his throat and the Legionnaire died under him. A young Legionnaire, not old enough to shave, thrust his sword through Brimhilt's back. Brimhilt stood and turned, the Capan sword still thrust through him, before dropping to his knees. He dropped his sword and the trumpet. He coughed up blood and held the Legionnaire's sword with both hands, trying to ease the terrible pain that he was enduring.

The four surviving Legionnaires scampered away from Brimhilt, afraid that the armored knight might rise once more. They watched him fight for his last breaths as the moans of their wounded friends filled the air. Thirty Legionnaires had ambushed the Oakbridge party. Now only four remained. The survivors did not know who this swordsman was, but he was the finest any had ever seen. Ragonious and Cyprian walked over to Brimhilt, and Cyprian sneered at his old nemesis. Brimhilt's eyes widened with rage after he recognized Cyprian. He tried to curse at the Capan, but it was too painful. He slumped his head, disgusted by his failure to not save Aemon.

"Looks like you are not immortal after all, Paladin. Not like me anyway," Cyprian whispered into Brimhilt's bloody ear. He looked at the blood dripping down from Brimhilt and smiled. The Paladin had suspected that he and Tadius were hunting Elves before Capa had betrayed them. He had never been able to prove it, and Brimhilt's face burned red with rage upon hearing the lying, treacherous Capan's words. Cyprian walked around, wanting to look into the Paladin's eyes as he died. Brimhilt's head was lowered, but through the slit in his helmet, he could see Cyprian's legs. He summoned all his remaining strength, and with all his willpower, he suddenly stood. Brimhilt ignored the flaming tendrils of pain and grabbed Cyprian's neck with both of his hands. The Paladin started squeezing, and he saw Cyprian's eyes bulge.

The four remaining Legionnaire's and Ragonious attacked Brimhilt, but he did not release his grip. Cyprian tried to knock the Paladin's arms away, but Brimhilt held on, his thumbs pressing into Cyprian's throat. Ragonious thrust his sword repeatedly into Brimhilt's exposed back, bringing the Paladin to his knees. He kept his grip through, and Cyprian's legs shook wildly as the Paladin choked the life out of him. Cyprian's bladder unleashed its contents before he died with the Paladin's hands around his throat. Brimhilt saw Cyprian's wide eyes frozen with fear and knew he had killed the Elf hunter. He released his grip, and the Capan's ceased their attacks, shocked at their leader's sudden death. They backed up, once again fearing Brimhilt would rise.

Ragonious and the four surviving Legionnaires cautiously watched Brimhilt as he labored for breath. The Legionnaire who had lost his eye collapsed in front of Dalir and Dobervist, who was lying on the ground, still tied. "Grab his sword," Dobervist whispered to Dalir, who was closer. Dalir quickly rolled over to the short sword the Legionnaire had dropped and grabbed it. He wiggled across the grass, back to Dobervist. He awkwardly clutched the sword with his bound hands, which were still tied behind his back. Dobervist instructed Dalir to remain still as he cut his rope binds. In a matter of seconds, the sharp Capan sword sliced through the bonds, and Dobervist stood, taking the sword from Dalir. He cut Dalir's bonds, and Dalir scrambled over to Talar and Mona.

Dobervist brought the short sword behind him before hurling it end over end at the Legionnaire standing next to Ragonious. The blade impaled the unsuspecting Legionnaire, and his companions turned in shock. Dobervist waved at the Capans that he hated and started heading towards them. He picked up a Capan spear as Ragonious and the three Legionnaires charged towards him. Dobervist hurled the spear, and like a bolt of lightning, the lead Legionnaire was thrown back from the impact. Another Legionnaire swung his sword, but Dobervist easily side-stepped the blow. The Dwarf grabbed the Legionnaire's elbow and wrist and snapped his forearm. The Man fell screaming. The last Legionnaire thrust his sword at the smaller Dwarf, but Dobervist dodged the blade. Dobervist punched the Legionnaire in the jaw, sending him stumbling towards his fallen comrade. Dobervist broke the stunned Legionnaire's neck with a brutal kick to his throat. The Legionnaire with the broken arm scrambled away and ran back towards Oakbridge.

Ragonious stepped over the corpses that lined the Great Road. His sword was raised, and he pointed it at the Dwarf. "You know, I was champion of the Arena before you Dwarf," Ragonious said confidently. He had defeated more than two dozen challengers during his reign as champion. He circled around Dobervist, who was unarmed. "Your luck has run out, Dwarf! You have finally met a real swordsman!" Ragonious said before he twirled his sword. Dobervist did not look impressed. Unlike any other Arena champion, he had defeated both Ogres and Cyclops. The wounds from those bouts had been terrible, but his victories had taught him not to fear Men any longer.

Dobervist had been taught by his Capan weapon trainers to delay killing his opponents. He had been taught to wound his foe multiple times, then slowly kill him to the delight of the blood thirsty Capans. The Dwarf was in no mood for such antics today. Ragonious raised his sword and advanced towards Dobervist. He twirled his sword arrogantly as he did so. The Dwarf dived at Ragonious feet, and he felt the Capan's sword slice his back. The blow had not been enough to stop the Dwarf's momentum, though. Dobervist lifted Ragonious off his feet and slammed him into the cobbles. Ragonious was shocked at the strength of the stocky Dwarf, and he desperately tried to stab Dobervist, who was climbing on top of him. Dobervist grabbed his wrist and twisted it until he heard the bone break. Ragonious screamed out in pain. The former Arena champions' screams were cut short when Dobervist's fist smashed into his jaw. Ragonious spit out a few teeth before looking up at the

Dwarf. The last thing he saw was the open palm of the Dwarf's hand. Dobervist grabbed Ragonious' head and bashed it upon the cobbles, killing the last Elf hunter.

Dobervist stood up and walked away from the carnage that he had created. He surveyed the area but saw no more Legionnaires standing. Dobervist looked over and saw the young Koristan, whose name he could not remember, kneeling next to the Prince of Stonedom. The Prince looked dead along with the young, red-haired Woman. Dobervist's heart sank. Dobervist heard the Paladin wheezing and looked back at Aemon, who was still lying unconscious. He was about to run over to Aemon when he heard the Paladin speak. "Dwarf, Dwarf! Come here," Brimhilt gasped, and the Dwarf jumped over fallen Legionnaires. He stared in wonder at the Paladin, who clung to life despite the sword embedded within him.

Dobervist leaned over, his ear next to the wheezing Paladin. "Bring him to me. Bring the Prince to me," Brimhilt rasped. The Dwarf obeyed, hearing the urgency in Brimhilt's voice. Dobervist ran over to Talar, and Dalir looked up at him fearfully.

"Mona is dead! I fear Talar is dying too!" he exclaimed as he tried to stem the flow of blood from Talar's wound. The Dwarf gently pushed Dalir away from Talar, who was still holding Mona's hand.

"Wake the Elf. Now!" Dobervist commanded. Dalir nodded, then sprinted over to Aemon and began shaking him. Dobervist bent over and picked up Talar. The Prince of Stonedom awakened from the movement. He immediately spotted Mona's lifeless body and felt her cold hand grasping his. He tried to scream as Dobervist ripped him away from Mona.

"Let me die, Dwarf. She is gone!" Talar said. The blood from his wound muffled his words, and the Dwarf ignored the bleeding Prince as he carried him across the Great Road to Brimhilt. He placed Talar next to the kneeling Paladin, who embraced the Prince with his right arm.

"We are brothers, Prince. We are knights of the north. My time is ending now, but yours is just beginning," Brimhilt gasped. Dark clouds suddenly began forming. Dobervist looked up in awe, for just a moment ago, the sky had been clear. The sky darkened, and the wind began to swirl. Thunder erupted from the black clouds. The swirling wind picked up in intensity, blowing Dobervist's long black hair.

Talar shook his head and wept. He tried to turn around to look at Mona, but Brimhilt restrained him from doing so. Brimhilt turned, so they were looking eye to eye. Brimhilt removed his helmet, and blood poured down his face afterward. "You will take an oath now, young knight. Then you will be the Paladin," Brimhilt whispered to Talar.

Talar sobbed and shook his head. "She is dead. Mona is dead. I do not wish to live," Talar whispered, his voice faint but audible over the swirling wind. Talar saw Brimhilt's eyes fill with pity before he smiled slightly.

"Do you want revenge? Where is your anger? What about your honor? Brimhilt asked mockingly, repeating Talar's words from the night before. Talar shook his head, to overcome with grief and pain to speak. "What about your brother, Prince. Do you wish to see him again?" Brimhilt asked wearily. He could feel his life leaving his body. Talar thought of Cynfor and then nodded as he wept. "Repeat my words, Prince. You will live," Brimhilt whispered. Talar nodded as the storm above them worsened. More thunder crashed through the valley, awakening Aemon, who struggled against his metal bonds.

"I will defend the weak. I will defend the Elves. To the death," Brimhilt whispered, and Talar repeated the words. Brimhilt then repeated the words that Henrik, the first Paladin, had whispered into his ear as he lay dying. He did not understand the words, nor could he remember them before this moment. The strange words filled Talar's ear, and he whispered them back to Brimhilt. Dobervist looked up in wonder as the dark clouds parted above Talar. A bright beam of light shot down from the sky, illuminating Talar with its brightness. Brimhilt smiled. He had fulfilled his oath. He looked up at the towering Stone Mountains as his breath became more ragged. Brimhilt looked across the valley and spotted his beloved Gweneth waving at him. She was in her wedding dress, and Brimhilt smiled upon seeing her. She gestured for him to join him. Brimhilt nodded, took his last breath, and left this world for the next.

The light blinded Talar, Dobervist, Dalir, and Aemon. The pain within Talar vanished as a new life force entered the Prince of Stonedom. Talar could feel energy buzzing within him, and his arms shook as his strength returned. A final clap of thunder boomed across the valley. The bright light from the sky and the clouds disappeared instantly. Talar looked over at Brimhilt. His blue eyes were staring across the valley, and he was smiling. Talar shook his head, confused at what had happened. He stood and unwound the Capan cape that Mona had used as a bandage. Dobervist stared in wonder, for the Prince's skin was unblemished where the gaping spear wound had been. Talar shook his head, then looked back at Mona, who lay against the cart motionless. He rushed to her side and cradled her in his arms. Tears flowed down Talar's cheeks. He mumbled Mona's name over and over.

Dalir found the keys to the metal bonds around Tadius's neck, and he ripped them from the dead Elf hunter's neck. He ran over to Aemon and unlocked the struggling Elf. Aemon had witnessed the transfer of eternal life from Brimhilt to Talar, and now he rushed over to Brimhilt. The kneeling knight was still staring across the valley when Aemon reached him. Aemon sighed at the sight of his dead friend and brother-in-law. He saw the smile on Brimhilt's face, and that comforted the Elf. Aemon spotted the silver horn that he had given Brimhilt as a wedding gift. He picked the trumpet up, along with Brimhilt's sword. Aemon examined the silver trumpet before raising it to his lips. He blew the trumpet to honor his fallen friend, and its tune filled the valley once more. To Aemon's surprise, the silver trumpet's call was answered. In the distance, a group of horsemen was riding hard towards them.

Dobervist looked around and spotted a Capan sword lying in the grass. He picked up the blade, ready to fight. Dalir squinted. His eyes were beginning to shut from the beating the Capans had inflicted upon him. He saw the green and white flag of Stonedom flying as the horsemen neared. He walked over to Dobervist and urged the Dwarf to lower his weapon. Aemon saw the flag of Stonedom, then turned his attention to Plumo, who was whining softly. The black horse was lying on the Great Road, covered in blood. Aemon rushed to his side, knelt over, and quickly healed the magnificent stallion. Plumo got up on his hooves immediately, nickering loudly. He trotted over to the Elf and licked his face.

Sigrid walked out of the birches and aspens, carrying Stripe in her arms. The dog had been cut by a Capan spear on his front left leg and had run off into the woods. He had returned, limping over to Sigrid. He licked Sigrid's face until she woke up, and now, she saw for the first time the carnage that Brimhilt had wrought. She spotted Dalir and the Dwarf, and she waved, getting their attention. Dalir and Dobervist rushed down the hill towards her as the Stonedom cavalry thundered down the Great Road towards them.

King Cynfor Stoneking slowed his twin column of knights and surveyed the battleground in front of him. A merchant from Stonedom had ridden in the night before, informing the King of his brother's location. Lifeless Legionnaires and Oakbridge townsmen covered the Road, and he pulled his mount's reigns back to stop. The King of Stonedom had never seen so much bloodshed before. He had never witnessed a tempest form and disappear so quickly either. Cynfor looked to his right and saw a young Koristan, a tribeswoman, and a Dwarf holding a brown and white dog. He turned his head back to the bloodbath in front of him. It was then that he spotted his brother cradling Mona. Cynfor immediately dismounted and rushed over to his younger brother. He had hated himself ever since ordering war on Capa, for he knew his order would put Talar in danger. The Elves and Dwarves had told him they had spies in Capa that would aid Talar, but the decision had still torn at Cynfor's soul.

"Talar! Talar! Are you hurt?" Cynfor asked. Talar did not respond. Cynfor's captain, who was also Hartwin and Alwin's cousin, pushed past the confused King, who did not know why his younger brother did not respond.

"My Prince, My Prince! You are bleeding," the captain exclaimed, grabbing Talar by his shoulder. Talar turned and looked up into his older brother's eyes. Cynfor saw the pain and rage in Talar's eyes. He knew his younger brother had changed since he had left home.

"He is a Prince no longer," Aemon said, and the captain and Cynfor turned to look at the tall stranger. Cynfor saw Aemon's starry eyes and recognized him as an Elf instantly.

"What do you mean? He is Talar, Prince of Stonedom. He is my brother," Cynfor stated with conviction. Aemon looked at the captain, then at the King of Stonedom, then he shook his head.

"He is not a Prince," Aemon said. For seventy years, he had been looking for the protector of his people. In the end, Brimhilt had fulfilled his oath, despite lapsing from his duty. Aemon looked down at Talar, felt the rage in his eyes, and he knew that Talar would fulfill his oath. The Elf had found who he had been looking for. "He is not a Prince," Aemon repeated loudly, so all could hear him. "He is a knight! He is the guardian of the Elves! HE IS THE PALADIN!".

You have reached the end of the The Lost Paladin!

The Paladin will ride again...

Printed in Great Britain
by Amazon

33840828R00172